My Name is Randa

My Name is Randa

Marg Watland

Dear Laura,
my special friend.
Your belief in me
helped.
love Marg

❧Inscript

Bladensburg, Maryland

My Name is Randa

Copyright 2023 by Marg Watland

All rights reserved

No part of this work may be reproduced or transmitted in any form or by any means, electronic or mechanical, including photocopying and recording, or by any information storage or retrieval system, except as may be expressly permitted by the 1976 Copyright Act or in writing from the publisher. Requests for permission can be addressed to Inscript Books, a division of Dove Christian Publishers, P.O. Box 611, Bladensburg, MD 20710-0611, www.inscriptpublishing.com.

Paperback Edition
ISBN 978-1-957497-25-9

Inscript and the portrayal of a pen with script are trademarks of Dove Christian Publishers.

Published in the United States of America

This is a work of fiction. Unless otherwise indicated, all the names, characters, businesses, places, events and incidents in this book are either the product of the author's imagination or used in a fictitious manner. Any resemblance to actual persons, living or dead, or actual events is purely coincidental.

O God, thou art my God; early will I seek thee: my soul thirsteth for thee, my flesh longeth for thee... Because thy lovingkindness is better than life, my lips shall praise thee. Thus will I bless thee while I live: I will lift up my hands in thy name. Psalms 63:1,3-4 KJV

Chapter 1

Chicago, Illinois

Saturday, May 16, 1953

Quinn Edwards slit open a small handwritten envelope and read the first two lines of childish script. He sucked in a deep breath and began again. His mouth hung open as he read the letter.

> *Dear Reverend Quinn Daniel Edwards,*
>
> *John, my stepfather, thinks you are my uncle.*
>
> *My mama's name was Sarah Jean Edwards when she married my father, Leland E. Shepherd, in 1936. My father was killed in a railroad accident before I was born. My birthday is September 30, 1940, and I am twelve years old.*
>
> *Mama married John Reynolds, my father's best friend, a year later. When I was eight, we moved from Yuma to Minneapolis to help take care of my Grandpa Reynolds.*
>
> *Mama died last year on December 28, 1952. She wanted me to live with you after she died. John asked Reverend Bennett to help us find you. If you don't want me, John said I could live with him until I turn eighteen.*
>
> *We won't send you any legal stuff until we're sure you are Mama's brother.*
>
> *John said I should tell you I'm religious. Reverend Bennett told me to put his card in this letter.*
>
> *Sincerely yours,*
>
> *Miranda (Randa) Shepherd*
>
> *PS. I could be your housekeeper. I can cook pretty good.*

Quinn smoothed a trembling hand over his dark, short-cropped beard, then looked toward heaven and whispered, "Oh, Mother, she had a child."

He would never forget the high pitch of his mother's voice when she called that day. "Quinn, we can't find your sister. We got home from a funeral, and Sarah Jean wasn't in the house. We searched everywhere, then we checked her room again. Her closet and dresser drawers are all empty."

Quinn sat on the edge of his chair and stared blindly at the wall in front of him. How did Sarah Jean get clear down to Arizona? Why did she leave?

Had she fought with their father? Quinn learned the hard way that he couldn't win an argument with that man. When he told his father he wanted to be a teacher, his dad demanded Quinn stay home on the family farm and till the land. The old man yelled, "Don't you know this farm will be yours when I die? I'm not going to waste my money on college when I can teach you everything you need to know."

Quinn had shouted back, "I'll pay my own way through school." He *would not* live under his father's thumb.

It was the week before Christmas break when his mother wrote, saying she had convinced his father to pay for his schooling. She ended the letter, begging him to come home for Christmas.

Outside, a lawnmower roared to life, jolting Quinn out of yesterday and into the present. He ground his teeth together until his jaw hurt, trying to push those unhappy memories from his mind. He slid the letter into the envelope, shoved it into his briefcase, and left the church for home.

At home, Quinn went directly to his study to call Drew, his best friend from seminary. "This is Professor Patterson."

Quinn massaged the tight cords at the back of his neck and said, "Drew, I received a letter today that I want you to hear."

"Sure. Go ahead."

He choked on *twelve-years-old*. Quinn stopped reading and cleared his throat. "Sorry, my emotions got away from

My Name is Randa

me." He continued reading to the end and said, "She was alive all those years, had a child, married twice, and *never* contacted us?

"My sister erased our family from her life and broke my mother's heart. After Sarah left, I called Mother once a week, and she never once talked to me without mentioning Sarah Jean's name."

He flung his arm in the air with the letter in hand. "Now, out of the blue, I get a letter that says Sarah has named *me* to be her daughter's guardian."

Drew asked, "How long has it been since she ran away?"

"Sarah left in '32, twenty-one years ago."

Drew whistled. "Unbelievable. Would you read it to me again?"

When Quinn finished reading the letter, Drew said, "It sounds genuine to me. What do you think?"

"I agree, but Drew, I don't know how to raise a child. If my Arlene was still alive, she would be ecstatic. She longed to have a child, but it wasn't to be."

Drew laughed. "Madeline and I didn't know how to raise our children either, but we learned one day at a time. Trust in yourself, Quinn; you're good with kids. I know you're scared, but you can do this." After a few moments of silence, Drew said, "I wonder if you might need some legal advice?"

"That's a good idea. There's an attorney in my congregation. I'll call him."

"Yes, call and see if you can talk to him *today*. It would be easier if you had some direction from him before you have to preach tomorrow." Drew ended their conversation by praying God would quiet Quinn's anxious thoughts, then said, "Keep me posted, my friend. We will be praying."

Quinn put the receiver back in its cradle and said to the empty room, "What kind of stepfather would allow a child he'd raised for ten years to move away from her family and friends?"

His stomach rumbled. It was almost three o'clock, and he hadn't eaten since breakfast. After devouring two bologna sandwiches and half a bag of potato chips, he called attorney Thor Olsen, who said he'd be over after dinner.

Quinn began pacing. He traveled to the kitchen, wiped crumbs off the countertops, then moved on to the living room. The morning newspaper lay open on the floor. He folded it together and placed it on the bottom shelf of an end table. Then he moved back to the study and stood for a moment staring at the letter before making the room neat for company.

***

After Thor left, Quinn sat at his desk and ran his finger down the list of the attorney's suggestions: call an emergency board meeting, ask for a month's leave of absence, leave for Minneapolis on Friday … He folded the paper and tucked it into his Bible.

Where should he put Miranda's letter? In his desk drawer? No.

In his briefcase? No, it might fall out and get lost.

In his shirt pocket right up against his heart? Yes! He needed to keep it safe, never out of reach. Quinn carefully folded it to fit into his pocket.

It was bedtime, but would he be able to sleep? Maybe some hot tea would help. His mother always drank tea to calm her nerves.

Quinn finished his drink, prepared for bed, and dropped to his knees, like he and his mother used to do when he was a boy. "Lord, please clear my mind while I preach tomorrow." He rested his head on his clasped hands and repeated the question that kept circling in his mind. "How can I, a fifty-two-year-old widower, raise a girl who thinks she's old enough to be my housekeeper?"

Chapter 2

Sunday, May 17

*I*t was still dark when Quinn woke on Sunday morning. He dressed in a flannel shirt, plopped a Chicago Cubs baseball cap over his thick hair, and drove to a nearby park. With legs stretched out in front of him, Quinn sat on his favorite bench near the water's edge and watched a thin line of light appear on the horizon.

His mind circled, repeating one of his many questions. How could he raise a child, especially a *girl?* Quinn looked toward heaven and said, "Lord, she deserves better than me. I work long hours. I don't know how I'll find time for her."

The light widened with a yellow glow that deepened and reflected gold on the water. Streaks of purple colored the morning sky, and the water changed to a reddish-orange. The sun rose higher, a blush pink nestled between the purple streaks, and slowly night turned to day.

The tension in Quinn's muscles eased, and the beauty before him blocked the anxious questions from his mind. Birds in the trees greeted the day with a joyful song, and Quinn rejoiced with them. He raised his hands in praise to God, the creator of heaven and earth.

The heavens' expanse turned blue, and Quinn walked back to his car.

***

When he arrived at church, the choir was practicing their special number for the morning worship. His assistant Reverend Paul Richards and secretary Ramona Schrader were in her office, putting together pages of a handout for the youth group.

Marg Watland

"Good morning. I'm happy to find you here. Yesterday, I received some correspondence that requires an emergency board meeting. We have some work to do before the meeting. I'll come in tomorrow around ten and fill you in on all the details."

***

Monday morning, Quinn waited until nine o'clock to call Miranda's reverend.

A voice said, "Reverend Bennett speaking."

"Hello, this is Reverend Quinn Edwards. I received a letter from Miranda Shepherd."

"Yes, we've been hoping to hear from you. My wife and I want to help you and Randa in any way we can. I'm Ralph and my wife is Bertha."

Quinn exhaled and said, "Thank you. I'm in shock. Do you know what caused my sister's death?"

"She caught a cold that went into pneumonia and died of congestive heart failure."

Quinn's voice cracked. "Heart failure?"

"Sarah told us she had rheumatic fever when she was eleven. The fever damaged the valves in her heart. The doctors said it would shorten the length of her life, but they didn't know how much."

"Really? I knew she had the fever, but I thought Mother was overreacting. Sarah was born the year I graduated from high school, so I didn't really know her." He told the reverend about Sarah's disappearance.

"My, that's quite a story." Ralph cleared his throat. "Let me tell you about Sarah and Randa.

"The two of them came to our church in July of 'fifty-one. After the morning service, Sarah came to me with tears in her eyes and asked me if I could come to her house, saying

My Name is Randa

that she needed spiritual help. I suggested that my wife Bertha and I would be happy to come visit on Tuesday.

"Sarah told us that her doctor said she had one, maybe two, years to live. Then she told us she ran away from home when she was sixteen. Sarah said she was raised in a Christian home but hadn't darkened the doors of a church since she left home. She told us she wanted nothing to do with her parents, but she needed to forgive them and to get right with God."

"Did she tell you why?"

"No, she wouldn't answer questions about her parents, but I believe she genuinely forgave them."

Before they finished their conversation, Ralph insisted Quinn stay with them when he came to Minneapolis.

"That's very kind of you. I appreciate it."

"We wouldn't have it any other way. Bertha and Sarah became very close, and Randa … she's a sweet girl and we are going to miss her."

"Thank you for caring for my sister and her daughter. God bless you. I plan to arrive Friday, in the late afternoon. I'll see you then."

***

Quinn slid Miranda's letter into his shirt pocket and then headed to church. Paul and Ramona stood when he opened the door. He waved them into his office, closed the door, pulled the letter from his pocket, and said, "I don't like to share my family's personal business, but in this case, I have no choice. Please keep this confidential." He finished reading Miranda's letter, then told them Sarah's story.

Paul and Ramona sat in their chairs with shocked looks. He continued, "An investigator of Thor Olson's verified the information in Miranda's letter. She is, without question, my niece.

Marg Watland

"I want to spend the weekend with Miranda and her stepfather, then return home Monday. Paul, that leaves you to do the Sunday services.

"I'm going to ask for some time off. I can't leave my niece alone at the house while I go to work. I don't know how I'm going to do this. Please pray for us."

Paul broke in. "Let's pray right now." He took a deep breath. "God, we pray for this young girl who is going to be moving away from everything she knows. We pray you give Quinn wisdom as he figures out how to make Miranda a part of his life ...."

Quinn's eyes filled, and he thanked them profusely. "I asked Roland Harris to call an emergency board meeting for seven tomorrow night. I'd like the three of us to put together a schedule for the month of June, showing how our staff can operate in my absence and an upgrade of all the department leaders and their substitutes. We have the rest of today and tomorrow for Romana to have it ready for the board members when we meet."

***

Before Quinn left for the day, Ramona suggested he buy Miranda a welcome home gift, so here he stood in McKee's Drugstore with no idea what to buy.

He wandered up and down the aisles, looking for an idea. What would a twelve-year-old girl like? Several brands of bar soap caught his eye. Maybe she'd like some smelly soap. Arlene liked Camay. Quinn dropped two bars into his basket, then wandered down another aisle with nail polish and lipstick; no, she wasn't ready for that yet.

Toothpaste? He liked Colgate, but if she liked something different, he'd get used to it. They'd have to go shopping together, *or* he could give her some money and let her do her own shopping. Money! Did she get an allowance? Did

My Name is Randa

she have to earn it? He knew nothing about allowances. His dad didn't believe in them.

Quinn turned down the next aisle. Ah hah, stationery. Miranda could use some pretty stationery. He chose a box that had a border of flowers across the top of the paper. At the check-out counter, he smiled at the clerk and asked, "Would you wrap this and twenty stamps in some pretty paper suitable for a teenage girl?"

***

He carried his purchases into the house and admired the pink package as he walked into the guest room. Quinn stood the package on end against the pillows and glanced around a room with ivory walls and a white chenille bedspread. Would Miranda like his home? Would it be welcoming to her? How would he make them a family? Quinn thought for a moment and nodded. Miranda was old enough; they'd work it out together.

Chapter 3

Tuesday evening, May 19

*E*very member of the board was present. Quinn stood at the head of the table and said, "Thank you for coming. I've called this meeting to share a private issue that I ask to be kept confidential." He held up Miranda's letter. "I received this letter on Saturday. I will read it first and then explain further.

"Dear Reverend Quinn Daniel Edwards.

John, my stepfather, thinks you are my uncle ..."

The men stared at Quinn with open mouths. He didn't acknowledge their expressions but continued reading to the end before explaining.

"My sister was 4 months old when I graduated from high school. We barely knew each other, but this letter says Sarah Jean wanted me to be Miranda's guardian.

"Sarah ran away from home at age sixteen. The police never found her. We didn't know if she was dead or alive.

"Now, after twenty-one years, I learn she died this past December, leaving a twelve-year-old daughter that I didn't know existed.

"I don't know how to be a parent, but a friend tells me you learn one day at a time. Please pray for us. I'd like a month's leave of absence while Miranda and I learn how to live together as a family.

"I plan to go to Minneapolis this weekend to meet my niece. Paul is prepared to fill the pulpit in my absence."

Hiram Humphrey, the eldest member of the church board, stood. His hand quivered as he pointed a finger at Reverend Edwards and said, "You aren't to be the one telling Paul he can do Sunday services without our approval.

My Name is Randa

We don't know if Paul can write a sermon on such short notice, and you are in the middle of a sermon series. Will Paul continue with that series?"

"Yes, he will," Quinn said. "When I do a series, Paul and I discuss the subject at length, then both he and I write a sermon on the topic. Sunday will be lesson five in a six-week series, and Paul and I have already reviewed it.

"Tomorrow, we'll collaborate on the sixth sermon, and Paul will finish the series. Reverend Paul Richards is a graduate of Western Theological Seminary in Holland, Michigan and came to us highly recommended."

Ernest, the Sunday School Superintendent, raised his hand, "In cases like this, we usually hire an interim reverend to take your place."

Roland jumped into the conversation and said, "Excuse me. Let's deal with Reverend Edwards' request for a month's leave first. May I call for the vote?"

The majority voted "aye." After much discussion, they gave Quinn a leave starting Thursday, May 21st through June.

Quinn held his hands up to silence all the conversation and said, "Ramona is passing out an updated list of all the department heads, their substitutes, and any special events the leaders have planned for June.

Roland thumbed through the pages and said, "This is too much information for us to work through tonight." A special planning meeting was scheduled to prepare for Quinn's leave, then Roland closed the meeting with a prayer.

Hiram was the first one to leave for home.

Roland glanced at Paul and Quinn and said, "Don't worry about Hiram; he'll get over it."

Quinn laughed. "He is in for a surprise; Paul writes excellent sermons."

Mary Watland

***

Back at home, Quinn headed to his study and called Drew. "They gave me a leave of absence through the month of June, but it wasn't easy."

Drew hesitated, then said, "I've been thinking; you work long hours. Is it possible your church is too big for you now that you have a child to raise?"

"It could be. I wouldn't mind serving in a smaller church. I'll pray about it while I drive to Minnesota. Thanks for helping me through these last few days. I'll call you when we get back."

Quinn bounced a pencil on his desk. Did Miranda have dark Irish eyes like Grandma O'Reilly? Was she soft-spoken like his mother? A frown crossed Quinn's brow. Or was she a chatterbox that would drive him crazy with all her words?

"Oh, Lord, teach me how to give her father love."

Chapter 4

To Minneapolis

Friday, May 22

*R*anda Shepherd strode in long steps down the street to Bertha Bennett's. She wanted time for a last visit with Bertha before her uncle arrived. Tears welled up and trickled out of the corners of her eyes. She had to quit crying. Uncle Quinn wouldn't want a crybaby.

She turned the corner, checked the driveway for a strange car, and breathed a sigh of relief. He wasn't here yet.

Randa opened the screen door and called out, "Knock, knock."

The little round woman saw Randa's red eyes and pulled her close. "Your uncle called when he crossed the border into Minnesota. He should be here in the next 10 or 15 minutes."

Randa laid her head on Bertha's shoulder and said, "I'm going to miss you so much." They shed a few tears, and then Randa pulled away. Bertha used her hanky to dry Randa's face.

She kissed the sweet girl's brow and said, "We'll continue to pray for each other every day, and don't forget, I expect to get a letter from you at least once a month."

"I will, don't worry." Randa tightened her arms around the woman who felt like a grandma to her and said, "Bertha, I'm scared he won't like me."

"I know, Honey, and my guess is he's scared *you* won't like him. Let's sit in the living room and watch for him." Randa sat on a dark leather chair, pushed out of her sandals, and slid them under her seat.

Minutes later, a dark green car stopped in front of the house. Bertha patted Randa's shoulder, then pushed open the screen. "Hello Quinn, I'm Bertha Bennett; come on in."

Marg Watland

She stepped aside and watched the nervous pair. They stared at each other for a few heartbeats before Quinn smiled and said, "Hello Miranda, I'm your Uncle Quinn."

She jerked, and Bertha said, "Go ahead, Honey, tell him."

Randa's eyes focused on her uncle's chin. She couldn't believe it. He had a beard. It wasn't very long, but ...

"Miranda was my Grandma Shepherd's name. Everybody calls me Randa. That's what I like to be called. My middle name is Jean, and that's my Grandma Edward's name."

"Oh, I've been thinking of you as Miranda. If I forget, please remind me to call you Randa."

"Okay. Do I look like anyone?"

Quinn studied her face. Then his forehead creased as he looked at Bertha for an explanation. He didn't know the popular movie stars.

Bertha laughed. "She means, does she look like any of your relatives?"

He turned back to Randa, and with a wave of his hand, he gestured toward a mirror on the hall wall. "Our eyes are the same color. Let's look in the mirror and see what you think."

Reverend Bennett came in the back door. Bertha stopped him, and they watched Quinn and Randa decide if their eyes were the same color. Quinn asked, "What color do you say yours are?"

"Brown, but yours are black, and your hair is darker than mine, too. Maybe my eyes will get darker when I get older." She dug her big toe into the thick pile of the area rug. "Is my grandma alive?"

"No, I'm sorry. She died in 1951. Your Grandpa Edwards and my wife Arlene both died in 1948. I've been living alone for five years. Now you and I will be a family."

My Name is Randa

Quinn turned toward Reverend Bennett and said, "And you are Ralph?" They strode toward each other and shook hands. He winked at Ralph and said, "I've just now noticed that Randa and I have the same webbed feet. Our second and third toes aren't separated all the way down. We got that from my father."

"Really?" Randa laughed. "John teases me about my toes."

Quinn cocked his head to one side and said, "As to whom you might resemble, I'll have to think about that for a while."

***

That night, Quinn lay in bed thinking about the God-inspired mirror idea. It reminded him of when Sarah was five or six and he'd come home for Easter weekend. She sat beside their mother, sneaking looks at him out of the corner of her eye, exactly like Randa when they stood in front of the mirror. Tomorrow, he'd tell Randa about that Easter.

His thoughts turned to Randa's stepfather, who said very little during dinner and was careful of everything he said and did.

John seemed like a responsible person, so why would Sarah want to take Randa away from him? He'd invited John to go out for breakfast, so they could get better acquainted. John agreed, but Quinn was sure Sarah's husband would rather eat nails than have breakfast with him. It was too soon for a question-answer session, but he had so many questions.

Quinn slid out of bed and dropped to his knees. He prayed, "Heavenly Father, Sarah has brought John and me together. Help us break down the barriers that would keep us from becoming friends."

Chapter 5

Friday, May 22

$\mathcal{R}$anda knocked, then opened the door and popped her head into the Bennetts' house. "Hi, Uncle Quinn; John's waiting for you in the car. Sophies Café has 3 flavors of syrup; you'll like their pancakes."

Quinn raised an eyebrow and said, "Okay, I'll see you later."

He opened the passenger door and climbed in. "Good morning."

John nodded and shifted to first. "Randa picked the place where we'll have breakfast. It's not far."

It sounded like John wanted to be in control today. He'd have to be careful. He hoped they would be a little more at ease by the time they left the restaurant.

A waitress seated them and poured coffee. John said, "I'll take pancakes, two eggs and bacon."

"I'll have the same," said Quinn. He fiddled with the silverware, deciding on how to start the conversation. "I was shocked when I got Randa's letter. We thought Sarah must have died."

"Yeah, and Reverend Bennett said you didn't know she had a bad heart. Randa said your folks and your wife died, and you've been alone for five years. Sorry about your wife. Sarah and I were counting on you having a wife. Randa needs a woman in her life." John's face crumpled, and by sheer force, he didn't weep.

"John, everyone grieves differently, but I *know* how much you are suffering. I felt like Arlene was snatched out of my arms and there was a hole in my soul that nothing could fill.

My Name is Randa

"For weeks, I cried myself to sleep. I thought it would never end. I promise you; it *will* get better."

John took a sip of coffee and said, "It sounds like your parents died about the same time as mine. I have a sister too. Her name's Dorothy, and we're close. She and her husband Tom live on the other side of Minneapolis. They have two boys. Jimmy's ten, and Mike is eight."

The waitress came with their meals, and John said, "You probably better pray before this food gets cold."

Quinn prayed, then reached for his coffee. "Randa's letter said you were in Yuma. Is that where you were raised?"

"No, I grew up in Minneapolis. My Dad worked for the railroad, so when I graduated from high school, I followed in his footsteps. I worked here for a few years, but I wanted to see more of the country. So, when I heard they needed help in Yuma, I applied for the job.

Quinn wanted to talk about Sarah, but John kept the conversation impersonal. He waited for an opening and said, "John, I'm concerned about how Randa is feeling about leaving her home and all her friends."

"Yeah, well, she promised her mama she'd go live with you." John filled his mouth with a big bite of pancake and took his time chewing.

Quinn didn't know what to say, so he waited.

John fidgeted, took a sip of coffee, then said, "Sarah wanted you to raise her because you're religious. I'm not. I tried praying, but it didn't work. Sarah died anyway."

"Thank you. That answers why Sarah chose me. I couldn't understand why she'd want me to be her daughter's guardian."

"Yeah, well, that's why."

Quinn looked at John's bowed head and said, "Throughout the Bible, it says that God loves us. That means you, too.

Mary Watland

When Arlene died, it was God who helped me heal from the grief."

John poured syrup on his pancakes and asked, "Do you have kids?"

"No, Arlene, couldn't have children."

He looked Quinn in the eye, and his lip trembled. "I know you must be wondering. I didn't want Randa to call me dad, because I wasn't her father. Lee was my best friend, and Randa was *his* baby girl. Sarah was seven months along when Lee was killed in a railroad accident, and there was no family around, so I became her family. I was at the hospital when Randa was born."

A waitress refilled their coffee. When she left, Quinn said, "John, you were my sister's husband. That makes me your brother-in-law; you're the only brother I'll ever have. You are Randa's stepfather, and I am her uncle. We are a *family!*"

John's chin quivered, and his eyes watered. "Thank you."

***

John dropped Quinn off at the Bennetts' so Randa could direct Quinn to their house. She climbed into Quinn's car and asked, "Did you like Sophie's Café?"

"Yes, I tried the berry syrup, but I like maple better."

She directed him to a white bungalow with a massive oak tree that shaded the front of the house. The first thing he noticed when he walked into the house were two stacks of boxes butted against the wall.

John motioned toward the boxes. "Sarah picked out the things she wanted Randa to have, and Bertha boxed them up for her. I told Sarah I'd do it, but she said I already had enough to deal with her being sick and all. She was a good wife. You missed out by not knowing her."

Randa pointed to a box on top of the stack labeled *Keepsakes*. "Mama said to put this box in the attic, because it's

My Name is Randa

things I might want to have when I'm grown up." She squatted and pushed a box closer to the wall. "This has kitchen pans, cookbooks, and things we baked with. John said to take them because he didn't plan on doing any fancy baking."

Quinn's eye was drawn to a striped blanket with multiple bright Mexican colors that lay across the back of a beige couch, much too bright for Quinn's taste. He asked, "Would you show me the rest of my sister's house?"

Randa took his hand and led him away from the front door. "Okay, we need to start with the kitchen. That was Mama's favorite room. We baked together all the time. She taught me how to make all her special recipes."

John stepped over to the stove and pulled the oven door open. "She wanted a big gas range. We saved up and got her a real good one. I ended up having to change the cupboards around." He set his jaw and swallowed hard. "I don't know what I'm gonna do with that big monstrosity now that Sarah's gone."

They left the kitchen, and John led the way down the hall. The first door was his bedroom. He paused, his hand on the doorknob, then opened the door. "A couple months ago, I asked Dorothy to clear out anything that somebody else could use." He opened the door, sat down on the bed, and stroked the cover, a Mexican blanket. "We went to Nogales and bought this cover for our bed. Sarah liked the bright Mexican colors, but she knew I didn't. This is what we chose." He rubbed his hand along the vertical stripes of muted gray, purple, and white that covered his bed. There were bright purple pillowcases in one of Randa's boxes.

They moved on to where Randa stood. "This is my room. When I was ten, they bought me a new mattress. John painted my walls blue, and Mama made me ruffly curtains."

21

John fiddled with the scarf on Randa's dresser. "Are you expecting to get everything in your car? There's the furniture and a bike in the garage."

Quinn shook his head. "I waited until I got here to decide. I have plenty of furniture and bedding at home. Randa, unless your furniture has special meaning to you, we could leave it here for John. We'll do whatever you want. You don't have to decide today."

John raised an eyebrow. It took a moment for Quinn to realize he had forgotten to tell them his plans. "I'm sorry, I told the Bennetts, but I forgot to tell you the church board has given me a leave of absence, so we won't leave until early Monday morning. I thought she would like to go to her church one last time."

Randa looked from one man to the other and finally said, "John needs the furniture for when he has company, but I'd like my Mexican blankets, if it's okay." Tears filled her eyes. She spun and ran to the bathroom.

Quinn wanted to hold her in his arms until there were no more tears.

John shrugged. "She always runs away when she cries. I don't know what to do."

"I don't either, but I'm thinking there will be times when I'll be crying with her."

"We might as well go sit in the living room until she's done. My sister is bringing a picnic supper over here tonight at six for a goodbye time. We thought you'd have to leave on Saturday to get back to church. They want to meet you. I think I'll call her right now. Tomorrow would be better for them."

He called Dorothy and suggested they change their plans. Randa came back into the room while John was talking to his sister. He hung up and said, "We're changing the farewell picnic to tomorrow."

My Name is Randa

"Okay. What should we do now?" Randa asked.

Quinn said, "I'd like to take some flowers to the cemetery."

John averted his eyes. "Take Randa with you. She can show you the way. Monday, after you leave, I'll tell Sarah everything that happened while you were here. I don't know if she can hear me, but just in case—She'd want to know." John turned and hurried down the hall to the bathroom.

"Sometimes he goes there to cry," Randa said. "Let's go. I know a place to buy flowers."

Quinn chose a mixture of flowers for his bouquet, and Randa chose pink and white daisies with one dark red carnation in the center. She pointed to the carnation. "Mama liked pink and red together."

***

At the cemetery, Randa pointed to a place for him to park. She hopped out and said, "We go this way." When she turned left, Quinn, lost in thought, continued going straight ahead. Randa ran back and took his hand. "It's over here."

Three grave stones later, she dropped his hand and squatted down, pressing her hand on the sun-warmed stone. Quinn kneeled beside her, placed his flowers across the corner of the stone, and then traced Sarah's name with his finger. Randa laid her flowers on the other side. "Is it all right if we talk to her?"

"I don't know why not? Nobody really knows if our loved ones in heaven can hear us."

She sat cross-legged on the grass and began talking. "Mama, here's Uncle Quinn. He came to get me. We're going to Chicago on Monday, so I won't be able to come here to talk to you anymore." She burst into tears. "I miss you,

Mama." She dipped her head down to her shirt tail and dried her face. Quinn swiped his eyes.

Randa had more she wanted to say, but she pushed her grief back and jumped up. "Okay, let's go."

When they got to the car, she opened the door and stood, trying to decide what to do. "Uncle Quinn, would it be okay if I went back and talked to her a little longer by myself?"

"I think that's a good idea. Stay as long as you like. I'll sit under that tree up ahead. Don't hurry; I don't mind waiting." Randa closed the door and ran down the path toward her mama's resting place.

***

Quinn sat in the shade and prayed. "Lord, I didn't expect so much grief. Help Randa and me learn how to grieve together. I pray for John, who will be all alone."

***

When they returned to the house, John was making sandwiches. While he and Randa put food on the table, Quinn stared out the kitchen window at a neglected backyard.

John came up behind him and said, "I haven't taken care of my yard like I used to. I got behind, and now I can't seem to make myself go out there and clean it up."

"I understand. When Arlene died, it was months before I could make myself pack up her belongings and give them away."

Quinn stared at the unkempt yard and said, "John, would you let me help you clean up your back yard? A friend once told me the best way to get to know a man is to work beside him."

Randa came into the room and said, "Yeah, that would be fun. Let's do it."

My Name is Randa

John was about to refuse, then he looked at Quinn and Randa's grins and let go of his pride., "Okay, if that's what you want. It'd feel good to have this place cleaned up, but first, we'd better load your car with all of Randa's stuff."

Saturday morning, Randa answered Quinn's knock with a big grin. "Come in. Guess what, Uncle Quinn? We're going to have a real family workday. When Aunt Dorothy heard what we planned to do, she said it should be *all* the family. They're coming too."

An old Ford truck rattled into the driveway, and the rest of the *family* piled out of the truck. John hugged his sister and then turned to Quinn. "This is my sister Dorothy and her husband, Tom Evans." He grabbed the boys around their necks. "These two monkeys are my nephews, Jimmy and Mike."

The five men, boys included, pruned and trimmed, weeded and replanted, and dug and replaced. They filled the bed of Tom's truck and got to the dump before it closed.

Dorothy and Randa visited while they washed the windows inside and out, did two loads of wash, and put together their favorite Mexican meal of enchiladas and a green salad.

When the men finished, they sat under a shade tree and admired their work. Dorothy and Randa brought dinner out to the picnic table. Quinn had never eaten Mexican food, so when the hot sauce came to Randa, she spooned a small amount on his plate and suggested he taste it first. Everyone watched as he put some in his mouth. His eyes grew big, and he grabbed for his Coke.

At the end of the meal, Quinn said, "I liked the enchiladas, but I'm not sure I need that hot stuff."

They all laughed, and Tom said, "When John and Sarah moved to Minneapolis, the same thing happened to us. If you keep trying, you'll get used to it."

When it was time for goodbyes, Aunt Dorothy hugged Randa and whispered, "I like your Uncle Quinn; he's nice. Be sure to write and tell us how you're doing." They both shed a few tears. Uncle Tom squeezed her tight and told her to be good. She hugged Jimmy and Mike in a group hug, but they wiggled out of her arms and ran to get in the truck.

John put his arm around Randa, and she waved goodbye until they were out of sight. When Randa turned back to the house, tears glistened in her eyes.

Chapter 6

May 24

Sunday morning, Randa knocked on the Bennetts' door with a happy smile and a sparkle in her eyes. "We have a surprise!"

Quinn followed her to the car. John, who sat behind the wheel dressed in a suit, said, "Thought we should go as a family today."

Randa crawled in the front seat and bounced with happiness. "John and I decided I'll write to him one week, and he'll call the next week."

When they arrived at church, John chose the next to the last row. Randa slid in beside him; Quinn followed. She took both of their hands and whispered, "I love sitting between you. I feel extra safe."

Quinn said, "I appreciate that. Thank you for telling us."

John squirmed in discomfort. "Yeah, thanks."

She scooted back against the pew and listened to the organ prelude. Randa wondered if her mama was listening to this kind of music in heaven. Did Jesus see John was at church with them? She prayed. "Jesus, if it's okay, would you let Mama know John went to church today?"

During the announcements, her mind wandered. Yesterday, John had given her Mama's ratty suitcase. When she and Bertha finished packing her clothes, there was a church dress hanging in her closet, and the clothes she'd need for today and tomorrow were on top of the empty dresser.

Reverend Bennett began preaching, but Randa didn't hear his sermon. She hoped John and Uncle Quinn would like each other—a lot. She was going to try very hard to be

Marg Watland

good when she went to Chicago. What if she got scared? No, she wouldn't think about that.

After the service, John stopped the car in front of the Bennetts' house and said, "I don't want to go to any restaurant until I get out of these clothes." He yanked on his tie. "I hate ties and I don't like suits any better. We're going home to change and then come back to pick you up."

***

The restaurant John chose was well known for their fried chicken. The waitress came with menus, and Randa said, "We all want fried chicken." Quinn winked at John before he had time to correct her.

The men asked for coffee, and after they had their first swallow, Randa asked, "Can we do something fun today?"

Quinn smiled at her and said, "That sounds like a good idea, just so it doesn't involve driving. We have a long drive home tomorrow. What do you think, John?"

They walked out of the restaurant into bright sunlight. John opened the car door and grinned. "What do ya think, Randa? The zoo?" He glanced at Quinn. "When we moved to Minneapolis, that was the first place we took Randa. She came home chattering like a magpie and wanted to know when we could go again."

Randa pulled on John's arm. "Can we go to the amusement park, too? It's close to the zoo. I want you guys to go on the Ferris Wheel with me."

***

Quinn stood under the shade of a tree and watched Randa laugh at the swinging monkey's antics. He hadn't been to an amusement park since college. Those things were a waste of money. No! That sounded like his father. He wouldn't

My Name is Randa

do that to her. He needed to loosen up now that he had a teenager to raise. With his heavy schedule, how would he find time to play?

Randa's happy spirit spread over to Quinn; he relaxed and enjoyed the zoo with her. When they came to the snake display, John winked at Quinn and tugged Randa's pony-tail. "Come on, Randa; you've never seen the snakes. You don't want to leave Minneapolis without seeing them."

"No, no! I hate snakes. If you want to go in there, take Uncle Quinn with you."

John turned to Quinn with a challenge on his face. "Well, what do you think?"

Quinn laughed. "I might as well."

***

Randa sat on a bench and waited. She liked that Uncle Quinn and John went to see the snakes. She wanted them to be good friends. She hoped Uncle Quinn would go on some rides with her. Mama would have loved this day.

There was a breeze when they walked into the amusement park. Randa led them to the Ferris Wheel. She sat in the middle seat, and the men squeezed in on either side. Two teenage boys were next to be seated, and it wasn't long before their seat rocked from all the horseplay going on below. Just before they rounded to the top and began down the other side, John winked at Randa. "Well, it looks like your uncle isn't afraid of heights."

Quinn laughed. "No, but I *am* afraid of teenagers." It was dusk when Quinn stepped off their last ride on the Octopus. He staggered, and John and Randa laughed.

They finished the day eating German sausages with sauerkraut and double-decker ice-cream cones.

When they dropped Quinn off at the Bennetts', he said, "Thanks John; I think it was a good family day."

"Yeah, it was. I need to get this kid home. She has to get up early in the morning."

Quinn walked into the Bennetts' house, dropped on a chair, and said, "Randa wanted to do something fun. They grinned at me all day. I haven't done their kind of fun in years. I think John was testing me, and I don't know whether I passed or failed."

Ralph and Bertha laughed.

***

Monday morning, John stood at the kitchen windows watching for Quinn when he pulled into the driveway.

John came out of the house carrying one last box. Quinn opened the back door, and John pushed things around until there was room for it.

He turned to Randa, put his hands on her shoulders, and looked into her eyes. Tears ran down his face. "This is what your Mama wanted, so this is what we'll do."

She looked back at him. "Yes, this is what Mama wanted." He pulled her into his arms, and they hugged and kissed goodbye. She stepped back. "I promise I'll write to you tonight before I go to sleep." She turned on her heel and climbed into the car.

Quinn reached out his hand, but John seemed to have shriveled in front of him, so instead, he put both arms around the man and hugged him. "I'll take good care of her, brother, I promise."

As they drove away, Quinn looked in the rear-view mirror, where John stood alone in the middle of the street.

They'd gone two blocks when Randa's hands covered her face, and she sobbed. Quinn pulled over. "Honey, I think the best thing for us to do is, I'll drive, and you cry until there are no more tears." She nodded, and Quinn shifted into drive and headed toward the interstate.

When her tears subsided, Randa curled up into a ball and slept until Quinn stopped for lunch.

Chapter 7

Park City, Wisconsin

Monday, July 27

Neil Johnson, the tall, stocky chairman of the church board, walked into Park City Community Church, dropped a fat manila envelope on the secretary's desk, and said, "Nora, the Search Committee has found a promising candidate to be our reverend, and we'd like you to do the interview."

Nora Montgomery stood in the storage room doorway with her mouth hanging open.

"There are some personal questions that have to be asked; that's why we think you would be the best person to handle the interview," he said and walked across the room to take a box of stationery supplies from her arms.

She stared straight ahead at the third button on his shirt, then looked up into his eyes with a look of horror. "Me!?"

What was he thinking? She'd been the church's part-time secretary for seven months, and now they wanted her to interview a *reverend*? Her eyes turned to the envelope, and she sucked in a deep, shuddering breath. What was in there that was so unusual?

Neil tapped the packet. "This is his resume. I'd like you to look at it and then meet with us Wednesday after Prayer Meeting. You'll understand when you read it. We've decided to go to Chicago this Sunday to hear him preach, and we're hoping you'll go with us." He smiled and patted her shoulder. "I'll see you Wednesday. I have to get back to work."

***

My Name is Randa

Nora walked the three blocks to her house, in the blistering sun, with the envelope clutched to her breast. Her eyes brightened when she saw her daughter Julie's car parked in her driveway. When Nora opened the front door, the buttery aroma of grilled cheese sandwiches greeted her.

She lay the envelope on the kitchen table, snatched a napkin from the holder, and wiped her damp forehead. "It's hot out there," Nora said, vigorously fluffing her thick auburn curls.

"Hi, Mother," Julie said, carrying glasses of sweet tea to the kitchen table. "Tim is waiting on a part for the tractor he's repairing, and I'm to pick it up at one. I decided I'd come in early and make lunch for you."

"What a pleasant surprise; thank you, Honey." The mother-daughter look-a-likes hugged, and Nora patted the growing mound that was her first grandchild.

"We might have found a new minister. The Search Committee is going to Chicago this weekend to hear a reverend preach. They want me to go, too. Neil thinks I should do the interview."

Julie placed her hands on her hips and said, "Really? They want *you*, Nora Montgomery, to go to Chicago and interview a *reverend*, neither of which you have done before?" She grinned, and the cleft in her chin deepened.

Nora laughed. "Well, I've never done an interview, but your father and I left you with my parents and went to Chicago for the World's Fair in 1933. We had a glorious time.

"All I know is, Neil thought I'd be the best one to ask the questions, whatever that means." Her gaze flipped to the ominous envelope, and she said, "I guess I'll find out when I read what's in there."

***

When Julie left to pick up Tim's tractor parts, Nora settled in her favorite chair. She scanned the pages that contained Reverend Edward's clerical background and the letters of recommendation. Then she carefully read the page entitled, <u>Why are you interested in serving at Park City Community Church?</u>

I grew up in a farming town in Michigan. The minister, and the people in our small congregation, taught me how to walk with God. I've missed that kind of intimate ministry.

I'd like to teach the saints in my congregation how to encourage new converts and help them grow in their faith.

I'm fifty-two years old, have been a widower for five years, and have no children of my own. In May, I received a letter from twelve-year-old Randa Shepherd, saying she was my niece. She wrote that her mama, my baby sister, died in December and wanted me to be her guardian.

My parents and I never heard from my sister Sarah Jean after she left home, so this came as a surprise. We thought something happened to her, and she died.

My niece has been living with me since June. I'm not comfortable raising her in a large church. She needs to grow up in the safe environment of a community where everybody knows her. I want us to be in a small congregation where it will be easy for us to get to know you and you to know us.

Nora's heart went out to the young girl who not only lost a mother but now lived with an uncle—a stranger. She couldn't imagine how a man his age was handling the challenges of being a parent.

Did his sister have a child out of wedlock? Is that why she didn't contact her family? Neil was right. The pulpit committee couldn't make a decision about Reverend Edwards until they knew why Sarah didn't communicate with her family. They needed to know more.

My Name is Randa

So, that is why the committee wanted a woman to do the interview, but why her?

The wheels in her brain rolled to the future. If the church approved of this man, it would be easier for his niece if they moved to Park City before school started in September. Nora pulled a steno book out of her bag and started a list of things they'd have to do before a new minister came, just in case. The manse had been closed for over a year.

It disturbed Nora that the applicant's sister had died in December. He moved his niece to Chicago in May, and now they were considering another move. That child needed stability.

Later that afternoon, Nora remembered another circumstance very much like Randa's. She dialed a friend. "Hello, Ginny. I know of a twelve-year-old girl whose mother died and is now living with her mother's brother. I thought of your sister, Mimi. Would you give me her phone number? I'd like to talk to her about what they had to deal with when they brought Charles' great-niece home to live with them. The only thing I remember was Brandi had nightmares."

Chapter 8

To Chicago

Sunday, August 2

A large choir filed in through the side door, and Reverend Quinn Edwards, a man of medium build with black hair and a short-clipped beard, followed. Nora couldn't think of a minister in Park City with a beard, but there were a couple of mustaches.

He sat on a high-backed chair behind the pulpit. There were a few streaks of silver in his thick hair, but he looked younger than fifty-two.

While the music director led them in familiar hymns, Nora practiced, in her mind, how she would conduct the interview. First, she'd ask the committee's questions, and then she'd soften the tone to a conversational manner for the personal questions.

Nora listened intently to a message that challenged her to examine herself before God. Not all the sermons she'd heard during the past year had spoken so directly to her. He was good! The people in her church needed to hear Reverend Edwards.

When the service ended, Neil found the church secretary and introduced himself. "My name is Neil Johnson, and I'm from Park City."

She smiled. "I saw you come in and wondered if you were from the church in Wisconsin." She led them into the reverend's office. "I'll let him know you're here. It shouldn't be more than ten or fifteen minutes."

***

My Name is Randa

Reverend Edwards opened the door of his office and greeted them. "Good morning. I'm glad you came."

Neil stood, introduced each person who had come with him, and said, "We wanted you to know we came to hear you preach. Now we need to set up a time to do an interview."

"Okay. I'm available on Mondays—my day off." He sat down at his desk and opened his calendar.

"Monday's good," Neil said. "We've asked Mrs. Montgomery, our church secretary, to do the interview. I know this is unusual, but Nora was born and raised in our church, and while we've searched for a new reverend, she has kept our church running smoothly. We think she's the best person to ask some of our questions. Nora came prepared to stay; in case you were available on Monday. "

Reverend Edwards paused a moment, then said, "Ahh. Yes, tomorrow would be fine." He grinned. "You don't believe in wasting any time, do you?"

The committee members left Quinn's office with directions to a nearby restaurant and a hotel for Nora. They were excited about Reverend Edwards' preaching skills. Neil waited until after the waitress brought their food and then pointed his fork at Nora. "I think we shocked the reverend that we'd chosen you to do the interview." He chuckled. "You'll do fine, Nora. You have a good way with people. I hope you get a chance to talk to the niece."

Neil's wife Agnes squeezed her hand. "We'll be praying for you, Nora."

Nora's hand trembled when she cut into her slice of ham. "Pray for Reverend Edwards and his niece, too."

***

That evening, Nora sat in her hotel room, trying to find the right words to gently ask what they needed to know concerning his sister, but none of them sounded right. She closed her eyes and prayed. "Lord Jesus, I'm going to trust you to give me the right words."

Nora shook her head. That beard was going to cause some comments. Most ministers she knew were clean-shaven. Maybe he had acne scars under his beard. She was sure of one thing; there would be a rash of widows visiting their church if he accepted the call. It had been five years since his wife had died. He must have figured out by now how to handle husband-hunting women.

That child must miss all her friends. Maybe Charles and Mimi's story of becoming guardians to a ten-year-old great-niece would help Randa feel more comfortable answering her questions.

Nora tried to clear her mind of the anxious thoughts whirling around in her head.

At nine-thirty, she prepared for bed and slid in between the sheets. Her head barely touched the pillow before she fell asleep into a disturbing dream.

She stood, staring at an apparition in a mirror. A young man's image filled the glass. Nora blinked and looked again. He was still there, dressed in a chambray shirt. He smiled at her and said, "Hello, Nora."

"Who are you?"

"I'm your guardian angel. God has given you a heart filled with love. Don't be afraid to love them. Remember, I'm always close by, watching over you."

"Thank you. I didn't think my guardian angel would wear a chambray shirt."

"We wear whatever's right for the occasion. It's time for me to go," he said and blew her a kiss. "Goodbye, Little Mother."

Nora jerked awake, turned on the light, and looked at her watch. Ten o'clock. She sat on the edge of the bed and thought about the dream. What had just happened? Was it just a dream, or did she see her guardian angel?

Suddenly she said out loud, "LITTLE MOTHER! He called me Little Mother."

Chapter 9

The Interview

Monday, August 3

Nora put her notebook aside and said, "Reverend Edwards, we can't make a final decision about you without knowing more about your sister and your relationship with your family."

Quinn tensed and looked over her head. "I'll tell you about my sister, but I don't want this to be common knowledge."

"This will go no further than the five men on the committee."

He took a deep breath and said, "Sarah Jean, my baby sister, ran away from home when she was sixteen." He poured a glass of ice water. "She didn't leave a note, and we never heard a word from her."

"Oh, my." How his parents must have suffered. "I'm so very sorry, Reverend Edwards. Do you know why she left?" She watched his muscles tighten.

"I don't know. I know my father was *old country* strict. Laws and judgments controlled every decision he made in his Christian life.

"When I graduated from high school, Sarah was a baby. I had a scholarship to Western Michigan University in Kalamazoo, and from then on, I rarely went home except for holidays.

Nora nodded. "My husband's grandparents were like your father. Carl hated having to visit them. Thank you for answering my questions. We have covered everything I needed to know about Sarah. I assure you again, this will go

My Name is Randa

no further than the committee. Do you know if Randa was raised in a church-going home?"

"Their Pastor told me my sister had nothing to do with church until she learned she didn't have long to live. Then Sarah Jean and Randa began attending church."

"That means Randa's had no Sunday School background. The things we learn in Sunday School enhance our faith in Jesus." Nora paused. "I'm sorry, I got on a soapbox, but that early learning is so valuable in a child's life."

"I agree with you. I'm still considering how I'll help her catch up. I know only bits and pieces of Randa's life. She'll be talking to me about nothing important and then say something that answers what I've wondered about for days. Often, all it does is open another set of questions."

Nora smiled at him. "Thank you for disclosing those private things we needed to know about your sister. I believe that concludes my interview. I would like to meet Randa and, with your permission, talk to her about her mother."

"I'd like Randa to choose how much she wants to tell you about her mama. I don't think she will mind." He pushed back his chair. "My secretary suggested I invite you to have lunch with us. She brought cold chicken and a salad to our house this morning. Would you like to join us?"

"Thank you. I'd like that very much."

When they arrived at his home, Randa opened the front door before Quinn got around the car to open the door for Nora. Randa waited on the front porch and said, "I've been watching for you. Come on in."

Nora entered the house, and Quinn said, "Mrs. Montgomery, this is my niece, Randa Shepherd."

He put his hand on Randa's shoulder. "Honey, Mrs. Montgomery is representing the church in Wisconsin."

Marg Watland

Nora stepped forward and took both her hands. "I'm so happy to meet you. I've been praying for you and your uncle ever since I read his application. Please, call me Nora."

"That's a good idea, Nora, and I'm Quinn. All the members of my staff use my first name."

Their dark eyes left no doubt that Quinn and Randa were related. Randa hadn't reached her full height yet and was already taller than Nora's five feet.

"We're really excited you came, Nora," Randa said.

Quinn and Randa worked together, bringing the food and drinks to the dining room table adorned with a lovely bouquet of roses.

After Quinn prayed, Nora winked at Randa and said, "Quinn, you and I have something in common. We have matching birthdays."

Randa looked from one to the other. "When is your birthday, Uncle Quinn?"

"Saint Patrick's Day. I'm fifty-two."

"And I'm ten years younger," Nora said.

"I spent the morning answering Nora's questions," Quinn said. "Maybe she wouldn't mind if we learned some things about her. Randa, do you have a question?"

"Yes. Nora, have you lived in Park City for a long time?"

"I was born and raised there, and my grandfather was one of the men that started our church. I have one daughter, Julie. Last year, she married a southern boy from North Carolina. No woman has a son-in-law any better than my Julie's, Tim."

"Does Tim have a southern drawl? I love listening to southern people talk."

Nora couldn't help smiling. She had forgotten how many questions could come out of a young girl's mouth. "Oh my, yes. The day Julie brought him home to meet me, I suggested

My Name is Randa

he call me Nora. He said his southern upbringing wouldn't allow that; it wasn't proper. Tim named me Little Mother.

"My husband, Carl, died in the spring of 1951, and Tim helped Julie and me heal from our grieving. Now, they're expecting a baby in December. I'm excited to be a grandmother."

Randa had never heard that getting over grief was like healing. She missed her mama so much. Was she going to cry forever?

Quinn picked up the empty plates and said, "Randa made chocolate chip cookies for dessert. Would you like some coffee?"

"Do you have tea?"

After lunch, Quinn suggested they move into the living room, where Randa insisted Nora sit in her uncle's favorite chair. She and Quinn sat across from Nora on a brown leather davenport.

Nora smoothed her skirt and settled herself in Quinn's chair. "After I read your uncle's application, I called my friend Mimi. Several years ago, she and her husband, Charles became guardians to his ten-year-old great-niece, Brandi. She lived across the country in a little logging town in Oregon. Her parents and four-year-old brother died in a car accident."

Randa sat forward. "Was Brandi in the car, too?"

"No, she was at school. Brandi had relatives that lived nearby, but none of them could take her in. She lived in a foster home for two months before they located Charles and Mimi.

"Brandi was younger than you, Randa. Mimi told me Brandi was very fearful and didn't like to be left alone for even five minutes. She wanted a light on when she went to bed, and Mimi often slept half the night with Brandi because of her nightmares."

"Where did Brandi's uncle live?"

"In Iowa, and he was about the same age as your uncle."

Quinn sat back and watched them chatter away. It surprised him that Randa was so comfortable with Nora. She was usually tentative around adults. Then it hit him. Bertha Bennett and Randa were close, and Nora and Bertha had similar caring personalities.

Nora asked, "Randa, would you tell me a little about your family and your mother?"

Quinn slid his arm around Randa's shoulder. "Honey, if it makes you too sad, you don't have to answer Nora's questions."

He wasn't sure how Randa would respond, but he knew she'd not want to cry in front of a stranger. He couldn't believe how many tears he and Randa had shed when she talked about her mama. It broke his heart to see her suffer.

"Okay. I'll tell her, but I might cry."

"I'll probably cry with you, honey," Nora said.

He suggested she start where Sarah learned about her heart's serious condition. Randa leaned against him and began. "Mama got so tired she had to go to the doctor. When John and Mama came home, their eyes were red, and they were sad. That night, Mama told me she had a terrible fever when she was about my age, and it made her heart have to work a lot harder. Mama said the reason she took long naps was because her heart got tired." Tears trickled down her cheeks.

Quinn handed his handkerchief to Randa, and Nora pulled a hanky out of her pocket to dry her eyes.

"When Mama got up the next morning, she told us she needed to get right with God. She wanted to find a church, and she wanted us to go to church with her. John, my stepfather, said he didn't want anything to do with God, but he'd see to it Mama got to church if that was what she wanted.

My Name is Randa

I'd never been to church, but if Mama wanted to go, I told her I'd go with her." More tears crept down Randa's face.

Quinn kissed the top of her head. "Are you alright?"

She nodded and snuggled closer to him. "I'm okay. I want to tell Nora about Mama."

There was the answer Nora was looking for. Sarah wanted her brother to raise Randa in a Christian home. Sarah and her husband must have suffered when she made that decision. Nora admired the stepfather's commitment to his wife. He could have chosen not to search for Quinn.

Randa wiped her cheeks and said, "The first Sunday Mama and I went to church, she asked Reverend Bennett to come visit us. Mama told me she asked them to come because she hated her parents, and that was wrong. She wanted to quit hating them and get right with God. Reverend Bennett and his wife Bertha came the next week. Would you like to see a picture of my Mama?" She jumped up and disappeared around the corner.

Randa came back with a small gold frame that held a snapshot of Sarah and Randa in front of a climbing rose bush. She put her Mama's picture on the end table and went back to sit beside her uncle.

"So, Randa, did your mama get right with God?"

"Oh yes, Bertha came to visit us every Tuesday, and she showed Mama a whole bunch of Bible verses about forgiveness. It took a while before Mama told me that Jesus helped her forgive her parents."

The phone rang. Quinn excused himself and left the room.

Randa continued. "Mama told me we're all sinners, and that God sent Jesus his son to die for our sins. Every time Bertha came, she'd teach us things about Jesus, and give us verses to memorize. One day, I prayed and asked Jesus to forgive my sins and come live in my heart. Mama and Bertha both cried and said they were very happy for me."

45

Quinn came back and pulled Randa close.

"Mama told me her heart was too tired to live as long as other people, but she would be in heaven with Jesus, waiting for me. Bertha looked up everything she could find in the Bible about heaven and helped Mama and me know what heaven was like." She dabbed her eyes with Quinn's handkerchief.

"With Bertha's encouragement, Randa has memorized a great number of verses. I'm trying to catch up with her," Quinn said. "She's helping me memorize her verses."

Randa laughed at him. "He knows most of them, just not every single word. I like to memorize. It's fun. My favorite verse is Psalms 91:4. 'He shall cover thee with his feathers, and under his wings shalt thou trust; his truth shall be thy shield and buckler.' I like the feathers part. It makes me feel safe."

"I like that verse too," Nora said, picking up a Bible off the coffee table. "Let me read another verse I like in Isaiah 41:10: 'Fear thou not; for I am with thee: be not dismayed; for I am thy God: I will strengthen thee; yea, I will help thee; yea, I will uphold thee with the right hand of my righteousness.' I've memorized that verse; it tells me I don't have to be afraid because God is always with me."

It delighted Nora to hear Randa received comfort from the Word. Often, after Carl died, it was scripture that helped her get through the devastating days of grief.

"I miss my Mama a lot, but I'm happy she's in heaven with Jesus, and she can breathe okay now. I think I cry too much, but Uncle Quinn says it's okay for me to cry. Sometimes he cries with me." Quinn squeezed her shoulder and kissed her forehead.

Nora wiped tears from her face. "Thank you for telling me about your mama."

My Name is Randa

It surprised her how well Randa was doing. She was a brave girl to share her mama's story. If given the chance, Nora wanted to be there to help Randa when grief overwhelmed her.

She hesitated a moment. Randa's clothing looked snug. She and Randa had been getting along famously, and that young girl needed a woman's help. Would she be out of line?

"Quinn, I have a question. Have you purchased new school clothes for Randa? If not, I'd be happy to take her shopping."

Randa jumped up. "Oh, I would really like that! Some of my clothes are kinda tight. Could she, Uncle Quinn?"

His cheeks flushed. "Oh, Honey, I didn't even think about getting things for school. Thank you, Nora. If you don't mind, we'd appreciate your help."

Nora stood. "All right, Randa, let's check out your wardrobe and make a list of what you need."

Randa opened her bedroom door, and Quinn heard her say, "I hope I find a friend in Park City. I don't have any friends here."

Chapter 10

Wednesday, August 5

Nora stepped off the bus.

Her son-in-law, Tim, gave her a hug. "It's good to have you home, Little Mother. We brought supper to your house."

"Thank you. I had an early lunch, so I'm starving."

He helped her into the truck and stowed her bags in the back. "How'd your interviewin' go? Did you like the reverend?"

"Yes, we heard an excellent sermon. He'll be preaching here on Sunday."

"Did you like his wife?"

She shook her head. "He doesn't have a wife. He's fifty-two and has been a widower for five years."

"Whoa, I think Julie needs to hear this, too."

"You're right. I have quite a story to tell."

Tim grinned. "So do we," he said, turning into Nora's driveway.

The kitchen door flew open, and before Tim could get around the truck, Nora and Julie were in each other's arms. "Welcome home, Mother. Supper is ready to dish up."

Tim took her bags upstairs and hurried back to help Julie, while Nora sat at the kitchen table and watched them dish up southern fried chicken.

She rehearsed in her mind what she would tell her kids. Quinn's privacy was important, and she didn't want to reveal any of his sister's tragic story.

After Tim prayed, Nora asked, "Did anything exciting happen while I was in Chicago?"

Tim squeezed his wife's hand, and Julie said, "We've been looking at baby names, and we have three choices. The

My Name is Randa

first is Rosie May and Josie Louise, and the second is Rose-ann Elnora and Jordan Henry."

Tim took his turn. "The third is Adam Carl and Austin James."

Nora eyed the enlarged girth of Julie's stomach and asked, "Are you telling me two babies are in there?"

"We found out Monday," Julie said, "and we've been keeping it a secret for three days. We wanted you to know first."

"Did you tell Aunt Esther?"

"No, I thought you'd like to tell her. I know she will be so surprised, and I wanted you to see her face."

"Well, I'm too tired tonight. My sister will have to wait another day to hear your news," Nora said.

"Mother, why did you decide to shop in Chicago? What did you buy?" Julie asked.

"It wasn't for me; it was for Randa."

Julie and Tim said, "Who?"

"Let me explain. Reverend Quinn Edwards is the man I interviewed. The Reverend's baby sister, Sarah Jean, died last year, and she named Quinn to be Randa's guardian. The search committee wanted to know how a fifty-two-year-old uncle and a twelve-year-old niece were managing.

"Quinn has a congregation of five-hundred members in Chicago. Now that he has Randa, Quinn wants to serve in a smaller church where it will be easier for them to adjust and become a family.

"When I finished the interview, Quinn invited me to have lunch with him and his niece. Randa warmed up to me right away. I'd forgotten how many questions a girl that age can ask."

Nora emptied her plate. "I need to change into something more comfortable."

"You go ahead, Mother, we'll do the dishes."

When Nora returned, the kids had the kitchen in order, and a glass of sweet tea sat on the end table beside her chair. "I told Quinn I'd like to ask Randa a few questions about her mother. He was hesitant. He worried it might upset her. When I asked Randa, she was eager to tell me her mama's story.

"Randa said her mama came home from the doctor and told her the valves in her heart were wearing out, and she wasn't going to live much longer. Then she said she needed to find a church because she needed to get right with God.

"One of their neighbor ladies went to Reverend Bennett's church, so they started going there, too. Bertha Bennett came to visit them every Tuesday, and Randa said her mama cried and asked for God's forgiveness.

"I'm guessing Randa's been a Christian for about a year."

"But you told me on the way home he's fifty-two," Tim said. "That's kinda old to be raising a twelve-year-old girl."

Julie frowned. "Mother, that's ten years older than you. Couldn't one of his children raise her?"

"He doesn't have any. That's why I stayed another day. When I walked into their house, I noticed Randa's dress was too tight. I thought the seams would pop open any minute. When Randa finished telling me about her mama, I asked Quinn if they'd gone school shopping. He was embarrassed. It hadn't occurred to him to shop for school clothes.

"Randa took me to see her wardrobe, and nothing fit. My guess is Randa's family was so focused on her mother's dying, they didn't think about new clothes."

Julie wiped a tear off her face. "That poor man. Do you think the congregation will like Reverend Edwards?"

Tim cut in. "Should you be calling Reverend Edwards by his first name?"

"He asked me to. His staff in Chicago call him Quinn. When he comes to preach, I'm going to ask Don and Ruth

My Name is Randa

Thompson if they will house them. Their daughter Molly is about Randa's age." Nora reached for her notepad and wrote Thompson on her list.

Tim pushed up from his seat. "Well, Little Mother, the committee was right. You were the best person to do that interview. I don't know about anyone else, but I'm ready for dessert. Julie made a pineapple upside-down cake. Both of you are too tired. I'll dish up."

Nora had a first bite of cake, then sat holding up her empty fork. "I have a question. What do you think about guardian angels?"

Julie shifted, and her smock popped up. Tim's hand covered her stomach. "I think it's an elbow. Quick, Little Mother, come feel." Nora didn't make it in time. Tim assured her those babies punched Julie regularly.

Nora said, "Let me explain. Sunday night, I had a dream. I saw this man in a mirror. He told me he was my guardian angel and then said he wanted me to love them. I don't know what to think. Many people wouldn't understand."

Julie yawned.

Tim took their tea glasses to the kitchen. "That's quite a story. I think we'll have to think on it. Right now, my wife can hardly keep her eyes open. It's time to take Julie and those tiny babies swimming around in her belly home and tuck them into bed."

***

On the way home, Tim's mind churned. That poor little girl not only grieved for her mama, but they had taken her away from everybody she knew. Could a fifty-year-old reverend give her the love and compassion she deserved? He flipped his wheel to avoid a rock on the road. If they came to Park City, Little Mother would be right in the middle of their lives, helping in any way she could.

Julie slept with her head on his shoulder. He wondered if she had ever considered that her mother might marry again.

Chapter 11

To Park City

Thursday, September 3

A month and a day after the Search Committee visited his church in Chicago, Quinn stopped his car in front of Nora Montgomery's house. He stepped out, stretched his arms above his head, and lifted a silent prayer.

Randa watched him. "What are you doing, Uncle Quinn?"

"I'm praising the Lord with a verse from Psalms 63. Maybe you could memorize it, too." He raised his arms. "'Because thy lovingkindness is better than life, my lips shall praise thee.'"

"Okay, then, I can raise my hands and say it with you."

She perused Nora's beautiful yard. There were pink and red dahlias along one side of her house. Her mama would love those. Across the street, there were yellow roses climbing up a trellis, just like the ones at her house. She brushed tears from her cheeks. No, it wasn't her house anymore; it was just John's house.

She looked up at her uncle and said, "I think we'll like living in Park City. Molly Thompson is already my friend, and I didn't have any friends in Chicago."

He took her hand, and they cut across the grass to the front door.

Nora pushed the screen door open. "Come in where it's cooler. How was your trip?"

"Good. I saw pickups in front of the manse," Quinn said. "Should we go over there now? I don't think our guys have arrived yet."

"No, they're setting up tables under those big sugar maple trees in your backyard. We'll have a potluck later. I need to tell you there's a deep freeze in your garage. The farmers in our congregation will bring you more produce and meat than you can eat. Check the freezer before you shop."

Randa tucked herself into the corner of Nora's sofa and asked, "What's a manse?"

"It's our new home," Quinn said. "Most churches supply the reverend with a place to live. It's called a manse."

"Oh. I like Nora's house; it's cozy. It feels like a place where you can snuggle up with your cat and read a book."

Quinn sat beside her. "Cat? Did you have a cat?"

"Yes, a big fat cat that purred all the time. I called her Prissie. She died of old age a couple of months before Mama passed." A solitary tear escaped down her cheek.

Quinn would have to break one of his dad's rules: "Cats are mousers. They live in the barn." A house cat would be company for Randa. It was the least he could do for Sarah's child.

Randa asked Nora, "Is Molly Thompson coming to help today? We've been writing to each other ever since Uncle Quinn came here to preach. I think we are going to be good friends."

"Yes, she called me last night and asked permission. She didn't want you to be alone with all those adults." Nora pointed to a pine tree close to the back corner of her house. "You can see your street if you stand under that tree."

Randa jumped up and bound out the door, and Quinn followed close behind. Randa pointed. "Look, I see the Thompsons' brown pickup. Oh, and look, there's our truck. Can I go now, Uncle Quinn?"

He laughed. "Of course; we don't want her all alone with all those adults."

Nora laughed at her excitement. "I prayed Randa would find a friend, and it's already happened. Ruth and Molly Thompson asked me for advice on how to be Randa's friend

My Name is Randa

while she's grieving. I warned them Christmas would be hard for her. I'm thinking every Christmas season for the rest of her life, Randa will re-live the year her mother died. Time might soften the pain, but the memory will remain."

"Thank you for your prayers and all the things you've done to make this an easy move." Quinn pulled his keys out of his pocket. "May I give you a ride?"

"Yes, let me get my dish for the potluck."

He parked in front of his new home. Getting out of the car, he said, "Could you help me find a big fat cat that purrs? I don't want a kitten." His experience with cats produced scars on his arms from the wild barn cats, who would scratch their way out of his grip.

Nora chuckled. "You're a wise man. I'll discreetly ask around. If you made it public knowledge, dozens of cats would be sitting in boxes beside your front door."

Randa and Molly were waiting for them on the sidewalk. Molly said, "You're here! You're here! Welcome to Park City."

"Thank you, Molly. We are happy to be here." Quinn turned as two men lifted his desk out of the truck. "You will have to excuse me. I need to show them where to put my desk."

Randa laughed. "Uncle Quinn and I took the measurements of our rooms, and we drew a floor plan of where we wanted our furniture. That's why he left us. He doesn't care about his bedroom, but he wants his study just so."

Agnes Johnson parked close to where the girls were standing. "I see they got here safely."

"Randa, this is Mrs. Johnson," Nora said. "She has offered to help you unpack your kitchen things. You girls can go along with her and help empty the boxes."

The girls followed Agnes into the house.

55

Marg Watland

Randa smiled at the older woman. "I didn't know people were going to help us unpack. That's really nice of you, thank you. Bertha, my minister's wife back in Minneapolis helped me pack when I moved to Chicago with Uncle Quinn. We write to each other."

Randa looked at the long, narrow kitchen. She was glad a woman was helping. "My mama said arranging where everything goes in a kitchen is the hardest job you'll ever do. Mama rearranged our kitchen twice after she got her new gas stove. She was really particular about where things went."

She watched Mrs. Johnson put the electric mixer in a lower cupboard. Randa wanted to say that was wrong. The mixer belonged on the counter across from the stove. Then, Mrs. Johnson put all the spices from two boxes into a cupboard close to the sink. She'd have to change things all around after everybody left. Randa hoped she could remember where everything was in Mama's kitchen.

Jim, the church janitor, pulled a box of raspberry jam out of his car and said, "Hello, Nora." He motioned to the row of raspberry bushes along the fence. "We picked all the ripe berries, and my wife made jam for the reverend and his niece. That's a healthy row of bushes. We pruned and mulched them for the season." He pointed to a tree loaded with apples. "Come October, they'll need help with all that fruit."

They walked toward the front door. "The neighbor next door brought those pots of red geraniums over as a welcome gift to the reverend. They look good by the front door. Ain't that nice of them?"

"Yes, it is. Thank you, Jim. You and your family did a wonderful job on the outside work." Nora wondered if Quinn liked to garden.

My Name is Randa

Nora's elder sister, Esther Henderson, got out of her car. "It looks like everything's moving along just like clockwork." The women looked nothing like each other. Esther had wavy grey hair, stood four-foot-seven, and was skinny as a rail. Nora's hourglass figure was the envy of her female acquaintances.

Esther opened the back door of her car and handed Nora a quilt and a colorful crocheted afghan, then pulled out another quilt and two packages of sheets. "Have they brought in the bedroom furniture yet?"

"I don't know. Let's go see."

Molly warned Randa and Reverend Edwards that they were not allowed in their bedrooms until the ladies were through putting on the final touches.

They finished Quinn's room first. Molly said, "Come, see your bedroom, Reverend Edwards." A rail fence quilt in shades of brown with a wide, dark-brown border complimented the ivory walls.

"Thank you, ladies, for all your hard work; I'll enjoy sleeping under that nice warm quilt this winter."

Randa grabbed Quinn's hand. "Come on; I want to see my room."

"Of course; I understand it has ruffles. I'm glad they didn't put girly curtains in my room."

Molly made Randa close her eyes and pulled her new friend into the room the ladies of Park City Community Church had lovingly prepared for her.

Her mouth dropped open when she saw the quilt. "Ooh," she breathed. Blue prints of every imaginable shade were pieced together in different designs on a white background. The twelve-inch blocks were surrounded with strips of royal blue fabric.

"It's called a sampler quilt," Molly said. "Our high school colors are royal blue and white."

57

Randa turned around, looking at the pale blue walls, the colorful quilt on her bed, and the braided rug on the floor. She couldn't believe this bedroom was hers; it was so beautiful. Her face scrunched up, tears oozed from her eyes, and she ran out of the room.

The conversations stopped, and everything turned silent. Quinn saw Randa standing in the hall, hiding her face in her hands. He strode over and wrapped his arms around her.

"What's wrong, honey?"

"I wish Mama could see my pretty room," she whispered.

"I do too. Who knows, maybe she can."

"I'm sorry I cried. I didn't mean to."

"It's fine. It's perfectly okay if you have to cry." Quinn pulled out his handkerchief and dried her tears.

Randa took a deep breath. "Will you tell them why I cried? I'm so embarrassed."

Quinn held her close against his chest and said, "Randa cried because she couldn't show this beautiful bedroom to her mama. She's fine now, just a little embarrassed."

She turned in his arms and said, "Thank you for my pretty room. I love it!" Randa whispered to Quinn, "I better go wash."

Molly put her arm around Randa, and the two girls walked down the hall. "Mom uses a cold washcloth on my face when I cry. She says it helps the red go away."

Randa groaned when she saw her splotchy red face. "I can't believe I did that in front of all those people!" She turned on the cold water.

Molly handed her a washcloth. "I think you need to redo your ponytail, too."

When the girls entered the living room, everyone except Nora was outside. "Quinn said he'd wait until you could join us." They stepped outside, and Quinn took Randa's hand on one side, and his warm fingers covered Nora's hand on the other side.

Quinn said the last goodbyes, then looked for Randa. He found her in the kitchen, taking the spices out of the cupboard. "What are you doing?"

She scowled at him. "I put the spices in two separate boxes, and Mrs. Johnson mixed them all together and put them in this cupboard by the sink. Now, I have to separate them all over again."

"Why?"

"Uncle Quinn, you don't use the spices when you're standing by the sink. The baking spices go in a baking cupboard, and the meat spices go into a cupboard next to the stove. We need to have a functional kitchen."

"Oh, where did you learn that?"

"From Mama. She would probably be up half the night rearranging this kitchen if she was here. Mrs. Johnson is a nice lady, but she doesn't do things like Mama."

Quinn stood in the middle of the kitchen, not knowing what to do, then said, "We have had a long day, and we're tired. Why don't we leave all of this until morning?"

After Randa went to bed, he sat in his new study and thanked the Lord for Park City Community Church. He was confident those who had helped them move in were praying for the girl who missed her mama. The love and compassion of a community were why they were here.

Here, they would have more time together. She'd climbed into his heart and was a joy in his life. Already, he loved her like a father loves his daughter.

Quinn prayed, "Lord, each day I learn something new about her life. I'm so afraid I'll do something wrong. Please help me be patient with her." Then Quinn reached for the phone and called Drew.

Chapter 12

$\mathcal{R}$anda woke to the sound of water running in the shower and jumped out of bed. She ran to the bathroom and banged her fist on the door. "Uncle Quinn, don't use all the hot water. I need some, too."

Quinn groaned and turned off the water. Minutes later, Quinn rapped on her bedroom door. She opened it and stood with her arms across her chest. "I'm sorry, honey. We didn't have that problem in Chicago."

"Yes, we did. I waited for the water to get hot. I can't wait now that school has started."

"Our water heater is too small. I promise I'll go to the hardware and order a larger water heater before I go to work."

Randa muttered, slipped past him, and the bathroom door banged.

Quinn was stirring pancake batter when the bedroom door slammed. He winched.

She was dressed for school when she walked into the kitchen and sat at the table. "Thanks for the pancakes," she grumped, "but I'd rather have a bigger water heater. I hate cold showers."

She looked down and said, "Doesn't it say somewhere in the Bible you're supposed to go to your closet to pray?"

Quinn's eyebrows rose. "I've read that, but I don't remember the chapter and verse at this moment. I promise I'll go to the hardware store this morning."

Randa finished her pancakes, grabbed her books, and breezed past him. "If it's not here tonight, I get to shower first tomorrow."

***

My Name is Randa

Nora smiled when Quinn walked into the office. "Good morning."

Her greeting stopped him in mid-stride. "Oh no, I apologize. I forgot to let you know I'd be late." He sat in the chair by Nora's desk and said, "Randa's not happy with me, and it's my fault. She's been this compliant little girl ever since she moved in with me, but today I'm in the doghouse."

"What did you do?"

He blushed. "I prayed in the shower."

"Wha…"

"I used all the hot water, and she slammed the bathroom door *and* her bedroom door. She told me she gets the shower first tomorrow. I'm buying a bigger hot water heater, but it'll be at least a week before we get it."

"Ahh. But you told her you were sorry?"

"Yes, more than once. I made blueberry pancakes, too. She told me I should pray in my closet."

***

As Nora walked home from work, a smile spread across her face as she recalled Quinn's penitent face. She'd make a batch of brownies. Randa was sure to stop by on her way home from school.

When Randa knocked at the kitchen door, Nora said, "Come in, honey. How was your day?"

"Terrible. I yelled at Uncle Quinn. Do you know what he did? He has his morning prayers in the shower, and he used *all* the hot water. I slammed doors and was kinda mouthy too. Have you ever washed your hair in ice-cold water?"

It sounded like she'd been steaming all day. "I heard. Let's have a snack first, then we'll talk about it. I made brownies for our snack."

Randa poured a glass of milk, and Nora brought a cup of tea to the table.

"Do you think he'll send me back to John? Molly and I are friends, and I like it here. Molly is teaching me how to milk a cow. What am I going to do?"

Nora pushed flying wisps of hair behind her ears. "Honey, your Uncle Quinn loves you. Don't worry; he'll change his ways for you." She handed her Bible to Randa. "I want you to read Ephesians 4:26 to me."

Randa read, "Be ye angry, and sin not: let not the sun go down upon your wrath."

"Honey, that means never go to bed angry. Talk it through and forgive him. You two need a plan that works for both of your schedules. It'll be fine. And Randa, promise me you'll tell him you're worried he'll send you back to John. He loves you very much. He would never send you back. Trust me; talk to him."

The phone rang. Nora answered, then handed the phone to Randa. "He's been looking for you."

Randa took the receiver. "Hello. No, I haven't been home yet. I had to talk to Nora. Yes, I think she helped me. Oh good. I want a Denver sandwich. Okay, I'll go home now. Bye."

While Randa and Quinn talked, Nora filled a paper sack with brownies.

"Uncle Quinn is getting sandwiches for our dinner. I have to go home. Thank you for everything."

Nora put her arm around Randa and squeezed. "Take these brownies with you." She gave Randa a little push and sent her on her way.

***

Was Uncle Quinn mad at her? She tried so hard to be good, but she still felt a little mad.

When Quinn entered the kitchen, Randa was making a salad. "We are supposed to eat vegetables twice a day,

My Name is Randa

and our Health teacher said the stuff in a sandwich isn't enough."

"Vegetables aren't my favorite foods. Salads are okay, but I'd rather have meat, potatoes and gravy, chocolate chip cookies, and ice cream." Quinn sighed. "The new water heater won't be here for at least a week. Let's enjoy our food, and then we need to talk."

After dinner, they made a shower schedule. Then Randa showed him the verse in Ephesians.

"Are you still angry with me for using all the hot water?"

She looked down. "Well, maybe a little. Are you mad at me?"

"No, I'm ashamed that I was so thoughtless. Will you please forgive me? I promise I'll leave hot water for you from now on. However, I don't approve of slamming doors."

"Okay, I forgive you, and I'm sorry I banged the doors. I won't do it again."

She peeked at him through her lashes. "Uncle Quinn, Nora told me to tell you I'm worried you'll send me back to John if I'm not good. I've been trying so hard to be good, and then today, I kind of yelled at you. I want to live with you. Please don't send me back to John." Tears spilled out of the corners of her eyes.

Quinn dried her tears with his hanky. "Let's go to the living room, where it's more comfortable."

They sat together on the davenport. Quinn tipped her face up and looked into her eyes. "Sweetheart, you are a gift to me from God. I would never send you back. I love you, and I hope you love me, too."

He released her face and slid back into the seat. "My little sister chose *me* to guide you through your teenage years. I think of you as a daughter. I am so blessed to have you in my life. Honey, we are a family. Sometimes I'll be thoughtless, like this morning, but that will not change the fact that I love you. You are the most important person in my life, and I will love you no matter what."

Uncle Quinn loved her like a real father? How did that happen so soon? They'd only been together for three months.

She turned and wrapped her arms around his waist. "I love you too, Uncle Quinn. I'm so glad we had this talk."

He kissed the top of her head. "Do you like puzzles? I have a box of puzzles in the garage."

Randa picked a scene and emptied the box on the dining room table. The border pieces were in place, and half of a sunset was showing before Randa yawned.

Quinn sent her off to bed, then headed to his study. It was time to call Drew.

Drew teased, "Pray in your closet? Is there room for a kneeling bench? Maybe the Catholic priest in your town would have an extra one you could borrow."

Before calling it a night, Quinn quietly walked down the hall to Randa's room, opened the door, and stood watching her sleep in the middle of her double bed. A cool fall breeze blew in through her open window. He pulled a blanket up and tucked it around her shoulders. Tonight, they had crossed a hurdle. There had been anger, and together they resolved it. She knew he loved her no matter what, but he wanted her to feel secure enough to trust him with her anger.

Chapter 13

Monday, September 21

Quinn turned into the Thompsons' driveway a little before their children would arrive home from school. He needed Molly's advice on a gift for Randa's 13th birthday.

He eyed Don's fields and admitted to himself that he missed the physical labor of farm work and the satisfaction of a job well done. He could have had his father's farm, since he was the only son, but he preferred teaching and preaching.

Ruth met him on the porch. "Hi, Reverend. Come on in. The coffee will be ready soon."

"Where's Don?"

"He'll be in any minute. Don stops for coffee when the kids get home. He likes to hear about their day while it's fresh in their minds."

Quinn followed her to the kitchen. "Umm, I smell cookies." He sat at the oak table and watched Ruth pull a pan of oatmeal raisin cookies out of the oven. She poured milk for the kids, sat three mugs on the counter beside the coffeepot, and then brought a plate of cookies to the table. "Help yourself, Reverend."

He took a bite. "These taste like the cookies my mother made. She loved to bake. Randa does too."

Quinn couldn't believe he'd mentioned his mother. He hoped Ruth wouldn't ask questions about his parents.

Brad and Molly burst into the kitchen, talking up a storm with their father. Don pulled off his cap and flashed his dimples at Quinn.

Ruth hugged her daughter. "Honey, Reverend Edwards came to see you. He needs help with Randa's birthday."

Don laughed. "Last year, Molly had three girls over for a slumber party. They giggled all night."

"Nora told me girls like slumber parties, but we haven't lived here long enough for that." He didn't think she had three friends yet. Besides, the daunting thought of a house full of giggling teenagers made him cringe.

"Randa wants Nora and Molly to join us for dinner at Jane's Diner. Then we'll have cake and ice cream at our house. She insists on making her own birthday cake. Since Randa came to live with me, all our desserts are homemade."

Ruth set steaming cups of coffee on the table. "The last time Randa stayed overnight, she and Molly made a delicious breakfast cake. We ate it hot out of the oven, but she told us it would be better the next day."

Don and Brad said, "It was."

Quinn blew on his coffee. "I thought it'd work better if we waited until the weekend, but Randa said her family *always* celebrated on the day of her birthday, so that's what we'll do. I don't know what to give her for a gift. I've never shopped for a teenager. Molly, do you have any suggestions?"

Brad tipped the cookie jar towards Quinn. "My Mom makes the best molasses cookies ever. There's a few left. Would you like one?"

Quinn bit into a soft, spicy cookie that tickled his tongue. He closed his eyes and chewed. "It's delicious."

Molly tapped the table with a pale pink fingernail. "I know this is really dumb, but she told me her favorite room in the house is the kitchen, but yours is yellow, and she doesn't like yellow very much." Molly reached for her milk, then looked up at Quinn. "She wishes your kitchen was white like her mama's. It had white walls with red gingham curtains and a red apple cookie jar like ours. She says you have

My Name is Randa

nice stuff but none of her mother's things, and she doesn't want to forget her mama."

Quinn jerked upright. "Oh no, of course, she wants to remember her mother. I didn't think." He felt like he'd been punched in the gut. He should have known.

Molly blushed. "You didn't do anything wrong, Reverend Edwards. You didn't know. She loves you, and she likes living here."

She swiped a tear. "I'm really sorry, Daddy. I shouldn't have told him."

Don took her hand. "Honey, Reverend Edwards became Randa's guardian in June. Parenting is new to him, and he doesn't always know what a child wants or needs."

"Molly, thank you for telling me." Quinn glanced at the family. "My sister had their reverend's wife pack some boxes for Randa. They're in the garage. Bertha said I'd know when it was time to open them. I guess now is that time."

Quinn hoped they'd find some decorative things in those boxes. He'd wait until after her birthday. When she opened them, they'd need time for her to remember, and then she'd probably grieve. He wanted to help her through her sadness. She lost her mama, and he lost a sister he barely knew.

His mother was thirty-nine when Sarah was born. He'd thought of his parents as being closer to fifty. What else did he remember incorrectly? One thing he *remembered* was the embarrassment of having a baby sister at his high school graduation.

Quinn checked his watch. "I need to go. I have an appointment with our music leader in half an hour. We're choosing the music for my next sermon series.

"Molly, would you make a list of personal things that you think Randa might like and give it to Nora on Sunday? She's going with me when I shop for Randa's present. That child

Marg Watland

needs a happy birthday. And Molly, why don't you and your family call me Rev."

They nodded.

The two men shook hands, and Quinn said, "Thank you for your insight, Don. I'm sure we'll talk again."

"Anytime, Rev. Anytime."

***

Wednesday morning, Nora stashed her purse in the desk drawer and picked up the ringing phone.

"Good morning, Nora; this is Don Thompson. Rev is going to do some painting, and I'd like to help him. I'm sure he'll tell you about it this morning. Could you let me know his plan and please keep this between you and me?"

"I'd be happy to. I'll call you."

She started coffee, and soon the enticing aroma filled Quinn's office. Five minutes later, Quinn walked in and said, "When you finish what you're doing, would you come into my office? I want to tell you about my visit to the Thompsons."

Before she sat down, he began talking, "There's glossy white paint in my trunk and a new ladder in the garage. I'll come into the office on Monday, then I can take Wednesday off, and as soon as Randa leaves for school, I'll paint the kitchen."

Nora opened her mouth to respond, but Quinn interrupted. "Did you know Don stops for a coffee break when the kids come home from school? He wants to hear about their day. I'm impressed. I think I'll suggest Randa stop by the office after school so I can hear about her day."

Later in the morning, Quinn leaned against the door frame of his office. "You know, we didn't really celebrate birthdays in my home. Mother would make a cake on my

My Name is Randa

birthday, hand me the first piece, and say, 'Happy Birthday, son, today you're a year older.' That was it.

"When Arlene and I married, she made a fuss over my birthday. She'd buy me a present, make my favorite food for dinner, and bake a carrot cake. On her birthday, I bought her flowers and took her out to a nice restaurant. I haven't been to a teenager's birthday party. Would you help me?"

Nora smiled at him. "I've been hoping you'd ask. Randa's been through so much; it'll be good for us to celebrate her life and show her how much she's loved. Didn't you want children?" Nora asked.

"Arlene couldn't have children. She was a pediatric nurse and said the sick kids she cared for would be her children. That didn't stop me from falling in love with her. We talked about adopting, but she got sick, and it didn't happen. I'm still in shock at how God works. After living alone for five years, Sarah Jean turns my life upside down by making me Randa's guardian.

"Nora, I appreciate your help. Thank you."

Nora hoped Quinn realized this would be a hard day for Randa. A thirteenth birthday is a special event in a girl's life, and sometime during this celebration, Randa would grieve for her mother. She prayed God would help him comfort Randa when the tears of grief came. "Ask her to tell you about the birthday parties she's had in the past. You don't have to do exactly what they did, but it's a starting place. It's her first birthday with you. Let her know how much you love her. You'll do fine."

"Randa wants to make her own cake. I asked her why, and she said she always helped make her birthday cake. The more I hear about my sister, the more I think she was an excellent mother."

***

Marg Watland

With a list in her hand, Molly caught up with Nora before Sunday morning worship began. "Reverend Edwards told me to give you this list. Some I thought up, and others Randa's talked about."

Nora gave her a quick hug. "Thank you, Molly. This will be very helpful. So, I understand we're invited to her birthday dinner. This is the first time Randa will be celebrating a birthday without her mama. If she cries, give her time to empty out all her tears."

"I know. You told Mom and me to hug her if she cries. I hope I don't cry too."

Nora touched Molly's arm. "Honey, let me have your Bible for a minute." She turned to Romans chapter twelve and handed the Bible back to Molly. "Read verse fifteen to me."

Molly read, "Rejoice with them that do rejoice, and weep with them that weep."

"Crying with Randa will comfort her. The twelfth chapter of Romans teaches us how to live the Christian life. I encourage you to read the entire chapter."

Molly put the bulletin in her Bible to mark the place and said, "Thank you, Mrs. Montgomery. I'll read it today."

"We need to concentrate on making her birthday happy. I'll see you Wednesday, if not before."

***

It was mid-morning when Quinn entered Ernie's Second-Hand Store. The front half of the store was filled with rows of dishes, glassware, pots and pans, skillets, cutlery, crocks, and butter churns. Ernie Murdock came around the front counter and said, "Good morning. May I help you find something?"

"Yes, I'm Reverend Edwards. Nora Montgomery suggested I look for a birthday present for my niece in your

My Name is Randa

store. I've been thinking she could use a chair for her bedroom."

"We have several chairs over in this corner." He led Quinn to the furniture section and said, "How about this blue velvet rocker?"

Quinn examined the rocker; it might look good in her room. "I'd like to bring my secretary in to look at it in a couple of hours. I'm new at buying things for teenagers."

"Okay, I'll put a sold sign on it."

Thirty minutes later, Quinn and Nora walked into the store. She took one look at the chair and exclaimed, "It's perfect."

He grinned at her and made arrangements with Ernie to have the chair delivered Wednesday morning while Randa was in school.

Nora took his arm when they walked out the door. "See, you made a good choice. I think you are doing a fine job of planning Randa's party."

Chapter 14

Tuesday evening, September 29

*R*anda had the ingredients lined up on the counter, ready to make her birthday cake. She unscrewed the lid on the Watkins pure vanilla. The phone rang. Her hand hit the corner of the cabinet door, and vanilla flowed everywhere. She answered the phone, choking out. "Hello."

Nora said, "Randa, your uncle asked me to call you. He won't be home for another hour."

"Okay, thanks," she said and hung up. Her chin quivered, and tears flowed down her face. Randa looked down at the brown puddle and, with hands pressed against the counter edge, she sobbed.

When the sobs slowed, she stumbled to the phone and dialed Nora's number. "Mama didn't want us to borrow stuff, but I c-can't make my cake without vanilla."

"Randa, is that you? Are you crying? What do you want to borrow?"

"Vanilla."

"I'll be right there with vanilla."

"Okay."

***

Nora opened the kitchen door. Randa stood in the middle of the room with a stained towel in her hand. "The vanilla s-spilled ... it's all gone."

With arms around the weeping child, Nora said, "It's okay, honey. I've brought more vanilla."

When Randa calmed, Nora led her to a kitchen chair, then filled a glass with water. "Here honey, drink this. All those tears emptied your body of fluid. It needs to be replaced."

My Name is Randa

Randa chug-a-lugged every drop and handed the glass back to Nora. Nora shook her head in amazement. "Would you like more?"

"Yes, please." She shuddered and drank another half-glass of water.

How many times had Julie brought Nora water after a long siege of weeping? Carl died at forty-four without warning. He'd gone to bed to sleep off a migraine, but when she went to check on him, he wasn't breathing.

Randa picked up the hem of her blouse to dry her face.

Nora said, "Let me help. I'll clean the floor while you finish your cake." She rinsed out the towel and knelt to sop up more of the liquid.

Quinn opened the kitchen door and gasped when he saw Nora washing the floor on her hands and knees.

Randa stood at the mixer, cracking an egg on the rim of the bowl.

He scowled at his niece. "Why is Nora scrubbing the floor?"

Nora broke in. "I offered to wipe up this spot while she finished her cake."

Quinn reached out to help Nora up and asked, "Why?"

Randa burst into tears. "I'm sorry, Uncle Quinn. I spilled the whole bottle of that expensive Watkins Vanilla. You weren't home, so I called Nora."

Quinn's face paled. He stepped around Nora and pulled Randa into his arms. She put her face into his shoulder and said, "I'm sorry."

"It's all right, honey, I just didn't understand."

Nora whispered, "I'll take over in here. You can hold her while she cries."

He led the weeping child away to the living room.

***

Later, Quinn joined Nora in the kitchen. "She's asleep, but she's still shuddering. I'll wake her up after a while and give her something to eat."

"I noticed your list of menus for the week. Dinner is ready. She needs to sleep more than she needs food. I'll just invite myself to dinner, and then we can help her into bed. In another fifteen minutes, the cake comes out. I've set the table, so everything's ready to dish up."

In the middle of their meal, the timer sounded. Nora put the cake on a wire rack to cool. Quinn finished his meal and said, "I've never eaten tuna casserole with peas before. I'm not big on vegetables, but that wasn't bad." He picked up the dishes and said, "You cooked, so I'll clean. That's how we do it at this house.

"I'll carry Randa into her bedroom. Please help her get undressed and into bed."

Quinn gently laid Randa on the bed and kissed her forehead. He whispered, "Thank you, Nora," and left the room.

"I don't think she'll remember us putting her to bed," Nora said later. "She had two long hard bouts of crying. I suspect she'll sleep all night and be fine in the morning. A good breakfast for tomorrow would be pancakes with ham and eggs. That should fill her up.

"Leave the bedroom doors open so you'll hear if she wakes up in the night. If she wakes, give her another glass of water. With all those tears, her body is a little short of fluid." She patted his arm and said, "Goodnight."

"Thank you, Nora. God bless you for being such a good friend to us."

Quinn watched her taillights disappear down the street and prayed, "Lord, thank you for putting Nora in our lives."

He peeked in on Randa. She lay on her back in the middle of her bed. He left the door ajar and went into his study. It was nice having dinner with Nora. Tomorrow he'd have flowers sent to her at the church, and he'd stay home to paint the kitchen.

Chapter 15

Wednesday, September 30

A knock on the kitchen door caused Quinn to look up. Don Thompson, dressed in faded overalls and his cap turned backward, peeked through the window.

Quinn called, "Come in."

With an armload of painting equipment, Don sidestepped through the door. "Mornin' Rev; thought I'd help."

They covered the counters and floor with Don's old paint-spattered tarps. Don stirred the paint and asked, "You paint much?"

"When I was a teen, Dad and I painted our house inside and out."

"Hmm. That much, huh?"

"We didn't do a very good job. Mom's comment was, 'At least it's clean.' I appreciate your help, Don. You teach, and I'll be the pupil."

Don nodded, poured paint into a pan, and handed Quinn a roller. "I'll show you how to use a roller, and I'll do the brushwork." He pushed open the kitchen windows and said, "Ruthie said I should invite you to have Christmas with us."

"Thank you. We'd like that. I'm sure Randa will want to help with the baking. I'll have her call Ruth."

Don said, "While we work, you can give me a plan on how to read the Bible and make sense out of it, and I'll tell you about living with a teenager."

"Those two subjects will take much longer than the time to paint my kitchen." Quinn raised a brow. "We might have to see each other on a regular basis."

My Name is Randa

"My daughter loved helping you pick out make-up for Randa. She thinks you are very special."

"She's my niece's best friend. I wanted to get acquainted with her. I also felt safe with whatever Ruth allowed Molly to use. You have a sweet daughter."

Don skillfully finished cutting around all the cupboards, without a speck of paint spatter showing anywhere.

"Thank you for coming today. I appreciate your friendship." Quinn dipped his roller in the pan. "I have few real friends; I'm too private for my own good. Molly has been an answer to our prayers. Randa tells me Molly is her best friend."

"Yeah, Molly says the same." Don chuckled. "We read the birthday list she gave to Nora. It should cover Randa's birthdays and Christmas for the next couple of years. What's she getting from you?"

"I found a rocker for her bedroom. Someone's supposed to deliver it this morning."

A truck door slammed outside. "I think our chair has arrived."

Don held up his hand. "You're covered with paint. I think it'd be best if I answered the door."

Ernie Murdock brought in the chair, then hurried away to open his store.

Quinn wiped a drip of paint off his shoe and said, "My dad wasn't the best painter, but he *was* an excellent farmer. One year he got Farmer of the Year."

Did he just brag about his father? Quinn shook his head in disgust. He moved the tray. "We grew soybeans and winter wheat on our farm in Michigan." He stood and stretched. "It looks like you're going to have a good crop of beans."

"Yep. A new refrigerator is on order for Ruthie, and she's pushing me to buy a new truck. Brad has his license and is looking for a car. We're going to match what he saves, but

Mary Watland

he has to pay for everything else. His job of pumping gas doesn't make much, but he's good about saving."

Quinn watched Don brush white paint on the kitchen door. "I don't talk about my dad much; a lot of bad memories."

"My mother didn't talk about her dad either. She said there were better things to talk about than a mean drunk. You'll meet my folks at Christmas. Dad had to quit farming, bad lungs. Two or three times a year, they spend a week with us. He likes to play farmer while he's here. I save a project for us to do together. We have a good visit, and he goes home happy."

"You are blessed to have good times with your father."

***

Quinn sat in the clean white kitchen and waited for Randa and Molly to come home from school. He heard their chatter when they came up the steps.

Randa opened the kitchen door, and her mouth dropped open. Molly peeked over her shoulder. He grinned and said, "Molly told me you don't like yellow. Be careful; it's not totally dry."

"She told you?"

"Don and I painted it. I'm glad he came to help me. He gave me a lot of tips on how to paint."

Randa hurled herself into his arms. "Thank you, Uncle Quinn. It looks like Mama's kitchen."

"You're welcome."

Molly said, "It looks good. My great grandfather Thompson was in the Navy. He taught Dad how to paint. I guess they did a lot of painting on the ship."

"You girls put your things in the bedroom, and we'll have a snack."

My Name is Randa

Quinn winked at Molly and followed them down the hall. Randa squealed when she opened the door. "Oh, a rocking chair. It's beautiful. I love it!" She sat down and pushed with her toe. "I love to rock."

"It's not new. I found it at Ernie's Second-Hand Store."

"That's okay; Bertha said old chairs are filled with wonderful stories. It's fun to sit and rock and wonder about the stories it would tell."

The phone rang. Quinn answered, listened for a minute, and handed it to Randa.

"Hi John, thank you for the money. I'm going to buy a rose sweater I saw in the Penney's store ...."

Quinn led Molly into the living room. "It's her stepfather. I'll get Nora while they're talking, and then we can go to dinner."

***

Millie, the owner of Jane's Diner, led them to a back corner of the dining room. A table draped with a white tablecloth held a beautiful bouquet of red carnations and baby's-breath.

Quinn watched Randa's face. Would this be another night of terrible grief? "Lord, give her a happy night. Help her know we all love her. Show me how to give her a good life, one filled with joy. Thank you for giving me this child, this wonderful gift."

***

When they returned home from the diner, the phone was ringing. Randa ran for it and said, "Yes, this is Randa. Thank you. Okay, if you want me to. We've had dinner, and now we're going to have cake and open my presents. Okay, goodbye."

She mimicked her uncle's raised brow. "It was your friend in Canada. He called to wish me happy birthday, and he said I should call him Uncle Drew. How did he know it was my birthday?"

"Oh, I might have mentioned it. I'm ready for dessert, aren't you? Ladies, we'll bring cake to the dining room."

Nora and Molly sat at the table and enjoyed the sweet fragrance of Randa's flowers.

Randa and Quinn served plates of vanilla pound cake topped with ice cream and a drizzle of raspberry jam. He pulled a pale blue candle out of his shirt pocket. "There isn't room for thirteen candles, but we can sing with one candle." He pushed it into her piece of cake, struck a stick match with his thumbnail, and they sang "Happy Birthday."

The red gingham curtains Molly made for the kitchen were a hit. "Where are the curtain rods, Uncle Quinn? Will you hang them now so the kitchen looks finished?" She loved the dark blue throw Nora crocheted for her. "This winter when it gets cold. I'll wrap up in this and be nice and toasty."

The girls dumped a new puzzle on the dining room table while Quinn and Nora relaxed in the living room. Randa's laughter made them smile. "Oh, Quinn, she's so happy. It's hard to believe, after last night's tears."

Chapter 16

Sunday, October 4

*R*anda set plates of green Jell-O salad on the table, and Nora lifted a pot roast out of the oven. A red pickup pulled into the driveway. Nora said, "They're here."

Julie held open the front door, and Tim stepped into the house with a big box that rattled. He carried it to a corner of the living room.

"It smells good in here," Julie said and smiled at the dark-eyed girl staring at her. "You must be Randa. I'm Julie, and this is my husband, Tim."

"You look just like Nora, except she's not going to have twins."

Julie laughed. "No, I get to have twins all by myself. We're so happy to meet you." The young couple entered the kitchen, and Randa watched them give Nora hugs and kisses.

Nora said, "Tim, we'll take care of dinner today, and you and Quinn can get acquainted."

He saw a dark-haired man with glasses and a beard walk toward the front door carrying a large grocery bag. Tim opened the screen door and said, "Good morning; you must be Reverend Edwards. I'm Tim Hunter. Finally, we meet Little Mother's new reverend."

The two men shook hands.

Julie stepped out of the kitchen.

"And this is my wife, Julie."

Quinn grinned at Julie. "Your mother told me you were look-alikes. She's right, but not completely. When you smile, there's a cleft in your chin. I've seen Nora smile many times, and she doesn't have one."

Randa joined them.

Quinn handed the grocery bag to her. "Nora calls me Quinn. I think the rest of her family should do the same."

"I usually help in the kitchen, but Little Mother said today you and I should get acquainted. We might as well have a seat in the livin' room until it's time to eat."

With a raised brow, Quinn said, "I've heard a great deal about you, Tim. You're the son-in-law who is nearly perfect."

Tim grinned. "I love her, too." He pointed to the box in the corner. "Everyone knows I like red, so we received a lot of red duplicates as wedding presents. We heard about the white kitchen with red gingham curtains and thought Randa would like some of them."

"Thank you. We don't have a lot of color in our house. Now that Randa lives with me, things are changing. She says she's making it cheerful."

"We heard about the vanilla. I think God put Little Mother in your life at the right time. She grieved powerful hard when Carl died. She's the right person to help Randa through her grievin'."

Quinn stretched out his legs and crossed his ankles. "You're right. I've never been a parent, so without Nora's help, I would be lost. When Randa grieves, Nora told me to let her cry until she's through. Randa hasn't cried like that since the day we drove away from her home in Minneapolis. I drove while she sat beside me and sobbed. I thought she would never stop. Since then, she's cried, but last night her grief broke my heart."

Tim hung his sports jacket in the hall closet. "It was time for her to have a good cry. After Little Mother and Julie had a hard cry, they always felt better. I courted Julie while they were grievin'. Her daddy died in May, and Julie and I started going together in October. I asked Aunt Esther how to

My Name is Randa

help them while they grieved, and she said to let them cry it out and hold them when they needed a shoulder. I think I have a stronger love for both of them because of it. I'm blessed to be part of the Montgomery family."

Hearing about Nora's grief reminded Quinn of Arlene those last days gasping for breath before she died. He was a shell of a man for too long.

Now, with Randa, his life echoed with joy and laughter. He was whole again.

Julie poured water into the glasses with one hand on her round belly. Two more months and this young couple would have twins. Nora was so excited.

Parenting one teenager shouldn't be nearly as hard as caring for *two* babies.

Tim breathed in the smell of roast beef, garlic, and onions. "We're having Little Mother's Sunday pot roast. I most always have seconds and sometimes thirds. Everything she cooks is good."

"Yes, she's exceptional. We've had several meals here." Quinn loosened his tie and opened the top button of his shirt. "I like the relaxed peacefulness in this house."

"Are you beginning to feel like Park City is home for you and Randa?"

"Yes, I think we are. Randa likes her school. I wish she'd start making some more friends. So far, Molly is her only friend. She trusts me and has started asking me when she needs something. She was all smiles the evening of her birthday. I guess she got all of her grieving out the night before. My sister died three days after Christmas. Nora warned me that Christmas would most likely be a hard day for Randa."

"That's a terrible bad thing to remember," Tim said. "No wonder she cried so hard. Julie told me a girl's thirteenth birthday is a special day; and Randa had to celebrate it without her mama."

They sat in silence for several minutes.

"Thanksgiving was terrible hard for Little Mother. She always had their Christmas cards ready to mail by Thanksgiving, but that year she hadn't even bought them."

Quinn chuckled. "Nora is the most organized woman I've ever met. Who else has Christmas cards finished by Thanksgiving? I think her list-making is rather amusing, but I have to admit both Randa and I seem to have picked up the habit."

Tim burst into laughter. "Those lists are very important to the Montgomery women. Be careful what you say, sir. I've learned not to tease my wife about them.

"Julie cried when her father's favorite Christmas song played on the radio. When the cards started coming in the mail, they both cried. When it snowed, Julie cried because she and her daddy loved winter best of all. She cried at the most unexpected times. I kept a little towel in my truck to sop up her tears."

Randa had already mentioned something about getting ready for the holidays and making Christmas cookies. Quinn knew what was coming next. She'd want to send Christmas cards to the family and would need the names and addresses of all their relatives.

Tim continued to tell Quinn about some of Nora's other difficult days. "Little Mother didn't want to decorate for Christmas. Aunt Esther says everybody grieves different, but that's the way Little Mother grieved. It was hard to watch. Without Carl, their favorite Christmas traditions didn't work. They asked me how my mom decorated our house. I told them about the year she filled our tree with frosted Christmas stars. They liked the idea, so that's what the three of us did. You wouldn't believe how many cookies I frosted. I did everything I could think of to help them through those days."

My Name is Randa

Julie perched on the arm of Tim's chair. "What days?"

"The holidays. Quinn is worryin' about Randa and Christmas."

She nodded. "I suggest you and Randa tell each other about your past Christmas' and make new traditions that will please both of you." She stood and tugged on Tim's hand. "Right now, it's time to eat. Remember, I'm eating for three, and we're hungry."

Nora directed Tim to the head of the table and asked Quinn and Randa to sit on his right, and she and Julie sat on the left.

Tim reached his hands out to Julie and Randa. "Let's join hands, and I'll pray.

"Father in heaven, thank you for this Sunday dinner Little Mother has made for us. Thank you for her gift of being a good cook. Thank you for our special guests that came to eat with us today ...."

Tim filled his plate and buttered a roll. He closed his eyes and savored the soft yeasty piece of homemade bread, then turned to his mother-in-law. "These are your best rolls ever."

"I can't take credit for the rolls. Randa made them. She's quite the baker."

Tim's look of astonishment caused them to laugh. "You just turned thirteen, and you make homemade bread? Do you make cinnamon rolls, too?"

Randa blushed. "Yes, I make them every week."

Quinn beamed. "Every Saturday morning, around ten o'clock, we have, just out of the oven, cinnamon rolls. The first time she made them, I thought I'd died and gone to heaven. Randa takes after my mother. My mother made the best bread I ever ate. When I was a kid, I'd sit at the kitchen table waiting for the bread to cool enough so she could cut it. She'd cut me a fat heel, I'd smear on a thick layer of butter, and heap Mother's strawberry jam on top. She made me eat it over a plate to catch the jam that dripped off my chin."

Quinn quirked his mouth. "I used to tell this story to the first graders at Vacation Bible School. After I ate the bread and jam, I'd clean my face with my tongue." His tongue ran a circle around his mouth; then he stuck his finger in his mouth. "I cleaned the jam off my plate with my finger until it was shiny clean. Then I'd tell Mother she could put it back in the cupboard."

Tim bent over his plate and laughed. "I can't believe Little Mother's reverend just said that."

Julie held her stomach while she laughed, then erupted from her chair and ran to the bathroom, hollering, "Don't say another word until I get back. I can't wait any longer. One of these babies kicked me in the bladder."

Quinn blushed. What got into him to tell that story after all these years? What was Randa thinking? She told him he was a dignified reverend.

When Tim and Randa emptied their dessert plates, they stuck their finger in their mouth and tried to clean their plate until it was shiny clean. Tim chuckled, and Randa giggled.

The four adults found comfortable seats in the living room. Randa knelt in the middle of the floor and opened the flaps of Tim's box. She squealed in delight. "An apple cookie jar just like Mama's."

They laughed at her joy.

Julie said, "Take anything you want."

Randa stacked the things she liked on the coffee table. She chose white feed sack dish towels with red floral borders, red ceramic birds to hang on the wall, and four Christmas placemats and napkins in red and green plaid.

A big smile stretched across Quinn's face. He thanked God for Randa's joy. He was pleased that she warmed up to Julie and Tim right away.

My Name is Randa

Randa hugged Tim and Julie. "Thank you so much."

Julie asked, "Do you do all the cooking at your house?"

"No, I'm not very good. Uncle Quinn and I take turns. Mrs. Nordstrom, our housekeeper, puts dinners in the deep freeze for us."

Julie slipped off her shoes, rested her feet on the coffee table, and said, "But you bake bread."

"When we lived in Yuma, Mama worked part-time in a bakery. When we moved to Minnesota, Mama stayed home with me. People heard she could make wedding cakes and fancy birthday cakes, so she asked John to buy her a good gas stove. At Christmas time, she sold boxes and boxes of little gingerbread-boy cookies from Grandma Edward's recipe, and fruit cakes from Grandma Reynold's recipe. It seemed like she baked all the time, and I helped her."

"How old were you when you started baking with your mother?"

"Mama said I was three or four. They bought me a stool to stand on. I made biscuits first. Well, really, I cut the biscuits with a heart cookie cutter. When I got a little older, she taught me how to mix oatmeal cookie dough with my hands. That was a lot of fun. After I got it all mixed together, I got to lick my fingers."

Quinn's mouth hung open as he stared at his niece. "I didn't know that. You haven't said a word about Sarah Jean being a baker. I remember those little gingerbread boy cookies; they were my favorite."

"When Mama started taking long naps, John said she had to quit her baking business. That's when John took her to the doctor. The last thing Mama taught me was how to make bread." Tears welled up in her eyes. "It was Halloween time, and she'd sit at the kitchen table and lean her head against the wall because she was so tired. She had me make bread every week. John ate my terrible dry holey bread. I finally got the knack of kneading, and now my bread is light and soft."

If Quinn had been alone, he might have bawled, but he steeled himself and remained dry-eyed. Sarah was preparing Randa for life. He couldn't imagine how difficult it must have been for his sister to know it was the last thing she'd teach her little girl.

They all watched, but Randa remained calm.

"Do you know how to decorate a wedding cake?" Julie asked as a lump showed up on her belly.

Tim's hand covered the lump and whispered *a foot*, but his eyes didn't leave Randa's face.

"I can do a simple one. I can't do the fancy ones Mama made, but when I grow up, I want to go to Paris and learn from a famous pastry chef. That's what Mama wanted to do, and that's what I'm going to do."

Julie's eyes were nearly closed when Tim said, "It's time I take you home, darlin'. You need a nap." He stood, reached for Julie's hands, and pulled her off the sofa.

The two men shook hands, and Tim said, "We're havin' a Gospel Sing at our church this coming Saturday, if you like Southern Gospel music."

Tim put his arm around Randa and said, "Thank you for bringing those rolls. If I showed up at your house some Saturday mornin' around ten, could I sample one of your cinnamon rolls?"

"Sure. Bring Julie too."

They waved goodbye to the young couple.

Randa said, "I like Tim. He's really nice, and I love his southern drawl."

Nora drew Randa close. "All the women like his drawl. You are full of surprises, young lady. Today, we learned new things about your mama, and now I understand why you're such a talented baker."

My Name is Randa

Quinn wondered how many more gaps in Randa's life she'd drop, like a bomb, at some unexpected moment. That girl seemed to keep him off balance regularly. France was Sarah's dream. Somehow, he'd help Randa find her own dream.

Chapter 17

Saturday, October, 10

Quinn and Randa sat at the kitchen table eating warm cinnamon rolls.

"Can we go to the Gospel Sing at Tim and Julie's church tonight? Nora told me Tim plays the banjo and guitar, and he sings with three other guys."

"I thought we might. Do you know what Southern Gospel music is?"

"A man and wife in my church sang that kind of music. I liked their songs. We had a record by The Blackwood Brothers that Mama played all the time. She said it gave her peace. I think they were gospel singers."

"You're right. If we go tonight, we have to get all our Saturday chores done early. It's my turn to clean the bathroom. You get the laundry."

***

That night, Pastor Baker came forward and greeted the audience. He thanked them for coming, said a brief prayer, and turned the evening over to the Gospel team.

They began with "In My Heart There Rings a Melody." The crowd clapped with vigor. Randa turned to Quinn with a big grin as they clapped along with the others.

After a few numbers, they encouraged the audience to sing along. Quinn discovered Randa knew only a few of the songs. Maybe Nora could give him some suggestions on how to help her catch up. Did he have a record player in one of those boxes in the garage, or had he given it away?

My Name is Randa

The last song was "I'll Fly Away." The crowd sang joyfully, clapped to a rapid beat, and ended with rousing applause.

When the concert ended, Randa asked, "Should we go up front and tell Tim we liked the music? I like the happy songs; they make me feel good. Can we go to the next Gospel Sing?"

They threaded through the crowd and found Tim squatted down, putting his banjo in its case. "We enjoyed your music," Quinn said. "Randa wants to come again."

"Thank you, Randa. I'm glad you liked it. Julie baked some apple pies today. Would you like to come over for pie and coffee?"

Randa whispered, "Can we go, please?"

Quinn nodded and thanked Tim for the invitation.

They followed Esther's car into Tim's driveway and walked with Esther and Nora into the kitchen. Nora insisted Julie sit and watch while she and Esther helped Tim.

The phone rang.

Tim answered. "Sure, come on over. We're getting ready to have pie and coffee." After ending the call, Tim said, "The Calhouns are coming," and handed Nora three more plates.

Julie said, "We'd better have dessert in the dining room. This table isn't big enough."

Tim brought a quart jar of cream from the refrigerator and whipped some for the pies. Randa had never seen anyone turn the handle of an egg beater as fast as Tim.

Doors slammed outside. Six-year-old Pansy Calhoun opened the kitchen door and ran to Tim with her black ponytail flying. He scooped her in his arms, and she gave him her usual loud smack. Then she slid down and ran to Julie for a hug. Pansy rubbed her hand across Julie's extended tummy. "I feel it. I feel it kicking."

Julie moved her hand up higher. "Here's the other one."

Quinn had never felt a baby kicking in its mother's womb. Arlene grieved because she couldn't carry his child, and he showed her, in every way he knew how, that she was enough.

They had a happy ten years together, and now he had a child. Sarah's child.

Quinn had experienced too many deaths in the past few years. Then Randa sent him a letter, and she replaced his sorrow with excitement and joy.

Tim introduced Bert and Mavis Calhoun to Quinn and Randa, and then sent everyone to the dining room. Nora and Esther brought in plates of apple pie topped with whipped cream, and Tim followed with the percolator.

Quinn swallowed his first bite and said, "Julie, you make delicious pies, just like your mother."

Bert wiped whipped cream from Pansy's face, then asked, "Reverend Edwards, do you like football? There's a game on Friday, at Milton."

"Baseball is my favorite, but I make it a practice to go to all the high school games if I'm free. We plan to go to the next home game."

Pansy piped up. "I always go with Uncle Tim and Daddy."

"Sorry, I don't think I'll go this time," Tim said. "Julie is having false labor, and I don't want to leave her alone."

***

On their way home, Randa said, "I must know a hundred people here in Park City. I've never known so many people in my whole life."

Chapter 18

Sunday evening - October 11

Quinn stood in front of the stove dressed in jeans and a flannel shirt, waiting for water to boil. He needed to talk with Randa about something that might make her cry. He was making tea because his mother always made tea when she was worried or didn't feel good.

Randa slipped into the kitchen and dipped her hand in the cookie jar. "Uncle Quinn, do you think it would be all right to ask Julie if I could feel her babies?"

"Well, she let Pansy, so I don't think she'd mind. If you're not sure, ask Nora." He wouldn't mind feeling those babies move himself, but it seemed too intimate. He'd be embarrassed.

"Okay, I'll ask Nora. I want them to have a girl and a boy, and I want the boy to be born first so the girl can have a big brother. I've always wanted a big brother. Someone to play with and watch out for me. Sometimes being an only child isn't very fun."

He wondered if Sarah ever wished for a big brother. She had one, but he was off at college, relieved he didn't live at home anymore. He was in seminary the year she started school, and when she turned thirteen, he had a church in New York state. Quinn never once considered that Sarah might want to have a big brother to protect her. Down deep, he moaned with regret.

Quinn put tea bags in cups from his fancy dishes, poured boiling water over the bags, and dipped them up and down until the tea looked the right color. "Randa, I'd like to talk to you about the holidays."

Marg Watland

He brought the cups to the table and sat beside her. "I think this is a good time for a cup of tea."

Randa ran her finger across the pink roses on the side of the cup. "So, what do you want to talk about?"

He shifted in his chair. "The Johnsons have invited us for Thanksgiving dinner, and we're going to the Thompsons for Christmas. I thought if we told each other how we celebrated those two holidays, we'd have a starting place to make some traditions for us as a family."

With elbows on the table, she rested her chin on her hands. "Okay. Thanksgiving is easy. We took turns having it at either our house or Aunt Dorothy and Uncle Tom's house. After dinner, us kids played games. What about you?"

Quinn remembered Aunt Etta and her family coming to their house for Thanksgiving. But all his dad talked about was the Bible and how everybody that didn't go to church and get saved was going to hell. Uncle Norman said Aunt Etta could teach the kids all the religious stuff she wanted, but he would not go to church with them. By the time Quinn was in junior high, none of the relatives came to their house for anything. Randa didn't need to hear that.

"Since Arlene died, I've had dinner with whoever asked me first. You know, I should have talked to you before accepting this year's invitations. I'm sorry, honey."

Randa looked down and spoke in a somber tone. "When I think about Christmas, it makes my stomach hurt, but I guess it's going to come, anyway."

"You're right; we can't very well cancel Christmas. Honey, any time Christmas gets too hard for you, I'd like you to come to me so I can hold you, and we'll go through it together."

She wiped tears off her face with the heels of her hands.

My Name is Randa

"Randa, I promise you; it *will* get better. One day you'll wake up and realize you can't remember the last time you cried. I don't know how long it will take, but it *will* happen."

She looked up. "Thanksgiving will be okay. Mrs. Johnson told me her daughter and family will be there. They have two little girls. I'm going to make some sugar cookies for the kids."

"People don't expect you to bring food. The women can do that."

"I know, but Mama never went to anybody's house without baking something. I want to do like Mama."

Because of Arlene, Quinn had good memories of Thanksgiving. Her family lived in Kentucky, and his in Michigan. So, while they lived in Indiana, they invited people who were alone on the holidays. Their guests told them sweet stories, heart breaking experiences, and funny accounts. Some of them became dear friends.

In this new church, he and Randa were being embraced and loved by the families. He thanked the Lord for bringing them to Park City Community Church.

"How would you feel about sending a picture of us in our Christmas cards?" He might as well quit stalling. He needed to contact his family. They deserved to know about Sarah and her daughter. He'd write a letter to Aunt Etta tomorrow.

"Okay. We have lots of pictures to pick from. It'll be fun to pick out the best one. Have you bought the cards yet?"

Quinn shook his head and grinned. "No, how about going to the drugstore tomorrow after school, and we'll choose a card we both like? I always have my name printed on the cards I send out to the church members. Arlene insisted we buy some for family and friends, without the printing. We signed those and wrote a personal note. I suppose you're going to want us to write a note in the family cards?"

"Of course, Mama said we had to write at least a sentence to make them personal. It'll take me just a few minutes to count how many cards I need. I'll bet you haven't even started your list."

"No, I'll talk to Nora. I need a list of the church membership." He'd also talk to her about the church's Christmas and Thanksgiving traditions. He didn't want to step on anyone's toes. People got attached to things the church did in past years. When he visited his first church in New York, he suggested they change their Christmas Eve service from midnight to six o'clock. It almost ended in a world war. Quinn hoped he was wiser now.

"Uncle Quinn, do you have an open house at Christmas time and invite all the people in the church? Bertha told me they did one every year. She had to miss one of her visits to us so she could get ready for it."

"When Arlene was alive, we had an open house, but nobody expects us to do that this year."

"So, what do you want to know about Christmas?"

Quinn put his cup down. "Did you still get presents from Santa? How about stockings? What kind of Christmas traditions did you have at your house?"

Randa pushed her chair away from the table and said, "I'll be right back." She returned with a pad of yellow-lined paper and sat beside him with pencil poised. "I'd like to think about this for a while. I want to know about your Christmas when you were a little boy and your Christmas with Aunt Arlene."

"That's a good idea. I'd like to know what your favorite Christmas present was. How about we have our questions ready by Monday night, and we can meet right here after supper with our answers? At the bottom of the page, let's put, 'It wouldn't be Christmas without …'"

My Name is Randa

"Okay. That sounds like fun, but all that remembering will make me miss Mama." Her eyes filled. "I just don't want to be a crybaby."

He pulled a clean hanky out of his hip pocket and handed it to her. "You are *not* a crybaby; it's normal for you to cry when you miss your mama. Any time you're too sad to talk about Christmas, we'll stop and do it another time."

Things were getting emotional. He needed to change the subject. He put his arm around her shoulder, and she lay her head on his arm. "It's too late to write our questions tonight. We need time to think about it. Okay?"

***

That night, Quinn lay in bed wide awake, facing an ugly reality. He had been nothing to his baby sister. All he wanted to do was to get out of that joyless home.

Sarah wanted *him* to raise her child. She should've hated him for having a brother who almost never came home to visit. When Sarah ran away, he placed all the blame on his parents. He felt no responsibility toward his sister.

Randa's desire to have a big brother opened Quinn's eyes. Sarah was an embarrassment to him; he didn't want a little sister *sixteen years younger* than him. He had never thought of what she would want. He only thought about himself. Quinn realized he had committed a multitude of sins toward his family. He flipped the pages in his Bible to Jeremiah 31:34 and read, "… for they shall all know me, from the least of them unto the greatest of them, saith the Lord: for I will forgive their iniquity, and I will remember their sin no more."

Quinn tiptoed down the hall and peeked in Randa's room. She lay asleep in the center of her bed, curled up in a ball. Then he went to his study, closed the door, and confessed the sins he had carried for years. Quinn tore a page from a small notepad and wrote:

October 11, 1953
Lord, I've been self-centered, resentful, thoughtless,
unloving, unforgiving, and mean. Lord, I don't
deserve your forgiveness, but I ask you to forgive my sins
and remember them no more, as you have promised.
Signed, Quinn Edwards

He placed the note in his Bible and whispered, "Sarah Jean, if you can hear me, I'm sorry I wasn't a big brother to you."

Quinn closed the Bible and slid down to his knees. "Lord, I hold resentment in my heart toward my dad. Forgive me. Thank you for your promise in Jeremiah."

Chilled, he returned to his bedroom. It was close to dawn before his eyes closed in sleep.

Chapter 19

Traditions and a Letter

Monday, October 12

*B*acon sizzled, coffee perked, and Quinn sat at the kitchen table writing Christmas questions. Randa entered with her yellow pad and schoolbooks in her arms. "Morning."

She leaned over his shoulder and read what he had written. "The bacon smells good. Can I have some?"

"What, no peanut butter?"

"No. I'll have a breakfast this morning. Ca..." Quinn's brow twitched. "*May* I have an egg too?"

He dropped two slices of Wonder Bread into the toaster, kissed her cheek, and said, "Good morning to you too, honey. Do you have any more of those yellow pads? I've celebrated Christmas Eve with several families. I think I'll start there."

"Okay, I'll start there too. I'm going to work on my questions during study hall. Molly said she'd help me. There's another yellow pad on top of my dresser."

"If Molly's going to help you, I think I'll have Nora look over my list. I keep thinking of more questions. This might take a while."

"I couldn't go to sleep last night," she said. "I kept thinking of things I wanted to tell you. It's going to be fun. Usually, kids don't get to decide how the family celebrates Christmas." She looked at him with tears in her eyes and whispered, "I might have to cry."

He took her hands in his and stroked her knuckles with his thumb, "No doubt we'll both shed some tears. I'm so sorry I didn't know your Mama. This year we'll grieve, and next year will be a little easier."

Marg Watland

Randa wiped her face with the heel of her hands, jumped up from her chair, and said, "I have to go." She grabbed her books and yanked open the door. "Bye," she called as she rushed down the steps.

Quinn poured another cup of coffee and prayed, "Lord, I've avoided discussing my childhood with anyone, but Randa wants to know about Christmas when I was a kid. I have carried hatred for my father all these years, and last night, you made me face my sin. Lord, please show me my father's good qualities and help me love him again. I regret I can't go to Dad and, face to face, ask him to forgive me."

There was a new peace in his heart as he continued to write more Christmas questions.

At nine o'clock, Quinn headed to church with his freshly written pages. He couldn't wait to tell Nora.

When he walked into the outer office, he saw a tea cup on its side and a puddle of tea on Nora's desk. Her chair stood against the far wall. In his office, his chair lay on its back, and a woman's bottom protruded from under his desk. At first, he wondered if she was stuck. He bent over his desk to get a better look and grinned to find his proper secretary crouched on her hands and knees with her cute little stocking-clad feet resting near an empty cup that normally held his pens and pencils. "Are you alright?" he asked.

Nora backed out from under his desk with her hands full of pens and pencils. She raised her head a few inches too soon and cracked it on the drawer. "Ouch!" she exclaimed, then pushed up and stood in front of him with a red face, dust on one cheek, and natural curls all awry.

"I dropped the cup, and everything rolled under your desk," she said. "What are you doing here today? This is your day off."

Quinn picked up the cup and held it out for her to fill.

"Excuse me," she said and made a dash to the restroom.

My Name is Randa

Quinn called out, "Meet me downstairs."

When she came out, Nora found the chairs back in place and her tea cup missing.

Downstairs, Quinn stood at the stove waiting for water to boil in the big aluminum teakettle. He grinned at her with a twinkle in his eyes. Two pages of yellow-lined paper lay on the table beside her empty cup. Quinn brought the kettle to the table, dropped a tea bag in the cup, and filled it with hot water.

"Randa and I are going to write about how each of us celebrated Christmas in the past. That should give us ideas about what holiday traditions we'd like. Molly is going to help her, so I decided I'd show you what I wrote. I filled these two pages early this morning, and I've already thought of more."

While Nora read, Quinn stared at her hair and tried to imagine what it would feel like to bury his fingers into the curly mass. He sat back in his folding chair and wondered where in the world a thought like that came from.

"You need to keep this list," she said. "It'll bring back precious memories. The two of you will have wonderful stories to tell about this year." She read on. "So, there were no gifts under your tree until Christmas morning, and you like to ice skate?"

"Yes. When I was a teen, my friends and I skated every day during Christmas vacation. I'm giving Randa a pair of ice skates this year. If she doesn't know how to ice skate, I'll teach her."

Nora handed the pages back to Quinn and said, "At my house, I put the packages under the tree as soon as I wrapped them. We told Julie not to touch presents, and she usually obeyed. When Julie was little, she'd lean over, put her hands on her knees, and stare at the packages. I have a

101

Mary Watland

picture of her with her little bottom sticking up in the air, staring at all the presents.

"Esther had four boys, and those little scamps poked at their packages until the paper tore, and then they loosened the Scotch tape enough so they could see what was inside. The year George Junior was two, she gave up, put all the presents in a storage room in the basement, and locked the door. Esther's house was bedlam, and she loved every minute."

"Have I told you that Bertha, Randa's pastor's wife in Minnesota, gave her a diary to record her thoughts that last year and a half before Sarah died? Now we are recording our thoughts while we learn to be a family. Bertha said someday we might want to write Randa's story. I'm keeping that in mind when I write in my journal. You're right; we'll want to keep these memories."

Nora nodded and took a sip of her hot tea. "Quinn, I'm proud of you. Randa is adapting to her new life with you very well."

He laughed. "I've done some adapting, too. I have to eat vegetables twice a day. We're looking for a house cat, and I've been told I should pray in the closet instead of the shower. As for Randa, she's too mature for her age. Molly is her only friend. She bakes delicious desserts, and my clothes are getting snug."

Nora giggled and said, "And that is Randa's fault?"

***

When Randa came home from school, Quinn was standing by the car. He said, "It's time we picked out our Christmas card. Put your books inside, and we'll go shopping downtown."

Upon arriving downtown, Quinn opened the drugstore door and asked her, "Would you like to choose our cards?"

My Name is Randa

They had a lengthy conversation about which card represented them. Randa chose the card with a bright star shining down on the little town of Bethlehem. Quinn ordered duplicates of their favorite photo and a hundred cards printed with their name to give to the congregation. They left the drugstore with a bag of cards for their family and friends.

When they arrived home, Randa grabbed the cookie jar and set it on the table. "I'm starved." Quinn made coffee, and Randa poured a glass of milk. They munched on cookies, and she told him about her day.

When she finally slowed down, Quinn said, "Honey, it's time I write to my family and tell them about you and your mama. When I finish the letter, I'll let you read it. You can pick a picture of us to put in the letter. I'll send it to my Aunt Etta; she can send it around to the family like a chain letter."

Randa didn't understand why he hadn't written the letter before now, but she was afraid to ask. Maybe, at first, he wasn't sure he wanted to keep her. Now she knew he loved her no matter what, and she loved him too, more and more every day.

"I'm so glad you're going to tell them about me," she said with a big grin. "Is there anybody my age? Etta is a funny name. I've never heard it before."

"Her name is Henrietta. When we were little, it was too hard to say, so we started calling her Aunt Etta, and now everybody calls her Etta. I don't think there's anyone your age, but I haven't kept in touch with my family, so I don't know for sure. There are several great aunts and uncles and all kinds of cousins. Your mama was the youngest of the first cousins. There's a box in the garage with your Grandma Edwards' photo albums. I'll look for it, and you can see pictures of all our relatives."

In the next few days, Quinn wrote and tore up several pages before, with Nora's help, he finally completed the letter. Randa read it and handed him three pictures. "I couldn't choose between these three," she said.

The first picture was Quinn, Randa, and John in front of Sarah's home in Minneapolis. The next one showed the two of them in their backyard the day they moved to Park City, and

Millie took the third one on Randa's birthday.

He spread them out on the dining room table. The pictures told the story of their four months together. "I can't either. We'll have to send all three."

Chapter 20

October 15-27

Christmas stories filled their evenings. Quinn spoke of toy trucks and shooting at squirrels with his slingshot. She told him about tea sets and her favorite, a Raggedy Ann doll. Randa loved to watch the bubble lights on their Christmas tree. Quinn explained that when he was a boy, they clipped little candle holders on the branches and filled the holders with candles.

"Dad allowed us to light them only once. He worried the tree might catch fire and burn the house down."

Tuesday, Quinn came home with a big smile. "You'll never guess who called me at the office today?"

Randa perked up. "Was it John? He hasn't called in almost a month. The last time he called, I think he'd been drinking beer at the pool hall. He talked silly."

"No, honey, I'm sorry he didn't call. Reverend Bennett told me he's having a hard time catching John at home. We need to pray God will keep John safe. We know grieving is hard, but he doesn't have God to comfort him."

"Okay, I'll pray for him right now." She took his hand, and Quinn listened to Randa's trusting faith that Jesus would watch over her stepfather.

Why hadn't he asked her to pray before? From now on, he would. She had the innocent trust of a newborn Christian. Her prayer blessed him.

Quinn added his prayer for John. They had each other, but John was all alone, grieving for Sarah and missing Randa.

"So, who called, Uncle Quinn?"

"My Aunt Etta. She told me she mailed us a letter, but she had more questions. She wanted to know about your father. I had some answers, but not all. Do you know where your father was raised?"

"Uh-huh. In Missouri, but he didn't have any relatives because he was an only child, and his mother was an only child. Just like me."

No wonder Randa wanted to know about the Edwards family. The only relatives she *knew* were from John's family. Quinn prayed, "Lord, I've been so wrong. For years, I've tried to forget my family. Now, Randa's in my life, and she *wants* a family."

"What else did she want to know, Uncle Quinn?"

"I'm sorry, honey. I wrote her questions on a scrap of paper but forgot to bring it home."

Monday afternoon, Quinn found Aunt Etta's letter in their mailbox. She had filled the two pages with excitement about Sarah's child. She'd sent his letter out as a round-robin, so each member of the family could read the news.

When Randa arrived home from school, he handed the letter to her. It was difficult to read, but she finished it and ran a finger along the written words. "This handwriting's all jagged. It's hard to read. Is she shaky?"

"Yes, she has a tremor. Do you need help?"

"No, I figured it out. She sounds nice. I'm glad she wants to see me. Can I take the letter to school tomorrow so Molly can read it?"

He nodded. "Why don't you start a letter to her, and I'll write some at the bottom. Tell her some happy stories about you and your Mama, and John."

It felt good to talk to Aunt Etta and have her back in his life. He had Randa to thank for giving him the desire to be reunited with his family.

My Name is Randa

Randa said, "Okay, but I have homework tonight. It's math, and I might need help. I'll write to her tomorrow when I get home from school. Did you remember about the teacher's conference on Tuesday, and then Friday, we're going to the football game?"

"Teacher's conference?"

"I left the paper on your desk last week. She headed down the hall to the study, with Quinn following close behind. She lifted a reference book and pulled out a green paper from under it.

He skimmed the letter then reached for his pocket calendar and noted the time and date. "It looks like we might need another system for school letters."

"You need to write football on Friday, too. Maybe I should leave the school notices on the kitchen table."

"That sounds like a good idea. Now, both the school conference and football are on my calendar. It's time for a snack, and then you can do your homework, and I'll make dinner."

Quinn decided he could call himself a parent, now that Teacher's Conference was on his calendar.

***

On the day of the conference, Miss Jarvis, Randa's teacher, said, "She is doing well. I'll continue sending extra work home when I find a gap in her schooling. She's having trouble in math, and I suspect the two months she was out of school is the culprit."

Quinn suggested a tutor.

She shook her head. "From the things you said in your letter, I think it would be better if you helped her. It's amazing how much I learn about my students while I'm helping them. She's a sweet girl, and I'm pleased at how well she is adjusting."

Quinn went along with Miss Jarvis' suggestion but wasn't so sure he was the best person to help Randa with her math. It hadn't been his favorite subject. Being a parent was becoming a full-time job.

Chapter 21

October, 29-30

Thursday, Quinn came home a half hour early with a big grin. "Remember the day we moved here, and you told us your cat Prissie died of old age?"

She nodded and pulled enough silverware out of the drawer to set the table.

"I asked Nora to help me find a cat that purrs. She's found a cat named Goldie who needs a home. Her owner, an elderly woman named Mrs. Solheim, has recently moved into a nursing home. She is worried about her cat."

There was a loud clatter as the silverware spewed across the table. Randa jumped up and down, shouting, "Really? Really?"

"Yes, really. If you're interested, we have an appointment to meet her daughter Clara at the nursing home tonight."

"Oh, thank you, Uncle Quinn. Now, I won't get so lonely when you're gone."

***

When they entered the nursing home, a tall woman in her thirties stood and faced them. Quinn asked, "Are you Clara?"

"Yes, I'm Clara Larkin. You must be Reverend Edwards and Randa. Could we tell my mother you'll keep Goldie until she goes back home? Mother doesn't know. It's just a matter of time."

"If that's what you want." He preferred to be honest with people who were dying, but he'd follow her lead. "I come here once a week and visit some of our elder parishioners. May I add your mother to my list?"

109

"We aren't religious, but if Mother doesn't mind, I guess it'll be all right."

She led them down the hall to room thirty-nine. A white-haired woman lay in the bed with covers tucked under her chin. Clara whispered, "Mother, are you awake?"

The woman opened her eyes and smiled at her daughter. She gazed at Quinn and Randa. "You brought them."

"Mother, I want you to meet Reverend Edwards and his niece Randa. They've been looking for a big fat cat that purrs. I think Goldie fits the bill. They said they'd keep her until you go home."

Randa stepped forward and took the woman's hand. "My cat Prissie died a year ago. She purred all the time. I'd really like a cat to keep me company. I promise I'll take very good care of Goldie, and I'll come back and tell you how she's doing."

"Oh, thank you. I've been so worried about her." Her eyelids slowly closed, and in a faint voice, she said, "Irene, you can call me Irene."

Quinn stepped closer. "You rest now, Irene. We'll come see you again." He'd have to learn how to live with a house pet. He'd been raised on a farm where animals lived outside and worked for a living.

Clara leaned over and kissed her mother's cheek. "I'm going to take the Edwards' over to pick up Goldie. I'll be back to see you tomorrow afternoon." Irene's eyes remained closed, but a tiny smile crossed her lips.

They followed Clara's car to Irene's little bungalow. When Quinn stopped the car, Randa said, "She's dying, isn't she?"

"I believe so."

When they entered the house, a tabby appeared at Clara's feet, and meowed with a questioning sound.

Randa dropped to her knees and stroked the cat. "Hello, Goldie, you aren't gold. Your fur is mostly black and brown

My Name is Randa

and white, and your stripes are all broken up and scrambled."

Clara finished filling a box with Goldie's possessions, then squatted down beside Randa and said, "The vet says she's a mackerel tabby."

Randa hung Goldie over her shoulder, grinned at her uncle, and said, "Thank you, Mrs. Larkin. I promise I'll take good care of her."

Quinn picked up the box, and Randa carried Goldie to the car. They waved goodbye, and he drove away with a satisfied smile on his face.

She talked to Goldie all the way home, telling her new cat about their house.

When they walked into the kitchen, Randa put Goldie on the floor and dumped her coat on a chair. Quinn's eyebrow raised. She got the message and took her coat to the closet, muttering under her breath, "He's just like Mama."

Randa closed the closet door. "Come on, Goldie, we'll go down the hall first." She opened Quinn's bedroom door and said, "Uncle Quinn, I want you to sit on your bed and pet her."

"This is Uncle Quinn's room, and he keeps his door closed all the time. Uncle Quinn doesn't know anything about pets, so we'll have to teach him. He had cats on his farm, but he said they were feral. I looked up feral in the dictionary, and that means they were wild." Goldie looked from Quinn to Randa, then followed her across the hall.

"This is Uncle Quinn's study. He's pretty particular about how he wants things in this room." She turned his chair around and crooked her finger. Quinn sat in his chair and watched Goldie sniff around under the desk and then peer in the wastebasket.

"That's enough of this room. Come on, Goldie, next is my room."

111

Goldie trotted down the hall behind her. Randa sat on her bed, lifted the cat onto her lap, and stroked Goldie's multi-colored fur. Quinn smiled at Randa's earnest conversation. It appeared as if Goldie was hanging onto every word she said.

He didn't know she had been lonely but was certain she wouldn't want him to get someone to stay with her. Had she ever been afraid when he wasn't home? Did the house creak and make eerie sounds? Did the trees in the backyard make scary shadows?

She picked up the cat. "Now, you can check out the living room. I'll let you explore and decide where you want to sit. My friend Molly told me there's a new show on TV called Topper and it's really good."

Randa turned on the TV and parked herself on the davenport. Goldie acquainted herself with the furniture, then jumped up on Randa's lap and plopped down. Their attention turned to the TV program that sported a couple of ghosts. Randa stroked Goldie's soft fur, then Goldie closed her eyes and switched on her purring motor.

Quinn laid his head back and thanked the Lord for giving Randa a companion.

***

Friday night, the Thompsons, Quinn, and Randa arrived at the football field early and lined themselves on the third row. The high school band members were assembling and tuning up to play "The Star-Spangled Banner." Quinn recognized a few of the players but didn't know their names. Randa saw Pansy standing at the other end of the bleachers with Tim and Bert and waved. It wasn't long before they sat down in front of them.

Pansy said, "I told them we needed to sit close to you so we could visit."

My Name is Randa

Randa introduced Pansy to Molly and told her Molly's brother was on the team.

"What's his name?" Pansy asked.

"Brad Thompson."

"My Daddy says he's a pretty good player, not scholarship material, but good. He missed a couple of plays last week. Hope he does better tonight."

Bert's ears turned red. He turned to Don and Ruth, and they both grinned at him.

Don winked. "Every parent needs to have one like that to keep them humble."

When Bert turned around, Don nudged Quinn and said in a low voice, "I've heard about her."

They chuckled under the noise of the crowd.

Quinn said, "I met Pansy at Tim's after the gospel sing. She announced they were going to have a baby in April, and she would be a big sister. She doesn't look like either of her parents."

"No, she's Bert's daughter. His first wife was part Sioux. Bert married Mavis two years ago."

The flag bearers marched onto the field, the crowd quieted, and the band played the national anthem. The game was a redeemer for Brad. He didn't miss any plays, and Park City won 20 to 17.

***

That night after the game, Randa plopped down on the davenport and said, "Whew, living in Park City keeps us busier and busier."

"I'm sorry, honey. We haven't had enough time together lately." Quinn pulled out his pocket calendar, turned the page to Saturday, and handed it to Randa. "Nora and I talked about it, and she said I should write your name in my calendar. I'll continue to go to the office early Saturday morning, but when I come home for cinnamon rolls, the rest of the day will be ours."

Randa turned to each Saturday in the booklet and saw her name. Her smile and the sparkle in her eyes were a beautiful sight. Yes, with Nora's help, he was learning how to be a good parent.

Chapter 22

November, 2-3

The director from the nursing home called Quinn, saying a patient would soon pass. Even though his family weren't churchgoers, they asked for a minister.

When Quinn arrived, he encouraged the patient's two granddaughters to hold their grandfather's hand and say goodbye to him. "Later on, showing your love to him at the end of his life will be a precious memory."

Ten minutes after the girls came out of his room, the nurse stepped out, saying, "He's gone."

On the way out, Quinn walked by room thirty-nine and saw Irene was awake. "May I come in?" he asked.

"Yes, please," she said. "My daughter doesn't want me to know I'm dying. She doesn't know God, but I do. Would you put her on your prayer list?"

"She's already there." He reached for his pocket Bible. "May I read to you?"

"Yes, Psalm 23."

Quinn took her hands in his. "The Lord is my Shepherd; I shall not want ..." Irene mouthed the words with eyes closed.

Clara walked into the room. Quinn smiled at her but didn't stop quoting the Psalm. When he finished, Irene opened her eyes and said, "Thank you. I'd forgotten some words. That gives me so much comfort."

Quinn offered his hand to Clara. "Would you like to pray with us?"

She hesitantly put her hand in his and Quinn prayed, "Lord, thank you for the comfort you give us in the Psalms.

Mary Watland

Thank you for Goldie, who brought us together. I pray that today, Clara and Irene will have a happy visit ..."

Tuesday morning, Quinn sat in the kitchen with his first cup of coffee. He heard Randa moving about in her bedroom, noisier than usual. Drawers slammed, the bathroom door banged, and then the shower went on. Quinn glanced at the calendar, poured a second cup of coffee, and prepared himself for a confrontation.

Randa stormed into the room barefoot and wearing a bathrobe. "Uncle Quinn, I can't find anything to wear. I finished my math assignment, but I'm not sure it's right and I really don't want to go to school today."

"You did the laundry and the ironing on Saturday," he said. "What's wrong with your clothes?"

"They're too tight and I don't like them." She flopped down on a chair across from him and cried.

Quinn stood, filled the teakettle with water and put it on the stove. He dropped a tea bag in one of Arlene's rose bud teacups. "All right, Randa, let's talk about what's happening here. Arlene and I were married for ten years, so I know about female problems. The only color on your face is that nasty pimple on your chin, and I suspect your stomach hurts. Am I correct?"

Randa looked at her uncle with a red face. Her mouth hung open. "You know?"

The teakettle whistled and Quinn stood to make the tea. He set the steaming cup in front of her, gently squeezed her shoulder and said, "When I didn't feel good or was sad about something, my mother made tea. She said it would make me feel better."

Randa warmed her hands on the teacup and said, "That's what Mama said."

"Have you taken something for your stomach?"

"I took aspirin, but it still really hurts."

My Name is Randa

"I'll stay home with you this morning and go to the office after Nora leaves. Do you have enough supplies? I'm going to call Nora and ask her to go to the drugstore for us. You can tell her what you need."

Quinn called Nora and asked her to find something stronger than aspirin for cramps, then handed the phone to Randa. He dropped bread in the toaster and put peanut butter and jam on the table.

After lunch, Randa curled up in a corner of the davenport with Goldie sprawled across her stomach. Quinn asked, "Do you feel any better, honey?"

"Yes, the pills helped and Goldie laying on my stomach feels really good. I forgot to ask Nora to get me a hot water bottle, but I guess I don't need one."

"Call me if you need anything. Nora has a meeting this afternoon, but she said she'd stop by afterward." Quinn leaned over, kissed her, and scratched Goldie behind her ears.

Right after Quinn left, the phone rang. It was Drew.

"He just left; he'll be in his office in five minutes," said Randa.

Drew said, "I called to find out how you two are doing. What's happened since your birthday?"

Randa spent the next twenty minutes telling him about Christmas traditions, Great Aunt Etta, and Goldie. When they finished talking, Randa wished she could meet him. He was really nice.

Later in the afternoon, Nora arrived and found her in the kitchen making a cake for dessert.

The phone rang. Randa answered it and after a minute, said, "No, I took a meatloaf out of the deep freeze." She whispered into the phone, "Nora's here. Can I invite her?"

She hung up the phone. "Uncle Quinn said I could invite you to stay for dinner. We're having meatloaf. Before he comes home, he's going to check on a lady that had surgery."

Nora welcomed their invitation. She treasured their friendship. His call this morning was embarrassing. Thank goodness he was on the phone when she delivered the supplies. Would she ever get over being exceedingly modest?

Goldie appeared at the door when Quinn walked into the kitchen. She meowed, and he leaned over to fluff her fur. He grinned at Nora. "I think she likes me. She welcomes me home every day. I'm sorry I'm late. It took longer for Mrs. Schmidt to wake up than I expected."

They had an enjoyable meal, then Randa served pineapple upside-down gingerbread topped with whipped cream. Quinn said, "I can't believe it. My mother used to make this."

Randa nodded. "Mama made it too."

"Randa, I suggest you make this for our next potluck, and put a little sign in front saying, 'Grandma Edward's recipe.'"

Nora took another bite. "I've never heard of this combination, but it's very good."

Nora remembered her mother's pineapple upside down cake. They used a yellow cake instead of gingerbread. She was glad that even though Quinn's mother had passed, he still enjoyed her recipes. It must be a comfort to him.

It was after eight when Nora went home. Quinn joined Randa on the davenport. "Think you'll go to school tomorrow?"

"Yes, I feel much better tonight. Thank you for making it easy for me to talk to you." She hugged his arm. "You're the very best uncle ever." Goldie climbed over Randa, squeezed in between them, and rubbed her head on Quinn's arm.

My Name is Randa

He tugged on Randa's ponytail and said, "Thank you. I love you too. I almost forgot to tell you; Aunt Etta called today. She said the news about you has spread through the family like wildfire. She had more questions. I jotted down the ones I couldn't answer. It sounds like it's time for you to write to her again."

Friday afternoon, Quinn and Randa went to see Irene.

Randa said, "When Uncle Quinn comes home, Goldie welcomes him by winding herself around his legs. He built her a bedroom between the garage and the fence, with a roof and everything."

Irene smiled and said, "That's nice."

When they left, Randa said, "Irene's almost ready to go to heaven, isn't she? She looks like Mama did when she went to the hospital. Do you think Irene will tell Mama about Goldie?"

Quinn turned into the driveway. "We don't know. It's a nice thought, isn't it? Are you okay, honey?"

"Uh-huh. I'm glad they found us to take care of her cat."

***

Saturday morning, Clara called to say her mother passed peacefully in her sleep. "I think Mother needed to know Goldie was all right before she died."

Tuesday afternoon, Randa stopped at church to have her afternoon chat with Uncle Quinn. A brown car was running with the trunk lid open. Pam, a classmate at school, came out the church door carrying a potted plant in her arms. Behind Pam was Clara Larkin with a large bouquet.

Randa frowned and asked, "Was Irene your grandma?"

Pam nodded. "Do you live with Reverend Edwards?"

Clara said, "Pam, this is Reverend Edwards' niece and Goldie's new owner. I'm sorry girls, there's family at our house. We have to go."

"I'll talk to you tomorrow," Pam said, putting the plant in the trunk and shutting the lid with a bang.

***

That evening, Randa told Quinn she and Pam Larkin were in the same grade. "Could I invite her to come visit me? It might make her feel better about her grandma if she saw Goldie."

"Yes. you may, with one stipulation. Anytime a friend comes over, their parent must know you're at the house alone. Let me know when they will arrive and when they plan to go home. Okay?"

"Okay."

Quinn turned off the lights and made ready for bed. He didn't say it very well, but Randa didn't object to the guidelines Nora had suggested. He thanked the Lord for Nora's wise advice.

Chapter 23

Tuesday, November 10-18

*R*anda stopped by the church and said, "Uncle Quinn, can we talk about a Christmas open house again? Bertha Bennett told me they have one every year to thank their members for the kind things they do for them. The people here in our church have been really nice to us."

"Honey, preparing for an open house is a lot of work."

"Could we talk to Nora about it? Please. Her car is out front. Is she downstairs?"

Quinn sighed. "All right, you may ask her."

She dashed out and ran full tilt down the stairs. He agreed it was a good way to say thank you, but the job was way beyond Randa's capabilities. It was a job for a minister's wife, and he didn't have a wife, nor did he want one. Well, maybe someday, but not soon. He had enough on his plate.

Quinn heard Randa's animated chatter as she and Nora climbed the stairs. She came through the door, beaming.

He frowned and said, "Randa doesn't have time to make hundreds of cookies. She's a seventh grader who has homework. I want her to have time for friends and Goldie."

"You're right," Nora said. "The women in the church would be happy to bake cookies and help organize an open house. Randa wants to make gingerbread boys to give as gifts. Would you let her do that?"

"I could start baking them now," Randa said, "and put them in the deep freeze. They're easy to make. We sold hundreds of them at Christmas and that's how we did it."

Quinn stood taut and thought for a moment, then his shoulders relaxed. "Well ..."

Marg Watland

Within minutes, Randa and Nora had the whole thing planned, along with the date, December nineteenth. Quinn shook his head in disbelief; Nora had a solution he could accept.

Randa bounced in front of him. "Can Nora help us decorate? Shouldn't our house be fancy with red and green everywhere?"

"Yes, Nora, we'll need help to do anything fancy. Arlene preferred decorating by herself; she said I got in the way."

Nora laughed at him. "Then we will change things. There are only two people in your home. I'll teach you how to decorate fancy." She turned in Quinn's direction and whispered, "All Randa has is school clothes. A fancy Christmas dress would be nice."

Randa heard, stopped dancing, and stared at him with eyes open wide.

He grinned. "We could go shopping this Saturday. Arlene liked me to go clothes shopping with her. She said I had good taste."

Randa slammed into Quinn and hugged so hard she squeezed the air right out of him.

***

That night, Quinn's first question was, "Do you know how many dozen gingerbread boys you'll need?"

"Nora said to plan for around a hundred people, so we decided fifty dozen. That's seventeen batches."

"I'm impressed; you did a lot of math to figure that out. How long is this going to take?"

"I learned how to do the figuring from Mama. She made sure there was enough time to fill an order before we agreed to take it. On the nights I don't have homework, I'll make two batches. I should have them finished in two weeks."

122

My Name is Randa

"Two weeks is acceptable with me, but I have some rules: homework first, and on Saturdays, we plan time away from the kitchen."

***

On Friday, Quinn arrived home as Randa took out the last pan of cookies for the day. He searched the rows of cookies and filched a boy with a misshapen foot. "When I was little, Mother let me eat the broken ones," he said and chomped off the head. "She would be so proud to see you baking one of her recipes."

Randa laughed. "Mama told me Grandma Edwards accidentally on purpose broke those cookies. I didn't accidentally mess up that *boy's* foot, but if Mama was here, you would have found broken ones for us to eat."

"I've decided we should go shopping first thing in the morning, before you do any baking," Quinn said, and broke a perfectly shaped gingerbread boy in half. He crunched away with a silly smile on his face. Randa stood in front of him with her arms crossed and they laughed together.

Late in the afternoon, the sixth batch of *boys* were cooling. Quinn said, "That's all for today. You can start baking again on Monday."

"But..."

He held up his hand. "Randa, when I was growing up, it was a rule at our house to rest on Sundays. Dad told me God worked six days and rested on the seventh day and we were to do the same. I preach morning and evening. It's the busiest day of my week. I need to rest between those two sermons, and you need a day when you aren't baking. Besides, the sound of all your activity in the kitchen wouldn't be restful to me."

***

Marg Watland

That evening Ozzie and Harriet were on TV, but Randa didn't laugh, not even one time. She didn't like Uncle Quinn's day of rest rule. Sunday at her house was catch up day, and they often baked all day. She missed baking with Mama. What would she do while Uncle Quinn was being restful?

Sunday afternoon, Randa lay on her bed with Goldie and moped. She whispered, "If he'd let me bake on Sunday, I could finish the cookies a lot faster."

Goldie jumped off the bed and meowed at the door. Randa headed down the hall to let her out, but Goldie turned at the living room and jumped into Quinn's lap.

Randa shrugged her shoulders, went back to her room, and spent the afternoon doing her homework. She hoped he didn't catch her because she was pretty sure she'd be in trouble. It wasn't fair, she didn't want to be restful, baking didn't make *her* feel tired.

In the living room, Goldie turned on her purr motor and curled into a ball on Quinn's lap. He stroked her fur and was thankful for the cat's presence. He didn't know what to do. Was he being unreasonable? No, he didn't think so. Should he try to reason with her? No, he'd already done that. Randa was acting like a teenager. He was glad she was acting her age but didn't know it would hurt so much.

Monday evening, Goldie perched on the windowsill in Quinn's study, preening. Quinn worried about the conflict in his home. Randa spoke to him, but under her words there was a silent sulk. He needed to take a stand and stick with it, but ... He prayed, "Lord, I didn't know it would be like this." He'd told Randa he would love her, no matter what. Down deep in his soul, he heard *love her.*

Wednesday, after school, Randa trudged up the church stairs to Quinn's office. She peeked in her uncle's office window, saw he was alone, and knocked as she opened the

My Name is Randa

door. "Uncle Quinn, can I come in?" Her mouth was a grim, straight line and her eyes showed a bit of fear.

"Always. Come in." He waited for her to speak.

She stood in front of his desk and said, "Yesterday, I told Nora about your rules. She asked me what Mama would say, then sent me home to think about it." She sucked in a breath. "Mama would say I pout when I don't get my way. I'm sorry I pouted and made you sad."

He pushed his chair back and held his arm out to her. Quinn patted his leg, and she sat down. "I'm really, really, sorry. I've been mad at you for four days and the Bible says I have to quit being mad before I go to bed. Nora made me memorize that when you bought the water heater. I already asked Jesus to forgive me."

She put her head on his shoulder and rained a sprinkle of tears on his neck.

Quinn put his arms around her and patted her back. "You know I love you, don't you?"

She nodded and asked against his warm neck, "Uncle Quinn, how do I be restful?"

"We need a diversion. We could work on our Christmas traditions, or I have a box of keepsakes from my childhood. Would you like to see them?"

"Yes, and you never showed me Grandma Edwards' photo albums. Mama said she thought I looked a little like my Great Grandma O'Reilly. Do you have pictures of her?"

Chapter 24

November 24- 26

$\mathcal{T}$he spicy smell of gingerbread met Quinn when he opened the kitchen door. Randa had changed his home from dark, cold, and empty, to bright, warm and welcoming. Every night, Goldie greeted him at the door and, after a figure eight around his legs, she led him to Randa.

The counter was filled with freshly baked cookies. On the Tuesday before Thanksgiving, Randa said, "Guess what? I'm done. As soon as I package these, I'll have fifty-one dozen gingerbread boys in the deep freeze."

***

School let out at two on the day before Thanksgiving, so Quinn left the office an hour early. When he arrived home, Randa was rolling out cookie dough on the breadboard. "You're making another batch of cookies; don't you ever tire of baking?"

Randa snickered. "I'm making a batch of sugar cookies for the Johnsons' granddaughters. I'm making stars and flowers for the little girls." She handed him the two cookie cutters, dried a cookie sheet from the drainer, and greased it with shortening. "You can help me by cutting out the stars. I told Mrs. Johnson I'd let her grandchildren help me decorate them."

The timer sounded. She opened the oven door, and the sweet smell turned on the juices in his mouth.

Quinn hadn't filled half the cookie sheet before he huffed and said, "They're sticking to the cookie cutter."

Randa looked at two ruined stars and said, "I'll take care of that. Come here and watch me." She patiently taught him

My Name is Randa

how to remove the hot cut-outs from the pan with a spatula and carefully place them on the dishtowel-covered counter. "Didn't you ever help Grandma Edwards with her baking?"

"No, my mother didn't want people in her kitchen while she was cooking, but after supper, I had to dry dishes."

***

Thanksgiving

When everyone was seated at the table, Neil Johnson said, "On Thanksgiving, we tell each other what we are most thankful for."

Randa said, "Can I go first?" She stood. "I'm an only child and all my life I've wished I had brothers and sisters. Uncle Quinn told me that people in a small church are like one big family, so he found us a small church."

She smiled at her uncle. "When we came that first time, we stayed with the Thompsons. Now, Molly is my best friend; we're like sisters. When we're with the Thompsons, they feel like our family." She took a deep breath. "Uncle Quinn was right; all of you feel like my family. I hope my Mama knows I have a big family now, and I'm thankful to be here."

When she sat down, Quinn put his arm around her and kissed the top of her head. He looked around the table and saw tears on the women's faces. The men sat still, taking in what she said.

Quinn cleared his throat, "I guess I should be next. Randa's desire to know her relatives has caused me to reconnect with my family. I don't know if we'll find any cousins her age, but those who have heard she is living with me are writing letters and saying they want to meet her. Years ago, I gave up having any children of my own, but God knew different." He grinned. "At least I didn't have to wait until I was a hundred like Sarah and Abraham in the Old Testament. Thank you for your love to us." He paused and stared at Neil with unseeing eyes, then said, "I am truly blessed."

Agnes said, "It has given us so much joy to watch you become a family, and we are blessed to have you in our midst. We love you." She pulled a hanky out of her pocket and blew.

"Thank you," Quinn said. "We're thankful for Nora, too. She's been a big help."

They ate a sumptuous turkey dinner with all the trimmings until they were full to the brim. Agnes picked up the turkey platter and said, "I made lots so we could send leftovers home with you, Reverend."

The little girls begged Randa to have a tea party with them.

Mary whispered, "I understand you have brought the girls a surprise. Go have a tea party with them, and we'll clean up the kitchen."

Later, the women peeked in the playroom, and Agnes said, "The kitchen is yours." They tied aprons on the girls, and Agnes said, "Randa has a surprise for you."

Randa grinned at her charges. "All right *ladies*, I brought sugar cookies that need to be frosted. Would you like to help me?" She took them into the bathroom to wash their hands. Three-year-old Janey and five-year-old Emily soaped up and chatted with Randa as if they had known her for a very long time.

They streaked to the kitchen and picked their favorite cutout. Emily chose the stars and sang "Twinkle, Twinkle, Little Star" with a lisp as she spread on yellow frosting. Janey liked the flowers and smeared pink frosting on everything within reach.

My Name is Randa

Their parents, Mary and Steve Dawson, peeked around the corner and watched their daughters, then returned to the living room. Mary said, "I wish that niece of yours lived on our block, Reverend. She's really good with children."

Quinn beamed with pride.

The Johnsons waved goodbye to their guests, then Mary asked, "Is there something going on between Reverend Edwards and Mrs. Montgomery? All afternoon it has been Nora this and Nora that."

Agnes said, "No, Nora told them she would be their friend after she interviewed Reverend Edwards." Agnes tilted her head to one side and stared at the wall. Neil glanced at his wife, then winked at his daughter.

Minutes later, Agnes grinned at Mary. "If there is, I don't think they know it, especially Nora."

Neil lifted Janey on his lap and spoke firmly, "Agnes, I don't want you doing any matchmaking. You hear me? Reverend Edwards is perfectly capable of taking care of his love life all by himself. Now Nora is another matter. I suspect if he's interested in her, he'll have to wake her to the possibility." Everybody laughed, and Neil said, "We'll just wait and see."

Chapter 25

Tuesday, December 1

The church phone rang ten minutes before noon. Nora answered, listened for a moment, and said agitatedly, "Oh, Tim, it's too soon. Yes, I know; but is she okay? No, you go, don't worry about me. I'm almost through here, and then I'll see you at the hospital."

She hung up the phone, covered her face with her hands, and burst into tears. Quinn rushed out of his office.

Nora said, "She's brushing her teeth when she should get in that car, so Tim can take her to the hospital."

Quinn pulled her up. She put her forehead against his chest and wept. He patted her back and said, "It'll be okay. Tim will take care of her. There, there ..."

Nora took a deep breath and tried to calm herself. She stepped back, and anger flashed in her eyes. "Carl had no business dying on me. He should be here when our grandchildren are born. I have to wait all by myself."

"I thought you told me Esther planned to sit with you in the hospital."

"She's at a meeting and won't be home until after four."

"I will not let you drive anywhere in the state you are in. I'll take you to the hospital and stay with you until she gets there. We'll drive by my house, and I'll leave a note for Randa. She can call Esther at four and let her know. Why don't you freshen up before we leave?"

Nora picked up her purse and obediently walked down the hall to the restroom. Quinn stood by her desk with keys in hand.

When she returned, he said, "I thought they were due the end of December."

My Name is Randa

"Twins are often early. We need to pray."

Quinn put an arm around her shoulder and prayed for an easy birth, healthy babies, and that Tim would be a strength to his wife. Then he drove Nora to the hospital as fast as the law would allow.

***

Nora prayed all the way, "Please, God, give us healthy babies."

When they arrived at the hospital, an older nurse said, "Hi Nora, Julie said you were coming. I'll tell her you're here."

Nora sat beside Quinn in the waiting room. He patted her hand. "I'm not leaving until Esther gets here. I told Randa she could come with Esther."

"That nurse looks familiar," he said.

"Marian's a member of our church. She works on Sundays."

Tim joined them and said, "I can stay with Julie as long as she's the only one in the labor hall." He looked pale and stuttered a bit. "Little Mother, they're m-making an exception for you. Marian said she'll come get you in a few minutes, as s-soon as they finish checking Julie." He turned and rushed back to his wife.

Nora worried about seeing her daughter in pain. When her babies were born, Carl wasn't allowed to be with her; she was terrified and felt abandoned. She was only five months along when Carl Junior was born. He was too small. He never cried. "Please, God, let Julie's babies be healthy."

It was different when she had Julie; they put her on bed rest for the last two months. Doctor Dan said it was a miracle she carried Julie for the full nine months. He said she would bear no more children.

131

Mary Watland

When Nurse Marian came to get Nora, she said, "Reverend Edwards, thank you for staying with Nora." She winked at him. "Sometimes first-time grandmas need someone to hold their hand. Come along, Nora. You can have a few minutes with your daughter. This is Julie and Tim's party, but you can see her before the hard stuff starts. If Julie continues to progress, like she is now, I expect those babies will come sometime after supper, but understand, babies don't pay any attention to our predictions. Tim's helping Julie stay calm, so he can stay for now."

Five minutes later, Nora was back. "Julie wants Tim to get something to eat. He'll be here as soon as she lets go of his hand. She's in the middle of a pain, and he won't leave until it's over."

Tim rushed into the waiting room and said, "I'm not leaving Julie. I don't care if she wants me to eat. It's late, and y'all haven't had lunch, so go and bring me a sandwich. I'm going to stay as long as I can. They told me another mother's comin' in."

The more Quinn saw of Tim, the more he admired him. Would he have been a calming force for Arlene if they had children?

At Rudy's Lunch Counter, Quinn ordered two club sandwiches and a roast beef with horseradish, to-go, for Tim. Nora tried to eat, but most of the time, she sat folding and smoothing out her napkin. When Quinn finished his sandwich, Nora asked Rudy to wrap up the other half of her sandwich for Tim.

They returned to the hospital and took the same chairs they had used before. Quinn was amazed at all the people who stopped to hear the latest news. Kids from the youth group filed in and settled down to wait.

Mavis and Bert Calhoun dropped in and stayed for just a minute. Mavis hugged Nora and said, "I want to hear the latest. I'll call Mom and let her know Julie's in labor. Call me when it's over."

Tim found a full waiting room and said, "Julie still has a few hours to go. Y'all go home and have your supper."

The teens did not want to leave.

Tim sat beside Nora, with moist eyes. "They won't let me be with her anymore."

Nora took his hand. "I'm so glad they broke the rules and let you be with her. Don't worry, Julie's healthy, and we are praying the twins are healthy too." Nora didn't want Tim to worry; she worried enough for both of them.

***

At four-thirty, Esther and Randa arrived. Randa carried Nora's knitting bag, and Esther had a sack of sandwiches and cookies. Quinn stood so Esther could sit next to her sister. She reached for Nora's hand, and Tim told them of Julie's progress.

Quinn put his hand on Randa's shoulder and said, "We should go."

"But Uncle Quinn, I want to wait until the twins are born."

He sighed. "I'll make a deal with you. We'll go home, feed Goldie, have dinner, and come back this evening. They said it would probably be after supper."

Esther hugged Randa and said, "I'll call you when it's getting close?"

"That's a good idea; thank you, Esther." Quinn put his arm around Randa. "Come along, young lady. Let's go home and wait for Esther's call."

***

Esther called at seven-thirty. "They're taking Julie into delivery."

Quinn and Randa bundled up and stepped out into the icy night. When they arrived, Quinn sat on the empty chair beside Nora.

A short time later, Tim and Julie's pastor, Mark Baker, joined the waiting family. Quinn greeted Mark, and the two men stood together and watched Tim make a path on the carpet.

A nurse's aide dashed into the waiting room and said, "Tim, baby one is a girl and baby two is a boy. The doctor isn't through with Julie yet. After he examines the twins, he'll be out to talk to you." She left before anyone had time to ask a question.

"... but Julie. How's Julie?" Tim asked the empty space. "Are my babies all right?"

Quinn asked Mark, "What do you say to him?"

Pastor Baker winked at him and headed toward Tim with his hand extended. "Congratulations Dad. Do you have names?"

The muscles in Tim's face relaxed. "Yes, sir, Rosie and Jordie; Roseann and Jordan."

Pastor Baker said, "We'll wait with you."

Nora slumped. Esther rushed over to help Quinn walk her to a chair. "I'm okay," she said. "One of each. Oh my, it's real. We have twins."

"You need tea," Quinn said.

Randa grabbed his hand. "What's wrong with Nora?"

Quinn rushed over to the nurse's station, Randa following close on his heels. A nurse took them to the staff lounge and helped him make a strong cup of tea. Randa stood as close as she could to her uncle. "She looks so white. Will she be all right?"

He picked up the cup. "Nora just needs some tea to revive her."

My Name is Randa

Esther took the cup and said, "Randa, give Nora a cookie. Julie doesn't need to see her ready to faint."

Dr. Daniel Cockrill met them in the waiting room, and everyone circled around. "Tim, your daughter weighs five-pounds-four-ounces. Her brother is four pounds-eleven-ounces. He needs a little help breathing, so we'll keep him in the incubator overnight. He's going to be fine, but we can't let him go home until he's five pounds."

"But Julie, how's Julie? Is there something wrong with his lungs? When can I see them?"

Doctor Dan motioned toward the hall and said, "Come along, Tim; let me introduce you to your family."

Randa pointed to the nursery window. "Nurse Marian's in the back, and I see an incubator."

Everyone gathered around the nursery window, straining to see the babies. They watched the nurse's every move. A few minutes later, Tim, dressed in a gown and mask, entered the nursery with Doctor Dan. The young father nodded his head from time to time while the doctor talked.

A chime sounded, announcing visiting hours were over. "When can we see the babies?" Randa asked.

"Not until tomorrow," Esther said. "Rosie will be close to the window, but we won't get a good look at Jordie until they take him out of the incubator."

Chapter 26

December 2

Wednesday morning, Quinn was in his office reading the morning paper when Nora arrived. She didn't even remove her coat but sat in the chair beside his desk. "Thank you for being with me at the hospital yesterday and making tea. I was distraught, and you helped calm me."

"I'm glad I could help. I've never sat with a family waiting for a baby to be born. When we got home, Randa hit me with questions I couldn't answer. I thought about telling her how a calf is born but decided against it. She wants to ask Nurse Marian."

"Marian is the perfect one. Thank goodness she didn't ask me," Nora said.

She fiddled with the strap on her purse. "I talked to Julie this morning, and she said they've taken Jordie out of the incubator, but Doctor Dan said it might be a week before Jordie gains enough weight to go home."

Nora put shaking fingers to her mouth and said, "Quinn, they're so tiny."

He took her hand. "Nora, it was a long day yesterday. Do only what is necessary and then go home."

The phone rang. Nora ran to the phone on her desk. The calls increased as people learned the Hunter babies had arrived.

She apologized, but Quinn laughed and said, "If I didn't already know, I'd be calling myself." He listened in on her conversation and wrote all the pertinent details, so he could help answer people's questions.

Nora worked past lunchtime. She wanted everything current when she took time off to help Julie with the babies.

My Name is Randa

Quinn stopped at her desk and said, "You were supposed to leave at noon. I'm going to Rudy's Lunch Counter. Let me bring you a sandwich."

She protested, but he stopped her. "You're a grandma now, and you need to keep up your strength. Tell me what you want."

"Oh, all right, ham and cheese."

Nora was downstairs when Quinn returned with their lunch. She poured tea and said, "Remember when I told you I would be your friend if you came to Park City? I didn't think about how that would affect me. You and Randa have become my wonderful friends, and I love mothering Randa."

He squeezed her shoulder and said, "We feel the same. I thank God you were there the night Randa baked her birthday cake. Thank you for being available when she has questions."

***

Wednesday evening, Nora stood at the nursery window, admiring her grandchildren. Rosie was asleep in her bassinet, and Jordie's arms and legs flailed while Marian changed his diaper. Marian finished her task and rolled his bassinet next to Rosie's.

Quinn and Randa came down the hall and stood behind Nora. Randa unbuttoned her coat and asked, "Shouldn't someone take care of Jordie? He's crying."

Marian heard and peeked her head out the door. "Don't worry, honey, he's had a bottle and a diaper change. Jordon seems to be one of those babies that cries himself to sleep." Marian grinned. "We've noticed he usually falls asleep in the middle of a wail."

Quinn saw Tim walk into Julie's room with a milkshake. "There's Tim," he said. "We should go see Julie."

137

He and Nora started toward her room, but Randa held back.

"I want to stay here and watch Jordie fall asleep."

When Randa finally showed up in Julie's room, she said, "I saw Jordie fall asleep in the middle of a cry. He cries so loud; it makes me laugh."

Quinn handed their gifts to his niece. "You decided what we should buy, so you should give it to her."

Julie opened the packages and held up a Raggedy Ann doll and a slingshot.

Randa said, "Nora told us your babies have enough clothes to last them until they are toddlers. Uncle Quinn and I are telling each other about our Christmases, so we can start making new traditions. These were our very favorite Christmas presents when we were little kids. We're pretty sure the twins will like them, too."

Julie fingered Raggedy Ann's red hair and said, "Thank you. We'll put these on a shelf in their room, and I promise you that one day they will send a thank you note."

Randa shook a finger in front of Tim's face. "And you are not to borrow Jordie's slingshot. It's already used. Uncle Quinn tried it out to be sure it worked."

Chapter 27

December 4-9

Friday morning, Nora was folding bulletins when she stopped abruptly and said to herself, "Of course. They should stay with me. If they stay with me, they can get to the hospital in minutes."

Quinn stepped to the door of his office. Before he could speak, she snatched her coat off the hook and said, "I'm going to the hospital to talk to the kids. Please pray I can convince them to stay with me until Jordie is ready to go home." She dashed down the stairs, and the heavy front door opened and closed before Quinn had time to gather his thoughts.

"Whew," he said to the empty office. "That woman can move like the wind." He laughed at the thought of Julie or Tim crossing her on this. It seemed like a logical plan to him. They were blessed to have Nora as a mother.

***

She was smiling when she returned from the hospital. Esther stopped by to hear the latest about the twins, and Nora said, "They're staying with me. As soon as I'm finished here, I'll go home and get my house ready for my family."

Esther grabbed half of the stack of unfolded bulletins and helped her sister. "You can borrow a crib from the church nursery. I have a dresser that is the right height for diaper changing. The next person who comes through that door with a truck can help us move it over to your house."

Don Thompson walked in to have coffee with Quinn. The sisters looked at each other and giggled.

"Don, you're just the man we're looking for," Esther said. "We need your truck. The kids are staying with Nora until Jordan can come home. I'll go now and empty the dresser." She pulled gloves out of her pockets and said, "Bring Quinn with you. I'm too short to help move furniture. Nora, you can clean the crib with Lysol and have it ready to pick up after you guys get my dresser."

The sisters left the room together.

Don burst into laughter as Quinn stood motionless, watching them vanish down the stairs. "Rev, it looks like you haven't seen how fast those two sisters can shift gears. What are we moving? We better go before one of them comes back and plows us under."

Quinn grabbed his coat and hat and joined his friend. "I've never seen anything like that in my life."

They hurried down the stairs. Don said, "Esther might sound bossy, but she can think through a plan faster than any person I've ever met. She acts and Nora asks with a please and a thank you. If you need someone to head up a project, those women are the best."

**

Saturday afternoon, Quinn and Randa drove to Nora's house to see baby Rosie. He worried Nora was taking on too much. He'd tell her to slow down but didn't think she would listen.

Randa fell in love with Rosie and said, "Nora, could I help you babysit when they get a little bigger. I don't know how to take care of babies."

On the way home, Randa said, "Nora's house is a mess. There's baby stuff all over. Can we go see Jordie?" Quinn turned the car toward the hospital to visit a patient who weighed less than five pounds and hadn't learned to talk yet.

My Name is Randa

***

Four days later, Nora called Quinn from home. "I'm sorry, I can't come in until afternoon. Julie is at the hospital nursing Jordie, and I need to pick up some ointment for her. Can you come over?"

When he arrived, Nora flipped a diaper over Quinn's shoulder, placed the baby in his arms, and led him to a rocking chair. "Sit here. You can rock her to sleep." She showed him how to hold Rosie so her back was supported and her head didn't bob about. "I won't be long."

She hurried out of the house before she got flustered and blushed. He didn't need to know she was going to the feed store to get Bag Balm for Julie's sore nipples.

Quinn watched Nora's car turn the corner and whispered to the little bundle nestled up against his neck, "Your grandma has more faith in me than she should." A resounding *wurrup* nearly put him in a panic. Rosie rubbed her face back and forth on his shirt and quieted. Quinn sang "Jesus Loves Me" and rocked. A wonderful feeling came over him, and Reverend Quinn Edwards fell in love with the little scrap of life in his arms.

That evening, Quinn told Randa about holding Rosie while Nora went to the store. "When she returned, I didn't want to give her back. I loved Rosie sleeping on my chest."

"I wonder if you'll be able to say that about Jordie. He's so loud." She turned to gaze out the window.

Randa's silence caused Quinn to ask, "What's on your mind?"

"Do you think you'll get married some day? I think Nora's really nice."

Quinn blushed and worked at making his voice sound normal. "I certainly wouldn't marry Nora. I'm too old for her, and besides, she's still wearing her wedding rings. She's not interested in marriage."

"Oh, I just wondered what it would be like if you married someone and had a baby."

"I'm much too old to be having babies. People my age have grandchildren."

"Okay, I was just wondering."

Where had that come from? Nora was too young for him, and besides, she hadn't been blinking her eyes at him like those women in his Chicago church. Getting married was his business, and he had enough to handle with a teenager in his house.

Chapter 28

Thursday, December 10-15

Thursday morning, Nora breezed into the office with a big grin. "Jordie will be discharged tomorrow. The kids are going home this afternoon, and I'll move in with them tonight. Tim's parents expect to arrive on Sunday the twentieth, so I will be gone from home for eleven days. I should be back in time for evening church on the twentieth.

"I'm sorry, Quinn, but I won't be available to help with your open house. I've asked Esther to take my place. If you don't like something, say so. She'd like to come over this evening and look at your Christmas decorations."

"Alright, we'll miss you." Quinn tried to give her a happy smile. "Enjoy the babies."

How would he and Esther, the living whirlwind, get along? Sometimes that woman intimidated him. He'd rather work with Nora.

That evening, Randa gave Esther a tour of the house. In the dining room, Esther opened a buffet door and said, "These are file folders. Where are your good dishes?"

Quinn headed to the garage.

Randa said, "We have lots of boxes in the garage. Uncle Quinn said one day he'd have to go through them. I didn't know we had good dishes."

With a grunt, Quinn stacked a second heavy box on the floor by the buffet. Esther opened the box and lifted a plate out of the top box. "Isn't this pretty?" She examined the white plate edged with silver and circled with a string of silver leaves. In the center was a small delicate nosegay of pink roses. "I've not seen this pattern before." She turned the plate over and read, "Petite Bouquet."

143

Randa brought a cup of the same design from the kitchen. "Uncle Quinn made me tea in this when I didn't feel good."

Esther put the plate back in the box. "We won't put these away until they have been washed.

"Quinn, you can put the Christmas boxes in the living room."

He trudged back to the garage, brought in a big box, and pushed it into a corner next to the davenport. "There are two more," he said, returning to the garage..

Randa tugged open the flaps and found ornaments in multiple colors. Goldie, with front feet on the box, peeked in at the colorful array, then looked up at Randa and meowed. She pulled her cat away. "No, you are not to stick your nose in our boxes." She held up a glass ornament. "You could accidentally break this and cut yourself." Goldie looked her in the eye as if she understood.

Esther handed Quinn a list of things he was to look for and said, "I'm through for tonight. Your house has little color, and that won't do for an open house. We need to fill it with Christmas colors."

They waved goodbye, then Quinn brought a small box labeled Christmas to the dining room and pulled out a stable with a bark roof. "Arlene and I found this nativity set in a little shop in Indiana. She loved the beautiful carved figures, and I liked the bark roof. We couldn't afford it, but we bought it anyway. Arlene called it our treasure."

Randa took out wooden figures painted in soft-washed colors and unwrapped sheep, donkeys, camels with elegant trappings, an angel on bended knee, shepherds, Mary, Joseph, and last of all, the baby Jesus lying in a straw-filled manger.

Randa touched the face of baby Jesus. "I love it. Bertha told me the story of Jesus' birth with her manger scene. I already knew the story, but she made it seem real when she

My Name is Randa

told it with the figures. I'm so glad you have a nativity set. Where should we put it?"

"We always displayed it on the buffet. Arlene would lay a cloth down and then place each figure in its own special location."

"Okay, Uncle Quinn, you can put all the figures in their special place, just like Aunt Arlene. That will be one of our traditions."

He smiled. "Yes, one of our traditions." He hadn't thought to bring out the nativity set since Arlene's death. "In the last five years, I decorated with a couple potted poinsettias."

Quinn feared that opening the boxes would bring back the grief of his loss, but with Randa beside him, he shared happy stories of his life with Arlene; the experience was a sweet remembrance.

He looked around his living room, thinking about Esther and Randa filling his house with bright colors. Nora's house had lots of color. Maybe he'd like a change.

***

Monday morning, Esther arrived early enough to see Randa off to school. She and Quinn stood at the dining room window and watched Randa give the neighbor's dog a pat before scurrying down the street. Quinn handed Esther a cup of coffee.

She took a sip, headed to the kitchen for sugar, and said, "I went to Ernie Murdock's store and asked him to let me in early. He's bringing some items I think would look good in your house."

When Ernie arrived, she sent Quinn out to help. They carried in an oriental rug with a multitude of muted colors. Esther said, "What do you think? I thought it would make the room feel homey."

Mary Watland

"You're right; I like it. Thank you." The men bartered on a price, and Quinn gave him a check. When Ernie left, Quinn handed Esther a house key. "Nora told me you'd do a good job. Thank you for helping us."

Quinn left the house with his head spinning. He had to admire the spunky lady. She had great ideas. That rug had some worn spots, but that added to the homey feel.

It was after four when Esther arrived at Julie's house to see Nora. They discussed all the changes Esther planned for Quinn's house. Julie handed warm bottles to the two sisters, and Esther whispered in Jordie's ear, "You can call me Aunt Essie until you're four and then I'm your Great Aunt Esther."

Tuesday afternoon, Julie answered a call from her Aunt Esther. She listened to her aunt, then responded. "Okay, I'll take care of it. Have her call me in ten minutes." Julie hung up, then picked up the receiver and dialed. She whispered a message to someone and ended the call.

Julie grinned at Nora and said, "Mother, there are a couple of people who miss you and want you to help them decorate their Christmas trees, so the Calhoun's are coming to help us with the babies. Randa will call soon."

A short time later, the phone rang, and Julie motioned for her mother to answer it. Nora listened a moment and said, "My daughter, who whispers in the phone, has called in help. I would love to." She hung up the phone and said, "Thank you. I can't wait to see what they've done.

"Randa says they'll pick me up around six-thirty. Quinn doesn't want me driving back after dark by myself. It's only been three days, but I've missed them."

When Quinn and Randa arrived at the Hunters' house, six-year-old Pansy Calhoun answered their knock with a diaper draped over one shoulder. "Come in," she said. "My

My Name is Randa

Mom and Dad are holding the twins. They need the practice 'cause we're gonna have our very own baby."

Jordie's deep cries echoed throughout the house. Pansy covered her ears and said, "We need to find a way to stop that boy from howling."

Quinn squatted to her level. "Hello, Pansy. Do you remember me?"

"Uh-huh, you were at the football game with Randa. You're her Uncle Quinn and you pray in the shower. Randa wants you to pray in your closet," she giggled. "Is it dark in your closet?"

He heard snickers in the living room and struggled to keep a straight face. Quinn winked at the little girl and gently tugged on one of her black braids. "Yes, but I keep the door open."

Nora floated down the stairs with a sweet smile on her face. "Pansy came to learn how to hold new babies."

Nora and Quinn stared at the empty tree in the middle of the floor. He said, "Esther suggested we wait for you to help us decide where to put it."

Randa bumped her way in from the utility room with a clothes basket heaped with popcorn. "We've been stringing popcorn for a week."

With a funny grin on his face, Quinn said, "We got started and couldn't quit."

The cogs in Nora's brain turned. Her tree-decorating ideas wouldn't work with all that popcorn. She tried to be diplomatic. "What did you have in mind?"

Goldie batted at the tree. Randa took her into Quinn's study and shut the door. "Well, one time when we strung too much popcorn, Mama had us start right up against the trunk, and we wound it round and round the tree. When we got through, you couldn't hardly see any green. John didn't like it so much, but I thought it was pretty."

Quinn and Randa wound and rewound the strings of popcorn until Nora was satisfied. Nora wanted equal amounts of white and green to show. Then they moved the tree to the far corner. She separated all their red decorations and said, "You'll need some more red ornaments."

Nora sat in Quinn's chair and sighed in contentment as she watched the two hang the red glass balls. When they finished, Randa leaned against her uncle and admired their popcorn tree. Yes, they were a family.

Nora and Carl wanted four children, but Julie was the only child her body would carry to full term. In Nora's heart, Quinn's niece was becoming her daughter. That child needed a mother figure. She prayed, "Lord, thank you for this sweet girl and all the joy she gives me."

Randa danced over beside Nora and said, "Before we take you home, I want you to see my Christmas dress. It's made of taffeta and rustles when I walk." Randa's face beamed when she returned to the living room and gave a twirl.

"You look like a princess," Nora said.

Quinn glanced at his watch. "It's late. We need to take Nora back to those babies. It's way past your bedtime. You have school tomorrow."

Nora removed two boxes of *Thank You* notes from her bag and handed them to Randa. "I suggest you make a list of all the gifts you receive and who gave them to you. You'll never remember unless you write it down."

Randa and Quinn carried fat grocery bags of strung popcorn when they walked Nora to the Hunters' door. Quinn apologized for bringing Nora home so late.

Randa clapped her hands. "Our tree is super beautiful. Thank you for helping us, Nora."

Quinn turned his niece around. "It's late, and you have school."

As their taillights disappeared into the night, Nora said, "Can you believe they had a clothes basket *full* of popcorn?"

***

After Nora went to bed, Julie said, "My mother doesn't know it, but I think she might be falling in love. She glows when he's around."

Tim laughed and kissed her. "I think you're right. Is that okay with you?"

"Yes, I think it is."

Chapter 29

Saturday, December 19

Saturday afternoon, there was a sign on the front door of the manse.

MERRY CHRISTMAS.
PLEASE COME IN.

Quinn, with a sprig of holly in his lapel, and Randa in her rustling red taffeta dress, stood close to the door and greeted their guests.

Esther asked a couple of women to help her keep plates of Christmas cookies replenished and the punch bowl filled. She couldn't remember a time that gave her greater pleasure than helping Quinn and Randa with their open house.

The generous members from the church brought gifts, and they oohed and aahed over the popcorn tree. The house remained full for three hours.

***

Sunday evening, Quinn looked out at the congregation and saw Nora sitting in her regular spot. He looked for Randa and saw her hurrying down the outside wall to join Nora. When they were standing together, he smiled at them. He was glad Tim's parents had arrived, so Nora could come back home where she belonged.

After the service, Nora asked Quinn if she could bring a box of gifts to their house. There were packages from Nora, from Tim and Julie, and even presents from the twins. Under the tree were packages from Quinn's Aunt Etta and Randa's family in Minneapolis. Several of Quinn's relatives sent money for Randa in their Christmas cards. The word

My Name is Randa

had gotten out that Randa wanted current pictures of her relatives, and nearly every card had photos enclosed.

On Monday, five days before Christmas. Quinn had coffee ready when Nora arrived at the office. He poured a cup and sat down on the chair beside her desk. Day off or not, he needed to talk to her.

She flashed a happy smile at him. "How did you like working with my sister?"

Swooping his arm in the air, he said, "She took our pictures off the walls, rearranged them, and added more. Almost every night, my chair sat in a different place. She decorated every room in my house, but the best thing she did was the oriental rug. She was right. That rug makes our house look warm and homey. One afternoon, Agnes Johnson came over to help, and she and Randa washed all the good dishes and put them in my buffet. Esther left a note saying the papers they found in the buffet did not belong in a dining room, and I needed to buy another filing cabinet."

"Well, if you don't want a filing cabinet, you'd better warn Ernie, or she'll be telling him to deliver the next one he gets to your house." Nora stifled a yawn. "I understand Esther gave you Santa socks."

"Yes, those socks helped me decide to have Santa come to our house." His father wouldn't have agreed, but Quinn thought it might please Randa.

Quinn was overjoyed to have Nora back in the office. His previous secretaries had gone on vacations, but he'd never missed them like he missed Nora.

She took the cover off her typewriter, and Quinn knew he should leave, but … he poured another cup of coffee and continued to sit in the chair beside her desk. He didn't care if it was his day off. He wanted to stay here with Nora.

"I think I'll review my New Year's sermon from last year and make changes to fit the people in this congregation."

Maybe she'd have lunch with him. When he asked, she agreed. He drove over to Rudy's, picked up their sandwiches, and stopped by the house to get a box of gingerbread boys for dessert. She was downstairs waiting when he returned.

Quinn said, "After we found Randa's Christmas dress, she asked me if I could afford fancy shoes, too. Later that day, she asked me how to be a hostess, and Esther helped me explain it to her. I've never seen a sweeter hostess than Randa was at our open house. I wish Sarah could have seen her. I was so proud of her."

"Esther told us she looked like a sweet young lady in her red dress," Nora said.

He frowned and ran fingers through his hair. "I don't want her to look like a lady. I want her to look thirteen. She's had to grow up too fast. She bakes instead of having fun. I'll not have her very long, and then she'll be off to college."

"Teenage girls want to look grown-up, Quinn. They are moody one minute and silly the next. Enjoy her today and tomorrow, and don't worry about college until she gets there. She's not going to change overnight. It takes time."

"So, you're telling me to be patient?"

"Quinn, the Bible says, 'rest in the Lord, and wait patiently for him …' That's what you are to do right now. It isn't easy being a parent. Sometimes we run ahead of our children, and other times they drag us to catch up with them. Wait and let the Lord do his work in her."

Quinn opened his mouth to speak, then his shoulders slumped. "Nora Montgomery, you are a wise woman. I want to talk to her about last Christmas. I've been asking the Lord to show me the right time. I don't want to get this wrong."

"You'll do fine," she said.

My Name is Randa

Nora came home from the children's Christmas Eve program and sat in her dark living room, wishing she could see Quinn and Randa's faces when they opened their gifts. The day would be bittersweet, but she prayed joy would overshadow their grief.

Chapter 30

Christmas morning

Randa woke early and dressed in a robe and slippers. Today was so different from last year. Uncle Quinn knew she'd be sad today, but they'd worked together to make it a beginning of new traditions. She quietly closed her bedroom door. On her arm was a green velveteen Santa sock lined with plaid taffeta. She tip-toed to the kitchen, made coffee, then snuck into the living room and stood Uncle Quinn's Santa sock on his chair.

Under the tree sat a Raggedy Ann doll on a large square package. A stuffed bright red velveteen Santa sock, lined with a candy cane print satin, stood on the floor propped against the colorful packages. He did it. Uncle Quinn figured out what would be the perfect gift for Santa to give her. It was her favorite doll when she was little, and now Santa gave her another one. Her Uncle Quinn was — she couldn't think of a word. Maybe she could use Pansy's words. He was the *bestest uncle ever!*

She shot down the hall and banged on his door with her fist. "Uncle Quinn, Uncle Quinn, Santa came to our house. It's time to get up. We have stacks of presents to open."

"I'll be out in a minute. Wait for me."

Five minutes later, Quinn found her pouring coffee into his favorite cup. He kissed her cheek and wrapped his arm around her shoulder, "Merry Christmas, honey."

She turned, put her arms around his middle, and squeezed tight. "Thank you for being Santa, and thank you for Annie."

My Name is Randa

"You're welcome. Let's have a bowl of cereal and a glass of orange juice before we open gifts. We'll need all the energy we can get to open that stack of presents."

Randa wolfed down her cereal. It was just like Uncle Quinn said. There was a fairyland Christmas in their living room. She'd never seen so many presents under one Christmas tree.

They went into the living room, and Quinn picked up the doll. "Molly thought you'd like a Raggedy Ann doll, like the one we bought for Rosie." They sat cross-legged in front of the tree and opened package after package. Randa noted every gift on the yellow pad beside her.

Nora had knitted soft wool sweaters in their favorite colors, blue for Randa and a light nutmeg for Quinn. Aunt Etta gave them a brown leather photo album with *Our Family* printed on the front. Randa opened a stack of packages from Quinn—clothes, a record player, and records.

He pushed up from the floor and lifted a package from behind the davenport. "This is something I like to do. I'm hoping you might enjoy it, too." Inside were ice skates he'd ordered from the Sears catalog.

"Ohhh," she squealed, "I can roller skate, but I've never been ice skating. Would you teach me?" Randa jumped up and kissed him on both cheeks. "Thank you. Thank you." Goldie ran to Quinn's study and crouched under his desk.

As the pile of wrappings increased, Goldie nosed under one paper after another. Suddenly she leaped up, pirouetted in midair, twisted a half turn, and dropped onto her feet. Then she calmly walked over to Randa and jumped into her lap.

"I think Goldie likes Christmas, too."

Molly's brother, Brad, had told Randa to give her uncle baseball things because that was his favorite sport. She bought each of them a royal blue Park City Bulls cap. When

Marg Watland

Quinn opened the package, she said, "Brad told me to get this stuff. I'm terrible at baseball, but he thought you could help me."

Quinn grinned and said, "I'd love to. He put on his cap and wore it the rest of the morning. Randa gave him a five-by-seven picture of the two of them. She knew he would like the dark leather frame.

"Thank you. It's a picture of us when we first became a family. I'll put it on my desk at work."

Goldie nosed around in the paper heaped in front of Randa, and a green ribbon tangled around her neck. She pulled and tugged at the string and shook her head back and forth until it nearly strangled her. Quinn picked her up, unwound the strings, and suggested Randa get a grocery sack for the ribbons.

She pushed the wrappings into a pile in front of the davenport. Goldie jumped into the heap, spewing paper all over the room. Randa picked up the rambunctious cat and lectured her about making a mess. Goldie jumped out of her arms and nosed around in Randa's stack of gifts.

Quinn pulled one more package from under the tree. He handed it to Randa. "We missed this one. It must be something else from Ledbetter's Department Store."

She ripped the paper and held up a flannel nightgown sprinkled with pink roses. She looked up at her uncle with tears streaming down her face. "Mama bought me a nightgown every year for Christmas."

Quinn didn't know if now was the right time, but with fear and trepidation, he asked, "Would you like to talk about last Christmas and your mama?"

She looked down and nodded.

"Come sit beside me." She snuggled next to him, and he put a box of Kleenex in her lap.

My Name is Randa

Randa pulled a tissue from the box and began, "Mama caught colds really easy, and John would take her to the doctor right away. He said that no matter what, Mama couldn't get pneumonia.

"Mama was sick with a cold the week before Christmas. We were going to celebrate Christmas later when she felt better. The day after Christmas, John took Mama to the hospital because she couldn't breathe good. She had pneumonia. John asked Bertha if I could stay with her for a couple of days. I kissed Mama goodbye and went home with Bertha. I never saw my Mama again." Quinn wrapped his arms around her, and she wept on his chest.

"I stayed with Bertha until after the funeral, then John took me home. People from the church brought us food. John stayed home from work for a week. I heard him crying in the night. I cried too." Randa sighed and said, "That's what happened. I've really wanted to tell you, Uncle Quinn, but I didn't want you to be sad."

"Sweetheart, thank you for telling me. I needed to know. I want you to tell me anything—sad or happy, funny or dumb. Tell me, okay?"

"Okay." He pulled out a couple of tissues and dried her face. She shuddered and said, "You know Uncle Quinn, sometimes I think I want to go home, but without Mama, there isn't any home. I need a father. John told me he was my dad's best friend and he'd take care of me and Mama, but he wasn't my dad; never would be. I think you are the closest thing to a dad I've ever had."

Quinn silently prayed God would help him be a loving parent to Randa and that she would feel safe with him. He hadn't been a loving brother to Sarah, and he hated his dad's hard old country ways. But the Christmas questions had reminded him of good memories of his dad teaching

157

him to ice skate and the two of them sneaking away to go fishing early on a summer morning.

Randa leaned heavier on his damp chest. He sat quietly and let her grieve. She relaxed, her breathing deepened, and she slept in his arms.

He pushed a strand of hair from her face and offered thanksgiving to his heavenly Father. "Thank you, Lord, that you forgave me. Help me forgive myself for all my hatred and anger toward my parents.

"I don't deserve my family's acceptance, but they have forgiven me. Thank you for blessing my life with Randa."

Chapter 31

Christmas Dinner

$\mathcal{M}$olly opened the door when they arrived at the farm. The heavenly smell of roasting turkey drew them into the house. Quinn's stomach rumbled. He hoped it wouldn't be too long before dinner.

The first thing they saw was the Christmas tree with garlands of gold beads and white lights circling the tree. Silver tinsel, meticulously hung from each branch, shimmered in the light. Gold ornaments hung like jewels from the branches. An angel, dressed in white velvet, topped the magnificent tree. Randa stared at the tree and said in a near whisper, "It looks so elegant."

Ruth, Don, and his parents came from the kitchen. Don said, "Mom and Dad, this is Reverend Edwards. He told us we could call him Rev, and his niece Randa." He turned to Quinn. "You can call my folks Dean and Wilma."

Ruth said, "Molly thinks we should open presents before we have dinner. Why don't you two girls pass out the gifts?"

Quinn knew Randa was excited about her present to Molly. She gave her a box filled with all the tools needed to decorate a cake. Randa was excited to teach Molly how to decorate a special birthday cake for her mom, who was born on New Year's Day.

Molly and Ruth gave Randa a quilted wall hanging for her room, with a gold calico cat in the center.

Don gave Quinn a pocket-size New Testament with Psalms and Proverbs, to replace the tattered one he carried in his shirt pocket. The gifts from their friends touched Quinn.

Randa made Brad a box of homemade fudge and gave Molly's grandparents two boxes of gingerbread boys. "Molly talks about you all the time," Randa said. "I feel like I know you. She says you are the best grandparents ever. Could I call you Grandma and Grandpa Thompson? I don't have any grandparents."

Quinn winked at Don, who had a pleased look on his face. The elderly couple flushed with surprise and then pleasure. They promised to tell their other grandchildren about Randa joining their family. That child of his was going to surround herself with a big family. He smiled in approval as Randa hugged Dean and Wilma.

He picked up a red and green package and handed it to Ruth. "It isn't brand new, but I polished it, so it shines. I think this will help with your communication problems." Inside lay a bright, shiny brass dinner bell.

Don stepped outside the front door and gave the bell a good shake. "Thanks, Rev. This is a good present for us. I'll hear this bell loud and clear."

Dinner was a feast of turkey and dressing, mashed potatoes and gravy, and all the other traditional foods served at Christmas dinner, along with three kinds of Ruth's wonderful pickles. Most everyone had seconds and left the table stuffed.

Molly had told her grandparents about Randa and Quinn choosing family traditions. Wilma talked of a Christmas light in the window, and Dean remembered horse-driven sleigh rides.

The girls helped clean up, then went to Molly's room to talk. Randa thanked her for suggesting Raggedy Ann. Molly said, "Mom likes to give me dolls at Christmas. This year I asked for a baby doll for my first little girl. Mom made doll clothes; they are so cute. Do you want to see them?"

My Name is Randa

The girls came downstairs, where Brad was telling the men about a play the football coach had taught him. Randa gave her uncle a quick hug, then she joined Molly.

They dropped to their knees in front of the tree, and Molly picked up a pink dress. "Look, isn't it pretty with all the ruffles? Mom said she liked me in ruffles."

Don asked Quinn if he played chess.

"I do," Quinn said with a twinkle in his eye. "It's been a while. I would enjoy a game."

Don went to the living room window. "Come on, Rev, and you too, Randa. Let me show you what my son gave us for Christmas. Remember when I told you Brad was making a table for his room in Shop? Instead, my son, the furniture maker, made us a game table. He copied the idea from a fancy mahogany one that he found in a furniture catalog. Brad made ours out of pine. Ruthie insisted we move all the furniture around before breakfast."

Randa told Quinn she'd already seen it. He praised Brad for the beautiful glossy finish and added, "Your family will get hours of pleasure sitting at this table. You did an out-standing job."

Quinn and Don sat at the dark-stained table. It had a checkerboard painted in the center of the tabletop and open shelves for games beneath. Brad and his grandfather brought chairs from the dining room to watch.

After Quinn's first checkmate, Don, with a raised brow, insisted on another game. When Quinn called checkmate the second time, Don raised his arms in defeat and looked at his father. "Dad, why don't you take a turn, and I'll watch."

Molly whispered to Randa, "Grandpa beats everybody. He has chess friends, and they play three or four days a week."

Within two moves, Quinn suspected he was playing with a master, and the game became intense. He carefully thought through each play and stroked his beard between moves.

Ruth rocked in a chair near the tree with a happy smile and tucked a lock of brown hair behind her ear. She picked up a tiny white nightgown that dripped with lace and rubbed the trim between her fingers. "Molly, this has been a special Christmas for me. I sewed doll clothes for my daughter and my future granddaughter."

Molly said, "I can't decide which outfit I like best."

Randa held up a little navy-blue sailor outfit. "I like this one." Throughout the day, Randa and the three generations of Thompson women kept returning to fondle the doll clothes Ruth made for her daughter.

Late in the afternoon, Ruth offered pumpkin, apple, and mincemeat pie. Quinn asked for a sliver of each. Randa turned her nose up at the mincemeat.

***

They left after nine because of a lengthy game of monopoly. Quinn didn't hurry their departure because of the joy on Randa's face. He thanked the Lord for her laughter on this Christmas day. They left with a package of turkey and an apple pie.

Quinn turned the car toward home. "This is the nicest Christmas I've had in years, even though Dean Thompson skunked me at chess."

Randa yawned. "Me too. Can Goldie have some turkey? They gave us lots."

Soon after they carried everything in from the car, Randa said, "I can't keep my eyes open; I'm going to bed."

Quinn read the front page of the newspaper, then folded it and put it aside. He opened Randa's bedroom door and watched her sleep. Raggedy Ann lay on the pillow next to her. He quietly closed her door, then slipped outside and

My Name is Randa

walked down the street until he could see lights on at Nora's house. He went back inside and called her. "I know it's late, but I wanted to talk about our day. Could I come talk for a while?"

***

Nora opened her door, and he stepped inside.

"Randa's asleep. She's had a big day. I left a note in case she wakes up. How did your southern and mid-western menu turn out?"

"Everything was delicious, except the cornbread dressing was kind of gluey. Tim ate three helpings of it. I probably could get used to it. We got through the main meal before the babies woke. We were on our own for dessert. It's good to come home to my house, where there is blessed quietness. How was your day?"

"I thought we'd never finish opening presents. Randa loved the doll. Thank you for the sweaters. We wore them to the Thompsons'. The grief surfaced when Randa opened the last gift, a nightgown. Sarah bought her one every Christmas. Nora, they didn't have Christmas last year.

"She fell asleep in my arms. I held her for two-and-a-half hours. I thought my arms would break, but I didn't let go until she woke."

Nora dabbed her eyes and said, "I'm happy she told you the rest of her Mama's story. How was your day?"

"Great. Randa asked Molly's grandparents if she could adopt them. I hadn't planned to stay so late, but the kids were having fun playing games."

Nora yawned.

Quinn said, "You're tired. I need to go. Let us know when you can come see all our *loot*. Goodnight."

Chapter 32

1954

Sunday, February 14

Total silence, like the earth holding its breath, woke Randa. The covers flew when she leaped out of bed and peeked around the blind. Randa yanked it all the way up and shouted, "Snow!" Four inches of new snow covered all the dirty stuff, and lazy flakes announced the storms near end. Early morning sun made the backyard a glittering fairyland.

With bleary eyes and hair in a scramble, Quinn knocked and burst into her room. "What's wrong?"

"It snowed. Can we make a snowman?"

He stood beside Randa and looked out. The neighbor's dog ran across their yard with snow flying in the air. "I don't think so; that snow is just powder."

"Well, we could make snow angels."

"Don't you think I'm kind of old to be making snow angels?" When her smile disappeared, Quinn decided he wasn't that old. "Okay, after church."

She clapped her hands. "Goodie, it'll be fun."

***

That afternoon, Randa told Quinn to lie on his back. He grinned at her, flapped his arms up and down, and moved his legs in and out. Cold flakes covered his glasses, and snow crept down his neck.

"Okay, Uncle Quinn, now get up and be sure to step over your angel."

He rolled over, pushed his body up with his hands, and walked across half a wing, then clipped the corner of the skirt. Randa giggled and led him to a clean spot. The second

My Name is Randa

time was no better. He walked over the head, tripped, and fell, destroying the right wing.

Then Quinn watched while Randa filled the backyard with angels. She insisted he judge her angels. He chose the top two, then washed her face with snow. Her giggles made the event a whopping success.

The warm house felt good. They changed, and Quinn made hot chocolate.

She lowered her eyelids and looked at him through her lashes. "Did you know Mr. and Mrs. Bates were watching us from their upstairs window? I think they had a camera."

He grinned. "Do you really think so, or are you trying to scare me?"

The phone rang as Nora drove into the driveway to pick up Randa. They had volunteered to babysit the twins while Tim and Julie got away for a romantic Valentine's Day dinner. Quinn grabbed the phone and called out, "Have fun."

Into the phone, he said, "I'm sorry. This is Reverend Edwards."

A familiar voice with a Canadian accent said, "Happy Valentine's Day."

"Drew." The voice triggered memories of when they were roommates in seminary. That scrawny, brainy Canadian who became his best friend. "How are things up across the border? We haven't talked since you called to wish us Happy New Year."

"Well, I'm on your side. Madeline and I are in Chicago. Her mum had gallbladder surgery this week. Madeline suggested I drive over to Wisconsin and have a visit with you. I want to meet your niece. The picture in your Christmas card was nice, but I would like to meet that young lady in person. How's the parenting going?"

"My secretary tells me we're doing okay. Randa likes to bake and is in the kitchen a lot. She thinks she's the woman

165

of the house. I want her to be a normal teen with lots of giggling girlfriends." He paused. "Shouldn't you be teaching?"

"I planned for another professor to take my classes for a couple of weeks. I'll come over Wednesday afternoon and go back on Monday. And Quinn, teens are not normal. They're extreme, either up or down."

***

Randa came home with funny stories about the twins. She dug in her jeans pocket and pulled out several bills. "They paid me for helping Nora babysit. I told them they didn't have to. I like helping. Tim said that every woman should have some money in her pocket for ice cream or bright red nail polish." She giggled. "I told him you didn't want me to wear bright red."

"I have a surprise for you. My friend Drew Patterson is coming to visit. He'll be here in three days."

"You mean Uncle Drew? I like it when he calls and talks to me."

"I'm glad. He wants to meet you," Quinn said.

"What's his favorite dessert?"

"Cookies—any cookies, but I think his favorite is peanut butter. How about one of those pound cakes with extra vanilla?"

"Okay. Don't you think peanut butter cookies are kind of boring? I'll make a couple of different kinds and put them in the freezer. What's your favorite cookie, Uncle Quinn?"

"Gingerbread boys, and we still have some."

"Where's Uncle Drew going to sleep? We don't have a guest room."

"On the davenport, it opens up. Arlene and I paid good money to get a comfortable davenport. He's slept on it several times."

My Name is Randa

Randa untied her shoes and bridged her legs across the coffee table. "I think I'll ask Nora to help me plan some meals for when he's here."

"Honey, we don't need to change the way we do things for Drew. We'll take turns cooking, and Drew will probably help us. It's fine if you bake some extra cookies, but that's all."

"But Uncle Quinn, wouldn't it be easier if we had some meals planned?" She looked about to cry.

"I'm sorry, honey, you're right; planned meals would make Drew's visit easier for us. Write your ideas and then take them to Nora to see what we missed. I'll call Mrs. Nordstrom and see if she can come Tuesday to clean."

Chapter 33

Wednesday February 17,1953

Randa answered the door and looked up. A man over six feet tall, with long skinny legs, stood before her. A mixture of gray and white curls sprayed across his head, and some crept down over his forehead.

"Are you Professor Drew Patterson?"

He smiled. "That I am, and you are Randa?"

"Yes. Uncle Quinn didn't tell me you were so tall. Come on in."

He laughed and set his cracked brown leather grip on the floor. Drew breathed in. "It smells good in here. I smell cookies."

"Yeah, the last pan is almost ready to come out." The timer sounded, and Randa said, "They're done," and dashed to the kitchen.

Drew called, "Where's your washroom?"

"Wash… Oh, the bathroom is at the end of the hall."

Drew found Randa in the kitchen. Rows of cookies on old tea towels covered the kitchen counter, and Randa was washing the baking dishes. He grabbed a dish towel and lifted a big bowl out of the rinse water. "Are those peanut butter cookies?"

"Yes, Uncle Quinn said they're your favorite."

When they finished the dishes, Randa said, "Would you like to see our house? Come on, follow me." She turned down the hall and opened Quinn's door. "The church ladies made us quilts. He wanted brown, so they made him a tan and brown quilt with a dark brown border. I think brown is boring." She pressed a finger to her lips. "Shh. Please don't tell him. It might make him feel bad."

My Name is Randa

At the next door, she said, "This is my room. The ladies made my quilt all blue and white, and each square is different. It's called a Sampler Quilt. Isn't it pretty?"

She picked up a Raggedy Ann doll from the bed. "Santa quit coming to my house when I started fifth grade, but don't tell Uncle Quinn. I love Annie. I can't wait to see what Santa brings me next year."

Drew watched her hug the doll to her chest and said, "Santa never came to your uncle's house. His father said Christmas was for celebrating the birth of Jesus, and he didn't want any fairy tales to be part of their Christmas."

Randa couldn't understand why a father would be so mean. Mama said her parents were stoic. Did that mean they didn't love their kids? Did Uncle Quinn have a grandma that loved him, told him stories? She had a Grandma Reynolds, who loved her and gave her hugs and kisses, but she didn't live very long. Mama said all her grandparents died before she was born. Randa wished grandparents would live longer, and she wished she had lots of aunts and uncles to love her. That would make her feel safe.

She grinned at Drew. "I already know what Santa will give Uncle Quinn next year. A dump-truck. When we went shopping for the twins, he told me when he was a boy, he wanted a red one." She picked up a picture off her dresser. "This is me and my mama with one of her wedding cakes. She taught me how to decorate, too, but I only do birthday cakes."

"That's a fancy cake." Drew took the picture and studied it. "Your Mama looks nothing like you, but you have Quinn's eyes. You are an Edwards."

"I know. It really surprised me when he came to get me. I could tell right away he was my uncle because of his eyes. He told me my Grandma O'Reilly had dark eyes like ours."

Mary Watland

Open reference books, a Bible, a yellow pad, and a pen covered the desktop in Quinn's study. She picked up a picture of the two of them. "Molly took this the day we moved to Park City."

"It amazed my wife Madeline and me when we got your Christmas picture. You hadn't been living together very long, and you already looked like a family. That's a lot to accomplish in five months. Your picture sits on our mantel to remind us to pray for you."

"We *are* a family. Uncle Quinn does a lot of things like my mama. He's more serious than her, but after all, *he's* a reverend."

Drew leaned over the counter and breathed in the sweet aroma of warm peanut butter cookies.

Randa said, "Help yourself. Uncle Quinn shouldn't be too much longer. Would you like some tea or coffee?"

"Tea, please, but don't use yours. I brought English tea. I'll get it."

Randa filled the teakettle, then reached into the cupboard for a white teapot with a pretty pink nosegay on each side.

He smiled and joined her at the counter. "We gave this teapot and a matching creamer and sugar bowl to Quinn and Arlene for a wedding present. I was his best man. You would have liked Arlene."

After the tea had steeped, they sat at the kitchen table, munching on the warm cookies.

"Mmm, these cookies are delectable. Thank you for making them." Drew looked around at the bright kitchen. "Quinn did a marvelous job paint job in here. He told me you didn't like yellow, but I'm surprised he painted it white. I thought he didn't like white."

"He doesn't. He says white gets dirty too fast. Molly's dad helped Uncle Quinn paint the kitchen on the day of my birthday. I wanted it to look like mama's kitchen, and my

My Name is Randa

best friend Molly Thompson made the red gingham curtains, and Julie and Tim gave me the red apple cookie jar."

She grinned. "Mrs. Nordstrom, our housekeeper, and I keep it spotless, so he won't ever see it dirty. When I miss Mama, I come in here. It makes me feel closer to her. I think it's cheerful."

Randa poured Drew another cup of tea. He said, "Honey, we have prayed for you since the day your uncle called and read your letter to me." He took both her hands in his and said, "I'm here to welcome you into *my* family."

Her dark eyes opened wide. "How many?" she asked.

Drew frowned. "How many what?"

"… are there in your family? My best friend in Minneapolis has two sisters and four brothers. I've always wanted a *bunch* of relatives like her. Sometimes it's really lonely to be an only child. So, if you are my uncle, do I have any cousins my age?"

Quinn opened the kitchen door, and Drew stood to greet him.

Randa poured tea into Quinn's favorite cup while the men answered her many questions. She refilled the plate of cookies. "Nora told me I should let you have time for yourselves. I'll go to my room and read a bunch of pages in my history book. Don't eat too many cookies. It'll spoil your appetite."

Quinn winked at her and mouthed a thank you. Randa gave him a little wave and disappeared down the hall. What would he do without Nora? She was always a step ahead of him.

Drew grabbed another cookie. "How are things going? I haven't heard about one of Randa's gaps lately. What's the latest?"

Goldie looked up at Quinn and meowed. He reached down and picked her up. "Randa speaks Spanish fluently.

171

Mary Watland

When they lived in Yuma, all their neighbors were Mexican."

Goldie jumped off Quinn's lap, nosed Drew's shoes, then trotted away to the study.

Drew laughed. "Did you see that? She checked me out and walked off. What does that mean?"

"Just wait. She'll let you know. Don't forget, she stuck close to me for three days while Randa pouted about not working on Sundays." He stood and headed to the refrigerator. "I'm the cook tonight."

While he worked on dinner, Quinn told Drew about Goldie's previous owner, Irene Solheim. He opened the oven door and put in a meatloaf and potatoes to bake, then handed Drew the empty cookie jar. "You can fill the cookie jar for me. I need this counter cleared before I start on the salad."

While Quinn chopped lettuce, he told Drew about the Larkin family. "Randa invited Irene's granddaughters to go Christmas caroling with us. Now, Pam Larkin is Randa's friend, and the family has been coming to church regularly since the first of the year. Pam told Randa her parents like our church. I think they are close to committing to Jesus."

Drew filled the cookie jar and stacked the remaining cookies on a plate. "So, your niece is helping with your ministry, bringing people in to hear God's word."

"Yes, I guess she is. It breaks my heart that Sarah blocked God out of her life for all those years. Randa was ten or eleven before she heard about Jesus. I don't think she knows any of the Old Testament stories."

"You could do an overview of the Old Testament books. I am sure a large number in your congregation rarely, if ever, read the Old Testament."

My Name is Randa

"I hadn't thought about that. Thank you. I've already done a four-week series on Nehemiah." He handed Drew a grater and the carrots he'd just peeled.

"That's fine. You don't need to lock yourself into keeping things in chronological order."

Randa set a yellow legal pad beside Drew's empty cup. "When you finish helping Uncle Quinn, would you write the names and ages of all your family? Are there grandparents?" She grinned at him and walked away to set the table for dinner.

Quinn chuckled, "She's serious. We make lists."

"That's right. Nora taught us to make lists," Randa said. "We have pages and pages of Christmas lists. The first ones were Christmas memories, and then they changed to Christmas questions. That's how we decided what we wanted for our Christmas traditions. It was fun." Her smile slid away, and she looked down. "Well, it was sad too, but Uncle Quinn hugged me close while I cried. He told me when I didn't have any more tears, I'd feel better, and I always do."

Drew explained his son was in college, one daughter was engaged, and the other daughter had a nine-month-old son. "I'm sorry, there's no one your age. Now that you want to know the names of all my family, I'd like you to help your uncle and me know more about you."

"Okay."

"You asked Jesus to come into your heart two years ago. Quinn tells me you have devotions together every morning. He's learning what you know in the Bible, but he's not sure what you don't know."

She sat quietly and stared at Drew for a time. "Well, I've read all of Mark and John, but mostly Bertha would have me read verses and chapters about Jesus and love and salvation and heaven and that kind of stuff. She gave me a notebook, and every day, I wrote down the verses I was memorizing. I'll go get it."

The two men looked at each other. Quinn breathed a sigh of relief and said, "Thank you."

Randa returned with a blue three-ring notebook. Quinn asked, "Is that the notebook that sits on your night table? I thought that was your notebook for school."

"No, that one is black." She handed the book to Quinn and said, "You can read it whenever you want. I don't write in it so much anymore."

***

After she went to bed, Quinn and Drew moved to the dining room table with her book and sat side by side, scanning the pages and discussing the list of verses Randa had memorized. When Quinn closed the book, Drew said, "The verses Bertha Bennett chose for Randa to memorize have given her a solid foundation for her walk with Jesus. This book needs to be put in her keepsake box."

Drew yawned and said, "It's been a long day."

Quinn pushed his chair back. "I'll make up your bed while you brush your teeth. You can keep your grip behind the davenport."

***

Later, Quinn sat in bed and reread the verses Randa had memorized. He'd buy Randa a small trunk and tell her it was her memory trunk.

Chapter 34

Thursday AM,

February 18

The phone rang. Quinn woke, rushed to the study, and spoke with a nurse at the hospital. The clergymen in Park City took turns being the hospital chaplain, and it was his week. This was the first night call he'd received since moving to Wisconsin. When Quinn came out of his study, Drew raised up on his elbow.

"That was the hospital," Quinn said. "There was a bad three-car accident near Evansville. Will you ask Randa to call Nora in the morning and tell her where I am?" He dressed and quietly slipped out the kitchen door.

Randa entered the room in time to see the car lights flash across the dining room window. "What happened?"

"Accident on the road near Evansville," Drew said. "Go back to bed, and I'll pray for the injured people."

***

Randa came into a sunny kitchen dressed for school. Drew sat at the table, waiting for the tea kettle to boil.

"I'll get the coffee ready, so Uncle Quinn can plug it in when he gets back," she said. "He likes his morning coffee. What would you like for breakfast?"

"I'll eat whatever you have. Quinn said you should call Nora and tell her he's at the hospital. It was a three-car accident."

"Okay. I prayed for them before I went back to sleep." It could be someone they knew. She hoped nobody died. Uncle Quinn had a hard job. He had to do so many things:

Marg Watland

preaching, visiting sick and dying people, going to meetings, studying, and she didn't know what else.

She called Nora and then looked at her guest with an amused smile on her face. "You'll eat what I fix for breakfast, huh?" She took peanut butter and jam from the cupboard, put a loaf of bread beside the toaster, and dropped in two slices. Randa poured a glass of milk and said, "My breakfast is three pieces of toast with peanut butter and jam."

The kettle whistled, and Drew stood to make a morning pot of tea. He shook his head. "I think I'll have a couple of those cookies you made yesterday and wait for your uncle, you silly goose."

She crunched on her toast and wiped jam from the corner of her mouth. "Uncle Drew, can I ask you a question? I keep hearing Uncle Quinn talk about my gaps. Is he mad at me?"

"No child. How do I explain this? Aha, I've got it. Imagine you are a book he wants to read, so he'll know you better, but there is something different about your book. It starts on chapter thirteen. He's frustrated because he can't read the first twelve chapters."

"Oh, that's why …

"My dear, you should be the one that's frustrated. Your uncle's book says volume three, and the first page is chapter fifty-two."

"Uncle Quinn told me he didn't have any close relatives, but yesterday I found out your big family adopted him a long time ago. That's one of Uncle Quinn's gaps, isn't it?"

"Honey, let me fill you in on the past five years of Reverend Quinn Edward's life. Your uncle's wife died in June, and his father died in August 1948. His mother died in 1950, and then you wrote last spring and said your mama died in 1952. Did you know all of that?"

"No. That's so sad … and now he has me."

My Name is Randa

"Yes, he has you, and he's a new man. I haven't seen him this happy in years. Randa, you can't imagine the joy I feel when I see the love you have for each other. Your uncle doesn't have any experience in parenting, but I think he's doing a good job. You've walked through so much sadness, and here you are, a well-adjusted young lady. I'm proud of him; aren't you?"

"I guess so. Nobody ever asked me that before."

When Randa left for school, Drew received a thank you and a kiss on the cheek.

***

Drew sat at the kitchen table with a cup of tea when Quinn walked in the door. His eyes were red, and his shoulders slumped. "This was a hard one. They're all from out of town. The driver of one car died on impact, and a nineteen-year-old boy needed extensive surgery. He's in critical condition and will be flown to Mayo Clinic as soon as he's stable. I stayed with the family until he got out of surgery. The doctors think he'll survive, but there'll be a long recovery. The family members said they weren't religious but wanted me to pray for them. I'll go back this afternoon sometime."

"Your prayers will comfort them. We should pray for the chaplain they'll get at Mayo Clinic."

Quinn nodded, checked the coffee pot, and plugged it in. "Have you eaten?"

"No. I told Randa I'd eat what she ate, and that kid offered me peanut butter and jam. A couple of cookies will hold me over until you make us a proper breakfast."

Quinn chuckled and rattled around in the fridge. "Before I forget, there's a men's Bible Study at six tomorrow morning."

"Count me in."

While they enjoyed ham and eggs, Drew said, "Did you know Randa feels guilty about her gaps? She asked me if you were mad at her."

"How did she find out?"

"If you've said it out loud, there's a good chance she's heard it. Kids hear much more than we imagine. Remember, frustration can look like anger. Be careful what you say. Tell me about Randa's gaps."

Quinn said, "I couldn't understand why a thirteen-year-old wanted to bake all the time. Four months after she came to live with me, I found out my sister had a cake-decorating business in her home."

"Yes, she told me. She gave me a tour of your house and revealed several things I hadn't heard before."

"There's a good chance I haven't either."

Drew nodded. "I discovered Randa knew nothing about your life. Now she knows that in the past five years, there have been four deaths in your family, two different churches, and a niece."

"I told her about all the deaths the day we met. She wanted to know if her grandparents were alive. I'm not surprised she didn't remember. It was an emotional day."

Quinn checked the clock and said, "I need to get going," and headed to the shower.

He returned, dressed for work, and asked Drew if he wanted to go with him.

"No, I plan to finish an article for the Presbyterian Record while you're at work."

Quinn cleared the top of his desk and left for church.

Chapter 35

Thursday afternoon

February 18

When Randa arrived home from school, she found Drew sitting at her uncle's desk with glasses perched precariously on his nose. His shirt sleeves were rolled above his elbows, and an ink blot stained the front of his shirt. Goldie sat on a nearby chair in the winter sun, cleaning her fur.

Randa picked up her cat and grinned at Drew. "I always have a snack when I get home from school. Would you like a cookie?"

"Sounds good. Give me another five minutes to finish this paragraph."

She left the room, asking Goldie about her day.

When Drew strode into the kitchen, he'd pushed up his glasses and rolled down his sleeves. Randa had two glasses of milk and a plate heaped with cookies. "Did you make all these cookies?" he asked.

"Yep." She pointed to the different stacks and said, "You like peanut butter, I like chocolate chip, and the gingerbread boys are Uncle Quinn's favorite. The boys are left over from Christmas. Uncle Quinn didn't want us to have an open house, but Nora helped me talk him into it. The church ladies helped us. I made Grandma Edwards' recipe, and we gave a dozen boys to every family that came."

"That's a lot of cookies. How many cookies did you make?" Drew asked.

"Fifty-one dozen, and I did it in two weeks. I could have finished sooner, but Uncle Quinn said we had to rest on Sundays."

Drew worked hard to keep a straight face while he listened to Randa's version of the open house.

Randa continued telling Drew about their Christmas. "Nora took a week off work to help Julie with her brand-new twins ... Nora helped us decorate our tree. I was really sad that she couldn't come to our open house.

"We went to Beloit and bought me a red Christmas dress. Uncle Quinn was the host, and I was the hostess. Uncle Quinn said I was beautiful, and Aunt Esther told Nora our open house was a success.

"We're going to Nora's house for Sunday dinner. We go there a lot. You'll get to see the twins. Sometimes I help Nora babysit; they're so cute.

Drew stared at Randa with his mouth open. Too many words were out there, waiting for his brain to catch up. "So, you like Nora."

"Yes, she's really nice. Nora watches out for us, and we watch out for her." Drew's question made Randa pause. Nora was more like a mother friend. She taught her how to take care of babies and change diapers, and that was hard.

Drew interrupted her thoughts. "Are you sure she wants me to come?"

"Of course. She knows you are coming. You will like her. Do you still have more work to do?"

"No. I'm through for today."

She washed down the last bite of cookie and said, "We shouldn't eat anymore. It's too close to dinner time."

They moved to the living room, where Drew sat in Quinn's chair and said, "Tell me about Nora."

My Name is Randa

"I'll show you pictures." Randa ran to the dining room and returned with a shoebox full of photos.

Drew moved to the davenport and, through Randa's eyes, began learning about their life in Park City.

"... and this is my friend Pam. Goldie belonged to her grandma before we got her. Pam and her sister come to play with Goldie."

He looked at picture after picture of Nora. The last photograph she showed him was Nora sitting at a kitchen table with a glass of tea in her hand. "This is at her house on the day we moved to Park City."

Randa sat the box on the coffee table and tucked herself into a corner of the davenport. Goldie jumped onto her lap and purred. Randa stroked the soft fur and said, "I'm glad we're part of your family. It's kinda hard for Uncle Quinn to be my only close relative. What if something happened? He says most of the Edwards family live in Michigan, but he doesn't know if there's anyone my age. I am writing to my Great Aunt Etta, who is really old and shakes."

Drew reached behind the davenport, grabbed his slippers, and moved back to Quinn's chair. He said, "You've lived in Park City for five months; does it feel like home?"

"Yes, I like it here, and I have friends. I didn't live in Chicago long enough to make any friends. It was lonely."

Drew slid his feet into the warm sheepskin slippers. "I've not heard anything about your father's family?"

"Mama said he never talked about his father. Maybe they were like Mama's family and didn't get along. Sometimes, I feel like Uncle Quinn and I are all alone, and it's scary. I can't tell him about being scared, because Mama said the Edwards' are worriers. I don't want him to worry."

Drew took both her hands in his. "Randa, listen to me. I don't think anything is going to happen to your uncle. He's a happy, healthy man. Let me talk to him about this. There are some legal things he can do, then you won't have to worry. After I leave, you two can talk about it. Okay?"

She looked down. "Mama died; Uncle Quinn could too."

Chapter 36

Friday Morning

February 19

*I*t was still dark when they left for church. Drew said, "I go to a men's Bible Study at home, but they're all professors. This will be men discovering God. These are my favorite Bible Studies."

"You're right," Quinn said. "We'll keep all your degrees under wraps. I've been working with Don and turned the Bible Study over to him six weeks ago. I think that all your titles would be more than he could handle."

He paused at the church door. "I don't linger afterwards. Randa deserves a hug before she leaves for school."

Drew nodded. "Sometime today, before she comes home from school, we need to talk. I have several questions to ask you."

***

After breakfast, Drew suggested they talk in the living room. He crossed one leg over the other and said, "I don't know how it happened, but I have become Randa's confidant. She said something yesterday that needs to be fixed. I told her I'd talk to you."

"I'm not surprised." Quinn sipped his coffee. "You're easy to talk to, and you listen. What have I done wrong?"

"You haven't done anything wrong. Tell me, do you have a will?"

"Yes, Arlene and I had one drawn up a couple years after we mar..." He jerked forward in his chair and stared at Drew. "I need a new ..."

Marg Watland

"Yesterday, she told me you were her only close relative, and if her Mama died, you could too."

Quinn sighed. "That's why she wanted a list of your family. Why didn't she tell me?"

"I don't think she withheld it from you. I'm not sure *she* knew before she said it. She's grieving her mother's death and learning how to live with you. The possibility of you dying would be more than she could handle.

"You need a lawyer's advice, Quinn. I'm guessing everything in your will needs to be changed. I'd start by showing him Randa's letter. Tell him she's worried about you. Don't wait on this."

"I'll ask my banker to recommend a good lawyer. Hopefully, I can get a Monday afternoon appointment."

"I'm delighted to hear Randa is writing to your aunt. Are you still carrying around anger toward your father?"

"Not any longer. Randa told me she'd always wanted a big brother who would watch out for her. Drew, it was like a punch in the gut. I was never a big brother to Sarah. I barely knew her.

"Like Sarah, I needed to get right with God. I spent most of one night asking for God's forgiveness. I'm ashamed it took so long for me to acknowledge my sin. It was a humbling experience, but now I have a new peace."

"We all need to be humbled now and again, but Quinn, remember, part of repenting is to forgive yourself."

"You're right. Even though I'm forgiven, Satan attacks me like my sins are a weed you can't kill. I call on Jesus with the words of Jeremiah, '… for I will forgive their iniquity… I will remember their sin no more,' and the nagging guilt goes away. You don't know how much I wish I could tell my parents I'm sorry, face to face."

Drew picked up a Zane Grey book from the end table and frowned. "Do you read westerns?"

My Name is Randa

"I read one. I wanted to be sure it was an acceptable book for a teenager." Quinn grinned. "Randa likes the love parts."

Drew chuckled. "There's another thing. Are you sure Randa's father had no family? I'd consider checking that out."

Quinn frowned. "What if they're deadbeats?"

"What if they aren't? You don't need to tell her what you're doing. Talk with her stepfather. See what he knows."

"That's a good idea, I'll ask John. What else have I done wrong?"

"There's one last thing. Would you quit nagging that child about being too mature for her age? She can't change the way she is. God took her Mama home, and God *allowed* Randa to become mature for her age. Just relax and keep your hands off God's work."

"Nagging, huh? You're right; she doesn't deserve that. I'll ask her to forgive me. Thank you for your advice, Drew. Thank you."

"She is a sweet, sweet girl. If I didn't know you would take good care of her, I'd pack her up and take her home with me," he said.

Quinn laughed, "She's mine. Sorry."

Drew's stomach growled. While Quinn made bologna sandwiches, the cookie jar magically moved to the kitchen table. He gave Drew a shove and said, "Everything she bakes is good."

Drew bit into his sandwich, then pulled the jar closer to his plate.

"Quinn, you're doing an exceptional job with that girl, and she's doing the same with you. I thank God for putting you together. Randa tells me one day the two of you plan to write a book."

"Yes, we're both keeping a journal with that in mind."

Chapter 37

Friday after school

The front door of the church opened, and Quinn heard Randa and Molly laughing as they climbed the stairs to his office. They burst into the room with rosy cheeks and red noses from the winter air.

"Molly and her family are going to see *The Robe* tonight. They invited me. Can I go?"

"I believe the question should be, may I go? Yes, you may. How are you, Molly?"

"I'm fine." She giggled and asked, "You really brought a Doctor of Theology, who's a professor at a seminary, to my dad's Bible class? He's thinking about never forgiving you."

He chuckled. "Ask your dad what he would have done if I introduced him as Doctor Patterson before he started teaching. Tell him both Drew and I thought he did a fine job. In our line of work, we rarely get to listen to someone else teach. We found it refreshing."

"Okay, I will. Dad's waiting in the truck. We'll pick up Randa around quarter to seven."

When Molly left, Randa pulled off her coat and mittens and sat on the chair by his desk. She rolled his yellow pencil back and forth. "Did Uncle Drew tell you I was worried? I'm sorry I told him." She continued to roll the pencil. "I should have told you first. I didn't know I was so worried."

Quinn rolled his chair over in front of her, knee to knee, and took both her hands in his. "Look at me, honey. Yes, Drew told me. I'm thankful you told him. Your Uncle Drew is a wise man, and he gives me excellent advice."

"But you said I'm to tell you first."

My Name is Randa

"Honey, if there's something you don't feel you can tell me, it's okay to tell someone else, like Drew or Nora or Molly's parents.

"This morning, Drew brought to my attention that I need a new will. We realized there are other legal matters, too, that affect you. When my mother died in 1950, I inherited everything she owned. We thought I was her only living child. Now I know my sister was alive. Half of that inheritance money belongs to you.

"I've made an appointment with a lawyer, and we will put your money in a trust fund for your college. Listen to me carefully. I'm changing my will and making you my sole heir. Your inheritance is our private business. It's my practice not to tell others my personal business, and I'm hoping you will do the same."

"Okay. Is there enough for cooking school in France?"

"Yes. If that's what you want. You have several years before you need to choose your vocation, and you might discover you have a different dream. Either way, there'll be enough money for your schooling."

Randa started to stand, but Quinn held up his hand. "Wait, I need to apologize for nagging you about being too mature for your age. I'm very sorry that I nagged you about something God allowed and over which you have no control. Will you forgive me?"

"It's okay. If you nag again, I'll tell you." She reached for her coat.

Quinn took it from her. "A gentleman always helps a lady with her coat."

She slid her arms into the sleeves, then turned around and wrapped her arms around his middle. "I love you, Uncle Quinn."

"I love you too. Now off you go. We have company at home, and it's your turn to make supper."

Marg Watland

When Randa arrived home, there was a plate of cookies on the kitchen table and two empty glasses. Drew came in from the study and asked, "Is it too late for cookies?"

"No, but remember, there's chili and cornbread for supper. I'm late because I had a talk with Uncle Quinn. He apologized for nagging me. I'm going to see *The Robe* with the Thompsons tonight."

Drew smiled. "Is that all he told you?"

"No. He told me I'm not to talk about our private personal business to anyone, and then he treated me like a lady and helped me with my coat. Have you seen *The Robe*?"

***

After Randa left, the men carried hot tea into the living room. Quinn told Drew about the appointment with a lawyer and his conversation with Randa. "Nora and I talked about who I should choose for her guardian. We decided Don and Ruth Thompson would be a good choice. I don't want her to move again."

"I'm glad you've found a lawyer." Drew leaned forward. "I have another question. What's going on with you and your secretary? Is there something you haven't shared with me?"

Quinn's voice cooled. "What are you talking about? She wants us to go to her whenever we need a woman's advice. Randa and I are both thankful that she is our friend."

"I haven't met her yet," Drew said, "but it seems to me there is more here than you're saying. Just think about it. Pray about it."

"No, Drew, you need to wait until you meet her. We are having Sunday dinner at her house."

Quinn grabbed their empty cups and left the room. Where did Drew get an idea like that? He didn't need to pray about his friendship with Nora. She was his secretary, and *he* was her boss.

Chapter 38

Saturday, February 20

Drew shambled into the kitchen at six o'clock Saturday morning, hair awry and without his horn-rimmed glasses. Randa and Quinn were at the table eating cold cereal. An empty bowl and spoon sat in his place. Quinn handed him a box of Wheaties and said, "Good morning. We eat light now. I go to the office to finalize my sermon, and then we eat again around ten. We've both showered, so the bathroom is yours." He stood and dressed for the cold. "See you later."

Drew poured cereal into his bowl and said, "I'll work on my article until Quinn returns. What will you be doing, Randa?"

"My usual Saturday baking, and I'm making a cake for tomorrow."

***

Drew lost his concentration when a sweet cinnamon smell wafted from the kitchen. He dropped his pen on the desk and followed his nose.

Randa stood at the sink, drying a large mixing bowl. She laughed. "I wondered how long it'd take before you'd be in here checking out what I've been doing."

"What are you baking? It smells wonderful."

A big grin spread across her face. "Cinnamon rolls. I make them every Saturday."

He sat down and leaned his head against the wall. "I'm not leaving here until they're out of the oven,"

My Name is Randa

Outside, a car door slammed. Quinn walked into the kitchen and laughed at the look on Drew's face. "I guess I forgot to tell you about Randa's bread-making."

The timer sounded. Randa pulled a large pan out of the oven and lifted saucer-sized cinnamon rolls onto dessert plates. Drew's mouth watered as she spooned sweet goo from the bottom of the pan and drizzled it over each roll. When she placed them on the table, he leaned forward and breathed in the heavenly aroma. "I wouldn't have believed it if I hadn't witnessed it myself."

He took a bite and rolled his eyes. "Mmm. Wait until I tell Madeline what this child can do."

Quinn grinned. "Saturday is my favorite day of the week. I think of Randa as my angel baker."

In a rushed voice, she said, "I'm not that hungry right now. I'll finish my English assignment and then make the pound cake for tomorrow. She hurried to her room, and Goldie followed.

***

Randa didn't want them to see her cry. Uncle Drew leaning his head on the wall triggered a painful memory. Her door clicked shut, and tears streamed down her face. She flung herself on the bed, and sobs shook her body as she remembered that day.

It was Halloween, and she was learning how to make bread. Mama tried to show her how to knead the dough but didn't have enough strength. John wanted Mama back in bed, but she refused. He helped her to a chair, where she rested her head against the wall. She sat there until Randa finished the push and pull of kneading, then let John carry her to bed.

***

191

The men finished the first roll and split a second one. Drew downed the last of his tea and left for the shower. Quinn followed down the hall to check on Randa. She didn't answer his knock, so he opened the door and peeked in. She lay asleep in her unmade bed, curled in a fetal position with Goldie tucked under her chin. A box of tissue sat next to her pillow. He pulled a corner of the blanket over her shoulder and quietly left the room.

***

Sunday, Nora served pot roast with potatoes, carrots, and onions—Quinn's favorite. They sat around the table after dessert, listening to Drew's stories about Quinn.

Tim's southern *yes sir* showed respect toward Quinn, as if he were the patriarch of their family. Drew watched Randa and Quinn interact with Nora and her family and understood why her name laced their conversations.

At three, Quinn stood and thanked Nora for dinner. "We'll go now, so you can have a rest." On their way home, he told Drew that she and Randa would babysit later.

***

After Randa left, Quinn asked, "Are you hungry for a sandwich?" He picked up a foil-wrapped package and discovered enough pound cake left over for two generous servings. "Or there's ice cream and the rest of Randa's cake?"

Drew filled the teakettle. "I can have sandwiches anytime. I vote for the pound cake. We wouldn't want it to get stale, would we?"

The kettle sang, and Drew made a pot of his English tea and put it on the kitchen table. Quinn dug out liberal scoops of ice cream to top the cake.

My Name is Randa

The men concentrated on eating Randa's delicious cake. They scraped every crumb from their plates. Drew wiped his mouth with a napkin and asked, "How old is Nora?"

"Oh, I think she's in her early 40s," Quinn said, shifting in his chair.

"She'd make a perfect wife for you, Quinn. Her family likes you, and when you talk about baby Rosie, you sound like a bragging grandfather."

"I'm too old for her. Besides, she's still wearing her husband's rings. When the twins were born, she cried because Carl wasn't there. She stood in the church office and spat out her anger toward him because he left her all alone. She's still grieving."

Drew shook his head. "It looks to me like she's more than a friend. You're in her life, in her family. Whether you realize it, you are. She's even more in your family. She mothers your niece and takes care of you. Nora is fulfilling you in the way that a wife would. How old did you say she was?"

"I'm ten years older." Quinn poured tea, and they carried their cups into the living room.

"There's nothing wrong with ten years," Drew said, setting his cup on the coffee table. "I know several couples that have a fifteen-year difference in their ages, and they have good marriages."

Quinn hadn't heard of anything so ridiculous. Nora was the best secretary he'd ever had. He wasn't interested in jeopardizing their friendship.

It was after eight when Nora's headlights flashed across the kitchen window. Randa stormed in, and the kitchen door banged. "Jordie threw up all over me, and then he peed in my hair and soaked the dry sleeper. Ya know what he did next? He smiled at me like some kind of little baby angel." She turned and stomped down the hall.

Marg Watland

Quinn's mouth hung open. He looked at his friend, whose face contorted in repressed laughter. He shook his head. "She was maad."

Drew's shoulders shook, then he whooped with laughter, and Quinn joined him.

Doors banged, and they heard the shower. Twenty minutes later, Randa crept into the living room in clean clothes, toweling her hair dry. She frowned at them. "I heard you guys laughing at me."

"Sorry, but you have to admit it *was* funny," Drew said.

Quinn quirked his eyebrow. "So, do you still want four children?"

She curled up in the corner of the davenport, and Goldie jumped on her lap. "Yes," she grumped, "I just won't have twins."

Drew rocked in Quinn's chair. "Randa, do you have any pictures of when you were a little girl in Arizona? I'd like to hear about your life in Yuma."

"Okay. Everybody on our block was Mexican except us. They helped Mama before I was born because she had to stay in bed. We were all very good friends. I have pictures of them. They're in the garage." She jumped up. "I'll be right back."

"Wait, Randa," Quinn said, "take a flashlight. The light in the garage isn't enough. Tell me, why was your mama in bed?"

She shrugged. "I don't know. Maybe it was because of her heart." Randa grabbed the flashlight and ran out the door.

He sighed. Why hadn't she told him about her pictures?

Drew nodded. "If your sister spent the last months of her pregnancy in bed, it sounds to me like she could have died during her labor."

Randa came inside with the photo album in her hand. "Come on, I'll show you." She sat between them on the dav-

My Name is Randa

enport and opened the book. The first few pages were pictures of Sarah and her husband, Lee. They tried to see a resemblance between Randa and her dad, but there was none.

"Mama said I didn't look like my father, but maybe it would show up in my children."

"Honey, why haven't you shown me these pictures? I showed you your grandma's pictures."

"You don't know these people. Why would you want to see them?"

"Well, because these are pictures of you, your family, and your friends. They are a part of you I know nothing about."

She flipped to a page that showed her first birthday party. Frosting covered her hand, and there was a hole in the fancy birthday cake. A sea of smiling Mexican children was gathered around her.

Quinn couldn't believe it. Sarah, with a weak heart, had a baby. What were they thinking? It was a miracle she survived.

Randa closed the album, and Quinn hugged her. "Thank you, honey, for showing us your pictures. I loved seeing you when you were little. Could we keep this album with our other family pictures?"

Chapter 39

Monday morning

February 22

Drew put his luggage by the front door and went into the kitchen. Quinn leaned against the kitchen counter with a cup of coffee. Randa, ready for school, put her arms around Drew and hugged him tight. He hugged her back and said, "Thank you for taking care of my best friend. You're good for him."

"Thanks for helping us. I hope I get to meet all your family sometime."

"You will, and that's a promise."

Randa picked up her books and opened the door. She looked at her uncle, dropped her books on the kitchen counter, and rushed into Quinn's arms. He kissed the top of her head and said, "I'll be here when you get home."

"I like Uncle Drew. He's nice," Randa said in a loud whisper and bounced out the door.

Quinn sighed and turned to his friend. "This has been ... Thank you for everything, for helping me see my mistakes, for loving my niece, for being a brother to me."

"You're welcome. We took care of quite a few things. There's one thing left to do. Look in your heart and find out how you feel about Nora. Is she just a good secretary, or is she more?"

Quinn shook his head. "Forget it. I've enough to deal with right now, and things are good the way they are. Today I'm busy seeing a lawyer."

My Name is Randa

When Drew's car turned the corner, Quinn picked up the phone and called the Thompsons. "Good morning, Ruth. Is it possible for me to come talk to you and Don?"

***

Thirty minutes later, Quinn sat at the Thompsons' kitchen table. "Randa told Drew that if her Mama died, then I could die too; I had no idea she was worried."

Ruth gasped. Don moaned, "Noo."

"Drew thought a will would help. I have one, but it's twelve years old. That's why I'm here today. I have an appointment this afternoon with Erik Larson to draw up a new will and whatever other legal things need to be done. If, God forbid, I were to die, I don't want her to move away from Park City. I don't have any close relatives that are the right age, and Drew lives in Quebec. I want to know if I could name you as her guardians? I don't need an answer today, but would you pray about it? It wouldn't be a financial burden for you. I have enough money to support her."

Don looked at Ruth. "I can't think of any reason why not, but you're right; we need to pray about this. What about her father's family?"

"Randa says he didn't have any family. Drew thinks I need to find out for sure. That's another thing I'll discuss with Mr. Larson. I worry about them being a bunch of deadbeats."

Tears trickled down Ruth's face. "That poor child. She's gone through so much."

Don gently wiped her tears. "Rev, you have turned that sad little girl into a happy teenager." He chuckled. "Not all teenagers are happy, but Randa is."

"I couldn't have done it without Nora. She has become like a mother to Randa. I thank the Lord for her every day."

"We'll pray about it, Rev," Ruth said. "She's already a part of our family. My tomboy daughter is learning how to bake because of Randa. You didn't get to see the birthday cake those girls made for me. It was beautiful."

***

As Quinn drove away from the farm, he breathed a sigh of relief. The burden was lighter now that the Thompsons knew.

Each member of that family was a blessing to them. Randa and Molly were like sisters. Quinn knew he was too closed mouthed to make many friends, but because of the girls, he and Don were close.

He looked for Ruth's example to know what was right and wrong for a teenage girl.

Brad was a good big brother to his sister, and at Christmas, he learned Randa went to him for advice.

***

Back at the house, he put sheets in the washer, righted the kitchen, and fixed an early lunch. Quinn smiled as he thought about Drew's visit. It wasn't a surprise that Randa warmed up to him right away. He was always good with kids. They learned many new things about Randa. Her sweet goodbye to Drew pleased him.

His smile faded when he thought about Drew's matchmaking tactics. He didn't have time or inclination to consider dating Nora or any other woman who might show up at his door. He needed to concentrate on being a good parent to Randa.

Chapter 40

Monday afternoon

February 22

Attorney Erik Larson, a forty-year-old Scandinavian with white-blonde hair, brows, and lashes, shook Quinn's hand and invited him to be seated. "How can I help you, Reverend Edwards?"

"Please call me Quinn."

"Okay, and I'm Erik." He moved a yellow legal pad to the center of his desk and reached with his left hand for a pencil.

Quinn took three envelopes from his briefcase and put them on his lap. "I need to start by giving you some background about my family. My sister Sarah Jean was born four months before I graduated from high school. My father wanted me to be a farmer, and his continued insistence was intolerable. I rarely went home, except for holidays. As a result, I barely knew my sister.

"Sarah ran away from home when she was sixteen and left no explanation. In May of last year, I received a letter from Sarah's twelve-year-old daughter, Randa Shepherd, saying Sarah had died and she wanted me to be Randa's guardian." He handed the three envelopes to Erik. "The top one is Randa's letter to me. The other two are from Sarah."

He continued, "Randa has been living with me for nine months. I haven't applied for legal guardianship yet. I'd like you to help me with that."

Erik read all three letters and said, "We'll need notarized papers from people who can attest that your sister was of sound mind when she wrote these letters."

"That would be Sarah's husband, John Reynolds, and Bertha Bennett, their minister's wife."

Quinn reached for a pen in his shirt pocket. Erik stopped him. "I'll give you a list of everything I want from you. I believe I heard you were a widower. Do you have children?"

"No, my wife couldn't have children. She died in forty-eight."

"Are your parents living?"

"No, my father died in forty-eight and Mother in fifty."

"Did you inherit anything at the time of your parents' death?"

Quinn shifted forward in his chair. "Yes, everything. I sold the farm and still have the government bonds. I realized yesterday that my sister was alive when my parents died, so half of that money legally belongs to my niece."

Erik nodded. "Correct. We'll add that to the list of things you'll want done. I'll make a list of documents I'll need. What else can I do for you?"

"I want you to draw up a new will for me, making Randa my sole heir. I learned last week she's worried I might die, like her mama. I've asked Don and Ruth Thompson to consider being her guardians if something were to happen to me. They're praying about it. The only thing Randa knows about her father, Leland Shepherd, is he was raised in Missouri and didn't have any close relatives."

"I'd like you to find out more about Randa's father. I can decide what to do with the information when I know more."

***

Quinn left the office with his mind awhirl. He muttered, "That man doesn't need another appointment for the next month, with me as a client."

After dinner, Randa and Quinn carried in boxes from the garage and searched for the legal documents Erik wanted.

My Name is Randa

Randa sorted through her mama's keepsakes and found her parents' marriage certificate. She shed tears but kept going. They didn't find all the documents on Erik's list, but there were more boxes in the garage.

Close to midnight, Quinn sat in his study, writing a list of everything he needed to do the next day. Drew's suggestion that he pray about his feelings toward Nora hovered in a corner of his mind. He went to bed unsettled and knew sleep wouldn't come until he talked to the Lord about Drew's ridiculous idea. He prayed, "Lord, Drew said, I need to pray about Nora. I'm sure he's wrong, but …"

The Lord must have smiled.

***

The next morning, Quinn stood in front of his kitchen window and watched the sun peek through the clouds as it announced a new day. Randa entered the kitchen and popped two pieces of bread into the toaster. "What's wrong, Uncle Quinn?"

He joined her at the table. "I'm sorry, honey. I think I'll go to Minneapolis to speed up the guardianship process."

"Can I go too?"

"No, not this time. You have school. Mr. Larson says I need notarized letters from John and Bertha to prove your mama's mind was clear when she wrote our letters."

"Mama's mind was clear all the time." Her eyes filled with tears.

He squeezed her hands. "I know that, honey. I'm sorry this makes you cry, but I need to be your *legal* guardian." He handed her his hanky. She wiped her face and gave him a weak smile.

"After dinner, I'll call both John and Bertha, and you can talk to them, too. I promise I'll take you sometime this summer. We'll see if you can stay with Nora while I'm gone."

"Okay, but I'd really like to see everybody. I'm worried about John. Why doesn't he call more often? Do you think he's glad to have me gone? Doesn't he love me even a little?"

"Honey, John is living alone in a house full of memories. He's not only grieving for your mama, but you are gone, too. I think he loved both of you very much. John is a special man to have honored your mama's wishes." Quinn glanced at the clock. "It's time you left for school."

She gave him a hug and ran down the porch steps.

Quinn watched her hurry down the street and out of sight, then poured another cup of coffee. The last days of Arlene's life welled up in his mind. He wanted to plug his ears when she told him to marry again, maybe even have children. Now, he had a child, a teenager, and that was all he could handle.

Nora greeted him with a sweet smile when he arrived at the office. He leaned against the wall and told her about his appointment with Erik Larson. "I plan to take the train to Minneapolis tomorrow and speed up the guardianship process." With his hands in his pockets and head down, he turned and said, "I need some extra prayer time. I'll be in the sanctuary."

Two hours later, a floorboard squeaked, and Nora sat down beside him. With his head down and an empty cup dangling from his finger, he said, "Do you think I can be a good parent to Randa? She deserves the best."

"She has the best. You!"

He picked up a piece of paper from the seat beside him and handed it to her. "These are the documents Erik needs."

She read the list, took the cup from him, and gave his arm a compassionate squeeze. Her soft hands felt good. He liked her touch. Quinn moved his arm away and chided himself for losing his concentration. "Randa cried when she looked

My Name is Randa

through a box of her mama's keepsakes." He handed her a second page. "I wrote this list last night."

Nora glanced at his list and said, "Quinn, listen to me. You have a lawyer taking care of your legal matters. You're trying to put your life in order. You can't do it by yourself. Have you asked the Lord to help you with this list?"

He stared at the little woman and, with a shamed look, quoted Proverbs 3:6. "In all thy ways acknowledge him, and he shall direct thy paths."

"No, I've been trying to tell God how I'll do it. I can't tell you how many times I've counseled people to let God direct their life and encouraged them to memorize Proverbs 3:5-6." His stomach growled.

"Did you eat this morning?"

He shook his head.

She patted his arm again and said, "I'm going home to make us some lunch."

Quinn breathed a sigh of relief and left the sanctuary for his office just as Don Thompson opened the front door.

Don dropped into the chair by Quinn's desk, took off his cap, and hung it on his knee. "Ruth and I have prayed about being Randa's guardian. I called my folks, and we all agreed. If anything happens, we'll take her and love her like our own. Dad said she is already their granddaughter. So, what do we do next? We'd like to tell our kids about this and get their okay. I know they'll say yes, but we think they deserve to know."

"I agree, but would you wait to tell the kids until we get everything in order? I haven't talked to Randa about this yet."

"Sure. I'm glad you have Erik Larson. He is a good man." He stood and winked at Quinn. "If I leave now, I think I can get home before Ruth throws out my lunch. Thought you'd like to know as soon as we decided."

203

Quinn stood and shook Don's hand. "Thank you. You're a good friend."

Don hadn't reached the first step before Nora opened the front door. They greeted each other, and Don left, leaving a draft of cold air.

Quinn joined her, and they went downstairs to their regular table, closest to the kitchen door. They lunched on roast beef sandwiches and filled each other in on what had been happening in their lives.

Quinn said, "If things go well in Minneapolis, I'll take the late train home. Could Randa stay with you while I'm gone?"

"Of course. You know she's worried about her stepfather."

"Yes, I know. I called John last night. He plans to take the day off. I want to talk to him face-to-face about failing to call Randa. She deserves an apology from him."

He rambled on. "I'd like to hear more about Sarah's life. All I know is what Randa's told me. I have so many questions."

Nora unwrapped a stack of heart-shaped cookies, pushed them toward Quinn, and said, "I'll pray John will listen to your reprimand and accept that he has wronged Randa."

They finished lunch. Quinn said, "Thank you for everything, Nora. I don't know what I'd do without you. And thank you for the roast beef sandwiches. They hit the spot. I'll see you in the morning."

***

Nora drove towards Julie's house with a smile. On occasion, her boss needed to be reminded not to worry about tomorrow.

Life had changed since Quinn and Randa moved to Park City; she wasn't lonely any longer, and she *loved* her job!

My Name is Randa

Chapter 41

Early Monday

March 1

The train slowed.

Quinn stood and stretched. He saw John on the platform, hunched against the cold early morning air.

They shook hands. Then John drove to his house through dark, empty streets. "Would you like coffee or a nap?"

"Coffee, please. I slept a little on the train." Sleep was out of the question. He had to confront John and not damage their new relationship.

Quinn looked around the kitchen and saw the same red cookie jar, white walls, and red gingham curtains that they had at home.

John filled his coffee pot, plugged it in, and joined Quinn at the kitchen table. "I'll make breakfast later if that's okay."

"That's fine with me." Quinn forced himself to stay calm. "Randa's worried about you. She writes to you every other week, but you don't call her. You haven't called in a long time. She told me the last time you called, it sounded like you'd been drinking."

John looked down and rolled his wedding ring round and round.

"Ralph Bennett told me about the widower who helped you stop drinking. We've been praying for you. I haven't said anything to Randa. It's not for me to tell. She deserves an explanation from you—and an apology."

John turned beet red. "What am I supposed to tell her? That I was the town drunk until Reverend Bennett sent Glen over to see me?"

My Name is Randa

"No, my brother, but now you have turned your life around, and she won't have to worry about you ruining your life by being a drunkard. She'll forgive you; she forgives me all the time."

John nodded. "You're right. I need to tell Randa the truth. I don't want to lose her, and if I start drinking again, you won't let me see her." His Adam's apple dipped as he gulped to push down a sob. "I didn't know how much I loved that girl until she moved away. I promise, I'm through drinking."

Tears streamed down John's face, "Randa says you cry together." He sobbed. Quinn rubbed his back while John grieved. When the storm of grief was over, John headed to the bathroom. "I need to wash my face."

When he returned, Quinn said, "My Dad told me to stop crying after my grandma's funeral. I was ten. The Bible says Jesus wept when his friend Lazarus died. If God's son cried, we can too."

"Well, *you* know what to do when Randa cries," John said. "Before you came, we went off by ourselves and cried alone. My Dad told me men don't cry. Quinn, you're a father to Randa. I never was. Thank you for being so good to her; she belongs with you."

"Thank you for those kind words, but she's part yours. You had her for twelve years before she came to live with me, and she loves you."

Quinn took a sip of coffee. "I don't know how to be a parent, but I have a friend who is a good father. I'm trying to follow his example. His name is Don Thompson, and his daughter, Molly, is Randa's best friend. I make mistakes, but I ask Randa to forgive me, and she hugs me and tells me it's okay.

"We're human, John. We make mistakes, and sometimes we hurt those we love the most. All you have to do is apologize. Randa will forgive you, and you'll both feel better."

John opened the drapes to the sun peeking over the horizon. He turned. "How's Randa doing in school? She stayed home with her mama most of November and all of December."

Quinn laughed. "I realized I was not only Randa's uncle, but I was also her parent when I went to the first Parent Teacher Conference. Her teacher, Miss Jarvis, is amazed at how well she is adjusting to her new home and pleased with her progress. She's giving Randa special assignments in math. I wanted to hire a tutor, but she said if I helped Randa, it would bring us closer together; and it has."

"Good, I'm glad to hear that. Dorothy has worried about her schooling, too. I go out to Dorothy's when I get a letter from Randa. We all miss her. She wrote about the gaps and your Christmas questions. We liked the question idea. You guys had quite a Christmas."

Quinn pushed his empty cup aside. "Randa wanted to know about me when I was a kid. Then she asked me about her grandparents.

When I thought about my dad, all I could remember was him yelling at me. The day I packed up all my belongings and told him I was leaving, I heard him yelling at me all the way down the drive. He wanted me to be a farmer. I wanted to be a teacher.

"Sarah's letter helped me realize I needed to get right with God, too."

"Did you forgive your parents?"

"I did. It took a good part of one night, sorting through all my rebellion, and asking for forgiveness. Jesus said, 'For if ye forgive men their trespasses, your heavenly Father will also forgive you.' I'm ashamed of the anger and resentment I

My Name is Randa

held toward my father. I accept my father's *old country* opinions as his, and now, I have a peace I've never had before."

John's eyes searched Quinn's. After a lengthy pause, he said, "Sarah got right with God. I know I'm not right with God; he took Sarah away from me. I guess I should be thankful for the years I had with her. The doctors couldn't believe she lived as long as she did." He pushed back from the table. "I think it's time to rustle up some breakfast."

Quinn thanked the Lord for his brother-in-law. He'd cared for Sarah and Randa from the time Lee died. He would make sure John was always part of their life. It amused him that John, who hated God, had two preachers in his life. He prayed, "Lord, help us love and care for this man. May he see Jesus in us."

John mixed up a batch of biscuits and put them in the oven. He stared out the window at his garage while he waited for the skillet to heat. His stance stiffened. "I think the skillet's hot enough; would you start the eggs?"

He dashed out the door to the garage. Minutes later, he came back with two pints of jam. John held up a jar labeled 1950 and handed it to Quinn. "This is the last of Sarah's strawberry jam. That one's for Randa." He opened the other jar and put it on the table. They piled generous amounts of strawberry jam on each biscuit they ate and didn't stop until the pan was empty.

John took the empty dishes to the sink and refilled their cups. "Thanks for keeping in touch. I don't deserve it, but thanks." He grinned. "Someday, I might have to go to Wisconsin and hear you preach."

"You're always welcome."

Chapter 42

Monday afternoon

March 1

Quinn showed John the letter he and Bertha needed to sign in front of a notary, then told him about the other legal documents he needed.

They met at Bertha's bank, and while they waited for the notary to be available, Bertha told how she helped Sarah with the wording in her letters. "She didn't want any confusion."

John nodded. "Sarah's mind was clear right up to the day before she died. She wrote my letter first, months before she died, and she made me promise to look for you. I read every one of those letters."

They went to the courthouse to apply for a copy of Sarah's death certificate and then had lunch in the city.

Quinn said, "We found the newspaper article about Lee's death in Sarah's box of keepsakes. How did she manage financially after Lee died?"

"Their insurance paid off the house, and she got a settlement from the railroad. The doctor put her on bedrest right after Lee's death. Carlita, her next-door neighbor, found someone to move in and take care of Sarah in those last months. Carlita and Juan Flores kind of adopted Lee and Sarah; they treated her like a daughter. Then when I married her, they took me in, too. They were really good to us," John said.

"She spent a month in the hospital before Randa was born. I was at the hospital when she started having labor pains. I

My Name is Randa

didn't leave until after the baby was born. She named Randa after their mothers."

Quinn yawned. "What can you tell me about Randa's father? She knows almost nothing."

"I don't know much; Lee hired on with the railroad in thirty-four, and they assigned him to my crew. My boss had me teach him the ropes; we hit it off right away. We were work buddies. He had a big old Harley Davidson and spent all his free time with his biker friends. Then in thirty-six, he came home from vacation married to Sarah."

After lunch, John turned the car toward home. "Lee told me he'd gone to a family get-together, and the guys partied all day and all night. He woke up the next morning in a hotel in Albuquerque—married. He couldn't remember much about their wedding night.

"Sarah told me she had a crush on him since she was seventeen, but Lee wouldn't have anything to do with her. I think Lee must have been sweet on her but thought he was too old for her. There was seven years difference in their ages."

"I don't understand. With her Christian upbringing, how could she get married in a drunken stupor?"

"I don't think she had anything to drink. I tried to give her a beer once, and she took a sip and spit it out into the kitchen sink. Another time I had her taste some wine, and she told me it tasted like rotten fruit. I don't know anything about what happened the day she got married, but I know my Sarah wasn't drinking.

"I have a few pictures of Lee and me before they married," John said, stopping the car in front of his house. "Give me a minute, and I'll find them."

***

Marg Watland

Quinn sat on the couch and tried to make sense out of John's story. Why would Sarah marry a guy that much older than her? What kind of person did she turn into? He knew Sarah was a good mother. Randa was proof of that. Things didn't add up.

Lee's motorcycle was in every picture John had. "He took me out in the desert, on his bike, for an overnight camping trip. I about froze. The desert gets cold when the sun goes down."

John straightened a picture on the far wall, then sat on the couch. He tried to control his leg from bouncing. "Quinn, do you think Sarah can see me? I'd hate to have her see how I drank after Randa left."

"Nobody really knows. We'll have to wait and see. I'd like my parents to know I'm sorry for all the hurt I caused them—but I don't know."

The two men sat for a time without speaking.

John broke the silence. "A few weeks after they married, Lee invited me over for the best supper I'd eaten in a long time. They were so happy. I envied them. He called Sarah his little princess. My family bugged me about settling down with a good woman. I couldn't seem to find anyone that wanted to marry me."

"Tell me more about Sarah and Lee."

"Okay, let me make some more coffee first."

Quinn followed him into the kitchen. They stood propped against the counter and waited for the coffee to brew.

"I kept waiting to hear that Lee and Sarah were expecting. A couple of years went by, and I asked, 'how come no baby?' Lee said she couldn't have kids. Then one day, Lee came to work white as a ghost. He wouldn't talk to me; he just kept muttering, *what am I gonna do*? When we got off work, I made him tell me what was wrong. He told me they'd found out Sarah was going to have a baby, but her

My Name is Randa

doctors in Michigan had told her it would be too hard on her heart to have children. I followed Lee home. And Sarah told me she had rheumatic fever when she was eleven, and it damaged her heart."

"Lee was scared she'd die having the baby. Sarah promised she'd do whatever the doctor told her. She was so happy about having a baby, and as time went on, her excitement spread over to Lee. He died dreaming of having a son."

Quinn's heart hurt for his parents and for Sarah. He understood how Sarah's excitement could overshadow Lee's concern, cause him to push the danger aside, and rejoice with his wife. They made a terrible mistake that could have jeopardized Sarah's life, but she survived for another twelve years. He prayed, "O God, thank you for this child you have given me to love."

They went into the living room with their coffee. Quinn had more questions. "Do you know why Sarah ran away?"

"Yes, your parents smothered her. They wouldn't let her do anything because of her bad heart. Sarah told me she couldn't live like a nun, so she ran away."

Would Quinn smother Randa if she was the one with a bad heart? He hoped not.

John grinned at Quinn. "I bet you don't know this. When Sarah started working part-time at the bakery, Randa stayed with Carlita's daughter, who had a house full of kids. It wasn't long, and she was speaking Mexican to everybody in the neighborhood and English to us."

"Do you think she can still speak Mexican?"

"I don't know why not?"

John leaned over, dropped his hands between his knees, and didn't look up. "When Randa left my house, I couldn't stand the emptiness. I missed my girls. I started going to the pool hall for company, and each time I drank more than the time before. I wanted to forget. One night, Reverend Bennett stopped by here, and I had a snort full. He said he wanted me to meet a man in his church, a widower like me. The next day I went to work hungover and fell asleep on the job. My boss told me if I did that again, he'd fire me."

Quinn nodded. "I remember after Arlene died, I'd walk into my house, and there was dead silence. I hated going home. I'm sorry. I should have had Randa call you more often. We were trying to do the right thing for each other. Our decision to move to a small town in Wisconsin has been good for us. Tell me about you and Sarah."

"I got drafted and sent to Camp Ibis in California for my boot training. I worried about Sarah all the time I was there. When I got home on furlough, even though Lee had only been gone a year, I asked her to marry me. We went to the courthouse and got married the next day."

"But I thought you loved her."

"I didn't think so, but we got along. Sarah told me she'd write every week. She wasn't much of a talker; I never knew what she was thinking. It bowled me over when she wrote about how much she missed me and that she loved me.

"I married her because I wanted to take care of my best friend's wife. She'd never once told me she loved me. I wanted to find a girl *like* Sarah, but instead, I got Sarah. I couldn't believe my good luck. I was overseas, reading her love letters, when I realized I'd loved her all along. No man ever had a better wife."

Quinn breathed a deep sigh. "Praise the Lord! I hoped Sarah had a happy marriage. Thank you for loving her."

John continued. "I told people Randa was enough. I didn't want any kids, but I lied. We were really careful."

Quinn said, "My wife couldn't have children; we had ten happy years together before she died."

My Name is Randa

"Sarah told me to find someone to love and have some kids." John's voice changed to a whisper. "No way; I'd be a lousy father."

"John, you've grieved for over a year, and you are a wiser man. You are too young to live alone for the rest of your life. It's time for you to find a woman to love."

John shook his head. "What about you? You and Randa love each other, but she needs a mother. Both of you talk about a woman named Nora. What about her? Would she be a good mother for Randa?"

Quinn raised his brow. "My roommate from seminary visited us a week ago, and he asked the same question. Nora is my secretary. Her husband died two years ago. I don't think she's interested in marriage. She's still wearing her wedding rings."

"Humph. Maybe you should talk her into taking off those rings."

Chapter 43

Tuesday, March 2

Quinn arrived home in the middle of the night and fell into bed. When the alarm rang, Quinn woke with John's last words swirling around in his head. *A man doesn't tell a widow to take her deceased husband's rings off.* Neither John nor Drew understood.

Nora was an excellent church secretary, but she had shown no sign she was interested in him. She probably didn't know any of the tricks widows pulled on eligible widowers. He soaped his beard, rinsed, and poured shampoo on his head. Randa wasn't home, so he could use as much hot water as he pleased.

***

Quinn entered the church office and blushed when Nora smiled and said, "Welcome home." He stood at the corner of her desk and looked at her, really looked at her. He didn't know she had green eyes. How did he miss something like that?

"Are you alright?" she asked.

He gulped and searched for something to say. "I think I'll close my door while I do some research." He winked and said, "Please keep the crowds away for a couple hours?"

"I'll guard your door with my life." She grinned. "I brought us sandwiches for lunch and can't wait to hear about your trip."

He went into his office, stacked a couple of reference books on his desk, then sat and stared at Nora. The clock on the wall showed ten o'clock, and he hadn't even opened his briefcase. All he'd done so far was watch Nora efficiently go from one task to another.

Could Drew be right? Had she become more than a secretary to him? What did John Reynolds know about anything? He hadn't even met her.

Quinn forced himself to get busy. He opened his Bible to Genesis and whispered, "Lord, please help me. I can't seem to get anything done today."

Nora walked by to get supplies out of the storage room. She hadn't been a distraction before, but now he had to figure out if he more than liked her. If he asked her for a date, she might reject him and say she still loved her husband. That would make both of them uncomfortable. Their friendship would suffer, and he didn't want that to happen.

His Bible lay open as thoughts of Nora circled around in his head. Quinn gripped his pencil and titled his sermon, *The Beginning*.

The words flowed, teaching his congregation about God the creator. Now, things were working right. The pencil slid across his paper, making a dark mark on his creation notes. He dropped the pencil, rubbed his aching fingers, then started on the second part: Adam.

Nora knocked and opened his door. "Is this a good time for lunch?"

While they ate, Quinn told her John and Sarah's story. They speculated on how Sarah got from Michigan to Arizona. Did she hitchhike? Had she made plans to leave home with a friend? Where did she meet her husband, Lee? As they climbed the stairs to the office, Nora said, "Quinn, there are dark circles under your eyes. You haven't had enough sleep. Your sermon can wait until tomorrow. Go home."

"Maybe I will. I'll wrap up here and sneak in a nap before Randa gets home from school." He filled his briefcase with

Marg Watland

what he needed to finish his sermon and hesitated in the doorway of his office, watching Nora type.

***

Randa plunked her suitcase on the kitchen floor and waved goodbye as Nora drove away. She called out, "Goldie. Where are you?" The cat came around the corner. She picked her up and walked into the living room to find her uncle stretched out on the davenport. He sat up, blinking, and reached for his glasses.

Randa stepped back. "Oh, I'm sorry. I thought you'd be awake by now."

"I should be. I think it's my turn to fix dinner."

"We have enough leftovers for dinner. I want to hear all about your trip. Did you see Bertha? Nora told me to remind you about a meeting at the hospital at ten tomorrow."

Quinn grabbed his pocket calendar, made a note, then followed her into the kitchen.

She stood looking in the fridge. "When do you want to eat? I'm already hungry."

"Come here." He pulled her toward him and closed the refrigerator door. Quinn put his arms around her and squeezed, "That's a hug from Bertha." He kissed her forehead. "And that's a kiss from John." Again, he hugged her tight and dropped another kiss on her head. "And that's from me."

She wrapped her arms around his middle and said, "I love you too, Uncle Quinn."

It was Quinn's turn to stand in front of the fridge with the door open. "Okay, we'll eat an early dinner, and I'll tell you about yesterday." He shoved his hand into the cookie jar, and it was empty. He tipped it over for her to see. "I think this means a trip to the deep freeze. Wait just a minute. John said you used to speak Spanish. Do you still remember it?"

My Name is Randa

Randa stopped, her hand on the kitchen doorknob. With a teasing light in her eyes, she said, "I speak Mexican. *¿Quiere usted galletas o biz cocho de chocolate?*" She laughed. "I asked you if you wanted cookies or brownies."

Quinn chose cookies, and Randa dashed out to the garage for oatmeal raisin cookies.

All the way through dinner, she peppered him with questions about John and the Bennetts. He answered her questions but refrained from revealing John's suggestion about Nora's wedding rings.

At eight o'clock, Randa turned on the TV to watch *The Ed Sullivan Show*, which helped him push Nora out of his thoughts.

***

Later, his head barely hit the pillow when everybody's comments came rushing back. John was right. Nora would make a wonderful mother for Randa, but that wasn't a good enough reason for him to ask her out. Dating at his age would differ from when he was younger. He had enough pressures in his life already, and there was no guarantee Nora would even be interested. Well, he didn't have to do anything about it right now. Tomorrow, he had meetings back-to-back and probably wouldn't be in the office until late afternoon. He'd try to concentrate on what needed his attention for the day.

Chapter 44

Friday, March 5

Quinn climbed the stairs to his office with plans to build his Easter sermon around the prophecies in the Old Testament. His study time was a disaster. He couldn't keep his mind on the sermon.

For three days, Drew and John's comments about Nora kept popping into his mind. Should he ask her for a date? How does a man date his secretary?

Everyone would be watching. Nora was born in this town. Those rings on her finger were an issue. How does a man ask a widow lady to take off her wedding rings? Nora seemed to enjoy being with him. It might be good if he suggested dating and then give her some time to think about it.

If she said yes, where would he take her? It should be someplace where they wouldn't run into people from church.

Quinn couldn't take it any longer. He needed to get this out in the open. He walked over to her desk and sat in the chair beside her desk. "Nora, our birthday is in two weeks. I'd like for you to consider us celebrating it together, just the two of us. It could be our first date." He hesitated, took a deep breath, and said, "You're still wearing your wedding rings, so maybe you aren't interested. You don't have to answer right now, but would you think about it?"

Nora stared at him and blushed. The phone rang. She answered it in a near whisper, then handed the phone to Quinn, saying, "Hospital."

He listened, then said, "I'll be right there."

My Name is Randa

Quinn grabbed his hat and coat. "Melvin Gray's at Emergency in terrible pain. I'd better go. We'll talk later," he said, hurrying out the door.

Nora glared at the office door. "I don't want to talk later," she said to the empty room. "I want you to come right back here and explain yourself." Her mouth settled into a childish pout. "Why does he want to ruin a good thing? My rings are my business. Things are fine just the way they are."

She turned to the typewriter and furiously banged on the keys. Two hours later, Quinn called and said Don Thompson had fallen off a ladder and had a badly sprained ankle and bruised ribs. He and Randa were going out to the farm to help Brad with the chores. Nora hung up and dropped her head in her hands.

The next day Quinn called to say Melvin passed a kidney stone and had gone home from the hospital. "Randa and I are taking cookies out to the Thompsons'."

Nora offered to type his sermon notes, but Quinn said, "No, that's not necessary. I'll make do with my hand-written outline."

Nora frowned and hung up the phone. That man would probably work way into the night before finishing his sermon. He didn't mention a thing about dating.

***

Sunday morning, Randa joined Nora in the second pew, directly in front of the pulpit. She whispered, "Molly isn't here today, and we're going to dinner at the Johnson's, so I'm going to sit with you. After dinner, we'll check on Don. Ruth told me he groaned every time he moved last night."

"You two have been busy this weekend," Nora said. Secretly, she wondered why Quinn hadn't called her. He needed to explain himself. Where did he get the idea that they should date? Did the professor have something to do with this? She heard Quinn's voice preaching his sermon, but the words were a blur. They needed to talk, and he didn't seem to have time. What should she do?

***

When the service was over, Nora said goodbye to Randa, slipped out a side door, and drove to the Park City Cemetery. She took her normal route across the grounds to the stone inscribed *Carl Montgomery, 1906-1951*. Nora didn't know where else to go and needed to talk to someone about this date thing. She stood and rolled her wedding rings round and round on her finger.

She scanned the area and, seeing no one, said, "Carl, I loved you with all my heart. I'm not removing these rings because you're no longer the man I loved, but I believe God has someone else for me to love. I'm scared, Carl. I thought I just liked him, but something is here in my heart for this man." She stood with her eyes closed and her hand on her chest.

Instead of driving home to an empty house, she turned her car toward Julie and Tim's. Halfway to their house, she slammed on the brakes and pulled to the side of the road. "That's what's wrong. He's scared! He's afraid I'll tell him to go fly a kite."

The babies were sleeping, so she ended up telling Julie and Tim about her birthday date. Tim laughed and said, "It's about time, Little Mother. I told Julie back in October that if you weren't careful, that man might court you. I'll bet his friend the professor helped this along."

Nora turned rosy.

"Tim, quit teasing my mother," Julie said.

***

My Name is Randa

After nine that night, Nora stood on Esther's front porch, hunched in her winter coat. Had she made the right decision? Before she could raise her hand to knock, Esther opened the door and said, "What on earth are you doing standing at my front door this time of night? Get in here out of the cold."

She stepped inside. "May I have some tea? I need to talk." She took two cups and saucers out of the cupboard and put them on the table.

Esther filled the teakettle, then joined Nora at the kitchen table. "So, tell me, what has you in such a tizzy?"

Nora stuck out her hand. "Just look at that. It's ugly! I can't go around with an empty finger. I've had Carl's rings on that finger for twenty-two years, and they left a dent. I think I'm interested, but …

"So, my baby sister *is* interested in our reverend? It's about time."

Nora stared at her in disbelief and then burst into tears. "I'm scared. What if he doesn't like me that way after we go out on a date? If we date, the entire world is going to be watching every move we make."

The teakettle whistled. Esther poured boiling water over the tea ball in the teapot and brought it to the table. "You're right; we've all been watching." She winked at her. "Believe it, Nora, he likes you."

"Who's been watching?"

"Most everyone. We rarely get to watch a reverend and his secretary fall in love. Did you come over here this late to tell me he asked you out on a date?"

"No, could I borrow one of your rings? None of the rings I have cover this dent, and it's so obvious."

In a teasing voice, Esther asked, "How long do you think you'll need it?"

Nora swiped the tears from her face and laughed. "I don't know. I hope it won't be too long. When you and George started dating, how long did it take?"

Esther giggled, slid out of her chair, and headed toward the bedroom. She returned with a two-layered carved jewelry box. "Let's see what I have." The sisters bent over the box, pushing the rings around, sliding one ring after another over Nora's finger. They chose Esther's birthstone ring, a dark blue sapphire mounted amidst gold scroll filigree. It covered Nora's dent.

"So, tell me. Why did you take off your wedding rings?"

"I can't go on dates with my wedding rings on my finger. Friday morning, Quinn told me he'd like our first date to be a birthday date. He told me to think about it, and I haven't seen him since. I'm scared and excited. I didn't even know I wanted this, but I do."

"Honey, we're all rooting for you. I can't believe it has taken all this time for him to get the picture."

"What are you talking about?

"Don and I were talking. He told me that a niece, a new church, and a sweet widow lady are a lot to dump on a man's shoulders all at once."

Nora stared at her sister and whispered, "Who's rooting for me?"

"The entire congregation, your friends, and all your family."

Nora covered her hot face with both hands. "Oh, no. This is so embarrassing." She started building up steam and spluttered, "What are we supposed to do now? This is our private business, and everyone has been talking about it before we even knew."

Esther laughed. "Just let nature take its course."

Chapter 45

Tuesday morning

March 9

$\mathcal{N}$ora, dressed in a navy sheath that complemented her hourglass figure, unlocked the church door. Her heart raced in anticipation. That man would not avoid her one more day. She'd been *thinking* about it for four days. Did he know people were watching them? How could they date in front of everybody?

Nerves clenched her stomach. She had slept little over the weekend, and some things she thought about were outrageous for a woman her age.

Nora looked at her watch; it was close to nine. Maybe she should check her hair once more. Those pesky curls popped up; she'd better check.

When she returned to the office, Quinn stood by her desk with a bouquet of baby's breath and pink carnations in a pretty glass vase. "I tried to call you several times yesterday. Where were you?"

She took the flowers, breathed in the sweet fragrance, and her eyes searched his face. He looked lost. Did he have any idea how much she needed to talk to him?

"I went to Julie's in the afternoon. The babies were sick. Thank you for the flowers. I like pink."

"I bought them yesterday."

She bravely held out her left hand. "Esther loaned me one of her rings."

Quinn glanced at the ring, turned her hand over, and his lips touched the borrowed ring. He looked into her eyes, took a deep breath, and said, "Thank you! Thank you for not keeping me guessing. Thank you for borrowing the ring."

Quinn was sure if he moved too fast, he might scare her away. He didn't know exactly when he started loving her, but he was *in love* with Nora Montgomery.

"Oh Quinn, Esther told me last night that everybody's been watching us fall in lo..." She covered her mouth with both hands and blushed until her ears were rosy pink. "Tim thinks the professor helped. Will we have any privacy?"

She wished he would take her in his arms and hold her. This conversation would be easier if his arms were around her. How long did she have to wait until he decided it was proper to hold her? She was ready and waiting to be in Quinn's arms.

"Let's go downstairs and take our morning break. I think we could use a cup of tea to soothe our nerves," he said. "I'll tell you what I know." He took her hand, and they walked downstairs together.

Nora made a pot of tea. Quinn found a piece of apple pie in a sticky pie tin and grabbed a fork. "What's your favorite part of a pie, the fruit or the crust?"

"The fluted crust with some fruit." She poured hot tea into their cups and dropped a sugar cube in his.

He cut a crumbling piece of the crust's edge with some apple filling and said, "Open up. I expect the same amount from you. It's my favorite too." He fed the sweet to her, handed over the fork, and said, "It's your turn now." Nora looked at him with a delighted smile on her face and cut a bite for him.

Quinn thought both Nora and Julie made better apple pie than this one, but it was fun feeding her. It would be even nicer to touch his lips to hers. How long would he have to wait for a kiss? The normal way was to date, then fall in love.

My Name is Randa

"Do you know where you're taking me for our birthday?"

"No. Do you have a suggestion?"

"I like Madison. Esther's eldest son Clyde has a church in Madison, and he and his wife Phyllis love having company. They have a big, old farmhouse with six bedrooms. Julie and I shop for clothes in Madison. We go over early one day, stay overnight, and return home the next morning. I could show you where Julie went to school and her favorite furniture store. The state capital is a beautiful building, and there's a museum at the University."

"That sounds good. We'll talk about this later. We need to go to work." He raised one eyebrow. "I have to tell Randa and find a place for her to stay while we celebrate our birthday."

Nora said, "From what Esther told me, I'm willing to bet she and Molly have had discussions about us. How long have you thought about me?"

"Well, Drew said I talked about you all the time. He got pushy and made me promise to pray about it. The Lord showed me how much I cared for you, but I worried you wouldn't feel the same." He followed her into the kitchen, and she quickly washed their cups. He lifted her chin so he could see her eyes. "Nora, I don't want to lose you."

She squeezed his arm. "You will not lose me. I'm right here." They silently climbed the stairs with his hand touching her back in a near caress.

He stood beside her desk and grinned. "I didn't expect this to happen to us; life has become exciting." He sat on the corner of her desk. "I'd like our first date to be just you and me, someplace where no one knows us. I think Madison sounds like a good idea."

***

Quinn sat in his office worrying over how to tell Nora about the demands of a minister's wife and the changes that would happen to her because she was the reverend's wife. He rubbed his forehead, trying to get his mind back on track, then started writing notes about the four patriarchs, Abraham, Isaac, Jacob, and Joseph. His thoughts flowed for a time, and then he lost his concentration and ended up back on the corner of Nora's desk.

She covered her typewriter and asked, "Is there something I can do for you?"

He took her hand and said, "No, but I'll miss you. It's lonely when you leave."

She looked into his dark eyes. "Oh my, I have a full afternoon today, or I'd probably find an excuse to stay. I'll see you tomorrow."

He lifted her hand and kissed it.

*****

That night, Quinn called Drew. "I prayed about it, and you were right. Our first date will be on our birthday."

Chapter 46

Tuesday Evening

March 9

Quinn couldn't get a word in during dinner. Randa had milked one of The Thompsons' cows by herself, and she wanted him to know exactly how she did it. Someday he'd have to tell her they had cows on his farm, and he didn't think milking a cow was all that exciting. He probably would leave out the *not exciting* part.

They were relaxing in the living room; it was time to tell Randa his news. He stretched his legs out and bumped into the coffee table.

Randa looked up from her book. "Did you need something, Uncle Quinn?

"Not anymore. Nora said she'd go on a date with me."

She turned back to *Ann of Green Gables* and stroked Goldie's fur. Suddenly Randa's head jerked. She jumped to her feet and shouted, "What did you say? Did you say date?"

Goldie streaked to Quinn's study and hid under his desk. He nodded.

She jumped and clapped. "You're going on a date? You and Nora? Molly and I have been praying and praying and praying that you and Nora would fall in love. We knew you liked each other a lot. She's perfect for you and for me. What took so long?"

Quinn stood and put his hands on her shoulders. "Randa, calm down. You're so loud people will hear you out on the street. I asked her for a birthday date. Esther told Nora everybody is watching us, so we're going to Madison, where nobody knows us. I'm asking you not to tell anyone. This is our personal business. Will you keep this a secret for me? It can be your birthday gift for us."

"Okaay, but I tell Molly everything. This will be really hard." Randa put her arms around his waist, squeezed tight, and said, "I'm so happy."

"Drew started this. I thought he was mistaken, but he made me promise to pray about my feelings for Nora."

Randa laughed. "You told me Uncle Drew was a wise man."

He nodded. "I prayed about it and had to admit Nora's become very special to me, but I hadn't realized how much."

"Molly and me prayed you'd fall in love with Nora and get married. Then Nora could be like a mother to me. You say she's the best secretary. Don't you think she would be the best wife, too?"

He laughed. "John thought so."

Randa bent over in laughter. "I wish I could tell Mol…"

Quinn waved his finger back and forth. "Not on your life, young lady, you promised. We'll figure out places to go with a semblance of privacy."

"Oh, Uncle Quinn, Molly and I could help."

"That's not necessary. We're grown adults. I don't think we'll need your help."

"Pleease."

He sighed. "We'll see."

Randa reached for her book. "Did I tell you John called me Saturday and told me about all the drinking stuff? I already knew he was probably drinking. He said you told him he had to apologize for worrying me. Do you know what else he said? He told me he loved me and missed me a whole bunch. I can't remember him ever telling me that before. He said he'd call me like we agreed when I moved to Chicago."

"And did you forgive him?"

My Name is Randa

"Of course! Didn't you know I would?"

"Yes, but John didn't think he deserved to be forgiven. It was a hard call for him to make. I think it would be nice if you thanked him for apologizing."

"Okay. I'll write him a letter." She opened her book, thought a minute, and said, "I went to see Nora today. I wanted to make her birthday cake, but she said she'd be out of town. She acted kind of funny. Did she know then?"

He chuckled. "Yes, I asked her last week."

***

Quinn went to bed thanking and praising God for Esther's ring and for Nora, who had such lovely curves. Thankfully, she couldn't read his mind.

He saw the love light in her eyes today. Did she see love in his?

Chapter 47

Wednesday, March 10

Wednesday morning, Quinn was sitting in his office reading the morning paper when Nora arrived.

She stepped into his office and said, "Good morning. Do you have an early meeting?"

"No, I couldn't wait any longer to see your sweet face," he said. "This morning, I realized you have started your days in a cold office for two years. I promise from today on, the office will be warm when you arrive, and coffee will be ready."

"Quinn, I love making everything ready for you and seeing your smile of appreciation. It's my way of taking care of you. Please don't take this little joy away from me."

He slid a finger along the side of her face. "Okay, but the office will be warm when you arrive. You can do the rest. Thank you for taking care of me."

She sat in the chair beside his desk, and he poured coffee. "Is Randa happy about our date?"

"She's ecstatic. She and Molly have been praying for us. I made her promise not to tell anyone about our birthday plans until it's over. I don't know what'll be worse, dating in front of my niece or dating in front of the entire congregation."

"That's easy. You have a certain amount of control over Randa, but I can't say the same about our congregation."

Quinn glanced at the clock and said, "It's time to put on our professional faces. Did you know I'm having trouble concentrating on my work when you're in the other room? You, my dear, are a beautiful distraction."

My Name is Randa

"I'll fix that," she said, then waved with her fingers and closed his door. It was sweet to hear Randa and Molly had been praying for them.

Later in the morning, Esther entered the office and immediately noticed the closed door. She whispered, "Why is Quinn's door closed?"

Nora blushed. "We just don't want anyone to know about us until after our birthday."

"Well, this won't work." Esther rapped on Quinn's door and opened it. "You're going about this all wrong. I love coming into this office; it's so friendly. You and Nora accomplish your tasks with the door open. Your interaction with each other gives the office a warm, welcoming feeling. Go back to the way you were."

Quinn breathed a sigh of relief. "Thank you, Esther. It was lonely in here."

She slapped her forehead. "Now, I can't remember why I stopped by. I'm leaving, but next time I stop by, that door better be open."

Esther left the office, and Quinn winked at Nora. "Checking on us, wasn't she?"

***

Thursday morning, Tim ran into Quinn at the post office and suggested they have coffee at the diner. "We're happy that you're courtin' our little mother," he said.

Quinn glanced around to see if anybody was nearby. "We're trying to keep this quiet until after we get back from Madison."

"Nobody heard me. I didn't talk that loud. You probably haven't met Clyde yet. He's Aunt Esther's oldest son. If you need advice or anything, Reverend Clyde Pearson is your man. Julie and I went to Madison for special dates. We'd stay overnight at their house and come home early the next morning. You'll like them."

***

Nora caught herself sitting on the chair beside Quinn's desk more often than necessary, and he took to sitting on the corner of her desk, so she rearranged the items on the top of her desk and made space for him. Sweet delicious moments entered their days, and the world stopped when they gave each other a secret smile. Or Quinn would look up, catch her glance and send her a secret wink.

The week progressed, and cherished moments ebbed and flowed as their love blossomed. He'd walk past her desk and brush his hand across her shoulder. She ran her fingers down his arm. Quinn thought she needed a kiss. They hadn't had their first date, and he couldn't wait to take her in his arms. He loved Nora. How long would he have to wait before she'd say she loved him?

The phone rang early Saturday morning. "Hello, Quinn. This is Julie. My mother tells me Randa promised to keep a secret and that she might explode at any moment. If Randa needs a place to stay overnight or for the day, she's welcome. Of course, you know our favorite topic will be your trip to Madison."

"Thank you, Julie. You're an answer to my prayers. If you could keep her on Tuesday and Wednesday night, I would appreciate it. I'm sure she could stay at the Thompsons, but I don't think she could keep her promise. That girl is like Yellowstone's bubbling geyser, about to erupt. We don't want anyone but family to know about us. Thank you for offering. I'm sure she'll be calling you when I give her the news."

Chapter 48

Tuesday, March 16

Quinn's freshly washed car faded into the late afternoon as he drove away from the Hunters'. Randa plopped her schoolbooks on the dining room table. "Uncle Quinn said to tell you I have homework. I'll do it after supper."

Tim put a finger to his lips, but it was too late. Randa hadn't noticed the twins asleep in their playpen. Jordie twitched and woke with a howl. Rosie whimpered, and Randa groaned. "I'm sorry."

The parents rushed to pick up their babies. "Don't worry; it was time for them to wake. You can help by heating bottles," Julie said.

Randa brought warm bottles into the living room and handed one to Tim and the other to Julie. The room quieted as the hungry babies latched onto their dinner.

Randa sank into the corner of the dark old horsehair couch with a sigh. "I love your old furniture. It wraps around me and is the most comfortable I've ever sat in. I made bell cookies for them to take to Madison. Uncle Quinn asked me why I used a Christmas cookie cutter. I told him it wasn't Christmas; I made wedding bells.

"At last, I can talk about their date. I have lots of questions. When Molly and I told her mom, we were praying they'd fall in love; she told us not to talk about it to anyone. She didn't want us to embarrass them, but I told Uncle Quinn after he said they were going to Madison for their birthday."

Tim put Jordie on his shoulder and patted his back. He glanced at his wife and said, "You go first."

"I understand you want to help them find places where they can have some privacy. I doubt they will need your help. They'll want to discover the depth of their affection privately."

Randa's smile vanished. "You mean they aren't in love? They just have affection? I thought they were in love."

Tim took over. "Honey, they like each other and work well together. Your uncle has asked our little mother for a date, and now they'll start learning who they are, away from work. I'm thinkin' they're both excited and a little scared. They're cautious people, so I 'spect it will take a bit of time for them to discover if they love each other."

"But if they kiss each other, won't they know they're in love? They know in my books."

Julie grinned at Tim and said, "May I remind you Zane Grey's books are fiction? My mother taught me girls don't kiss on the first date."

"You didn't kiss Tim on your first date?"

She laughed, "No. I hardly knew him, although I liked him from the first."

"But Uncle Quinn and Nora already know each other. I hope they kiss before they come home."

Julie grinned at Tim and said, "There's a good chance we'll never know when they have their first kiss. They're going to save many things they do as their own private memories. I know in the days ahead, you'll want to know how things are going in their romance, but it is their *private* business. When you have a question you think might be private, ask us first. Call me and we'll decide together if it's an acceptable question for you to ask."

Randa's shoulders drooped. "Okay, Uncle Quinn said I should ask you or Molly's parents or Aunt Esther." She sighed. "I have so many things I want to tell Molly, and ev-

My Name is Randa

erything is a secret. This dating thing is going to—It's hard to keep a secret from Molly. We tell each other everything.

"I've always wished for brothers and sisters. If Nora and Uncle Quinn get married, could I be your sister and Tim, my big brother? Uncle Quinn told me a long time ago he's too old to have babies."

"Well, that depends on how this dating thing works out. Let's wait and see what happens next."

***

Julie laid her head on the back of the rocker, in the middle of the night, and enjoyed the peaceful quiet while her babies slept.

Her mind flashed back to that horrible day, May 4,1951, when she learned her daddy died. Her mother was inconsolable for weeks. There were days they feared Nora wouldn't be able to climb out of her terrible grief.

Five months later, Tim came into her life, and he helped them heal from their grief. Today, Quinn and her mother looked so happy, and Randa was bubbling over with joy.

"God, thank you. Thank you for letting us watch them fall in love. Give them a wonderful birthday. Thank you for Randa, a little sister for us to love and watch out for. O Lord, my heart is full of joy for all you have done for us."

Chapter 49

To Madison

Tuesday, March 16

Quinn stepped into Nora's house. The drapes were closed, her suitcase sat on the shiny hardwood floor, and they were all alone. "Nora, I don't know how to start this."

She smiled at him with a slight tremor in her voice. "How would you like to start it?"

"I'd like you in my arms, and a kiss would be nice. I've been thinking about it for days."

She blushed and said in a soft voice, "I'd like that."

Quinn pulled her close and tenderly kissed her. Nora's hands slid up his chest and around his neck. She drew him down for another kiss, then tucked her head under his chin and said, "That was very nice."

He backed away, kissed the tip of her nose, and said, "I was afraid you'd be a believer that girls don't kiss on the first date. I didn't expect this. We seem to be a little further along than I dared to wish for. Nora Montgomery, I love you. I have for quite a while and didn't know it."

"I didn't either, but it…"

"My darling, we need to give thanks." He touched his forehead to hers. "Lord, thank you for this lovely woman in my arms. Thank you for kisses. Thank you for Drew, who opened my eyes. Thank you for Randa and Molly's prayers. Thank you for the love you've put in our hearts for each other. Esther says everybody is watching; show us how to be a good example in their presence …"

They drove away in silence while love seeped into their beings. Quinn turned onto the highway to Madison. "We

238

My Name is Randa

should stop someplace soon and have dinner. Do you know a place?"

"Yes, about ten miles ahead, there's a little café that serves wonderful beef stew."

***

Quinn waited until their meal came and said, "Nora, tell me what helped you accept my birthday invitation."

"It shocked me when you asked, and I wanted you to come back and explain yourself. I fussed for days before I realized I'd love to have a date with you. The week I was at Julie's house with the babies, I missed you so much. I can't believe I didn't figure it out then. The same thing happened on Christmas morning. I wanted to be with you and Randa, but the thing that convinced me was a dream."

"A dream. Did you dream about me?"

Nora nodded. "The night before your interview, I had a dream. I saw my guardian angel in a mirror wearing a chambray shirt... then he blew me a kiss and said, *Goodbye, Little Mother.*"

Quinn scooped a spoonful full of stew and held it in mid-air. "I've heard many guardian-angel stories, but none of them wore a chambray shirt."

Nora continued. "Saturday, I was at Julie's, and Bert Calhoun stopped by wearing a chambray shirt. That reminded me of what my guardian angel said."

"What did he say?"

She smiled. "That my heart was filled with love, and I wasn't to be afraid to love you."

A big grin spread across his face. Quinn buttered his bread but left it on the plate. "Thinking back, I believe I was already in love with you when Julie went into labor. I *had* to be there to take care of you while you waited for the twins

Marg Watland

to be born. Everybody prayed for the twins, but all I could pray for was you." He winked. "We could elope."

"Quinn, you're going too fast. I know the word marriage is in our dreams, but we don't really know each other. I know Reverend Quinn Edwards, but I don't know the man Quinn Daniel Edwards."

"My dear sweet Nora, I believe you know me better than you think."

"No, I don't." She sat up straight in her chair. "Neither of us have seen each other angry. Quinn, please, don't ever avoid me after asking me such an unexpected question. You walked out of the church office, went to the hospital, and I didn't see you for four days. First, it made me mad, and then I felt abandoned.

"It took two days—forty-eight hours—to get past the anger." Nora sat back in her chair with a tiny smile on her face and said, "Then I remembered you hadn't been yourself for several days. I think you were worried that I wouldn't want to have a date with you."

Quinn stared at her with his mouth gaping open. He hoped she felt better because he didn't. This was a Nora that he didn't know, and she would not let him get away with the way he treated her.

"I'm sorry. I didn't intentionally avoid or abandon you. Yes, I was afraid I would lose you. I didn't know if you would date an old man like me."

"You are *not* an old man. I think you're a handsome, exciting man. Sunday, I went to the cemetery and told Carl I loved you. I'm scared and happy and in love."

"I've never thought of myself as exciting, but I'm pleased you think so."

Quinn shifted in his seat. How does a man kiss and make up while sitting in a restaurant filled with people? He need-

My Name is Randa

ed to get her back in the car, so he could take her in his arms and show her how sorry he was.

***

As they drove towards Madison, Nora said, "Let me give you some more examples of things we don't know about each other. What is your favorite food? What do you refuse to eat? Do you like to read? Did you know I read mysteries, hate liver, and my favorite food is bread?"

"I read three different newspapers: Time magazine, Don's Farm Journal and several Christian periodicals, aside from the Bible, commentaries, concordances, and reference books that go with writing a sermon. I rarely have time to read for pleasure. I like biographies, prefer meat and potatoes to vegetables, and refuse to eat Julie's peanut butter and dill pickle sandwiches. Randa told me Julie offered her one."

Nora laughed. "Don't knock it till you've tried it. Everyone in my family eats them."

"Randa eats toast with peanut butter and jam for breakfast, and I've even succumbed to eating them when I'm in a hurry or have an early appointment."

Nora adjusted the borrowed ring on her finger and said, "Do you have special dreams you hope to accomplish?"

"Yes, I want to write my sister's story. Several people have said I should. I'm thinking of asking Randa to write it with me. What about you, Nora? Do you have dreams?"

"I'd like to go to the Holy Land and walk where Jesus walked and go to Washington DC in the spring and see the cherry blossoms."

He patted her hand. "I haven't been to Israel. We'll plan to do that, not this year, but I promise we'll go."

They drove in silence for several minutes, then Nora said, "Your beard isn't scratchy; it's soft and tickles a little. I like it."

Mary Watland

He turned and grinned at her, then had to jerk the car back to his side of the road. She slammed up against him. Quinn put his arm along the back of the seat. "Pretend you're a high school girl and scoot in real close."

"Reverend Edwards, I'm surprised at you. I'm a mature woman, and that is not at all ladylike." She settled herself directly in front of the rear-view mirror.

Nora enjoyed being close to him, but should she have told Quinn she loved him? She couldn't help herself; it just came out. He loved her, she loved him, and he *was* exciting.

***

On the outskirts of Madison, Nora directed him to turn into a tree-lined lane. He turned a last bend into the front of a grand old three-story farmhouse and said, "That house is huge."

"Phyllis inherited it from her grandmother. In another month, the early flowers will bloom, and the place will be spectacular. It's getting too dark to see tonight. I'll show you around in the morning."

The front door burst open, and three children ran out to meet them. The eldest said, "I'm Nancy, and these are my brothers, Edward and Thomas. My daddy's at church, and Mother's upstairs changing a light bulb, so we get to greet Aunt Nora's reverend first."

Quinn took Nancy's hand in his. "My niece Randa can't wait to meet you. She wants cousins her age. She has two boy cousins, the age of your brothers. All my relatives are adults or small children."

Phyliss called from the front porch. "Come in; it's cold out here. Children, help them with their luggage."

Phyliss led them to the living room and said, "We are so pleased to finally meet you, Quinn."

242

My Name is Randa

Outside, a car door slammed, and minutes later, Clyde entered the living room.

Nora said, "I'm sure your mother has told you all about Quinn."

"Yes," Clyde said, and winked at Quinn. "I've become well acquainted with you through my mother. It's nice to put a face to the man Mother says is changing the life of my Aunt Nora. Every time we talk, she has to tell me the latest news about you. Mother tells me you both have the same birthday."

"Yes, but I'm ten years older."

Phyllis laughed. "My dad is thirteen years older than Mother. He tells her he enjoys living with a young chick. It keeps him from getting old. So, you don't have to worry about the difference in your age. We're thrilled that you care for each other."

Quinn took Nora's hand, gazed into her eyes, and said, "More every day." He brought her hand to his lips. Time stopped for them as they smiled at each other. Their hosts watched in delight as they witnessed the joy on their faces and waited for them to remember where they were.

Quinn looked at Clyde and said, "Tim tells me you give excellent advice. We'd like to have a few dates before the whole congregation knows. When the time comes, I don't quite know how to tell them we're dating."

Clyde's deep laughter resounded in the room, and his eyes sparkled with amusement. "Quinn, you don't have to tell them anything. It's my understanding several have already figured it out. Mom tells us it's the talk of the church."

***

That night, Quinn stacked pillows behind his back and prepared to unwind. He opened his Bible to read a few of his favorite Psalms. An hour later, he shut his Bible and lay reviewing the things he and Nora had discussed. She was right. He didn't know her as well as he thought. What obstacles were they going to discover as they learned more about each other?

He straightened the pillows and closed his eyes. "Jesus, thank you for bringing Nora into my life."

Chapter 50

Wednesday, March 17, 1954

Quinn waited to hear voices downstairs before leaving his room. When he entered the kitchen, a chorus of "Good morning, Reverend Edwards" sang out from the Pearson children. Nancy poured him a cup of coffee and said, "Mother is getting dressed. She takes us to school on Wednesdays."

Quinn greeted the children, took a sip of coffee, then walked into the sitting room. The snapping of the wood stove reminded him of his home in Michigan. He sat in a chair near the warmth and watched the flames rise and fall through the glass window of the stove.

The Pearson family had left before Nora came downstairs. He stood with arms open. "Happy Birthday, my darling." She walked into his arms and tipped her face up for his kiss. "Mmm, you smell good."

She blushed. "Thank you. I spent extra time getting ready. I wanted to look my best for you. Happy Birthday to you, too."

He touched her hot cheeks. "You look beautiful, all pink like that. I love your curls, and your gorgeous figure, and your sweet lips, and …"

"Ooh …" She hid her rosy face in his neck and said a shaky, "Thank you."

He whispered in her ear. "Did I say too much, too soon?"

She peeked up at him. "No, I like it, but I'm not used to hearing some of the things you say."

This modest little lady was going to change his life. God had blessed him with the perfect woman. Why did it take so long for him to realize he loved her? He picked up his

245

testament and said, "I start my day with a Psalm. Do you have a favorite?"

"Yes, Psalms thirty-four. When Carl died, that was the chapter the Lord gave me. Often, I felt God's presence beside me while he healed me from my grief. No matter how bad it was, the first thing I needed to do each morning was 'bless the Lord and praise Him,' like it says in verse one. Verse four says, 'I sought the Lord, and he heard me, and delivered me from all my fears.' God brought me out of the hardest time in my life through those verses."

Quinn turned to the chapter and read it aloud. His heart soared with happiness. Today, he heard how the Lord spoke to her through the Psalms and got a glimpse of her inner thoughts. She'd expect the same from him. His reticent personality kept him from sharing personal thoughts, but with Nora, it would be different. He wanted her to know everything about him.

***

They drove around the University of Wisconsin and then along Lake Wingra. Quinn parked the car facing the lake and put his arm around her. "Nora, surely you know Randa adores you." He rested his chin on her head. "I love you and want to marry you, but it isn't because Randa needs a mother. My heart is full of love for you. I don't know how or when it happened, but it's there."

"I know." She patted his chest. "I see it in your smile; the way you look at me takes my breath away. I love you, too."

He drew her closer, and they sat quietly, letting their love grow.

Nora broke the silence. "Do you like old things? Family heirlooms?"

"I do. My dad's grandfather built the house I was raised in. There was furniture in our house from both my

My Name is Randa

great-grandparents and my grandparents. I'm used to old things. I miss living in a big old house."

"Carl and I bought a two-bedroom bungalow to start with. We planned to buy a bigger house when the children came, but that wasn't to be. I miscarried twice before I had Julie. The doctor said it was a miracle I carried her the full nine months, and then he told us I wouldn't have any more babies. I always dreamed of living in a big house filled with little Montgomerys, but with only one child, we stayed where we were."

The car shuddered from a burst of wind, and white caps lapped against the shore. Students hurried toward nearby buildings. Nora shivered and snuggled closer to Quinn's warm body. "I promised Julie I'd show the owner of Alhric's Heirloom Furniture pictures of the twins. The kids bought several pieces from Hubert for their home. Could we go there now?"

He started the car, turned the heater on high, and she directed him to a refurbished red barn.

Inside, Quinn looked around in amazement at the large inventory. "No wonder Julie likes this store. There's so much to choose from."

They walked up and down the aisles, and he pointed out simple pieces that had beautiful wood grains. When they came to the Victorian furniture, he said, "I don't like all those curves. They're too fussy and collect too much dust."

Nora said she didn't like the large oak pieces. "These are too heavy; they have no beauty in their lines."

Quinn didn't comment; but decided they might have to do some compromising when Nora started furnishing their home. He liked the sound of that, *their home.*

They wandered through both floors and took advantage of being the only people on the upper level, where there was a large grouping of rocking chairs. Quinn pushed a small rocker with no arms. "We had a rocker in our kitchen like this. I rocked that chair all over the kitchen. I got many a swat for making marks on the linoleum."

They chose platform rockers and reminisced to the ticking of an old pendulum clock as they rocked.

At dusk, they returned to the Pearson's, and Quinn suggested Nora have a rest.

By six o'clock, Quinn was dressed in his best suit and a green tie that he always wore on Saint Patrick's Day. He heard voices and went downstairs to greet the family.

Phyllis was putting food on the table when Quinn came around the corner. "Hi, I don't want to interrupt your meal. I saw the newspaper in the living room and thought I'd read it while I wait for Nora. Enjoy your dinner." As he walked by the stairs, he heard water running in the upstairs bathroom and knew Nora wouldn't be long.

He sat on a black Windsor bench that faced the stairs. Nora came down wearing an emerald-green dress that emphasized her shining eyes. She carried a package topped with a green bow.

"I don't want to carry your birthday present to the restaurant. I'd like to give it to you now," she said.

They sat together on the bench while Quinn unwrapped the package. He lifted the lid and saw her likeness in a dark leather frame.

"Oh, my darling, there is nothing I would like better. Thank you." With his finger, he circled her heart-shaped face, tipped up her chin, and just as his lips touched hers, he heard a rustle. Quinn looked up to see Nancy with a surprised look on her face. "Hello, Nancy; I haven't gotten used to kissing Nora in front of people yet, but she has given me my birthday present, and I want to thank her."

"Oh, okay. I'll close my eyes, and you can kiss her."

My Name is Randa

Quinn kissed Nora's soft lips. "Mmm." He looked up, grinned, and whispered in her ear. "Look at Nancy." She stood in front of them with hands over her eyes.

Nora laughed. "You can open your eyes now, honey."

Nancy took her hands away and said, "I'm sorry."

Quinn motioned her over. "Would you like to see my gift?"

She ducked her head and nodded before taking a step toward them. "You look real pretty, Aunt Nora."

Phyllis marched into the room. Nancy said, "I didn't see anything. I closed my eyes so I couldn't see him kiss her."

Phyllis mouthed, "Sorry," and turned Nancy around. "I see a present in Quinn's hands, and I believe they need some privacy." She gave her daughter a gentle push, and they disappeared around the corner.

From the kitchen, they heard Clyde say, "Nancy, we told you to stay away from them."

"But Daddy, I just wanted to see what they were wearing." The voices faded as the family moved into the sitting room.

Quinn and Nora struggled to keep from laughing. He handed her a small square box and said, "Part of it is on order, but I think you like this color."

She pulled the paper away, and earrings of pale pink crystal lay in the box. "Oh, they're so pretty, and I love the color. I have several things that will go with them. Thank you."

"I apologize. A necklace goes with it, but it didn't arrive on time."

Nora slid her hands up his chest. "Is there anyone behind me?" He shook his head. She touched her lips to his and tightened her arms around his neck. Quinn smiled when he heard a muffled "Mmm" against his lapel.

They took their presents into the sitting room for everyone to see. Quinn asked the boys if they would put the gifts in their rooms, and he and Nora left for the restaurant.

***

A young man sat at a baby grand piano playing a melody Nora didn't recognize. A pretty young hostess in a green floor-length dress led them into a candle-lit room. She seated them at a table facing a large window with a view of the city and the glowing capital building. Nora's eyes shone at the breathtaking sight. Quinn reached for her hand. "Clyde made the reservations for us and told them it was for a special occasion."

She looked around the elegant room. "I've never been here. It's beautiful."

"I'm glad. I wanted to take you somewhere nice, and I'd say this is more than nice." Most of the songs were Irish, which delighted Quinn. The pianist played a few bars of "My Wild Irish Rose" and then asked everyone to sing along with him.

The pianist announced there was a couple in the room who were both celebrating their birthdays. Four servers and the hostess approached Quinn and Nora's table, carrying a small cake topped with two lighted green candles. The quartet led everyone in singing "Happy Birthday." Nora's eyes sparkled.

Quinn asked their waiter if they could stay a while longer. "Yes, sir, stay as long as you want. This place is yours for the evening."

They finished their cake and Nora asked, "Quinn, do you know when you started caring for me?"

"No. When Drew asked if there was anything going on between us, his matchmaking irritated me. I didn't want anything to come between us. You're the best secretary I've ever had."

He looked thoughtful. "I remember once wishing I could dig my fingers into your curls. I've had to restrain myself from hugging you a few times. It never crossed my mind that I had feelings for you. The only thing I can figure is God sent Drew to our house to open my eyes.

"Nora, the love I have for you differs from any love I've ever known. How about you? Do you know when it started for you?"

"Not really. Maybe it was when you stayed with me while Julie was in labor, but I'm not sure. My biggest concern that day was Julie and those babies, but then you took me in your arms and promised you wouldn't leave me until Esther got to the hospital. I liked your arms around me; it felt like I belonged there."

"I didn't want to let go, and then when we got to the hospital, I wanted to hold your hand, but reverends don't hold their secretary's hand. It isn't proper."

"When you asked me for a date, I couldn't believe it. It was the furthest thing from my mind." She squeezed his hand. "I'm having such a wonderful time. I can't remember being this happy for a very long time. This day has been perfect."

"It's perfect for me, too, because you're with me."

Chapter 51

Thursday afternoon, March 18

Randa ran up the stairs, bounded into Quinn's office, and plopped on a chair. He looked at her animated face and saw a joy that equaled his. When Nora joined their family, Randa would have a father *and* a mother. He stood and gave his niece a big hug.

"Did you have fun? What did you eat for dinner? Was it a really fancy restaurant?" Randa said before taking a breath.

Quinn smiled and teased her with the bare facts. "We stayed with Esther's eldest son, Reverend Clyde Pearson, and his wife, Phyllis. They live in a six-bedroom house."

Randa's eyes opened wide. "Do they have servants?"

"I don't think so, but Nora said they have gardeners, and I'm sure they must have a housekeeper. Did you have fun staying with Tim and Julie and the babies?"

"Yes, we talked and talked. Rosie smiles the most, but Jordie makes bubbles. When you get married, I'll be an auntie. I can't wait. Have you propo..." Randa covered her mouth with both hands. "I'm sorry, that's probably private." She quickly switched to another question. "Tell me about the Pearson kids."

"I'm happy to report the Pearsons' oldest child, Nancy, is six months younger than you. She has two brothers, Eddie and Tommy. Nancy says almost all her cousins are boys, and she can't wait to meet you."

Randa's questions might become a problem for them. Nora didn't deserve an interrogation every time they had a date. He and Nora would have to discuss how to handle Randa's curiosity.

252

My Name is Randa

"Honey, we've only had one date. We aren't ready to talk about marriage. Proposing is between me and Nora, and it is definitely private."

She bounced in delight. "I can't wait to meet Nancy. Can I tell Molly now?"

"Would you wait a few more hours? I have invited Nora over for chili, and she's helping with dinner, so you need to check in with her before you go home. The Thompsons are coming for dessert at seven. I want them to know that Nora and I are dating."

"Okay, but Uncle Quinn, you didn't answer my questions."

"We went to a Geology Museum at the University of Wisconsin. I learned the state rock is red granite, and galena is the state mineral. I have a brochure that shows pictures of the rocks in Wisconsin." Quinn loved Nora for taking him there, but next time he'd take a man.

"Then we toured the state capital. I bought a picture postcard of the capital for you to see. It's a beautiful building. Someday, we'll take you to Madison with us so you can spend time with Nancy. I think you'll like her."

"Good, I want to see her house. Six is a lot of bedrooms. I would be happy if we had a guest room. I guess I better go see Nora about dinner." She gave Quinn a hug and left for Nora's house.

Quinn sighed in relief. The church returned to a comfortable quiet, with the familiar creaks and cracks expected from an old building.

***

Nora opened the front door, and questions tumbled out of Randa's mouth in rapid succession. Nora didn't have a ready answer, so she turned to the kitchen and said, "Would you like a snack?"

253

Marg Watland

Randa filled her mouth with a cookie, then gulped down some milk and said, "Julie and Tim told me not to ask any personal or private questions. She said you and Uncle Quinn would save some things for your own private memories, but you didn't answer any of my questions, and I was really careful."

"I think Quinn and I will tell you about our date another time. The Thompsons are coming to your house for dessert. Let's wait until Sunday when all the family will be together. We need to concentrate on tonight. I have made a Crazy Cake for dessert. Your uncle said he'd pick me up around five. I'd like for you to have the chili hot when we get there, so we can eat right away." Nora handed a cookie to Randa and said, "Here's one to eat on the way home. It will be a late night, so be sure to do your homework first."

Randa left, and Nora chopped cabbage for coleslaw. Dating had suddenly become more complicated. Private memories …? Personal questions …? As always, Julie and Tim were watching out for her. She looked forward to the joys of courtship and the memories accompanying it, but their kids waiting for the latest details would be a challenge.

***

That evening, when the Thompsons arrived, Quinn took their coats and invited them to sit at the dining room table. Once everyone was served, Quinn said, "I've asked you to come tonight because, as my good friends, I want you to know that Nora and I are dating. We went to Madison yesterday and celebrated our birthdays.

Molly jumped up but bumped her leg on the table and plopped back in her chair. She squealed, "They went on a date? Randa, why didn't you tell me?"

"Uncle Quinn wouldn't let me. He told me it was to be a secret until after their first date. I stayed overnight with Julie

My Name is Randa

and Tim, and *finally* I could talk about it, because, of course, they knew all about the date. Molly, it's been really hard to not tell you. He said we get to help them find places to go on their dates, where they can have some privacy."

Ruth sucked in her breath. "I think you need to…"

Randa interrupted. "It's okay. Julie and Tim gave me a jillion rules and said I can't ask personal questions and a whole bunch of other stuff."

Don exhaled and said, "Thank God for Tim and Julie."

"What about you, Nora?" Ruth asked. "What's your side of this story?"

"He asked me on the day Don fell off the ladder and told me to think about it. I didn't have any idea he had thoughts like that. It took me all weekend to realize I'd like to go on a date with him."

Quinn looked at the Thompsons and laughed. "That went well. I think you have a pretty complete picture of how I finally woke up to the fact that I love this woman." He took Nora's hand, kissed it, and said, "She says she loves me too."

Randa bounced in her chair. "You really love each other? I'm soo happy."

Don slipped his arm around Ruth and said, "Well, it took long enough. Are you going to announce it to the congregation on Sunday?" he teased.

In a serious tone, Quinn said, "No, Clyde said I should let them figure it out for themselves."

"*We* could tell them," Randa said.

Ruth and Don spoke in unison, "No."

When it was time to leave, Ruth hugged Nora. "We should get together soon. I expect it will take the two of us to keep those girls in line. You never know what they're going to dream up next. I'm happy for you. "

Don shook Quinn's hand. "Randa kinda stole your thunder, didn't she? I hope you know you're in for a pile of

Mary Watland

teasing. I've forgiven you for bringing that professor to my Bible Study. I'm thinking a longtime friend like him might have clued you in; somebody needed to. You can bring him to another Men's Bible Study any time." He called down the hall. "Molly, we're leaving."

They waved goodbye to their guests, and before Quinn closed the door, they heard Don's laughter resound through the night air.

Randa headed to her favorite spot on the davenport and said, "Did you know John didn't know he loved Mama when he proposed?"

"He didn't?" Quinn pulled Nora close and said, "I believe Randa is about to fill us in on one of those gaps from the first pages of her book of life. Would you like to stay a while longer?"

Nora laughed at him. "There is no way you can get me out of this house until Randa finishes what she just started."

"Well, John asked Mama to marry him when I was one. He told her he didn't love her, but he liked her a lot, and he wanted to take care of us. She knew he loved her, but he felt guilty for wanting to marry his best friend's wife. Mama didn't tell John she loved him until he went overseas."

"Why did she wait so long?" Nora asked.

"Because Mama wanted him to tell her first. She used to tease him about it. John isn't very good at talking about lovey-dovey stuff. He gets embarrassed."

"Do you know where he was stationed?" Quinn asked.

"A couple of different places, but I don't remember where."

Quinn couldn't believe Sarah would marry a guy that couldn't tell her he loved her. That man certainly had some hang-ups about best friends.

Randa grinned. "When John went overseas, Mama changed her mind about not telling him and started send-

My Name is Randa

ing him steamy love letters. Mama used to tease John about the letters they wrote to each other while he was overseas." Randa put her hand over her mouth. "Oh, oh, Mama told me I wasn't to tell anybody about that."

Nora blushed. "You, my young lady, are not any good at keeping secrets." She watched Quinn try to keep a straight face. She patted his hand. "I think it is time for you to take me home."

Quinn chuckled as he helped Nora into the car, and by the time he was behind the wheel, they were both laughing.

Nora caught her breath and said, "My daughter says I am modest beyond reason, and I want you to be careful what you say to me. Steamy letters are close to my limit."

At Nora's house, Quinn pushed the front door shut, and Nora moved into his arms. "Lately, everyone seems to laugh when they walk away from us. Are we being laughed at, or are people laughing with us?"

He kissed her waiting mouth. "My darling Nora, I believe they are laughing with us." He kissed her again and said, "Goodnight, my love."

***

Nora lay in bed, unable to sleep. She had lived an orderly life, and now her life was rushing out of control. He'd marry her next week if she agreed. They needed time between the first date and the wedding, but how much? If Drew was in the wedding, they'd have to wait until school ended. The soonest would be June, and that was barely three months …

Chapter 52

Friday, March 19

At eight-thirty Friday morning, Quinn sat in his church office, remembering Tim's words. *Courting means your intention is marriage.* He had joked with Nora about eloping. They talked about marrying, in a round-about-way, while they were in Madison. So, what next?

When Nora walked into the warm church office, Quinn pulled her into his arms and rubbed his soft beard across her cheek. "You smell good."

"And you smell clean, like soap." She patted the arm around her waist. "Reverend Edwards, we don't want to get caught romancing in the church office now, do we?"

He laughed, "My dear, Esther told you everybody thought we were falling in love. I looked in the mirror this morning and decided it's written on my face. I can't quit smiling. I'm a new man.

"It's early; have a seat while we talk." He rolled his chair a little closer. "The Thompsons weren't surprised last night, were they?"

Nora laughed. "Think about it. They're your friends. Don't you think they might have had an inkling?"

His mouth opened, then closed, and a sheepish grin crossed his face.

"Quinn, do you suppose we could keep this to ourselves for a few days? I need time to catch up. We've skipped the not knowing, the mystery, and the excitement that comes first in courting. You have turned my life upside down, and everything is out of order. What are we supposed to do now?"

My Name is Randa

He winked at her. I'm sorry, my darling, it seems I have skipped courting. We'll have to make up new rules as we go along."

Quinn took a step toward Nora and stopped. She looked nervous about something. Her mouth trembled. "How would you feel about Saturday, August 28, for our wedding?

A big grin spread across his face. "Five months! Thank you."

She stepped closer, and her curls co-mingled with his beard. Quinn thought his heart might beat out of his chest. This brave little woman would not make him wait for some impossible tradition before they could wed. "I love you, Nora Montgomery," he said and kissed her right there in the church office.

When Nora pulled away, he said, "If it's all right with you, I'd like Drew to marry us and Tim to be my best man."

"I'll ask Julie to stand with me. Let's think of something for Randa to do, so our entire family can be included." She tucked her head under his chin for a moment and said, "If we're not careful, someone is going to come into this office and find me in your arms."

"I can't help it. When the woman I love tells me when we can marry, I have to kiss her, even if I get caught." He dropped a kiss on her curls, then forced himself to release her.

The phone rang, and a woman asked to speak to Reverend Edwards.

When Quinn finished talking to her, he came out and sat on the corner of Nora's desk. "That was Erik Larson's secretary, and there's a report back from the private investigator. He wants to see me. I made an afternoon appointment on

Monday. Would you go with me? I don't want to read that report without you."

"Of course, I'd be happy to. I pray there aren't bad things in it."

Would Leland Shepherd's family be a bunch of losers? John and Lee were friends, but ... He sighed. Maybe he should give them the benefit of the doubt. John liked Lee, and Sarah loved him. It was possible his family were honest, hard-working people.

He glanced at his watch; it was past time to start work. Nora was removing the cover from her typewriter, but he had one more thing to check out.

Quinn turned to his bookcase and reached high for a dictionary, then squatted to take an old tattered one from the bottom shelf. He stacked five books on his desk; three dictionaries from different eras, an encyclopedia labeled R, and a thesaurus. He thumbed through each book and jotted words on a note card, saying them under his breath as he wrote, "love, deep affection, attraction, romance, wooing, excitement, flattering ..." Quinn slipped the card between pages in his pocket Testament, dropped it in his briefcase and whispered. "I messed up on the *courting*. Let's see if I can do a better job of *romancing*."

Chapter 53

Saturday, March 20

The next morning, Quinn called Warren Campbell and asked to see the old Heinrich place. He had driven by the boarded-up house on several occasions. It reminded Quinn of his old family home, and he wanted to see inside.

Warren swept his flashlight around the rooms and said, "The records show this house was built in 1872 by Emanuel Heinrich. The broken windows were boarded up five years ago, and nobody has looked at the house since."

They walked through rooms with gritty floors, sagging wallpaper, and a hand pump at the kitchen sink. The rooms were spacious, but it wasn't anything he could show to Nora.

***

That evening, Quinn called Drew. "Hi. Could you marry us on Saturday, August 28th?"

Drew laughed. "That soon, huh?"

Quinn grinned. "I suggested we could elope, but she wants to be courted."

"I would be honored to marry you and Nora."

***

The girls kept their secret on Sunday morning. They stood to the side with big grins and watched the people file out after church. Don and Ruth stood nearby. After Quinn finished shaking hands, he thanked them for being discreet and winked at Molly's parents.

Following dinner at Nora's, Tim and Julie put the twins down for a nap, and the family gathered in the living room to hear about *the date*.

Nora and Quinn had discussed what they wanted to be private and personal, and Quinn gave Randa a list of unacceptable questions. When Julie heard about the list, she winked at Quinn and asked, "Where's my list?"

Randa asked, "Did you go to a romantic place for dinner? Was it dark with candles on every table? What did you do all day?"

Nora took the first questions. "We had a candlelight dinner at The Stone House. It was elegant. Each table had white tablecloths, a shamrock plant, and green candles in pretty crystal candleholders.

"Clyde called ahead and told them it was our birthday, so after dinner, they brought out a little birthday cake with two green candles, and everybody sang happy birthday to us. When we left, the hostess handed us a shamrock to take home." Nora pointed to the plant. "I thought the coffee table was a good place for it."

Quinn picked up the plant and said, "The Irish Catholics say that according to Saint Patrick, the three leaves represent the Father, the Son, and the Holy Spirit. My Grandma O'Reilly said the leaves represent faith, hope, and love."

"Uncle Quinn, I think we need a shamrock plant for our house, because we're Irish, too."

Everybody laughed, and then Nora said, "Quinn tells me he has a collection of his mother's Irish records. I'll have to borrow a few. I'm not familiar with many Irish tunes."

Quinn took his turn. "I want to go back to Madison when Phyllis' flowers are in bloom. That place must be beautiful; even in winter, it looks like a park."

My Name is Randa

"Julie likes to go in the spring," Tim said. "I like the red flowers in the fall. Wait 'till the roses start bloomin'. You'll come back smelling like Julies' rose perfume."

Randa pulled Goldie into her lap and said, "Julie told me every bedroom in their house is a different color. I want to see all their bedrooms, but most of all, I want to meet Nancy."

***

On the way home from Nora's house, Randa wondered how long it would be before Uncle Quinn proposed. They looked so in love. Their happiness made her feel all warm and safe inside. Tomorrow, she would play some of her grandma's old Irish records; after all, she was Irish, and she needed to know what Irish music sounded like.

Chapter 54

Monday, March 22

Nora's hand rested on the menu, but she made no move to open it. Quinn recognized from the stance of her body that she was trying to work through a problem. He gave her time, then pulled change out of his pocket and held up a coin. "A penny for your thoughts."

She looked up. "Where are we going to live?"

"I'd like a two-story house with big rooms where we could have groups of people in for meals and meetings. Now that I have Randa, that will include parties for her friends. I'd like to buy us a house. Would you like that?"

"I'd love it." She was envious of Tim and Julie's big two-and-a-half-story, four-square house. A large home would be a dream come true.

Nora opened the menu and said, "Forgive me for ignoring you. I have so much on my mind. I was asking the Lord to help us blend into a family of three. We have to stay young for Randa. We'll need younger friends like the Thompsons. I like them, and I'm glad they're your friends."

"Yes, my darling, we'll make new friends, but right now, I feel ten years younger. Loving you has changed me."

"I know. When I think about you, I feel giddy." She blushed and looked around to see if anyone noticed her red cheeks.

Quinn chuckled. "You look beautiful, all pink like that."

She looked at him with a tiny smile. "If we look for a house, the secret will be out. Somebody will see us and start asking questions. I have to confess, I'm ready to have the secrets end. I'm sorry that I keep changing my mind. I guess

My Name is Randa

we can't do anything in the traditional way. I give up. I'll just have to enjoy whatever the day holds."

"Will that be so bad, my dear? We can look forward to each day being a happy surprise." He pointed to her menu and said, "Right now, you need some nourishment. We have an hour before our appointment with Erik."

***

When they arrived at Erik's office, Quinn glanced at the secretary's name plate and said, "Donna, this is Nora Montgomery. I'd like her to read the report with me."

"It's nice to meet you, Nora." Donna picked up a large manila envelope and led them to a conference room directly behind her desk. "Mr. Larson wanted to give you time to read the report before he meets with you. Let me know when you're ready." She handed the envelope to Quinn, then turned and closed the door behind her. They sat along one side of a beautiful oval cherry wood table. Quinn pulled the pages out of the envelope.

First was a copy of Leland's birth certificate. Together they looked at the certificate, and Nora gasped. She read, "Father Unknown. Oh, Quinn, do you think Lee's mother was forced? If that's true, she would have been shunned the rest of her life, and so would her son."

"I don't know. All Randa told me is he was raised in Missouri and didn't have any family. I was afraid of something like this. I don't want Randa exposed to riff-raff. She doesn't have to know about her father's family. I'm tempted to tear this up."

"We need to read the entire report before you tear anything up," she said.

"I know. I said *tempted*." He picked up another page, and they read a note from the investigator. "The following account was told by Sophia Shepherd Wagner, age 84 years, and recorded by my secretary May Barrett on March 11, 1954."

"My brother Elwin's wife Louisa was with child and bad sick with consumption when they moved to Colorado, a drier climate. Mother told me to go with them.

Their little baby girl was born early and was so tiny we made her a bed in a boot box. They named her Miranda Marie. Louisa died a month after the birth, and Elwin four months later. I took the baby home to my mother, and she and my stepfather, Joseph Olson, raised Elwin's baby.

Miranda was seventeen when she went to a dance, and some drunk guy laid her down in the dirt and made her a mother. "

Nora curled her arm around Quinn's. "I don't think these people were riff raff; they just had terrible things happen to them."

"Miranda named her son Leland. When Lee was five, my stepfather got real sick, and Mother told all of us we needed to help raise Leland. Miranda got a live-in housekeeping job.

I took him first. Every year a different relative took him in. Some of my brother's wives weren't very good to him. Leland went to a different school every year until he got to high school.

Not long after he graduated from high school, Leland and his friend Eldon Burton left for a job in Oklahoma.

"We heard he married some young girl, and then we heard he got killed in a railroad accident in Arizona, but we didn't know he had a child. That's nice they named the little girl Miranda after her grandma.

Signed by: Sophia Shepherd Wagner

My Name is Randa

"This is so sad," Nora said. Quinn picked up another page. It listed four generations of names and dates ending with Leland's death in 1940 and his mothers in 1946.

"Didn't you tell me Sarah and Leland had a happy marriage?" Nora asked. "That poor boy needed someone to love him." Her hand gripped his. "Randa doesn't need to know this, at least not now."

After they read all the pages, Quinn leaned back in his chair and said, "Thank goodness, there's no criminal record." He slid the pages back into the envelope and stepped out to tell Donna they were ready.

Erik came to the conference room and invited them back to his office.

Quinn introduced Nora and said, "I wanted her to read the report with me." He held up the envelope. "We can't show this to Randa."

"No, you can't. If she doesn't know you asked for a search of her father's background, lock it up and let it lay. You'll know if or when you want to give her this information." He smiled at Nora. "Are you Carl Montgomery's widow?"

She nodded. "Pease call me Nora."

"I worked with Carl on several occasions. He was a good man. I'm sorry for your loss."

Quinn looked at Nora, and she nodded. "Well, things have changed. You are one of the first to know. Nora and I are getting married the end of August."

"Congratulations, I think you'll be a fine addition to the Edwards family. Carl would want you to marry again."

Nora hadn't thought about what Carl would think. They'd never talked about his dying. She knew he would want her to be happy. Yes, Erik was right, Carl would want her to marry again."

Erik pulled two sheets of paper out of his drawer. "I don't believe you've had time to discuss a will while you were getting yourselves engaged, so here is a list of questions you will want to consider before you come back to see me."

***

When Quinn helped Nora into his car, she said, "Just drop me off. Randa has been home for over an hour, and she doesn't know where you are."

Quinn insisted on walking Nora to her door. He followed her inside and pulled her close. "I'm not leaving until I kiss my bride-to-be goodbye."

***

Randa stood waiting for him at the kitchen door. "I made roast beef sandwiches and a salad for our dinner," she said. "I'm really hungry. Can we eat now?"

"I'm sorry, honey. Nora and I went to see the attorney this afternoon to go over some papers, and it took longer than I expected.

He washed his hands at the kitchen sink and said, "Nora and I are talking about buying a larger home. How would you feel about moving one more time?"

They both added a generous amount of catsup to their sandwiches. Randa said with a full mouth, "I think that's a good idea. I thought it was terrible that Uncle Drew had to sleep in the living room. I'd like to have a white house."

He frowned at her poor table manners. "I'd vote for dark green, so it would blend in with the trees, but we need to know what Nora would like."

***

That night Quinn went to bed but couldn't sleep. He prayed God would show him how to be the father figure Randa longed for.

He rolled over and heard a gust of wind swoosh against the house. The windows rattled. Quinn wished they could find a new home before the wedding. An old house would probably need upgrades and would never be ready by August. Quinn burrowed his head in his pillow and prayed, "In your time, Lord. Your plan is best."

Chapter 55

Sunday, March 28

Following morning worship, Neil Johnson waited for his wife to join him in the sanctuary. He heard the snap of someone's fingers, looked up and saw Molly and Randa jerk upright, and their laughter stopped.

Agnes came toward him and asked, "Are you ready to go home?"

"I don't think so. Watch the Thompsons and those two girls for a minute and tell me what you think."

She peered at them. "It looks to me like they're ... What're they up to?" She took another look and shook her head. "It looks to me like Don and Ruth are standing guard over them."

"Yeah, I heard someone snap their fingers. I'm sure it was Don. Don't those girls look as if they've been disciplined?"

"Yes. I'd say so."

"Now, look at Reverend Edwards. Have you ever seen him grin like that before?"

"Well, come to think of it, no. Reverend Edwards usually smiles, but today he looks happy."

"A guy at work told me he saw the reverend with a realtor at the old Heinrich place. I think I'll find out what he was doing there."

She frowned. "Why would he be looking at that house? That makes little sense."

He winked at her. "Do you remember what Mary said at Thanksgiving?

"Oooh. Do you suppose?"

Neil took her arm. "Well, since I'm chairman of the church board, I think we'll just look into this matter." They waited

270

My Name is Randa

until all but the Thompsons were out of earshot, then Neil reached for Quinn's hand. "Good morning, Reverend. You look happy this morning."

"Yes, I'm having a good day. How about you?"

"I'm a little curious. I heard you were looking at old Gus Heinrich's place." Neil smirked. "Too bad they let it go to wrack and ruin."

Quinn stared at him for a moment, then glanced at the girls. "We've tried to keep it secret, but looking for a house has brought that to an end."

Nora overheard and moved over beside Quinn. He threaded his fingers between hers. She smiled up at him. "It lasted longer than we thought. I'm ready for our secret to be over."

Quinn tried to keep a straight face and said, "You're right, Neil. It's in terrible shape. We want a larger home, but not that one. Warren Campbell is going to show us another one this afternoon."

Agnes looked at their clasped hands, grinned, and said, "Mary told us at Thanksgiving there was something going on with you two. As soon as we get home, I'm calling her."

"You're the first ones to figure it out," Quinn said. "Would you not say anything until we're ready to tell everyone?"

They agreed, then Agnes hurried Neil away so she could call their daughter in Milwaukee.

Don and Ruth stood in the open doorway with them, watching the Johnson's leave.

Quinn asked, "If you don't have plans, could Randa spend the day with you? There are a couple of things I hoped Nora and I could do today."

Randa's mouth turned down. "But I wanted to go house hunting with you."

"I'm sorry, honey. I don't think that house is going to work for us, anyway. It's out of town, and I need to be closer to the church. I'll come pick you up if we finish early."

As she walked away with the Thompsons, they heard Randa whine, "I really wanted to go with them. It's not private or personal."

***

When they sat down to lunch, Quinn prayed, "Lord, my heart is filled with thankfulness for Nora's love and our wedding date. Thank you for the food she has prepared for us. In Jesus' name, Amen."

"I thank God for you, too," Nora said, buttering her muffin. "You looked at the Heinrich house? It needs to be torn down."

"I agree. It's bad, but the rooms are big." He leaned over and kissed her on the cheek. "I hope it doesn't take too long to find a house we like."

***

After lunch, they cleared away the dishes and went into the living room. Quinn chose the sofa and patted the cushion beside him. "Why don't you sit here with me?"

She joined him, and Quinn slid down to the floor on one knee. "Nora, I love you with all my heart, and I'm sorry Drew had to tell me you were more than a secretary to me." He pulled a velvet box from his pocket and said, "I want everyone to know I've asked you to marry me. Will you wear this ring now?"

Nora looked at him in astonishment. "You bought a ring? When did you do that? Oh, Quinn, it's beautiful. Yes, yes, I will! But the diamond it's … How …?"

My Name is Randa

"I went to Rockford last Tuesday. I wanted to buy a carat, but it seemed too big for your little hand. The jeweler agreed with me." By the time he finished speaking, Nora had removed Esther's loaner and Quinn slid the sparkling diamond ring on her finger. "My darling, I promise to do everything in my power to give you a happy life." He pulled her to him, kissed her and whispered, "I love you," in one ear and, "August can't come soon enough," in the other.

She gazed at him with eyes alight. Love filled her heart with joy. She took his face in her hands and gave him a kiss that left no doubt in his mind that she loved him. "Thank you for asking me. I'm honored that you want me to be your wife. It fits perfect. How…?"

He nuzzled his nose into her neck and whispered, "Esther."

***

Later, Quinn and Nora went through the house, located outside the city limits, but it didn't meet their needs.

Warren said, "I'll call you when we get a listing with large rooms. There's nothing out there right now." The men shook hands and went their separate ways. Quinn turned the car east, away from town.

"Where are we going now?" she asked.

He winked at her and, with a big grin, said, "To Tim and Julie's. They know we're coming. I'm sure you want Julie to be the first to see your ring. I've been thinking; would you like Tim to announce our engagement at evening service? He could do it after I finish preaching. I would never make it through a sermon if he announced it first."

"Oh Quinn, that's perfect. Everyone can be told at one time."

***

Mary Watland

Julie opened the door. "Shh. Come in. The twins are still asleep." They stepped inside, and Nora put her left hand out for Julie to see the ring. Tim leaned over his wife's shoulder and whistled. "Wow! That could blind a person. I guess y'all decided ta come out in the open. Congratulations."

Quinn drew Nora close to his side and said, "Nora is ready for everyone to know we're in love," Quinn said. "She accepted my ring today, so Tim, would you be willing to announce our engagement tonight at our evening service?"

Tim flashed his crooked grin. "Sure. I'd be happy to." He located pad and pencil and asked, "Have you picked a date for the wedding?"

"Yes," Nora said. "August 28."

While the men talked, Julie leaned over and whispered to her mother, "Your ring is gorgeous. That diamond is huge!"

Nora mouthed, *"Can you believe it?"*

Quinn stood and said, "I hate to cut this visit short, but Randa needs to see Nora's ring next. May I use your phone to call the Thompsons?"

When they stopped in front of the Thompson's house, Quinn beeped his horn. Randa ran out to the car and climbed into the back seat. "Did you like the house?" She leaned over and hooked her chin on the back of the front seat. "Nora, what did you do with Aunt Esther's ring?" Her voice boomed in Nora's ear. "Did Uncle Quinn give you an engagement ring?"

Nora pulled away. Quinn turned and said, "Don't yell; you'll burst her eardrum."

"I'm sorry. Can I see?" Nora lifted her left hand. "Wow, that's a really big diamond. Did you guys pick it out?"

"No, your Uncle Quinn went to Rockford and picked it out by himself. Isn't it beautiful?"

Randa was so excited; she was about to burst. Jesus answered her prayers. Nora was going to be part of her family.

My Name is Randa

She would have another mother, and they'd both take care of Uncle Quinn. She hoped Mama knew.

He shifted the car into reverse. "Stop!" Randa said. "We have to show Molly." She opened the door and jumped out. "Come on, you guys, the Thompsons have to see this before anybody else. They're our friends."

***

Quinn concluded his sermon and turned the service over to Bill Hubbard. The song leader grinned at the congregation and said, "Before we sing, Tim has an announcement."

Quinn stepped down off the platform, turned to Nora, and held out his hand. She took it and moved into the aisle beside him. They stood hand in hand and smiled in each other's eyes while Tim announced, "We'd like y'all to know that Reverend Edwards has asked our little mother for her hand in marriage, and she said yes."

"Woo Wee," sounded from the back. Someone shouted, "It's about time." Another started clapping, and everyone joined in. The sanctuary was filled with a buzz of voices.

Tim motioned Julie and Randa to come up front. They joined him, carrying Rosie and Jordie. He held up his hands to quiet the crowd. "We want y'all to know we're very happy about this. You're all invited to the weddin' on August 28."

Nora looked up at Quinn and whispered, "All our family is up here showing everyone they approve."

He squeezed her hand. "See, my darling, everybody is happy for us. They don't think we're moving too fast."

The voices faded for Nora when Tim finished speaking. The secret was out. She looked around the room at schoolmates, family, friends, and brothers and sisters in Christ; were all smiling.

275

The Johnson's grinned from ear to ear. Neil's smile was another assurance to Nora that she and Quinn were doing the right thing. Had she told Quinn that Carl and Neil were close friends?

Don winked at Quinn, put his arm around Ruth, and pulled her close.

Quinn tucked Nora under his chin. She looked up at him with pink cheeks. "Don't be embarrassed, my darling," he said. "Look out there and see how many men have arms around their wives."

Molly waved at Randa, then turned to whisper something to her mother. Nora couldn't wait to see what they'd come up with next. "Thank you, Lord, for Molly and Randa. Help Quinn and me be a good example before them."

Everywhere Nora looked, she saw delighted smiles. The pianist began playing *Let Me Call You Sweetheart*. Bill raised his arm and led in, singing the old song of love.

Rosie smiled at the crowd. Randa held Jordie in her arms, and his eyes grew big. He let out a howl. Tim took his frightened son, put the baby up on his shoulder, and patted his back until the love song diverted his attention.

Quinn and Nora stood at the entrance while the church members waited in line to tell them how happy they were that God had put them together.

Esther hugged and kissed, first Nora, then Quinn. "I'm delighted to see the joy on your faces. Welcome to our family."

Nora watched her sister go out into the night with a bittersweet smile. Their lives were going to change. They wouldn't have as much time together, and she wouldn't be sharing all her confidences with Esther. She must always be mindful of her widowed sister and find regular times for them to be together.

My Name is Randa

When the last person shook their hands and congratulated them, Nora patted Quinn's arm and told him she and Randa would go on ahead to her house.

"I won't be long," he said, then brought her hand to his lips and kissed her fingers.

Quinn noticed the janitor's family waiting for him and said, "Jim, go on home. I'll lock up."

He walked up the aisle and collected his Bible from the front pew. So much had happened to him in his seven months in Park City. He raised his hands and quietly quoted his favorite verses from Psalms 63, "Because thy lovingkindness is better than life, my lips shall praise thee. Thus will I bless thee while I live: I will lift up my hands in thy name."

Chapter 56

Monday, April 5

Julie called Nora at the office early on Monday. "Good morning, Mother. Yesterday, I was so excited about your ring, I forgot to tell you that Mavis had a boy on Saturday night. They've named him Andrew Albert Calhoun. He looks like a Calhoun, red hair and all."

"Would you like me to watch the twins this afternoon so you and Tim can go visit Mavis?" Nora asked.

"Not unless you can find someone to help you. The twins are teething, and they're fussy."

Nora hung up after assuring Julie she would find someone to help her.

Close to lunchtime, Quinn entered the office to find Nora with a deep frown studying her address book. He kissed the frown. "What's wrong?"

"Julie and Tim would like to go see Mavis Calhoun at the hospital. She had a boy on Saturday. Julie won't let me babysit alone because the twins are teething."

"I'll go with you; I have nothing planned for this afternoon."

"Oh, Quinn, I don't think that's such a good idea. I'm guessing you've not been around two crying babies." She was sure he had no experience and would be more trouble than help.

"So, they cry. I've heard babies cry. It can't be that hard. If it takes two, I want to be the one to help you. We'll play with them for a while, feed them, and then you and I can have some time to talk while they take a nap."

My Name is Randa

Nora opened her mouth to protest, then a resigned look came over her face. "Okay, we'll do it. Just remember, we're watching babies whose gums hurt."

***

Tim looked surprised when Quinn walked in behind Nora. He started to say something, then changed his mind. Julie came downstairs, saw Quinn, and looked at her mother with a raised eyebrow. "We'll check in with you in a couple of hours."

Quinn patted Julie's shoulder and said, "Take your time. We'll be fine."

***

Two hours later, Julie called to see how things were going. Nora suggested they go out for an early dinner before returning home. Upon their return, Tim carefully closed the door and stood listening to blessed silence. They tiptoed into the dining room to check on their babies, who were spread eagle, on their stomachs, in the playpen.

Tim frowned. "I can't believe it. What did you do to our children?"

Nora grinned. "We rocked them while they cried and fed them when they were hungry. They have been asleep about fifteen minutes."

Julie turned to Quinn. "I want to hear your version of what happened while we were gone, and I expect the truth."

He looked at Julie and considered what he should say. He wasn't about to tell her he was absolutely no help to Nora at all. "I think a person needs three hands to change a diaper. I hope Tim knows an easier way; it looks impossible to me." Quinn shook his head. "I have a new respect for you kids. Tim, thank you for helping Julie."

279

Marg Watland

"Jordie and Rosie are not just Julie's children. They are *our* children. We started doing things together while we were dating. The men in my family tease me about doing women's work, but I like to help my wife."

Quinn enjoyed watching the young couple work together and admired their devotion to each other. Tim adored Julie, and she was his happy bride.

Was it because they did things together? He didn't help Arlene that much. She always seemed so self-sufficient, and, as a reverend, he worked long hours.

***

When Quinn arrived home, Randa stood at the open kitchen doorway. Her eyes danced, but she kept a straight face. "*So*, you helped Nora babysit. How'd that go?"

He climbed the steps and said, "Not at all like I expected. She showed me how to change a diaper. Those babies are strong."

She laughed. "Rosie twists. She's stronger than Jordie. Nora taught me how to put my arm across her stomach to hold her down. Who did you change?"

"I didn't change either. I just watched. I told Tim I needed to see how he did it. There's no way I can do it her way."

She grinned. "I can't wait to tell Molly." Randa could hold it no longer; uproarious laughter erupted from her mouth, which was almost as loud as Jordie's howl.

"Could you please tone it down? Those babies are teething, they cried nonstop, and I have a headache."

That night Quinn couldn't get Tim's words out of his mind. *I like to help my wife.* His dad did the outside work, and his mother worked inside. He ministered to the people in his church, and Arlene worked in their home. He'd help if something was too heavy or needed to be repaired.

280

Now that he had Randa, they worked together in the kitchen, and they had wonderful talks. Yes, Tim was a good example for him to follow.

Chapter 57

Tuesday, April 6

Something white under the buffet caught Randa's attention. She squatted to pick it up and found it was a birthday card to her uncle from Great Aunt Etta. She dropped the card on the table and was halfway down the hall when she stopped.

Uncle Quinn was engaged. They needed to write another round-robin letter to the Edwards family. She whipped around, returned to the dining room, and slid their shoebox of photos out of the buffet.

***

When Quinn arrived home, Randa had rows of snapshots spread across the dining room table. "Come look at these," she said. "We need to write another letter to your aunt and tell her you're getting married. They'll want to know what she looks like. Come on, help me choose a picture."

He grinned. "Have I ever mentioned you're bossy?"

"That doesn't matter. Our family *deserves* to know."

Quinn picked up one picture after another. "It should be of both of us. I think the roll in our camera is almost full. I'll have Esther take a picture of us and send the roll in to be developed."

***

Thursday - April 8

Randa had walked past Erik Larson's office two days in a row. On the third day, she gathered enough courage to open the door. His secretary smiled at her and asked, "May I help you?"

"Yes, please. My name is Miranda Shepherd, and Reverend Quinn Edwards is my uncle. Mr. Larson is his lawyer, so I guess that means he's my lawyer too, and I'd like to talk to him."

"Okay, honey," she said. "Why don't you take a seat, and I'll see if he's available."

Erik Larson came into the reception area. "Wow! There's no doubt you are Quinn's niece. You have his dark eyes." He held out his hand. "Hello Miranda, I'm delighted to meet you."

Randa hesitated a moment before her hand shot out to his.

He led her to a beautiful room. Cherry wood bookcases lined the wall behind his chair. On the matching desk stood a family picture and a pipe rack with a collection of funny-shaped pipes.

She sank into a cushy dark leather chair, set her schoolbooks on the floor, and then took a deep breath. "Miranda is my legal name, but everybody calls me Randa. I like that better. I came to ask you a question. I never knew my father. He died before I was born, and my stepfather didn't want to be called Dad. Uncle Quinn's the first person who's ever seemed like a father to me. Now he's going to marry Nora Montgomery, who is like a mother to me. I'd really like to call them Mom and Dad, and I'm wondering if there is some way to make them my legal parents."

Erik explained at length about adoption, legally changing her name, and the exact cost of those legal procedures. "Randa, you can choose to call them aunt and uncle or mom and dad. You can have your name changed from Shepherd to Edwards. Your uncle has told me how important family is to you. Are you sure you want to replace your father's name with Edwards?"

Randa breathed in, and tears filled her eyes. "Oh. I didn't think about that. Mama told me about him and how excited he was to be a father." She looked down and picked at a hangnail for several moments. "If I changed my name, it would be like saying he never existed. I can't do that to him, can I?" Tears trickled down her face.

Erik picked up a box of tissue, moved to a chair beside her, and waited. When she looked at him, he handed her the box. "It sounds like the names you had for your parents were Mama and Father. I don't believe they would mind if you used Mom and Dad for your *second parents*. I suggest you think some more about what you'd like to do, and then discuss it with your prospective parents. I'll be happy to see you again if you have more questions."

Randa blew out a breath. "Thank you. I guess I need to think about it some more." She picked up her books, then stopped. "How much do I owe you? I have money in a trust account. I can ask Uncle Quinn to get some out of it to pay you."

"No, that won't be necessary. You just asked me questions, and I tried to help you sort things out."

"But ..."

Erik grinned and held up his hand. "I understand you make cinnamon rolls every Saturday morning. I'll be working here in the office this weekend. How about a pan of cinnamon rolls as payment?"

Her face lit up. "Okay, I'll bring them Saturday morning at ten."

He took her hand in both of his and said, "It was very nice to meet you. I'll see you Saturday."

Randa walked toward home, deep in thought. She wanted a mother and a father, but would her mama approve of having her name changed? Would her father? Mr. Larson

My Name is Randa

said she should talk to Nora and Uncle Quinn. Oh, oh, could she be in trouble?

She knocked on Nora's kitchen door and pushed it open. Nora held up her hand. "Stop, don't step on my wax. Go around to the front door. I'll finish this and be right in."

Randa was sitting in a chair with tears on her cheeks when Nora walked into the house. "What's wrong, honey? I'm not angry with you. I just didn't want you to make tracks in my wet wax."

"I talked to Mr. Larson today, and he told me to talk to you and Uncle Quinn. I think Uncle Quinn might get mad at me because he wants me to talk to him first."

Nora frowned. "Mr. Larson? Erik Larson?"

"I just want you and Uncle Quinn to be my parents. I want a mom and a dad just like everybody else." Tears trickled down her cheek. "I thought I wanted you to adopt me but ..."

Nora dried Randa's tears and listened until she could make sense of what Randa was saying. "Honey, your uncle and I need to hear this together, and he's in a meeting. Let's go to your house, and we'll wait for him there."

"Okay," Randa said and didn't speak again until Nora parked in her driveway.

***

Nora prayed the Lord would give them wisdom as, together, they dealt with their *daughter*. At least they wouldn't have to discuss the legal processes.

Quinn opened the door and found his two favorite ladies sitting at the kitchen table looking serious. He looked from one face to the other. "Aaah, what's up?"

Nora looked at Randa and waited for her to speak.

"I've been hoping you'd be ... well ... like my parents. Then I could call you Mom and Dad. I went and talked to Mr. Larson today to see if you could adopt me; if you want to."

He set his briefcase on the floor, crossed his arms over his chest, and scowled at her. "You went to my attorney? I'm your guardian. Why didn't you come to me?"

"Well ..."

He broke in. "It's your turn to fix dinner, so while you're doing that, Nora and I will talk." Quinn took Nora's hand and led her into his study.

Tears covered Randa's face. Uncle Quinn was mad at her because she didn't talk to him first. But she had legal questions, and their lawyer was the best one to ask. He was nice to her and answered all her questions. Could she be their daughter and keep her father's last name? She really wanted Uncle Quinn and Nora to be her mom and dad.

Quinn paced back and forth, and his arms flew up in the air. Nora sat and listened while he emptied his frustration. "Why can't she come to me with her questions? I'm her guardian. Why did she have to bother Erik? Where did she get the idea that thirteen-year-olds should go talk to a lawyer?"

Nora reached for Quinn's hand. "I don't think Randa should go to Erik without your permission, but it sounds like he gave her answers that neither you nor I know. You sounded grim out there."

Quinn lifted her hand to his lips and dropped into his chair. "I'm not so much angry as I'm disappointed that she doesn't come to me with her questions. What do you think? What should we do?"

"I'm sorry, Quinn. I think this is a problem you have been working with before I came into the picture. It would be better if you and Randa resolved this."

He stared at the wall, bouncing the rubber end of a pencil on his desk.

My Name is Randa

Nora remained quiet and watched him process his thoughts.

"You're right. This is between Randa and me." He continued to bounce the pencil. "I wish it didn't have to be dinner time. She's hungry, and we're all caught up in this problem. I have to do this now."

"Maybe I should go."

"No, Nora, please don't go. I'll do the talking, but I'd like her to see that we agree."

When they returned to the kitchen, Randa sat at the table with her head propped on her hands. Quinn had to steel himself not to pull her into his arms. He and Nora sat on either side of her. "Randa, thirteen-year-olds don't go to lawyers. Adults make appointments to talk to lawyers and then pay for their services before they leave."

Randa raised her head and started to speak, but Quinn stopped her.

"I'm not through talking." He took a breath. "Honey, Nora and I want to be your parents, but that means you will come to *us* when you have questions. If we don't know the answer, let us decide how to get the information."

Randa nodded. "Okay. I'm sorry I made you mad."

"That was my initial reaction, but more than that, I'm disappointed that you don't trust me enough to come to me first."

"Oh, Uncle Quinn, I trust you. I don't want to disappoint you. Please forgive me. I won't ever go to Mr. Larson's again, but I have to go there on Saturday. He said I could pay him with a pan of hot cinnamon rolls."

Nora screened her face with a hand to hide her amusement.

Randa's stomach rumbled. "Can we eat now? I didn't have a snack, and I'm hungry? Can Nora eat with us?"

Quinn got up from the table. "I think I need a hug first. We'll talk about what Mr. Larson told you after we eat."

She jumped up, plowed into him, and wrapped her arms around his waist. "I love you, Uncle Quinn. I'm really sorry."

Nora was proud of Quinn. He handled it well. He looked at her, and she smiled her approval.

Randa checked the stove timer. "We're having enchiladas. It's not real spicy. It will be done in five more minutes. Our neighbor lady in Yuma sent me the recipe in her Christmas card."

After dinner, Randa told Quinn and Nora all Erik had told her. "I don't think it would be fair to my father to change my last name. Is that alright?"

"Absolutely. You are honoring your father by keeping his name," Quinn said. "As for you calling us Mom and Dad; I think it would be best if you wait until after we're married."

***

Late that evening, Drew called to see how things were going. Quinn told him about Randa going to the lawyer and her payment of cinnamon rolls. Drew laughed and said, "Well done. I'm delighted to hear you and Randa have resolved your issues. You have worked hard to become a family, and adding Nora will make things easier. She is an answer to our prayers."

"Thank you. Nora and I have been talking about how to include Randa in our wedding ceremony. Do you have any suggestions?

"Let's see. How would you feel about some second-parent vows for the three of you? "

"Perfect. I knew you'd figure out something."

***

My Name is Randa

Quinn dialed Erik Larson's number the next morning at exactly nine o'clock. "Good morning, Erik. Randa told us she went to see you."

"Yes, she did."

"Thank you for seeing her. Nora and I had a long talk with her, and we're honored that she wants to call us Mom and Dad. She's going to tell everyone we're her second parents, and she's promised to come to us instead of others with her questions."

"Is she alright? Randa cried for her father yesterday."

"She's fine. Randa has decided to keep her father's name. Thank you for talking to her. Put the time you spent with her on my bill."

Erik laughed. "I can't do that. She offered to pay me out of her trust account, but I negotiated, and she promised to pay my fee with a pan of hot cinnamon rolls. Come with her, and we'll talk about how a trust account works."

Chapter 58

Easter Weekend

*F*riday afternoon, Nora stopped by the church to pick up a notebook she'd left on her desk. Quinn wasn't in the office. She'd seen his car outside, and the basement was dark.

Nora walked past the double doors to the sanctuary and glimpsed him through a small window in the door. Quinn was walking behind a pew with his head down and hand sliding along the top of the pew. She watched him move across the width of the sanctuary, his hand on each pew. Now and again, he'd stop, then continue on. His posture never changed, and when he came to the end, Quinn turned and started down the next row. That's when she realized what he was doing. He was praying for the people who would sit in those pews on Easter morning.

She needed to be in there with him but didn't want to disturb his prayer time. Nora opened a side door that he and the choir used and mimicked Quinn's actions. She prayed for each choir member by name and asked God that their ministry of song would touch the hearts of every person who attended.

She moved down a level to the high-back chairs behind the podium and rested her hand on the arm of Bill Hubbard's chair. Nora thanked the Lord for this talented young high school music teacher, who moved home to be close to his ailing father. Then she stepped over to Quinn's chair and sank to her knees. With elbows on the seat and face in her hands, she earnestly prayed for Quinn, their reverend.

He'd told her of butterflies in his stomach when he walked up to the pulpit and how they disappeared when he spoke. Nora prayed the Holy Spirit would give him the right words

My Name is Randa

on this resurrection day and that the people would recognize that his words were God's truth. She thanked God for their love for each other and asked the Lord to help her be a fit partner in his ministry.

A floorboard squeaked; he was close by. She turned, and Quinn, with tears in his eyes, cleared his throat and whispered, "Thank you. Your prayers mean the world to me. You are the perfect helpmate for me."

He reached for her hand, and she stepped down beside him. Without a word, they turned and looked at the empty pews. They visualized the people who would fill the sanctuary the next day and prayed for those who needed Jesus in their lives. When they started down the aisle, he checked to ensure there were name and address clipboards at the end of each pew.

After checking the last pew, Quinn pushed open the door and followed Nora out of the sanctuary. He stopped by a table stacked with bulletins. Isaiah 9:6 was printed across the cover. He picked up one that had fallen on the floor, took a deep breath, and said, "I think we're ready now."

***

Easter Sunday

Reverend Edwards stepped forward, lifted his hands, and said, "THE LORD HAS RISEN."

The congregation responded, "HE HAS RISEN INDEED."

He opened his Bible. "I am going to start today's message with the words of the Prophet Isaiah.

Quinn ended his sermon by quoting John 3:15-16. He joined the congregation in the center aisle of the sanctuary and asked those who wanted to follow Jesus to join him in the front. The first people to walk toward him were the Larkin family.

Clara held her hand out. "A few days before Mother died, she told me I needed Jesus and asked me to talk to you. A month later, Randa invited us to go caroling, and the people in your church were so friendly.

"Pam went to your house to see Goldie, and Randa talked to her about Jesus. Then when my girls saw your manger scene, they insisted we needed one, too. It changed our Christmas. I believe Jesus is God's son, and I want him in my life."

Quinn prayed with her.

She shed a few tears before she smiled and said, "Thank you. God has forgiven my sins, and I am washed clean."

Dave Larkin grabbed Quinn's hand. "Today, you told us the entire story, and now it makes sense. I want a new life with Jesus as my Savior."

Quinn prayed with him, and Dave wrung his hand until it hurt. Dave said, "Bill Hubbard and I work together. He's been talking to me about Don Thompson's Bible Study. I guess I better go with him."

Quinn released his hand and moved on to Pam. She said, "I came with my parents, but I've already asked Jesus to forgive me. Randa told me how."

Melinda stood rigid with her hands behind her back. Quinn sensed her resistance. "My Dad told us to come up here. I don't know if I want Jesus in my life. I might mess up, and then I'd go to hell. I just don't know …."

"I will not ask you to do something you aren't ready to do. I would like to show you some verses in the Bible to help you understand who Jesus is and how much he loves you." He glanced Nora's way. "Or if you'd like, Nora, my secretary, could talk to you. Would you be willing to talk with one of us?"

My Name is Randa

Melinda looked at him in surprise. "Is she the lady you're going to marry?"

"Yes, she is. Would you prefer to talk to her?"

"Okay. Pam says she's nice. I'll talk to her."

***

Easter dinner was at Tim and Julie's. Quinn thought it too much for Julie to have Easter dinner at her house, but that wasn't the case. Obviously, Julie, Tim, and Nora had worked together as a team. Everybody had their own job. Randa joined their team, and Quinn filled water glasses, mashed potatoes, and fetched things. Everyone's help made it a blessed family gathering. They enjoyed the traditional Easter dinner of ham, candied yams, salad, greens, and dinner rolls. Randa brought Tim's favorite, a devil's food cake with chocolate frosting.

Quinn already felt he and Randa were part of Nora's family. Tim and Julie honored Nora as their matriarch and listened to her wisdom. Now, they were doing the same with him. Tim's *yes sirs* and open, easy regard for his elders pleased Quinn. In his heart, the twins were already his grandchildren.

***

Later that night, Quinn praised and thanked God for those who came forward to ask Jesus into their lives. He prayed for those who might have been too timid to walk down the aisle, and also for Melinda, who would meet with Nora after school on Wednesday.

Chapter 59

Friday, May 7

Weeks passed, and Warren, their realtor, hadn't called regarding a house to show them. Frustrated, Quinn began driving up and down streets looking for houses for sale. One afternoon he turned onto Ninth Street and recognized the old place at the end of the block. It was on two acres of debris-filled land. He pulled over and parked. Dead weeds pushed between rocks that once defined a flower bed, and decaying tree branches lay on the ground. A broken board on the porch floor pointed upward. The screen door stood askew at the front entrance, and several windows were boarded up.

Behind the house, old man Heinrich had planted a grove of trees. Oak, white pine, and spruce grew along the north border of the property, and there were tall sugar maples grouped around the house to provide shade on hot sunny days.

Quinn sat in his car and considered the weather-scarred homestead. Could it be restored? When he looked at it in March, he was impressed with the sizeable rooms on the main floor and liked all the trees on the property. One morning soon, he'd drive over at sunrise to watch the sky turn red and listen to the sounds of nature awakening to a new day.

***

Days later, a noisy truck drove by the manse before daybreak and woke him. He threw his covers back and decided it was time. Quinn dressed in old clothes, filled a thermos with coffee, and drove to Ninth Street.

My Name is Randa

A thin line of pink pushed up along the horizon as he walked through the weeds to stand in front of the kitchen window. He leaned against the rough siding and listened to the earth wake up. Hues of coral joined the morning blush and spread out across the expanse. Birds flitted between the trees, singing their morning songs. Quinn stood in awe at God's handiwork. The bright yellow ball crept higher in the sky, announcing a sunny day.

The outer lines of the house were like his home in Michigan. It made Quinn homesick for his old childhood home. Some days, when the sky colored, he and his dad would stop doing their morning chores to gaze at God's glorious artistry. A forgotten piece of his childhood came to mind, and he remembered his father's words: "Stand still, son, and worship God with me."

He longed for a home like this. Could something be done with this place? Was he crazy? Well, there was only one way to find out. He'd make some calls. He wasn't ready to talk to Nora about this, but …

***

Randa was in the kitchen eating breakfast when Quinn returned home. "Where've you been so early in the morning?" she asked.

Quinn poured a cup of coffee and popped a couple of pieces of bread into the toaster. "We don't have a good view of the sunrise at our house, so I drove over a few blocks for a better look. I like to worship God as the sun rises."

That evening, Quinn grinned and handed Randa an envelope. "This is from my Aunt Etta. She, her daughter Lillian, and granddaughter Moira, are coming to our wedding. They plan to turn the trip into a weeklong vacation. I let Nora read the letter, and she copied the addresses of the relatives Aunt Etta thought should be invited to the wedding.

Nora suggested we invite Aunt Etta and her family to the rehearsal dinner. That way, you would have a chance to get acquainted with them before the wedding."

Randa jumped about, clapping her hands and shouting, "I'm going to have a whole row of family sitting with me. I can't wait!" She plopped down on a chair. "How old do you think Moira is? She has a funny name. I've never heard it before."

"Mother's family is Irish. My Grandma O'Reilly's name was Moira. Lillian's close to my age, so I'm guessing Moira's about Julie's age."

***

That evening, Randa asked, "Where do you go to see the sunrise?"

"Over at the old Heinrich place."

"You mean the dumpy old house on Ninth Street? I heard you talking to that realtor man on the phone about it, so I walked over there one day on my way home from school. It's awful. There isn't any lawn, and there's tall weeds everywhere.

"You're right, but there aren't any houses blocking my view."

Randa headed to the dining room table. "Do you want to start a puzzle with me? I'll let you pick."

He chose a farm scene with a big barn and cows grazing in a pasture. "I have an advantage. I've done all these puzzles before. You start on the border, and I'll do the sky."

That night, Quinn lay in bed remembering the beautiful sunrises he watched with his father when he was a boy.

Chapter 60

Saturday - May 15

Quinn met Warren coming out of the drugstore and said, "You know we're willing to look at older houses that need repair?"

"Well, I have one older home in the city limits, but it needs a lot of work. I'm free this afternoon. Why don't you bring Mrs. Montgomery to the office sometime today, and I'll take you over there?"

***

Warren drove across town to a tall, ornate Victorian house. Nora and Quinn glanced at each other, then politely followed him up the rickety porch stairs. They walked through tiny postage stamp rooms, and climbed three flights of stairs. Warren said, "Your niece might like the third floor; it's roomy."

As they walked to the car, Warren said, "I've shown you everything you might like. As soon as something else comes on the market, I'll call you."

When they returned to his office, Quinn thanked Warren and hurried Nora away to their car before bursting into laughter. "Didn't we tell Warren we weren't interested in a Victorian house?"

Nora laughed with him. "I'm glad Randa wasn't with us. She might have liked that third floor."

Since Randa would soon be home from school, Quinn took Nora to his house. "Would you like some tea and cookies while we talk?" She nodded, and he turned on the burner under the teakettle.

Marg Watland

She sat at the table and fiddled with a napkin. "I have a question. The day you moved to Park City; Randa said my living room was cozy. That's what I wanted it to say. What does your living room say?"

"Esther said it looked homey when Ernie brought over that rug."

"I think it's the rug that looks homey. If we took the rug away and put it back like it was, how would you describe the room?"

Randa came in from outside and said, "Boring, everything looks the same. There's nothing pretty to look at."

Quinn stared at her with a slack jaw.

She saw the look on his face and said, "I'm sorry, Uncle Quinn. I didn't mean to hurt your feelings. We'll just have to save up and buy some pretty things."

Nora groaned inside. That child didn't know she was making matters worse. "Randa, I think we need to find out why he chose tones of brown."

He looked from Randa to Nora with a bewildered look on his face. He didn't know how to answer her.

Nora squeezed his hand and said, "You don't have to answer right now. You can tell us later."

The teakettle whistled, and Quinn poured water into the teapot.

She continued to look at Quinn with a tender smile on her face and said to Randa, "Honey, we must remember not to gang up on your uncle. It's women who decorate a home. What's more important right now is for us to find a house.

"Quinn and I are having tea and cookies. Are you hungry?"

Randa took a cup and saucer from the cupboard and sat beside Nora. They munched and chatted about house hunting while Quinn listened and drank lukewarm tea. Nora

My Name is Randa

patted Randa's hand. "This feels like I'm having a snack with my family. I love it."

"You are," Randa said, "and I love it, too."

Quinn beamed.

Randa finished her cookie and left to change out of her school clothes.

Goldie came into the kitchen and butted her head against Randa. She picked up the feline and went to the living room, where they liked to play on the rug.

Nora reached over and took Quinn's hand. "My dear, teenagers speak first and think later. Parenting isn't for the weak." She smiled at him. "Nate King Cole sings you have to, *pick yourself up, dust yourself off, and start all over again.*"

He nodded, but remained silent for a time, then said, "My mother used to say brown was a good color because it goes with everything. Does my living room really say boring?"

"I want you to tell me what it says to you. I'm guessing it says more than that your mother's choice of color was brown."

"But I want to know what you think it says."

She tipped her head to the side and saw dejection on his face. "I think you have started with brown, but it's not finished yet." Quinn stared into her eyes but didn't speak. She broke the silence. "Talk to me, Quinn. You're upset. What are you thinking?"

"I'm embarrassed. Randa thinks our home is boring, and you think it isn't finished. I don't want her to live in a boring house, but I don't know how to finish it."

She raised a brow. "Is that all? Is embarrassment the only thing you're feeling?"

"All right, Randa hurt my feelings, but I'm not mad at her. I'm disappointed in me. I like my home to be functional and not cluttered, but she wants it pretty." His mouth quirked. "I've made it brown, and I'm going to let you girls finish it for me."

Nora laughed at him. "I'm not interested in decorating the manse. I'm going to put all my energy into decorating our new home. Oh, Quinn, I pray we find something before our wedding." She took her dishes to the sink. "It's time for me to go home. Esther has invited me to have dinner with her. She has too many leftovers in her fridge and wants me to help her whittle them down."

***

After dinner, Quinn washed and Randa dried while she told him about her home in Yuma. "It looked like all our Mexican neighbor's houses, with lots of bright, happy colors. In our kitchen, we had a plain wood table, but the chairs were painted pretty colors. Mama's chair was purple, John's green, mine blue, and the other chair was yellow. They had flowers painted on the chair backs. We sold all our furniture when we moved to Minnesota. Mama said we'd buy new American furniture." She folded the tea towel and hung it on a rack. "Uncle Quinn, Could I go watch the sunrise the next time you go?"

"How about next Saturday? You'll have to get up early."

***

Late in the night, Quinn sat in his chair, staring at his living room. He tried to imagine a home filled with vivid Mexican colors and shook his head. No, he would not ask that child to decorate anything he lived in. He liked Nora's house. Randa was right; it felt cozy. In the meantime, what *did* his living room say?

***

My Name is Randa

Monday morning, Quinn waited until Randa left for school and then called Norm Gustafson, a building contractor Warren recommended. "I'm getting married in August and we're looking for an old house with large rooms. I have a teenage niece, so we want a home where there's room for her to have her friends over for parties. I'd like to know if you could restore the old Heinrich house on Ninth Street. Everybody tells me they should condemn it, but I'd like to hear what you think."

They met after lunch. As they walked around the outside, Norm jotted down figures on his notepad. Norm pointed to the earth sloping toward the foundation, squatted down, and jabbed a pen in the wood. "There's dry rot here."

Norm scribbled more notes when they went inside. Quinn told Norm about the rooms he would like on the main floor. The estimates on certain jobs were alarming, and Quinn's mind spun. He needed advice on how much was too much.

Norm put his notepad away and said, "I can restore this house. It has good bones. All the dry rot appears to be in that one corner. We'll have to add an addition on one side for the extra rooms you want, and it will be expensive, but when I'm through, the value of your property will be considerably more."

After Norm left, Quinn leaned against the rough siding and watched the sun play peek-a-boo through the branches of a white cedar. His home in Michigan had several fireplaces, but the only fireplace in this house was in the living room. Next Christmas, they could hang their stockings on the fireplace mantle.

Dare he show the house to Nora?

He sighed and pushed away from the wall. He didn't think so.

Chapter 61

Monday, May 24

*I*t was the end of May, and they still hadn't found a house. Quinn stopped by Warren's office. "Nora has a small two-bedroom bungalow and loves it, but it isn't big enough for us. I haven't been in many bungalows. Would you have time to show us some?"

"I'd be happy to."

***

When he returned with Nora, Warren handed each of them a pad and pencil and suggested they take notes.

The first house had corner cupboards and stained-glass windows above the bookcases; that appealed to Nora. When they were ready to leave, Quinn stood in the doorway, looked back at the rooms, and said, "I like straight lines, and those corner cupboards aren't practical. They don't hold enough. It's too fussy for my taste."

Nora opened her mouth and then swallowed what she was about to say. Another time she'd tell him those corner cupboards were her favorites. That's where she put her precious teapot collection from Grandma Wilson.

At the next stop, the dark wood wainscoting was shoulder high. Quinn wrote on his pad, *too much wood, room's dark*. Nora wrote, *charming, like the wood*.

In the third house, the wainscoting and built-ins were a cream color. Quinn wrote, *like the paint, it makes the rooms lighter, don't like all that leaded glass*. Nora wrote, *the leaded glass windows are pretty. I want a kitchen large enough for a table and chairs*.

My Name is Randa

Quinn said, "All three bungalows had only two bedrooms and no room for a study." Warren suggested a rambler with three bedrooms. Quinn said, "No, we want an old house with spacious rooms."

They were quiet as they rode back to her home. When Quinn opened the car door for Nora, she set her feet on the ground but remained seated.

"Our tastes are so opposite; we might have to choose a different style." Her voice quivered. "We aren't going to find a house before our wedding, are we?"

"No, if we find an old house that needs repairs, it is likely to require months to complete the renovation. I know you would like to move into our new home when we marry. We'd both like that, but we can't count on it. I'm sorry."

She stood, and they went inside.

He pulled her into his arms. She said, "Would you hold me for a little while to help me get over the disappointment?" Quinn held her close while they swayed back and forth. She took the comfort she needed from him, then slid her hands up around his neck. The world stood still as their kisses softened the disappointment.

Nora pulled back. "I love you so much, Quinn Edwards, but now I have to let you go home to Randa. Thank you for holding me."

***

Quinn fought it for two weeks before he called Nora and asked her to put on her gardening clothes. She kept telling him she wanted to know what he was thinking. It was time to show her.

When he parked in front of the house, she looked at him in disbelief. "This is the Heinrich place. It needs to be torn down."

Mary Watland

"Give it a chance," he said , handing her a flashlight. They walked through the rooms, and he explained and dreamed out loud. "The kitchen and bathroom need to be gutted, and we'd need another bathroom upstairs. Norm suggested we add an addition along the east side. He is willing to do a walk-through with us. He does a better job of explaining than I do."

Nora shook her head. "All I can see is money flying out of your pocket. This Norm Gustafson would have to be a miracle worker to bring this house back to life. Has he told you how much it would cost?"

"No, he doesn't have enough information to give us a figure. Norm warned me it would be expensive."

"I think it's too risky. Can we wait another month and see if Warren can find us something?"

"If that's what you want, we'll wait another month."

He tried not to let Nora see his disappointment. If this was the right place for them, God would show her.

Quinn was home before Randa arrived. "Did you look at some houses today?"

"Yes, three bungalows, but they were all too small. How was school today?"

Quinn couldn't get the Heinrich house out of his mind, but Nora couldn't see past the dirt and disrepair. She was right. It was risky, but he could see the house redone in his mind's eye.

He imagined stepping outside, sitting in the backyard, and enjoying the sunrise. In the winter, he'd stand in the sunroom on a cold, cloudless day and look at the oak trees covered with snow. The sun would creep up above the horizon, God would spill soft, beautiful colors across the sky, and he'd worship God with his hands raised.

Chapter 62

Friday, June 4

Thursday afternoon, Randa stopped by Nora's. "I thought I'd come and have a visit with you. Remember when I told you Uncle Quinn has been getting up early and going someplace to see the sunrise? Well, I found out he goes over to Ninth Street, where that terrible house is. I'm going to go with him tomorrow morning, but we have to leave while it's still dark."

"Is that so?" He hadn't said a word about the Heinrich place since he showed it to her. She filled the teakettle, then stood with her back to Randa, drumming her fingernails on the counter.

Randa said, "Is something wrong?"

"I need a cup of tea. Would you like some?"

"Okay. I'll get the cookies." She reached into the jar and said, "Oh, oh, I better not; there's only two left. That's just enough for you to have for dessert."

Nora handed Randa two napkins. "We'll each have one, and then I'll get more out of the freezer later."

***

After Randa left, Nora worried over Quinn's sunrise visits at the Heinrich place. He had mentioned nothing about that house since she told him it was too risky. Maybe she hadn't been paying enough attention while he walked her through that dirty old place. They hadn't talked about finances at all. It was time they did, and the sooner, the better.

That evening, she called him. "Hi, Randa tells me you're going to watch the sunrise in the morning. I'd like to go too. I hope there's something to sit on."

He assured her there would be and sounded happy to hear she wanted to go with them. Nora set her alarm and went to bed early. She mulled over how to open a discussion about money.

When Quinn drove into her driveway, Nora came out carrying an old knitting bag. He hurried around to the passenger door, leaned over to kiss her, and said, "Good morning, my darling. I believe I learned an important lesson last night. Anything Randa knows, you know. Do we need to talk?"

She nodded and smiled at him. "Yes, we do. How about Monday?"

Quinn didn't know what, but something was going on. Nora's smile and her words didn't go together. Was she upset because he visited the Heinrich property to watch the sunrise? He parked in front of the old house and lifted three folding chairs from the trunk. Randa brought hot chocolate and two extra cups.

The three of them sat in a row, with Nora in the middle. She handed a bird book to Randa. "I thought you'd like to find out what birds we have around here. If you need a closer look, there are binoculars in the bag."

They watched night turn into day in glorious color. Pink turned to coral, and Randa said, "That's the color of the necklace and earrings Uncle Quinn gave you. Mama had a dress that color. It looked really good on her."

Nora smiled. "I like the dusty rose that fades along the edge. I'd like to find a shade like that for my wedding dress."

On the way home, they both thanked Quinn for taking them to see the sunrise and gushed over the beauty they had seen in the sky. He felt cheated by the noise of all their chatter. They spoiled his special quiet time with God. Nora wasn't acting right. He needed to find out what was going on with her.

My Name is Randa

They stopped at the manse first. "Randa, I'll drop you off so you can get started with your bread. I want to talk to Nora about some things, so we'll be awhile. Call if you need me."

Randa jumped out and ran up the steps to the kitchen door.

Nora insisted on fixing breakfast, but they ate in silence. He waited for her to tell him what was on her mind.

After breakfast, they entered the living room with a second cup of coffee. He sat on the sofa, and she joined him. "Quinn, you want the Heinrich house, don't you?"

He opened his mouth to answer her, but she interrupted. "I thought when I said it would be too expensive, we were through with that place." Her voice went up a notch. "How did you expect me to know you wanted it?" She pushed her index finger into his chest. "I need to know what you're thinking. Why didn't you tell me?"

Finally, she had a question that he could answer. "Because you suggested we wait a month. I want to buy you a house you'll love."

She looked him in the eye. "I think it's time we learn about each other's finances. Are you uncomfortable with that?"

"Of course not. You're going to be my wife, and all my money will be your money. If you would like, we could talk to Melvin Gray, at the savings and loan, about how much we should spend on a house."

Nora sighed in relief. "Thank you. I'll get all my financial papers together and show you what I have, and I'd like you to do the same, so we'll both know how much money we have."

"That sounds like a good idea. I'll pick up sandwiches at Rudy's, and we can have lunch together." He reached for her hand. "Nora, it feels like you are angry with me."

Mary Watland

She sighed. "I won't be angry if you tell me what is going on in your mind. Why do you want to buy that house? I think it's too far gone."

He waited a moment. It seemed she had finally said everything she had on her mind. She'd told him exactly how she felt, and it was like listening to Esther instead of Nora.

"I'm sorry, Nora." He pulled her into his arms and breathed in her essence. It was time. She needed to know about his finances.

***

Monday morning, Quinn stood at the door of Park City Savings and Loan and waited for them to open. Melvin got up from his desk when he saw Quinn headed in his direction. "Good morning, Reverend Edwards. Can I help you with something?"

They shook hands, and Quinn sat on the edge of his chair. "Nora and I are discussing our finances today. Sometime this afternoon, would you be able to talk to us about how much we should spend on a house?"

***

Quinn arrived at Nora's with a full briefcase, a photo album, and a bag of sandwiches. Her papers lay on the dining room table. Nora's financial status was about what he expected, but when she saw his figures, she was stunned. "You have that much money, but where …?"

"I inherited everything when my mother died. During the war, and even after, I bought savings bonds every month. I've tried to be a good steward with my money.

"We have an appointment with Melvin Gray at three," Quinn said. "I thought he could give us advice on how much we should spend on a house."

308

My Name is Randa

Nora nodded. "That's a good idea."

They gave each other their views on bill paying, borrowing, and saving. Nora gathered her papers and said, "Carl handled the money during our marriage, and you have proved to me you are the one to take care of our finances. I'm delighted to hand the job over to you." She pushed her papers aside and said, "I think it's time we had some lunch."

After lunch, Quinn picked up the photo album and said, "Let's sit in the living room. I want to show you some pictures." They sat on the sofa, and he flipped through the first pages and introduced her to his family. He stopped at a picture of a man and woman with a young boy standing in front of a large two-story farmhouse. "This is me and my parents standing in front of our home. I didn't realize it at first, but this is why I'm so attracted to the Heinrich house."

"Oh, my goodness, they look very similar." She grinned up at him. "Your father has a beard like yours. Show me more pictures and tell me about your family. We have half an hour before we go to the bank."

***

Melvin said, "If you want to restore the Heinrich house, do it. You can afford it. I recommend Norm Gustafson; he's a good builder. You can trust him." He told them the owners were asking too much for the property and suggested a counteroffer.

After they left, Nora asked, "Could we go through the house again?"

"I'd like that. I'll call Norm Gustafson and ask him to go with us. He'll help us see the possibilities of what he can do.

***

Wednesday, they met at Ninth Street and walked through the dirty rooms. Norm said, "I took another look at the place yesterday with one of my men. It's sixty-four years old, but it's well constructed. If you want to pay the price, we can do it." Norm showed Nora rough drawings of some changes he and Quinn had talked about and some suggestions of his own.

"If you do this," he said, "I want each of you to give me a list of the things you'd like to have in the house. Don't skimp. It's more expensive to make changes after we've started construction. We'll weed through your lists and eliminate those things that aren't practical or too expensive."

Nora smiled at Quinn and said, "We'll want the addition on the east side. Quinn loves the sunrise."

Norm left, and Quinn and Nora sat in the car, grinning at each other. "Now I understand," she said. "I won't be able to sleep tonight. It's going to be perfect. We need to tell Warren."

Quinn raised an eyebrow and asked, "Now?"

She nodded. "Yes, right now."

***

"Are you going to tear it down and build a new one?" Warren asked.

"No," they said in unison.

"Norm Gustafson is going to renovate it. We want a big old house with spacious rooms," Quinn said.

"Wow, I didn't expect that. Let me warn you, there are five Heinrich children involved in this. Don't be surprised if we don't hear anything for at least a month."

***

My Name is Randa

Quinn took Nora home with him, so they could tell Randa what they'd done.

She looked at their glowing faces and said, "Don't tell me you like that house now."

He held up a key. "Would you like to see what Norm is proposing to do? It's too dirty for sandals. You'll have to put on shoes."

"Okay, just a minute." Randa tied her shoes and wished Molly was going with her. Did people that were courting do crazy things sometimes? Really crazy things?

Before Quinn started the car, he turned around and said, "Randa, this is *private and personal.* Until we hear that the Heinrichs have accepted our counteroffer, this is nobody's business but ours. Do you understand? Not even Molly."

With turned-down mouth, she said, "Okay, not even Molly."

Quinn took a flashlight from the jockey box and handed it to Randa. She walked into the dark house with broken glass, grit, and debris on squeaky floors.

He said, "See how much bigger the living and dining room are? Next year you can have a slumber party here and invite as many girls as you'd like."

They walked into the kitchen, where some of the cupboard doors hung at an angle on loose hinges. Randa heard a scratching noise, and a mouse scurried across the floor. "Eek!" she screamed and grabbed at Quinn. "I hear mice in the walls. I don't like this place. I don't want to live here. Mice give me the creeps."

She could tell Uncle Quinn thought she was being funny, but she wasn't. They scared her. Randa tightened her grip around his arm and looked up at him with tears in her eyes. "One time, Prissie brought a mouse home and left it on the front porch. I almost stepped on it. I screamed and

311

screamed. John took it away, and then he told me cats like to eat mice. I don't want Goldie to *ever* eat a mouse."

"Listen to me, Randa. Norm and his crew will tear this house down to the studs, and the mice will have to find another home."

"What are studs?"

"They're long boards two inches thick and four inches wide that are used to frame a house. We call those boards two-by-fours." Quinn looked at the confusion on Randa's face and shook his head. "I'll call Norm and see if we can look at a place with exposed studs. I promise you, honey, there will be no mice in these walls."

***

Before Randa went to bed, Quinn told her Norm wanted each of them to make a wish list of what they would like in the house.

She didn't say *no mice*, but it was on her mind. "Could the bathroom upstairs have a crooked ceiling like the Thompsons'? You know, like the shape of the roof. Oh! I know what I want. Since my bedroom is upstairs, could I have a balcony?"

Chapter 63

Friday, June 18

*E*arly Friday morning, Randa called Nora. "Hi, I forgot to tell Uncle Quinn we wanted to see the sunrise with him, and he's already gone."

"That's okay. I'll leave right now. It isn't light yet. We'll surprise him."

A hint of pink was showing along the horizon when Nora and Randa arrived at Ninth Street. They lifted folding chairs out of the car and hurried down the path through the weeds.

Quinn heard them talking and met them, holding the thermos under one arm and a cup of coffee in his other hand. "Good morning, ladies. This is a surprise. I need to clarify something. I said nothing when I brought you over here the first time, but I come here to worship God. It's a quiet time for me when I commune with God and enjoy His handiwork."

Nora reached up and kissed him. "May we worship with you?"

He put his arm around Nora's shoulder and returned her kiss. "I'm happy to have you worship with me, my darling. We'll talk after God finishes painting the sky and a new day has begun."

Randa cut in, "Okay, Uncle Quinn. Just as long as we can talk after the sun comes up." She put her chair beside Nora's and looked toward the east.

Nora watched Quinn's countenance relax into a reverent mode. She quieted her heart and beheld the glorious sight before her. Randa didn't fidget but sat back in her chair, legs stretched out in front, silently watching God paint the sky.

As the beautiful colors faded and the sky turned blue, Quinn stood and raised his arms to the heavens.

Randa joined her uncle. "Is this a Psalm 63 time?"

He nodded. They looked toward heaven and repeated together, "My lips shall praise thee. Thus will I bless thee while I live: I will lift up my hands in thy name."

When they finished, Nora's eyes were closed, and her hands were raised. Quinn touched her. She opened her eyes and said, "That was beautiful. Thank you."

Nora glanced at her watch and said, "I think I'll leave you two here and go home. I'm a little behind at work and had planned to go in early today."

Quinn walked Nora to her car and said, "I have a meeting at the nursing home this morning, so I'll pick up lunch at Rudy's and see you around 12:30."

***

Quinn stopped his car at Nora's house and saw her standing in the doorway. She said, "I need to talk to you about something, and I can't do it in a public place. Could we have lunch here after we talk?"

"Sure." He brought the sandwiches and drinks in, put them in the refrigerator, and went into the living room. She sat on the edge of her chair. He didn't like the feel in the air. Something serious was wrong, and he had no idea what.

She joined him on the sofa. "Quinn, why didn't you tell us watching the sunrise was a private worship time for you? I was embarrassed because I didn't know if you wanted me there. Am I invited to worship with you at sunrise? I wouldn't want to do it all the time, but sometimes. Don't you want us to worship the Lord together?"

His mouth dropped open, but he hesitated to speak. How should he answer? He didn't want to spoil the precious time they had with God this morning. "I loved having you there;

My Name is Randa

it was wonderful. I've never shared that part of my life with anyone. It has always been my time alone with God. I didn't think about it being something we could do together."

"But you and Randa do it together."

"Not really. I lifted my hands and said those verses the day we moved to Park City. She asked me about it, and I told her I was worshiping God because he had answered our prayers so quickly. She said she would memorize the verses. This morning is the first time we've said them together."

Nora let out a breath of relief. "Okay, then I'll memorize them too, so we can worship together."

"I'd like that. It would be a blessing to me. I'm sorry, my darling, that you felt unwanted."

She burst into tears. Quinn wrapped his arms around her.

When Nora's shower of tears was over, she said, "Would you hold me a while longer?"

He held her close. "I'm sorry you felt bad. Thank you for telling me. Please be patient with me; I'll learn to share my thoughts with you. You've seemed so tired. I didn't want you to lose more sleep by getting up before dawn to see the sunrise.

After they had lunch, Quinn returned to the office. Nora stood at the front door and waved goodbye, pleased that Quinn wanted her to worship God with him. Maybe she had overreacted? She inhaled deeply, thinking a nap would be wonderful. She shook her head. Exhausted or not, there simply wasn't time.

***

Nora was filling a bag with worn tea towels and dishrags when Esther knocked and opened the kitchen door. "Hello, stranger. I've finally found you at home. Tell me what's happening in your life. How is the house hunting going?"

Nora laughed. "You're right; we haven't talked in ages. Would you like some sweet tea? We made a counteroffer on a... Oh dear, I can't tell you. Quinn told Randa this was *private and personal,* and she isn't to tell, even Molly, until we get an answer. The owners live out of town, so Warren thinks it will take a while before we hear."

Esther laughed. "I see. I'm guessing we will have to get used to that. He seems to be a close-mouthed person."

"Yes, he is, and I've had to take him to task about it on more than one occasion. I'm sure he wouldn't mind if I told you, but it will give me a free conscience with Randa if I don't talk."

Esther leaned back in her chair. "What's on your list for the rest of the day?"

"The linen closet."

"What about the linen closet? Are you packing? Nora Montgomery, are you getting ready to move?"

"I only have two months."

"That is ridiculous. This house is paid for. Leave everything here until you move into the new house that Molly and I know nothing about."

"But..."

Esther shook her finger at Nora. "There are bags under your eyes. You and Quinn have two more months of courtship. Don't mess up the time packing when you don't even have a house yet. I'm leaving, and I suggest you take a long nap." Esther stomped toward the door, stopped, spun around, and said, "We need to have some sister time. Come to my house on Tuesday at noon for lunch. I've missed you."

Nora called out to Esther's back, "Okay, I will."

Sunday following morning worship service, Nora visited with friends while Quinn shook hands with the church members. Abigail Babcock approached her and asked,

My Name is Randa

"What were the three of you doing over at the Heinrich place so early in the morning?"

"Quinn likes to go there to watch the sunrise, and Randa and I went with him. It was beautiful. Did you see it?"

"Land sakes alive, no. I like my nice warm bed at that time of day. I heard you've been looking at houses. Reverend Edwards has a perfectly good house already. There is no reason for you to find another one. You don't need to be using up all his money. He's already spent too much money on that ring you're wearing."

Nora put a smile on her face and asked the Lord to help her remain silent. Abigail rattled on. "I have to get home; my niece is coming for lunch." She rushed away.

Agnes Johnson stormed over to Nora. "Don't pay any attention to that woman. It's nobody's business if you and Reverend Edwards want to buy a house of your own. Personally, I would never choose one of those ranch-style houses like the manse. I love my big old four-square house, even if there's only the two of us anymore."

***

That night, Nora sat in her bed with a book on her lap. She ignored Abigail's opinions and prayed, "Oh God, help me be gracious and love the people who are critical of things we do." Maybe it was time for her to read Proverbs 31, the virtuous woman chapter.

Chapter 64

The week of July 11

Sunday, Esther and Nora brought plates of cherry pie to the table while Tim refilled coffee cups. Nora said, "We are going to Madison on Tuesday. Do you men think you can get along without us for two days while we do some wedding shopping?

"I'm excited," Julie said. "Aunt Esther and one of her granddaughters are going to help Tim with the twins."

Esther laughed. "I asked Gracie, and now she can't come. You would not believe how many of my granddaughters and some nieces have volunteered. I might have to put all their names in a hat and have a drawing."

Julie took a bite of pie and pointed her fork at Randa. "I understand Quinn took you through the Heinrich house. What did you think?"

She glanced at her uncle.

"It's okay," he said. "Everybody here knows about the counteroffer."

Randa sucked in her breath. "Well, the floors are gritty, the wallpaper has come unglued and is all torn, the bathroom stinks, the stairs creak, and a mouse ran across the floor in the kitchen. I hate mice; they give me the creeps. All I saw was dirt inside and garbage outside. It's aww-ful."

"That was how I felt the first time," Nora said, "Norm Gustafson went with us the second time and explained how he could restore it. Now, I can't wait. I promise, Randa, if we get that house, it will be wonderful."

Randa wasn't so sure; she'd have to wait and see. "We went over there yesterday and watched the sunrise with Uncle Quinn. It was very pretty, but tall weeds are every-

318

My Name is Randa

where, and there's junk all over the field. Uncle Quinn told me to trust Norm, and Nora says she can close her eyes and see how perfect it will be." She ducked her head and cut another bite of pie.

***

Tuesday afternoon, Quinn left the office early and went home to pick up Randa. Julie and Tim were already there when they stopped in front of Nora's house. Her car sat in the driveway with the trunk lid open. Randa gave Tim a bag of chocolate chip cookies and put another bag on the backseat of Nora's car. Quinn added Randa's suitcase to the others, closed the trunk, then hugged and kissed her. "Have fun," he said and asked if she had her money.

She patted her purse and nodded. "I'm so excited. We get to go to Madison and buy wedding things, and *finally*, I'll get to meet Nancy and see her big house." She climbed into the back seat and waited for the two couples to say their goodbyes.

Quinn opened Nora's door, took her in his arms, and whispered, "I already miss you." He rubbed his beard on the side of her face and held her tight.

Nora whispered, "I'll miss you, too," and then slid out of his arms and into the car.

Randa thought they spent way too much time saying goodbye. She was happy they loved each other, but the lovey-dovey stuff embarrassed her. Maybe she should have closed her eyes while they kissed.

Nora turned the car toward Madison. Julie said, "Esther and Georgia arrived at our house right after lunch." She hesitated. "Two days is a long time to be without my family."

"We'll be so busy you won't have time to miss them," Nora said. "You can call long distance if you get too lonely."

Randa's eyes opened wide when they pulled up in front of the Pearson house. "Oh," she said, "this is the most beautiful place I've ever seen. Look at all the flowers. This is a mansion. Is our house going to be this big?

"No, honey," Nora answered. "Ours won't be near as big, nor will we have a yard that looks like this one."

The Pearson family came out to greet them. Clyde and the boys took the luggage upstairs to their rooms. Randa handed a paper bag of cookies to Phyllis and said, "I brought cookies."

"Thank you. We've heard you like to bake." Phyllis gave Randa a hug.

Nancy hugged her next and said, "I'm so happy you came. We will be cousins on August twenty-eighth. I don't have any girl cousins my age."

"All I have are two stepcousins, and they are boys," Randa said. "Nora says when she marries Uncle Quinn, I'll have all kinds of cousins, but most of them are younger. I am so glad we're the same age. "

Phyllis led them into the kitchen and served cold drinks and Randa's cookies. The guys took a plate of cookies into the sitting room to get away from all the wedding talk.

Julie said, "I can't believe Mother doesn't know what color she wants for her dress."

"Well, I know what I don't want. I don't want a formal bridal dress. I don't know what colors are popular this year, but I want a dress I can wear later, for dressy occasions. We'll find my dress first and then decide on the colors for the wedding."

***

Tuesday evening, Quinn walked into an empty house. It wasn't worth it to cook for one person, so he had a big bowl of cereal. He paced the floor, and Goldie followed close be-

My Name is Randa

hind until he picked her up. "Alright, Goldie, let's watch TV," he said. Quinn sat back in his chair and stroked her silky fur. She turned her purring motor on so loud he had to turn up the volume. Whatever was on didn't interest either of them, so Quinn turned it off before the ending.

The next morning, Quinn woke up starving. He fried four pieces of bacon and three eggs over easy. The house was so quiet he could hear himself chewing. He finished breakfast, cleaned his dishes, and went to work early.

Later that morning, Don Thompson stopped by the church for a quick visit and found Quinn writing numbers on the pages of his day calendar. "What're you doing?" he asked.

"It's thirty-nine days until the wedding. As you know, the girls are in Madison, shopping. I'm all alone, and last night I talked to the cat. I didn't realize how much I'd miss them."

Don left the church laughing.

***

Nora, Julie, and Randa headed to downtown Madison with Phyllis' list of dress shops. At the first store, Nora tried on several dresses and said, "These dresses aren't for a wedding."

"Okay, Mother. The bridal shop is a block away. The least we can do is look."

Nora walked in, and all she could see was satin and lace. "No. These are for young first-time brides. I'm too old to wear this fancy stuff."

Their clerk suggested Marie's.

When they left the bridal shop, Randa whispered to Julie, "I thought the dresses were beautiful. She didn't even try one on."

"I know, but she's the bride. She must have a picture in her mind of what she wants. When you get married, we'll go to the bridal shop and get the fussiest dress they have."

Nora admired a rose dress with a pencil skirt in the window display at Marie's. Inside, a clerk found one in Nora's size. While she tried it on, the girls sifted through the racks, searching for dresses that would match rose. Nora came out of the dressing room with a radiant smile. The fitted lines complemented her buxom figure. Nora turned from side to side and said, "I love it."

She laughed at Randa's crinkled brow as she stared at the skirt that came down close to her ankles. "Don't worry, honey, I have to shorten all my skirts. It looks like I forgot to stand up, doesn't it?"

Julie squatted down and folded the skirt up to the right length. Randa breathed a sigh of relief.

"Let's look at hats," Nora said. "I want a veil over my face when I walk down the aisle." Randa plopped a broad-brimmed hat on her head and pranced in front of Nora with her eyes crossed. Julie giggled and socked Randa's arm. Not to be outdone, Julie followed with a creation that looked like a plate turned upside down with a circle of red flowers on the crown. She curtsied in front of her laughing mother, and it fell to the floor.

Nora picked up a white lace-covered pillbox hat with a birdcage veil that curved under her chin. Julie said, "Mother, it's perfect, and you won't have any trouble seeing through it. I could barely see out of my veil. I was so relieved when Tim lifted it away from my face." She giggled. "Tim was shaking so hard I was afraid he was going to yank it off my head." The three of them burst out laughing, and Julie shushed them. "I think we're getting too loud."

My Name is Randa

When Nora got her laughter down to a chuckle, she shook her finger at her daughter. "Julie Hunter, if I laugh when Quinn lifts my veil, I'll never forgive you."

***

After they completed their wedding shopping, Nora turned the car to Alhric's Heirloom Furniture. Randa opened her door and stepped out. "This is a barn. Is this where all the old furniture is?"

"Come and see," Julie said. The bay of the big red barn was full of furniture set in pleasing arrangements. Julie pointed to the open stairway. "There's a second floor, too."

Nora walked ahead of them with a smile on her face and climbed up to the next level. This place had become a precious memory. It was where she and Quinn rocked and talked about the incredible love that had been secretly growing in their hearts for months. She was shocked when he suggested eloping on their first date, even if it was in jest. The people in their congregation would never believe how impulsive he could be.

Randa thought this stop would be boring, but when they went upstairs, there was an entire section of bedroom furniture. Uncle Quinn had mentioned she might like to have new furniture, something more feminine. Her bedroom set was very plain. She wandered up and down the rows, trying to decide what she liked.

Julie joined her beside a maple dressing table. "Have you found something you like?"

"How do you decide? There are so many to choose from."

"First you decide on the color of wood. The flow of the grain helps me pick out my favorite."

Randa didn't know there were so many things you had to decide before you chose a bed and dresser. They would have to come back another day when there was more time.

Marg Watland

***

Thursday morning, Tim and Quinn were waiting at Nora's house when the three ladies drove in. Julie ran into Tim's waiting arms. "I missed you so much. Please take me home to my babies."

"Go on home," Nora said. "I'll bring Julie's packages out tomorrow."

Quinn helped his bride-to-be carry her parcels into the house while Randa moved her things from Nora's trunk to their car. He gave Nora a kiss and said, "I'll take Randa home and go back to work. Would you like to have supper at Jane's Diner tonight?"

On the way home, Randa talked non-stop, telling Quinn about the Pearson's house, shopping, and playing games with her soon-to-be cousins. He helped her with her packages and said, "I'll make bologna sandwiches, and you can show me your dress for the wedding."

Quinn had sandwiches ready when Randa danced into the kitchen in a pale aqua dress, with a full skirt, and spun around. It fit her perfectly and showed curves he hadn't noticed before.

"Julie's is aqua like mine, but it has a straight skirt like Nora's. I can't tell you the color of Nora's dress because she said it's a secret."

"You look beautiful," he said and sent her back to change. Quinn wished Sarah could see how lovely her daughter had become in the past year. He looked toward heaven and thanked God again for giving him Randa and Nora to love.

Chapter 65

Wednesday, July 28

Erik Larson called Quinn and said Lee Shepherd's aunt Sophia died and that a package was coming from the Shepherd family, with photographs and some of Leland's report cards. He offered to keep it at his office until they returned from their honeymoon. Erik promised he and his wife would be at the wedding.

For the third night that week, Randa sat alone in the living room while her uncle worked at his desk. She put her finger in the book she was reading and walked over to peek into his study. "Could I bring my book and sit with you while you work? It's kinda lonely out here."

Quinn looked up from his commentary. "I'm sorry, honey; give me 15 minutes and I'll stop for the evening,"

"No, that's okay. It's getting to the love chapter in my story, so you can keep on working and I'll read."

She pulled an old wooden chair with arms into the study. Quinn said, "I was a boy when that chair shifted and tossed me out on the floor. My father took baling wire, looped it around the legs, and pulled them back into place, making the chair secure and safe. It came from a dining room set of my grandparents. I took it with me to college."

Quinn returned to his research, and Randa read her love chapter in her great-grandparent's chair. Goldie jumped up on her lap, turned around once, settled herself in a curl, and purred. Each time Randa turned a page, the chair squeaked.

Thirty minutes later, Quinn gave up. The purrs and squeaks were too distracting. "I've come to a stopping place. How is your love story going?"

Marg Watland

"It's done, and Jonathan is out meeting up with Wetzel. Zane Grey's love chapters are too short," she said in disgust.

"That's funny. I always thought they were kind of dumb and more like a fairy tale than real life."

***

Thursday morning, July 29, Warren Campbell called Quinn to tell him the Heinrichs accepted his offer and he'd probably have the signed papers by Monday. Quinn couldn't wait to tell Nora the good news, but she wasn't home. When he called Julie, she wasn't there. He dialed Esther's number, and there was no answer. Frustrated, he gave up.

After work, Quinn drove to Nora's, but her car wasn't in the garage. Next, he went to Esther's place, and Nora's car sat in the driveway. He knocked on the door, but nobody answered. He peeked in Esther's garage window; her car was gone. Quinn wished he was a kid so he could kick something. He drove back to Nora's house, attached a note to her screen door, and went home.

It was almost eight when Nora turned into his driveway. Randa saw her first and rushed into Quinn's study. "She's here; Nora's here. Quinn bolted out of his chair and stood beside Randa at the front door.

***

Quinn went to bed that night and tried to push away thoughts about the package from the Shepherds. He had more important things to think about. When he asked Nora where she would like to go on their honeymoon, she said, "A nice place in Michigan, and I'd like to see the farm where you lived."

Tomorrow, he'd call and ask his cousin Lillian for advice.

Chapter 66

Noon on Saturday, August 14

Quinn knocked on Nora's door. When she opened it, he drew her into his arms and whispered in her ear, "Fourteen more days and you will be Nora Edwards." Quinn didn't like the circles under her eyes. He'd like to take her to a quiet place under the trees and let the soothing sounds of nature lull her to sleep, but he couldn't do it today. He had an appointment at three.

Nora offered to make some coffee. He followed her into the kitchen and sat at the table where her steno pad lay open. He turned six pages before coming to the end.

Quinn held up the pad. "My darling, Norm Gustafson told me building a house is very stressful on a couple. He said often they yell at each other, and some have divorced. I want you to have happy memories of being my bride-to-be. Please put your lists away and stop packing until after our honeymoon. You're trying to do too much. If we were married, I'd put my foot down, but I haven't figured out when or if I should do that."

Nora's pursed lips alerted Quinn he'd said too much. "I plan on being an obedient wife, but don't ever expect me to quit writing lists. That is the way I run my life, and I'm not stopping now. When we get back from our honeymoon, I'll be living in your house. That takes some planning."

He groaned inside and worked on pulling his foot out of his mouth. "You're right. I'm sorry, I didn't do that right. Please forgive me. I don't want you to quit writing lists; they keep you organized. Could we go through the list on your move to my house?"

With tears on her lashes, Nora said. "I love you, Quinn. I don't want to fight with you."

He took Nora's hand and pulled her onto his lap. Quinn ran his finger down her list. "Could we move the furniture when we get back, or maybe Tim could move it over while we're gone? How about just bringing your personal things and your clothes? That's enough for now."

Nora glared at him until he squirmed, then she grinned. "I guess that means I can't go through any more boxes in my garage, doesn't it?"

She offered to make lunch, but Quinn insisted they go out instead. He needed to help her slow down.

***

Most of the lunch hour crowd was gone, and it was peaceful. Quinn saw Nora's shoulders relax. She leaned back against the cushion in the booth and said, "Tuesday night, I have a bridal shower, but I think we should spend some time next week deciding where we want the addition on the house."

"No, my darling. That's the last thing we need to be talking about right now."

"Why not?"

"That isn't something we can decide in a couple of hours."

"But…

"Nora, it's going to be filled with too many decisions, and I suspect we're both going to do some compromising. I don't want us dealing with compromises and hurt feelings right before our wedding."

"How will Norm know what to do if we haven't decided?"

"I haven't called him."

"But I hoped we would be in by Christmas."

My Name is Randa

"Me too, but if it doesn't happen, so be it." Quinn raised his eyebrow and asked, "My darling, you are a very determined woman, aren't you?"

She sighed. "No, but I've noticed you are determined, too."

"You're right. Nora, I think we should stop this conversation and have a time-out."

"Could we at least let Norm know the house is ours?"

"Alright, I'll call him." Quinn took both her hands and prayed, "Lord, we need your direction with this. Help both of us be open to your leading."

***

Nora gripped the steering wheel as she drove to the church where her bridal shower was being held. The women of the church loved her, but they would tease her unmercifully. She hated to blush and could not understand why Quinn thought she was beautiful, all *flushed and pink*.

She sat in the empty chair between Julie and Randa, in a blue and green floral sheath, and eyed the women on either side of her. Ruth, Molly, Randa, Julie, Esther, and Mavis were all dressed in blue. Esther leaned around Julie and, with lips in a straight line to keep from laughing, said through her teeth, "We all received our marching orders from the youngest in the group."

Randa shrugged. "It's your favorite color. I thought we should all wear blue."

The first gift Nora opened was a slinky black silk nightgown that Esther had hemmed to the correct length. Whistles and laughter came from the group. Nora kept her rosy face down and opened the next package, a blue willow candle holder. Her cheeks barely had time to cool when she opened a sheer pink gown with a deep V. She thought the front was indecent, but Quinn would likely enjoy its lines.

Randa gave her a large leather-bound scrapbook. Inside, a large paper clip held the newspaper's announcement of Quinn and Nora's engagement.

The next two packages were nightgowns, a sweet pink and white floral, and the other a long white flannel garment that buttoned all the way up and triggered resounding laughter. Molly and Ruth made blue and white polka dot potholders and aprons for Nora and her two girls, plus bibs for Rosie and Jordie.

***

Esther helped Nora carry in all her gifts, then said, "Leave these things until tomorrow. You look dead on your feet. Go to bed."

Nora waved goodbye, sorted through the seven nightgowns she had received, and tried to decide which ones to take on her honeymoon. Her eyes squinted, and a wicked smile appeared on her face. Nora lifted a weekender suitcase from the storage closet and carefully wrapped each gown in tissue paper. The seven gowns filled the case, and with a twist of the key, she locked the blue piece of luggage.

Next, she found a small box, lined it with cotton, and placed the key inside. Nora wrapped the box with shiny green paper and tied it with a white satin ribbon. "Here, my darling, is your honeymoon gift," she said, tucking the little box in her make-up case.

***

Wednesday, after Prayer Meeting, Randa left to stay overnight with the Thompsons, and Quinn and Nora moved their chairs under the big oak tree in her backyard. They sat in silence, soaking in the peace as nature quieted the day to evening.

Nora said, "I have a long list of last-minute things to do before the wedding rehearsal. You were right. We don't have time to talk to Norm about the addition. Maybe there are things Norm can do that don't require decisions on our part."

"My darling, we have an appointment to meet with Norm on Friday evening, the day we plan to return from our honeymoon. I've given him Tim's name and number; in case he has questions while we're gone. Nora, I'm buying this house for us, but I want it to be your dream house."

Nora leaned back, closed her eyes, and thought about what he just said. *So, it's going to be my dream house. I'd like corner shelves and colorful pictures of sunrises in the living room. In another room, there could be pictures of trees by a river...*

Chapter 67

Friday morning, August 27

Quinn swung his legs over the side of the bed after less than three hours of sleep. A hot shower would feel good.

As the water washed over him, his mind wandered, recalling Aunt Etta's bony arm around his shoulder. If you were anywhere near, she hugged you. His mother showed her love with a pat, and his father rarely showed any kind of affection.

Randa would wrap her arms around his waist and wouldn't let go until he loved her back. She was going to *love* Aunt Etta.

What would Aunt Etta think of Randa? Did she have Sarah's personality, her mannerisms? He'd like to have a long talk with her about Sarah. He had so many questions, but there wouldn't be time on this visit.

A bang on the bathroom door startled Quinn, and he quickly turned off the shower. He didn't need to be in *her* doghouse today. "You caught me in time," he called. "I didn't use all the hot water. I'll be out in a minute."

She giggled.

When Randa entered the kitchen, Quinn had milk, cereal, peanut butter, jam, and bread on the table. She spun around, plopped on her chair, and said, "They'll be here in three more hours, and we've crossed off everything on our list. We're ready for them."

Quinn laughed. "I'll have to find something to keep you busy, or you'll be hopping around like a rabbit."

"That's okay. While I hop, you can pace," she said and gave her ponytail a flip.

My Name is Randa

He took her hand, bowed his head, and thanked God for their special family day. Randa wolfed down her food. He didn't think she would get much out of their devotions, so he left the little booklet they normally used on the shelf and opened his Bible to Matthew chapter six. "I thought we'd use the Lord's prayer for our devotions today. Let's say it together; '*Our Father which art in heaven ...*'"

***

A black Hudson stopped in front of their house. Randa's dark eyes sparkled. Quinn was proud of her. She looked pretty in her pink sleeveless dress and matching ribbon tied around her ponytail. He took her hand, and they went outside to greet their family.

Moira, Aunt Etta's granddaughter, helped Aunt Etta out of the car. She looked up and said, "Look, Grandma, they came out to meet us."

Etta spread her arms wide and said, "Come here, you two, and give me a hug."

They both put an arm around her waist. She squeezed them tight, and Quinn said, "Aunt Etta, this is Sarah's daughter, Randa."

"I'm so happy to have a great aunt," Randa said. "Uncle Quinn told me you were his favorite aunt, so you're my favorite, too."

Quinn's cousin Lillian exited the car on the driver's side. He broke away and gave her a hug. "It's good to have you here. The young lady helping your mother must be your daughter, Moira. She looks like you. I think Moira and Nora's daughter Julie must be about the same age. You'll meet her at the rehearsal. Randa's excited to have you here to sit with her at the wedding."

They walked into the house, and before they could sit down, Randa asked, "Would you like to see our house?"

Goldie jumped off her favorite chair in the living room and ran over to join the tour. Randa picked her up. "This is Goldie. Uncle Quinn thought it was funny that I showed Goldie all the rooms in our house the night we brought her home. A cat needs to see all the rooms when they move into a new house, just like people."

They all laughed.

Randa stepped to the open door of Quinn's study. "Goldie and I come in here and read while Uncle Quinn writes his sermons." She opened his bedroom door. "He likes brown, so when we moved here, the church ladies made him this brown quilt. Nora's favorite color is blue, so she's going to put a bunch of blue stuff in here too."

She opened her bedroom door and put Goldie on the bed. "The ladies made me a blue quilt. Isn't it pretty? And Uncle Quinn gave me the velvet chair for my birthday, and Santa gave me Raggedy Ann."

She turned to the dresser and picked up a picture. "This is Mama and me with the wedding cake she made for the Sorenson's. She let me help frost the cake, but she made all the roses. I have a book with all the wedding cakes Mama made for people. We always baked together. She made fancy birthday cakes too, and at Christmas, we made gingerbread boys from Grandma Edwards' recipe. People loved them, and we sold hundreds and hundreds of them."

Catching her breath, Randa pointed to the open door across the hall and said, "That's the bathroom. Now you need to see our kitchen. When we moved in, the kitchen was yellow, but Molly, my best friend, told Uncle Quinn I wanted the kitchen to look like Mama's. Uncle Quinn and Molly's dad painted the kitchen white for my birthday. Molly made the red gingham curtains, and Julie gave us the apple cookie jar and the red birds on the wall. Oh, I forgot about the dining room. We went to the flower shop yesterday and

My Name is Randa

bought a bouquet of pink and white daisies with a red carnation in the middle. Those were Mama's favorite flowers. She liked to put pink and red together."

Moira stood beside Quinn and whispered in his ear, "She's delightful."

Quinn hadn't been sure it was necessary to show their guests the house, but Randa's running comments were the perfect beginning for his family's visit. He suggested the women find a place to sit outside under the trees, and they would bring out lunch.

Moira shooed him out the door and told him to go visit with his family. She'd help in the kitchen. "Is Nora coming?" she asked.

"Later this afternoon. Nora thought we needed time to visit together by ourselves."

Randa opened the refrigerator and handed Moira a platter of fried chicken. They brought two salads, pork and beans, and sweet tea to the table.

Quinn asked everyone to join hands, and his prayer was full of thanksgiving. Randa thought he prayed a little too long, but after all, he *was* a reverend.

When they finished their meal, Randa carried a metal cake holder to the table. "I made a surprise for dessert for Great Aunt Etta. Mama said her favorite was a burnt sugar cake with burnt sugar frosting." She cut the cake, and Moira helped her carry the plates to each person.

Etta took a bite and said, "It tastes just like your grandma's cake."

"It's her recipe."

"That can't be," Etta said. "Would you show me your recipe?"

"Sure." Randa ran into the house, returned with a blue notebook, and handed it to her aunt.

335

"Mama told me she wrote all of her mother's recipes in this book before she left home. She wanted to have them when she found a husband. Grandma and Grandpa didn't want her to have dates or fall in love and get married because she had a weak heart, so she left home."

Everything got quiet. She looked up. They were staring at her. "What?"

Quinn swallowed and said, "Nobody knew why she ran away, honey."

How could Quinn's parents have demanded that of Sarah? Deprive her of love? It was unthinkable. What did they expect her to do while she waited to die? All this time, he'd thought she couldn't take all the rules and laws his father had inflicted on them, but she just wanted to live and be loved.

Would he have done that to Randa if she had a bad heart? Oh God, he hoped not.

They finished their dessert, and Lillian began stacking the dishes. She said, "We need to put this food away before it spoils."

Quinn joined her, and when Randa came to help, he suggested she visit with Moira and her grandma, who wanted to go in the house where it was cooler.

When Lillian and Quinn finished in the kitchen, the others were turning pages in Sarah's photo album. Etta said, "Look, here's Sarah and her class when she graduated from high school."

Lillian leaned over her mother's shoulder and said, "They're all Mexican except for Sarah."

Randa nodded. "Yeah, my father told Mama she should go to school and get her high school diploma. All our neighbors were Mexican except us."

Quinn chimed in. "And Randa speaks Spanish. Tell them about your birthday parties."

My Name is Randa

"They were lots and lots of fun. We'd sing and dance until we fell down. The best part was the piñata. We took turns hitting it." She spread her arms wide apart and said, "When the piñata broke, candy flew everywhere."

Lillian noticed her mother's eyes were drooping and asked Quinn where she could have a nap. Randa said, "Let her sleep on my bed," as she led them down the hall. Goldie followed and jumped up on the bed.

Etta stroked Goldie's fur. "I'd love her company."

They left the room, and Randa said, "Goldie will take good care of her."

Quinn and Lillian talked about times when they were kids. Moira and Randa paged through the pictures of Sarah's wedding cakes while Etta and Goldie slept.

A car turned into their driveway, and a tall skinny man helped his wife out of the car. Quinn sprang from his chair and strode to the front door.

Randa jumped up and followed him. "Uncle Drew." She paused at the doorway and watched Quinn hug a plump woman with white hair and glasses that hung on a chain around her neck. Randa turned back to their guests and said, "He's going to marry them."

Quinn led them into the house and said to his family, "These are my very good friends Drew and Madeline Patterson. Drew and I were roommates in seminary."

Drew put his arm around Randa's shoulder and said, "I'm glad you finally get to meet your aunt Madeline."

She reached out to Randa and hugged her. "I am so happy to meet the girl that bakes and stole my husband's heart."

Lillian excused herself to check on her mother. When they entered the living room, Quinn introduced his aunt Etta.

Drew said, "I have prayed for years that Quinn would reconnect with his family, and Randa has brought that about. I'm very happy to meet you."

"And I'm happy to meet you too," Etta said. "My brother Daniel was what my children call *old country*. He worked hard to give his son a profitable farm, but Quinn didn't want to be a farmer. He went away to college to be a teacher. That farm would have given him much more money than a teacher could ever earn."

Quinn grimaced; he had spent decades avoiding telling anyone about his family. He felt it was his private business, and nobody needed to know. In a matter of minutes, Drew and Aunt Etta had brought everything out into the open. He helped her sit in the davenport's corner and sat on the arm beside her.

She patted his arm. "Quinn, when your parents got your letter saying you were going to seminary, your father was so proud. He said his son was going to *reap souls* for Jesus. Daniel didn't have the right words in him to stop the feud between the two of you."

Tears welled in his eyes. "Sarah stopped the anger in my heart. She forgave him first, Aunt Etta."

"How?"

Randa broke in. "I need to tell them Mama's story, then she'd know how."

"Are you sure you want to do that today, honey?"

"Sure. Mama would want her to know."

Quinn glanced at Randa, sitting between his aunt and Lillian. "Lillian, could I trade places with you? I like to sit beside Randa when she tells Sarah's story." He left the room, returned with a box of tissue, and put it on the coffee table. Then he sat beside Randa and slid his arm across the top of the davenport.

She smiled up at him, then said, "Mama always took an afternoon nap, but her naps kept getting longer and longer, so John, my stepfather, took her to the doctor ..."

My Name is Randa

Reaping souls; his dad had forgiven him. Randa sat beside him, telling her mama's story. She was open, and he was closed. He had to change.

Randa wiggled into a more comfortable spot and continued to tell her mother's story. "Bertha, my reverend's wife, gave me a diary so I could write my thoughts about Mama getting ready to go to heaven. When I told Uncle Quinn about my diary, he liked the idea. Now we both have a journal, and we're writing about learning how to live together as a family. A bunch of people have said Mama's story should be a book. We're going to write it together, but we have to wait awhile because Nora's going to be in our story too."

Tears swam in the eyes of every person in the room. Etta's hands trembled so severely Randa helped her pull tissues from the box. Moira dabbed the places her grandma missed and passed the box to Madeline.

When Randa finished, Quinn's jaw jutted out. He straightened, and with determination, Quinn told *his* story.

"A couple of months after we moved here, Randa told me she'd always wanted a big brother who would watch out for her. I was Sarah's big brother, but I felt no responsibility toward her. When Sarah ran away, I blamed our parents. I had no compassion for them or my sister. When Randa told me Sarah had forgiven her parents, I was ashamed. I, a reverend, taught my parishioners to forgive, but I'd been holding hateful anger in my heart against my dad. I spent an entire night confessing my sins and asking for God's forgiveness. I regret I wasn't able to go to my parents and say, *I'm sorry.*"

Goldie jumped up in his lap, and Quinn stroked her fur.

Drew broke the silence. "I think this would be a great time to thank God for what's happened just now." He bowed his head. "Heavenly Father, we know that you are a God who heals not just our bodies, but also our relationships and our families. Thank you for the healing of this family. Thank you for Randa's willingness to share her mama's story. We also want to thank you for your love and how it penetrates and changes our lives. And we pray this in the name of Jesus, who forgave, even as he gave his life for us. Amen."

Randa looked around at her family and asked, "Uncle Quinn, shouldn't we lift our hands?"

"Yes, we should." The two of them stood, lifted their hands, and looked toward heaven. "*O God, thou art my God; early will I seek thee; my soul thirsteth for thee, my flesh longeth for thee. Because thy lovingkindness is better than life, my lips shall praise thee. Thus will I bless thee while I live: I will lift up my hands in thy name.*"

By the time they finished quoting the verses in Psalms 63, everyone had lifted their hands

Etta's voice quavered. "Thank you. I will never forget this day."

Everybody smiled, and Randa thought God must be happy to see all her family lifting their hands. She loved doing it at sunrise best; that's when she felt God was right there with them. Maybe Uncle Drew and Aunt Madeline would like to worship at sunrise on Sunday. She didn't think Uncle Quinn would have time on his wedding day. He'd been pretty twitchy lately. She'd ask Uncle Drew what they should do.

Quinn stood. "It's time for me to get Nora. She thought we should have a few hours together before she came. I'll be right back."

"Uh-huh." Randa laughed and raised her eyebrow, just like her uncle. "It might be a little longer than *right back.*"

Etta asked Madeline to come to sit by her so they could talk, and Drew went out to the car to get their luggage.

When he returned, Randa whispered, "Did you bring us some more of your good tea? It's too warm for a hot drink

My Name is Randa

today, so we bought extra milk, and I made sweet tea to go with our cookies."

He winked at her and said, "Of course, and I'm happy to hear there are cookies. I hope tomorrow you will serve your regular Saturday morning second breakfast?" He opened his grip and handed her a bag of English tea.

"Of course, the wedding isn't until one, so I have lots of time." She took the bag in the kitchen, and he followed her. "Uncle Drew, I want to ask you something. Could you help Uncle Quinn? He's been … well, kind of twitchety lately."

Drew smiled, then grinned, then laughed, and couldn't quit. He pulled her into a hug and kept on laughing. Goldie padded into the kitchen, and the women weren't far behind. Goldie stood at Drew's feet with her head tipped back as far as it would go.

He caught his breath and said, "I'm sorry, honey, but *twitchety* is a perfect word. Don't worry, the bride and groom get nervous just before a wedding. When they return home from their honeymoon, the *twitchety* will be gone."

Goldie went to the study and scrunched under Quinn's desk, away from all the noisy chatter.

Chapter 68

Friday afternoon. August 27

Nora opened the door to Quinn's knock, expecting to leave, but he stepped in and said, "I want you to know all that has happened before we go to my house." He walked into the living room and paced from one end to the other. He talked rapidly, and his arms flailed.

She sat in her chair and watched, trying to keep up with all he said. He was so excited he forgot to kiss her. He told her about the things Randa had revealed.

"I don't know how many times I've seen that notebook on the counter while she was baking, but I never picked it up and read it. When we looked at it today, it surprised me. The writing was neat and flowery. Sarah dotted her i's with little circles.

"I don't remember my dad ever saying he was proud of me. We didn't agree on anything. I would like to have heard him say, *reaping souls.*

"Can you believe Drew prayed for me all these years? I'll bet the rest of the family prayed too. Nora, it is so good to have my family here."

Nora marveled at how much had been revealed. She was glad his family heard *Mama's story.*

She squeezed Quinn's hand. "The biggest blessing is your father's pride at you becoming a reverend. I like the *reaping souls for Jesus.* I'm happy for you, my darling."

She was so beautiful with her sweet smile and sparkling eyes, which reminded him he hadn't kissed her. He pulled her up into his arms. She snuggled close. His kiss was hurried, but that changed when she put her soft hands on his face and pulled him toward her. They stood wrapped in

My Name is Randa

each other's arms while the things that had transpired at Quinn's house took root in their minds.

"I can see all of you lifting your hands to God. What a beautiful blessing that must have been to the Lord."

When they drove up, everybody watched Quinn help a little woman with auburn curls out of the car. He took her hand as they walked to the front door.

With his arm around her shoulder, he introduced Nora to each of them individually, beginning with Aunt Etta.

Nora had a special word for each of them. When they came to Madeline, Nora wrapped both hands around hers and said, "I'm counting on us becoming good friends." She reached for Drew's hand. "Thank you for insisting Quinn pray about his feelings for me. If you hadn't done that, I might still be just his secretary. Marriage never crossed my mind until Quinn suggested we have a date on our birthday. My life has been a whirlwind ever since."

The conversation blurred, and Nora thought of Quinn's warning that people sometimes expected more of reverend's wives than was fair. He assured her she'd make a perfect reverend's wife for him and their congregation. He said she had a meek and quiet spirit and was a wise woman. *What if I don't measure up to his expectations?* She wanted to be what he dreamed of her to be. Was she having pre-wedding jitters? Esther warned her that brides get jittery just before the wedding. She needed to talk to her sister.

Quinn and Drew were visiting, so Randa asked Moira to help put plates of cookies on the dining room table. Moira looked at all the cookies. "Oh my goodness, you made so many."

"I wanted to make four different kinds, and Uncle Quinn said to make them bite-size. What's left over I'll take to Julie and Tim's."

Everyone sat around the table munching on cookies while Lillian shared stories about playing in the barn. "Every time we saw Quinn, he had long scratches on his arms and face. He would not quit trying to catch those wild cats.

"When we were teenagers, I bought a deck of cards, and we taught Quinn how to play poker. Uncle Daniel said cards were of the devil. So, we hid them in the hay loft behind a board."

Aunt Etta sputtered. "Lillian, I swear I should take a switch to you."

Quinn laughed. "When Dad found those cards, he was furious. He thought they belonged to one of the hired hands. I didn't say a word. Dad threw the cards in the cook stove one at a time and didn't close the lid until he saw them catch fire and curl."

Everybody laughed with him.

Drew shared a memory. "When Quinn started coming home with me, he played ball like a girl. Our entire family loves baseball, so we taught him how to play like a guy. He's a good batter."

Randa was next. "At Christmas, Molly's brother told me to buy a ball and bat, so Uncle Quinn could teach me how to play. He's good at chess too, but he can't beat Molly's grandfather."

Nora slid her hand into Quinn's, and he squeezed. She liked his family. Tonight, they would practice for the ceremony, and tomorrow, they'd become one. She shivered and grinned.

Quinn watched Randa smile non-stop as she soaked in all the love-filled family stories. Those three women, his family, were wrapping their roots around him and Randa, and he accepted it with a happy grin. He'd not felt that kind of warmth for years.

My Name is Randa

That's why he liked Sunday dinner at Nora's. Quinn learned to let down his guard at her house. He could stretch his legs and relax. He didn't have to stiffen up and act proper like a reverend. The Montgomery family's love was strong, and early on, they had taken him and Randa into their fold.

Randa stretched her arms around Quinn and whispered, "I'm so happy, *Dad*. This is my dream come true."

He hugged her tight and said, "I love you, honey. Thank you for bringing my family back to me."

Aunt Etta watched Quinn smile at Nora and stroke her hand. She asked, "Where are you going on your honeymoon?"

Lillian patted her mother's hand and said, "Mother, it might be a surprise. If Quinn wants us to know, he'll tell us." They turned to him and waited.

"Mackinac Island," he said. "Nora's never been to Michigan, and I think that's one of the nicest places in the state. She wants to see our farm, so we'll drive down there, and she can see where I was raised. We'll only be gone a week. I've bought Nora a big old house that needs major renovations, and we want to be here for that. We'd like to be in it before Christmas, but ... it's a big job."

Randa piped up. "You don't want to see it now. It's awful, but Norm Gustafson promised me he'd make it all beautiful. He told each one of us to make a wish list. I want a balcony. Nora says it's going to be wonderful. The next time you come to visit, we'll have a guest room for you."

Nora marveled at the change in her soon-to-be daughter and the joy on her face. She prayed, "O Lord, my heart is full of thankfulness. I think you brought us together to be Randa's parents. She will make our union even sweeter."

***

Mary Watland

The rehearsal dinner hosted by the Johnsons and the Thompsons

Twenty people took their places around one of two tables, sitting in front of the place card with their name. Don stood at the head of one table and said, "When Quinn asked Neil and me to be ushers, our wives decided we should host their rehearsal dinner. Agnes and Ruth have been cooking up a storm today. You'll notice we put out-of-town guests across from someone they don't know, so we can all get acquainted."

Neil put his hand on Drew's shoulder. "We're happy to have you here for this special occasion, Professor Patterson. Would you ask the blessing on the food?"

Drew prayed, and Etta squirmed. As soon as he said amen, she said, "I thought you were a reverend."

Don laughed. "That's what *I* thought when they came to our Men's Bible Study. I was new at teaching, and when it was over, I found out he has a master's degree in divinity, is a Doctor of Theology, and teaches in the seminary where he and Rev were roommates. I was, well, let's just say, being good friends with Rev is a whole 'nother ball game."

Everyone laughed, including Drew, who said, "In a setting like this, I want to be Drew to all of you. I worked hard for all those titles, but it's refreshing to just be myself. We're here celebrating the coming wedding of Quinn and Nora. I'd be interested in knowing when you folks thought there was something going on between these two."

Tim raised his hand. "I think I might be the earliest. Little Mother invited Quinn and Randa to Sunday dinner on the fourth of October. On the way home, I asked Julie how'd she feel if her mother married again. Then in November, he brought her to the hospital to wait for our twins to be born and didn't leave her side until Aunt Esther arrived. That's when I knew for sure."

346

My Name is Randa

Esther was next. "After hearing *Quinn* this and *Quinn* that, for months, Nora showed up at my door late one night needing a ring to cover the dent on her ring finger."

Randa said, "For me, it was before Christmas. I asked Uncle Quinn if he'd ever get married and have babies. I thought Nora would make a good wife for him. He said he was too old for her and much too old to be having babies. We didn't think Uncle Quinn was too old, so Molly and I started praying that they'd fall in love."

Neil snorted, but Don couldn't hold it in. He laughed, and everyone laughed with him.

Randa didn't think it was *that* funny. Uncle Quinn and Nora both had red faces. Did she say something private and personal?

***

Nora went to bed with a smile. Randa would keep their life interesting. She was sure they'd have to make adjustments, but she'd not worry about that now.

Quinn was right. The house plans could wait until after the honeymoon. Tomorrow, she would marry the reverend she had met three weeks short of a year ago. He had four years of college and three years of seminary. She only had a high school diploma. Could she complement his ministry?

Nora sat up. "I need an advisor ... Madeline! She would be perfect. A list of books would be a good start."

Nora turned on her light and wrote a reminder on the pad sitting on her nightstand. She picked up her Bible, turned to the Philippians, and read chapter four. Several verses were underlined, but verse thirteen was the one she needed tonight. *I can do all things through Christ which strengtheneth me.*

Chapter 69

The Wedding

August 28, 1954

Professor Andrew Patterson led Nora and Quinn through their wedding vows and the exchanging of the rings. Then he said, "Now it's time for your parenting vows. Miss Miranda Jean Shepherd would like you to be her second parents."

Randa left her seat beside Etta and came forward. A few escaped ringlets had dropped from the mass of dark curls atop her head, and partially covered the fragrant white rose Phyllis had tucked in her hair.

Quinn gazed at his niece. She looked like a princess, his sweet princess. In a year and three months, she had changed from a grief-stricken child to a beautiful teenager.

He couldn't have made it without Nora. God had blessed him with a wonderful woman, and he planned to thank her daily for allowing him to be her husband. She gave him joy overflowing. Quinn's eyes searched the audience for the two guests Randa didn't know were coming.

Drew took Randa's hand. "Paul says in the sixth chapter of Ephesians, 'Children, obey your parents in the Lord; for this is right.' Do you promise to obey your second parents, Quinn and Nora?"

She grinned and said to the bride and groom, "I promise to obey you, my second parents."

"Do you promise to honor your mother and father?"

Quinn and Nora heard sniffles when Randa said, "Yes, I promise to honor you and come to you when I have questions."

My Name is Randa

Drew turned to the bride and groom and asked, "Quinn and Nora, do you promise to bring Miranda Jean Shepherd up in the nurture and admonition of the Lord?"

Together they said, "We do."

Drew squeezed Randa's hand and said, "Miranda Jean Shepherd, you may kiss your second parents."

She stretched up and kissed Quinn, then hugged him tight around his waist and said, "I love you Unc — D-dad,"

She turned and wrapped her arms around Nora. "I am so happy you are my mom."

Julie was braced for the exuberant hug. Randa's whisper was heard by all. "Now, you're my sister, and I love you very much."

Tim's arms curled around her. Randa's voice was muffled against his chest. "You are the best big brother I could ever have."

He patted her back. "Come on, little Sis, let's back up and let Professor Patterson finish this weddin'."

Drew winked at Randa, then said to the couple before him, "Quinn and Nora, I now pronounce you husband and wife. My friend, you may kiss your bride."

Nora was immediately tucked in his arms, then Quinn smiled down at his bride and gently kissed her waiting lips. They turned to a sea of smiles. Applause burst forth as they started down the aisle. Nora reached out to Esther, who stood and hugged her baby sister, and then her new brother-in-law. Molly rose when Randa came to her aisle, and they hugged and gave a little hop before Don tugged on Molly's skirt.

At the last pew, Quinn stopped and said, "Nora, here is the rest of my family. This is John, Randa's stepfather, and his sister Dorothy."

John stood and held out his hand, but Quinn wrapped his arms around his brother-in-law. "Thank you for coming."

Randa squealed. "John." Quinn stepped aside, and Randa and John were in each other's arms.

Quinn held his hand up and announced. "The rest of our family made it. This is John Reynolds, Randa's stepfather, and his sister Dorothy Evans."

SIA information can be obtained
ww.ICGtesting.com
ed in the USA
W072023110623
032JS00007B/203